HIGH GREEN

The Story of an Irish-American Railroader

by

Herb Cleaves

North Country Press

ISBN 978-1-943424-47-4
Library of Congress Control Number: 2019939566

North Country Press
Unity, Maine

High Green: The Story of an Irish-American Railroader

The youngest member of the train crew had built his fire well. The coal was tiered with care, and lined and trimmed across the firebox of the steam locomotive in a way that impressed the engineer. It was summer in the mountains, the hour was late and night had enveloped the cab of the train known as *Mountain Thunder*. The track descended sharply along the east slope of the Bitterroot Range, curved across a stream and led abruptly into another challenging hill on the other side. At the end of the curve stood a country depot and atop the structure was a signal light, one that an engineer on an eastbound train could not see from the right-hand side of the locomotive until he was almost upon it.

Engineer Glendon Lightfoot checked his gauges and valves, tightened his grip on the throttle and turned to the young fireman who was seated by his cab window to watch the track ahead.

"Okay, Johnny!" he yelled across the cab. "Watch for the hole in the big fir that sticks out from the forest. Holler when you see the light!"

"Yes, sir!" the fireman responded and fixed his eyes on the trees silhouetted against the moonlit mountain sky as the train raced into the curve. John Shanahan had turned eighteen that day in June of 1945 and was making his first official trip as a qualified railroad fireman although he had ridden before as a student observer. He knew that the color of the light atop the station was critical to the engineer's success in powering the train up the hill in the distance. A red signal would require a sudden stop and likely trouble on the grade. A green, uppermost on the signal mast, would allow Engineer Lightfoot to speed up immediately and take the hill in stride.

Suddenly the ragged fir came into view and a light flashed through the branches.

"High green!" John yelled.

"High green!" Lightfoot responded as he opened the throttle wide, yanked the whistle cord and turned his attention to the track ahead.

The fireman picked up his shovel and returned to the work of replenishing coal in the firebox. He was the first Shanahan since his great-grandfather, the Irish immigrant, to begin a railroad career as a working man. He was pleased with that thought and began to whistle a tune as he stoked the engine's fire.

Prologue: The Shanahans

By the fall of 1951 four generations of Shanahans had been associated with the American railroad industry for nearly a century. The first was an immigrant construction worker who died tragically during the building of track to open the West; the next learned the ways of finance and went on to shape the family's fortune in track and trains. His son carried on the tradition, but with a flair that dazzled the business world. The task left for the fourth representative, if he chose to follow in the footsteps of his forebears, was to cope with circumstances of great change at a time when highways and airlines were moving to the forefront of the nation's transportation network.

This is the story of John P. Shanahan III, that fourth generation representative of the Irish-American railroad family.

His great-grandfather, Patrick Shanahan, was twelve years old in 1847 when his uncle brought him to America from Ireland during the famine. The orphan grew up in the teeming immigrant quarters of New York City where he labored hard but lived in poverty. He married Matilda O'Connor when he was just eighteen and Mattie bore his only child, John Patrick, in 1854.

Desperate to improve his family's lot, Patrick followed friends to Illinois where visionaries were planning a transcontinental railroad and track builders were much in demand. He was a willing worker and signed on with a construction contractor. Patrick soon emerged as foreman of an all-Irish track-laying crew, where he was respected for his work ethic, his compassion for fellow laborers and his innate skill as a track builder.

Patrick faithfully sent money back to Mattie and the child. But tragedy struck just outside of Omaha, Nebraska, in the fall of 1856. An ill-timed detonation of explosives killed the young Irishman and many of his fellow workers.

Distraught and left to fend for herself, Mattie dedicated the rest of her short life to raising her son. Although frail, the young woman, also from Ireland, eked out an existence by working as a washerwoman in the tenement district until she fell gravely ill in the winter of 1871. On her deathbed, Mattie pleaded with 17-year-old John Patrick to get an education and to promise never to work as a railroad laborer.

John Patrick Shanahan took his mother's advice. He never sought employment in the railroad industry, opting instead to work for merchants in the city. He was a slight, scholarly lad and won favor with his employers for his selling and bookkeeping abilities.

John Patrick worked his way through business college and earned a graduate degree at the state university in 1878. He joined an investment firm upon graduation, learned the business quickly and went out on his own in 1882. An astute, hard-driving businessman, he invested heavily and wisely, mostly in railroad ventures, and over the next seven years amassed a fortune. Yet he was able to keep the promise to his mother because he never drew a salary from a specific railroad company.

At age 35, John Patrick moved his Shanahan Enterprises to Chicago to better manage holdings throughout the Midwest. His life was gripped by fear of failure, however, and he lived a spartan existence in a rented flat in a seedy South Side neighborhood. He continued to pour earnings into improvements that would pay off in years to come.

John Patrick met and married Claudine, a striking 20-year-old hotel maid, in 1890. There were few people less suited to marriage and their union was a short, stormy affair. He was 36 years old then, deeply set in his frugal ways and not about to spend lavishly on a wife. She expected more, of course.

Only weeks after their son was born in 1891, Claudine told John Patrick that she was tired of him and his business world. When she demanded payment for her services, he wrote a check for $10,000. He never heard from her again.

John Patrick Shanahan Jr. was raised by a series of nannies and groomed from youth to succeed his father in the investment business. He received the best education money could buy and in 1915, at age 24, became the corporation's chief financial officer. A year later, J.P., as he came to be known, joined his father as an equal partner in the firm. The Shanahans became major players in railroad operations across the country, and by 1920 were among the wealthiest men in America.

As flamboyant as his father was reserved, the younger Shanahan developed an uncanny ability to manage both people and money. While John Patrick preferred to work in the privacy of an austere boardroom, where he sealed deals by passing out cheap cigars, J.P. lavished in the limelight by debating business in the media and throwing parties to mark successes. He also developed something of a bond with railroad workers by riding trains long distances to work sites and conversing with his employees. His father steadfastly refused to associate with working-class railroaders.

J.P. convinced his father to move Shanahan Enterprises to better quarters in the business community of the city. It was against John Patrick's grain but he came to see the value in being in the presence of other major forces in the financial world. Father and son disagreed from time to time but never clashed. When J.P. decided he needed a personal business car to visit the company's many railroad holdings, John Patrick ventured that he could get a deal on a secondhand passenger coach from a longtime associate. J.P. said he preferred to have the car built entirely to his specifications. His father, who secretly admired the son's unique management style, warmed a bit and stepped out of character by suggesting that the car should be paneled with mahogany, "not some cheap, second-grade veneer."

When the business car was finished in the spring of 1924, J.P. had it taken to a prominent display site in Chicago for an official unveiling. The mayor served as keynote speaker and was joined on the outdoor podium by prominent city and state politicians. The car was christened *Matilda O'Connor Shanahan* for the grandmother he never knew, the mother his father deeply adored. Although the senior Shanahan avoided the limelight by stating that he had pressing business that day, he came by later for a drink and a private tour of the ornate car. As he prepared to leave, 70-year-old John Patrick turned to his son, embraced him and whispered hoarsely, "Thank you, son, for remembering her."

J.P. was looking into a prospective investment in a railroad in Helena, Montana, in June 1925, when he met Alicia McMahon in the city library. The shy, dark-haired 27-year-old library assistant was re-shelving documents in the railroad archives section when J.P. barged around a corner, a sheaf of business records in hand, and knocked her to the floor. He stooped, extended a hand to help Alicia to her feet and their eyes met for the first time. It was, J.P. would recall repeatedly over the years, the most magical moment of his life.

Alicia was clearly taken by J.P., who extended his stay in Montana, supposedly to work out details of the railroad purchase. Finally, an exasperated John Patrick sent a telegram from Chicago, demanding to know why the deal was taking so long. The son responded by wire: "Need more time to work things out. This is about the future. She's very special. You'll really like her. Send money. / J.P."

In September, Alicia and J.P. were married on the open observation platform of the *Matilda O'Connor Shanahan* in front of the railroad passenger station at Helena. Despite his advanced years, John Patrick packed sandwiches and took a lesser-traveled route to Montana even though he could have obtained passes on the best trains in the region. He was still the frugal businessman despite the fact that he was en route to a railroad wedding, the likes of which his peers had never seen. He offered a toast to the couple during a lavish reception on the station grounds and, in a private moment with his son, told J.P. that he had conducted excellent work, even if it had taken all summer. "She's a fine woman, son," he added.

The newlyweds purchased a stately home in an upscale Chicago suburb. Alicia was a homemaker from the start and the couple settled into a blissful relationship. A son, John Patrick Shanahan III, was born in 1927 and became the focus of their lives. His grandfather retired two years later, moved in with J.P. and Alicia and placed Shanahan Enterprises entirely in the care of his son. The wise management practices of a lifetime ensured the survival of the firm after the stock market crash and through the years of the Great Depression.

John P. Shanahan III lacked little in his youth. His grandfather spent a lot of time with the boy, often taking him to the neighborhood rail yard to watch the trains come and go, but the watching was always from a distance. It was the era of big steam locomotives and the youngster developed a keen interest in the industry, if only from its operational aspects. During their time together, John Patrick told the boy of his family, particularly his mother and her admonition never to seek employment as a railroad laborer. Surprisingly, he never pressured the boy to follow in the family footsteps. That was a mission left to John's father.

John Patrick died peacefully in 1941, at age 87. John was 14 then and his grandfather's passing left an ache in his heart that would last a lifetime. Not long afterward, J.P. felt the need to tell his son that he should think seriously about his future as eventual heir to Shanahan Enterprises. At that point, the boy had only one goal in mind and that was to be a locomotive engineer on a fast transcontinental passenger train. "Well, what will be will be," his father said thoughtfully.

In 1945, J.P. and Alicia traveled by train to the Northeast while John worked in locomotive service—both steam and diesel—on the Shanahans' line in Montana. He learned a great deal about locomotive operation, a skill built on practical knowledge of the dynamics of the machinery. That knowledge would come in handy in the years to come.

J.P. had learned of an about-to-be-abandoned branch line in Northern New England that led to an old slate quarry and an abandoned village in the hills. He scouted around for days, calculating all the time, Alicia later recalled. When the numbers added up to his satisfaction, he called an acquaintance in government who said yes, the place sounded like the kind of site the Army was seeking to set up a testing ground for trains.

So Shanahan Enterprises bought the 22-mile line, the township of Quarry and its village and slate workings, along with trackage rights in the New England Eastern Railroad Company's freight yard at Summit. J.P. also purchased a rambling car and engine shop at that yard as a place to maintain his equipment. On a lark, he also acquired an imposing Victorian station at Summit and leased parts of the building back to New England Eastern. From time to time, he would use a prominent turret of the structure as a personal business office.

In the village known as Quarry, the stately administrative building once used by the slate company was converted to a summer home by the Shanahans and was named *Seven Pines* for the tall evergreens that lined the property. The Army chose a site near the village and built special tracks upon which railroad equipment would be tested. The site was served through an interchange with Shanahan's Summit, Bolton and Quarry Railroad, leading J.P. to conclude that he had pulled off the railroad deal of the century.

J.P. had more in mind for his acquisitions in the North Country, as the region was called, but he could not define the specifics when asked to do so by associates at Shanahan Enterprises. "It's a work in progress," he would say, but it was one that never seemed to have all the details worked out.

Shortly after high school graduation John P. Shanahan III was a qualified steam engine fireman. He went on to college and studied to be a mechanical engineer but sought and secured work as a locomotive engineman on the Shanahan line in Montana during the summers and when classes were recessed for vacations. He finished college, graduating near the top of his class in the spring of 1949 and worked until July 1950 as a locomotive engineer. The obligation to serve his country nagged at him and he finally entered military service. He went to abbreviated transportation and officers' schools and was rushed through training. Another war was under way and he was posted to Japan and then on to Korea in the fall.

John's unit was deployed near the front—then deep in North Korea—in late October, a time when Chinese troops were entering the war in overwhelming numbers. The swift advance for the Allies stalled suddenly, then turned into a nightmarish scramble back to the south. John was seriously wounded in one of a series of desperate battles to evacuate Allied forces.

Months later the youngest Shanahan was released from an Army hospital and returned to Chicago. He knew that his wound would dash his hopes of being a locomotive engineer, and he was at a loss as to what to do and where to go. Disillusioned with his prospects, he agreed to take a short-term assignment with the family business before trying to find his place in life. That assignment would last much longer than he anticipated and provide the place from which to pick up the pieces and plan the rest of his life.

Table of Contents

Part I: A Journey of Discovery

Chapter 1: Seeking a New Direction

John Shanahan was weary. He had been awake since two o'clock in the morning when the business car *Seven Pines* was switched from an eastbound passenger train to a sidetrack in what had the appearance of having been a busy railroad terminal at one time. Then the passenger train pulled away from Hill Junction, a pair of red marker lights at the rear charting its course eastward into the night.

A yard locomotive snatched the business car and moved it to a spur track where it was attached to a steam line from the terminal's coal-fired power plant. Workmen, responding to shouted orders, banged pipes that hissed and clattered and spewed plumes of steam into the cold morning air. Train wheels squealed and a diesel horn blatted. A long freight train powered by several locomotives pulled in from the west, stopped briefly, and then moved on.

Ramon Martinez, an employee of Shanahan Enterprises, sensed his younger companion's discomfort and prepared a snack in the galley. Then Ramon retreated to his quarters and dozed off, quite oblivious to the commotion outside. He was accustomed to the sounds of train yards by then, having been around them for a dozen years or so. Ramon was 18 when his family left the Philippines just before World War II. Once established in America, his father took a position as a dining car attendant, and Ramon, who studied hard to master his father's calling, followed in his footsteps.

Ramon caught the attention of J.P. Shanahan on a transcontinental train trip in 1946 and accepted the financier's offer to work for the company in Chicago as a personal aide overseeing passenger train equipment and services. Ramon became a close family friend and took it upon himself to attend personally to the Shanahans' needs when they traveled in their private car. J.P. had asked him to accompany John on the trip to New England and show him around the company's holdings there.

The racket at Hill Junction subsided quickly and floodlights that had illuminated the freight yard went dark. Motor vehicles parked near the business car were started and headlights flashed on when shadowy figures fussing about the vehicles clambered inside. The cars and trucks were driven away into the night and all was quiet again.

The antique station clock at the end of the business car sounded three o'clock. John stirred uneasily in an overstuffed chair and pressed his face against the window. The darkness was stifling and he could not sleep. His left leg throbbed, a persistent reminder of injuries suffered half a world away, and his

1

thoughts flashed back to a hellish afternoon almost a year ago when events changed the course of his life so dramatically.

It was early in December 1950 and remnants of his Army transportation unit and others caught in the maelstrom of war were attempting to cover the withdrawal of Allied forces along a rudimentary roadway not far from the Chosin Reservoir in North Korea. It was desperately cold, and the Americans were under constant attack. There were still miles to go when an element of the enemy force burst out of the gray hills and riddled the hastily assembled rear guard with withering fire. His colleagues went down all around him and he stepped forward to rally the decimated defenders. They fought stubbornly, as they had for days, vowing to give no quarter.

As the firefight raged on, Shanahan sensed the end was near. He charged into the line of fire, praying aloud as the assault was taken to the enemy. Then a grenade exploded nearby and he fell and was overcome with excruciating pain.

A Chinese soldier was hovering over him, bayonet extended for the kill, when John saw an American leap from the smoke and fire and plunge a knife into the back of the aggressor. The American was a sergeant, small in stature, he remembered—a fierce warrior whose eyes burned black beneath his battle helmet. The sergeant grabbed Shanahan by an arm and dragged him under heavy fire to the side of the highway where he flagged down an ammunition truck. Another soldier pulled John aboard and the truck sped away.

Only semiconscious when he was carried aboard a rescue ship in Hungnam harbor, he heard a medic express doubt that his shrapnel-riddled left leg could be saved. Months later, however, First Lieutenant John P. Shanahan III, leaning heavily on crutches, limped out of a military hospital in Texas and struggled aboard a train for Chicago and home. Tucked in his duffel bag were a Purple Heart, a Silver Star and papers indicating that he was on leave from the Army pending recovery from his wounds. Despite repeated efforts during his long hospitalization, he was not able to learn the name of the soldier who plucked him from the battlefield. He would know that infantryman if he ever saw him again, but the odds of that happening, John knew, were infinitesimally small.

He was at a loss as to what to do with his life. He knew he could join the family business at any level he wished and attempt to learn any job he wanted. He wouldn't have to be proficient at anything; in fact, he wouldn't have to do anything and still get by. But the one thing he wanted to do—operate locomotives—was no longer possible. That option was taken from him in that last firefight in the hills of North Korea.

So John had agreed to make one trip to New England to help oversee the impending closure of a tiny Cinderella-like railroad holding that was his father's favorite. After that, he told the senior Shanahan, he would make other plans about his future.

"I want to go into a different business and forget about railroads," he said as they watched workers in Chicago outfit the Summit, Bolton and Quarry Railroad's *Seven Pines* for the long trip east. The business car, named after the estate in New England, was only five years old—modern when compared to the many 1920-era luxury cars still in use in America. Despite a design in stainless steel to match SB&Q's only passenger train in exterior appearance, the interior of *Seven Pines* retained many of the trappings of the Golden Age of railroad travel. One was the grandfather clock rescued from an abandoned station on another Shanahan line. The car also featured an open vestibule at the rear.

John expressed his reservations throughout the preparation for the trip. "New England's not a warm place. ..." His voice trailed off when he realized that J.P. really wasn't listening.

"You'll like it up there," his father offered after a while. "You'll never want to come back. Besides, it's cold here, too."

"I know. I guess I wasn't planning to spend the rest of my life here either," John responded sharply. "I'll do this job but then I really need to start planning for my future. ... Why don't you move this business to a place where it's warmer?"

"Well, maybe we can find you something somewhere else." J.P. was beginning to be annoyed. "You were fine with winter in Montana. Right now, we need to get this done. You'll want to talk to Henry Terrell when you get there. He's our manager of operations for the Summit, Bolton and Quarry."

And now he was in faraway New England and it was cold for October. Maybe this mission could be completed quickly and painlessly, he hoped as he slipped into a troubled sleep. As he dozed, night retreated into the shadows, yielding to an insistent dawn. Gray hills took form slowly against the eastern sky and the harsh sounds that had emanated from the darkness at the freight yard were gone. When the first fingers of sunlight flickered through the wooded hills, the place was eerily silent.

After a while the sun's rays reached *Seven Pines*, striking the windows with a sudden, blinding intensity. John pushed himself to his feet, fumbled for the cane that had replaced his Army-issue crutches and snatched a hooded jacket, which he struggled to put on. Then he walked unsteadily to the business car's enclosed front vestibule. He unfastened the latch on the upper section of the Dutch door, swung it out of the way and peered out. To the right stood the rambling wooden depot at the place called Hill Junction. To the left, the rails of more than a dozen sidetracks shimmered in the morning sunlight.

Leaning on the lower vestibule door, he took out a cigarette and lit it. He inhaled sharply and coughed. Bad habit, he thought, as he took another drag. Surveying the setting, John was struck by the stark, bleached landscape. It had been summer here not long ago, and should be only nicely into fall, but the chilly air and wind kicking up from the southwest suggested something more ominous. He grimaced as he inhaled again and flicked the cigarette into the crisp morning air. The butt landed on the station's asphalt platform, sputtered briefly and flickered out. Nearby, a station sign dangling askew from a bent stanchion creaked as wind whipped around *Seven Pines*.

3

John lifted the trap covering the stairwell, opened the lower vestibule door and stepped gingerly off the business car. He shivered as another blast of cold swirled along the platform and ripped at the hood of the parka that his father insisted he take along on the trip. The jacket was fancy but flimsy and the cold bit through it.

He walked by the steam outlet that had been attached to the business car and peered across the freight yard. He remembered reading once that this railroad had provided passenger train service to the border with Canada before falling on hard times. Now passengers from southern New England points who were bound for destinations along the 270-mile Hill Division were carried first to Sunbury, a small city twenty miles to the east.

There, after a wait of several hours, the travelers were transferred to a local passenger train that came back to Hill Junction in the morning before swinging north to Pleasant Valley, a mill town ninety miles up the line. Passengers had to get off at Gatlin station, which served the mill and the adjoining community across the Spanish River, and board another local train operated for New England Eastern by the Shanahans' Summit, Bolton and Quarry Railroad in order to reach Summit. From Summit, New England Eastern's local passenger trains continued to provide minimal accommodations across vast farmlands and through forests to the Canadian border village of Boundary.

But even that skeletal service was about to become a thing of the past.

When New England Eastern announced its intention to abandon all holdings north of Gatlin, the senior Shanahan reluctantly advised the Interstate Commerce Commission that if NEE were permitted to close its operations, the 22-mile-long Summit, Bolton and Quarry would be forced out of business. That was simply because the Eastern was its only direct connection to the rest of the nation's railway network. Although he had never been there, John knew his father had a special fondness for the SB&Q and had invested heavily in upgrading the line despite its meager traffic base. "It's really your father's hobby, and every man needs a hobby," his mother had confided years earlier.

The tiny line had a marginal freight business by that time but it was home to a passenger train of grand stature. At first, the *Northern Express* ran between Quarry, the tiny village that had been the site of a booming slate industry a half-century earlier, and Summit, the commercial-governmental center for the northern part of the state. Two years earlier, when New England Eastern proposed to end passenger service on the Hill Division, Shanahan negotiated an agreement to operate SB&Q's train through to Pleasant Valley's station at Gatlin if NEE would continue service between there and Hill Junction.

John had seen an artist's rendition of the *Northern Express* in the corporate headquarters in Chicago. The stainless steel-clad train consisted of a railway post office and baggage car, three coaches, a diner and the piece de resistance, a sparkling dome-observation-lounge that brought up the rear. The train's appointments rivaled the best railroad passenger conveyances that America offered at mid-century.

The coaches were named *Summit, Bolton* and *Quarry* for the principal communities on the line. The mail and baggage car, unlike many innocuous pieces of passenger train equipment of its kind, bore the name *Rural Delivery*. The diner was *Eden Valley*, named for the scenic river basin traversed by the SB&Q, and the dome car carried a particularly auspicious name, *Aurora Borealis*.

John was amused. Anyone but John P. Shanahan Jr. would have named the dome car *Northern Lights*. But John's father possessed a flair for the fanciful and the capital to bankroll any project he desired. Even so, the truth was that the Summit, Bolton and Quarry, a little-used former New England Eastern branch, was overbuilt, over-maintained and vastly over-equipped. The restoration was declared to be a grandiose venture by critics—and Shanahan had many in the financial world—but he paid scant attention to detractors. What SB&Q lost each year was made up by other holdings across the country.

In a novel move to fill seats on his local version of a luxury train, J.P. contracted to transport Eden Valley students to and from the region's schools at Summit. The train's schedule was adjusted to coincide with the opening and closing of classes and several school flag stops were added along the route.

A growing number of homesteaders in the valley frequented the train throughout the year and baggage car crews became accustomed to carrying more bags of grain and crates of baby chicks than travelers' trunks and valises. Heavier livestock and bulkier goods were transported by an irregular freight train that switched cars at the box and barrel factory in Bolton and served the government's needs at the Army test site in Quarry.

In the summer and early fall, SB&Q attempted to market the *Northern Express* primarily as a tourist train along the spectacular Eden Valley but success was marginal because the connecting service offered by New England Eastern was abysmal. A number of tourists drove up the roundabout Hackmatack Highway to ride on the Shanahan line.

Even that was about to end, John thought, as he stepped around the back of the business car. The sprawling Hill Junction roundhouse, its turntable and the fueling depot dominated the north side of the freight yard. A pair of diesel road switchers were idling next to the turntable and several other locomotives protruded from the engine shed. Two concrete coaling towers and a water tank attested to the region's long association with steam locomotives, an era that was over for all practical purposes.

A 150-ton railroad wrecking crane occupied a nearby siding, along with an array of passenger coaches that had been converted for use by equipment-maintenance crews. Wrecking cranes fascinated Shanahan as a boy. This one was the local version of "The Big Hook," he thought as he recalled similar equipment during his work in Montana. Behind the crane, he spied a car repair shop that appeared to be the worse for wear.

Long strings of refrigerator cars filled a number of sidings and John recalled that a succession of potato crop failures in the North Country had contributed significantly to Eastern's financial woes. Many of the reefers, as the freight cars

5

were called, looked as if they had been in storage for years. As the crises worsened, the Eastern's stock was merged under the umbrella of a New York holding company; one that seemed bent on deriving what profit it could from the railroad while spending minimally on upkeep.

And now the Eastern was in the process of seeking the permission of the Interstate Commerce Commission to abandon all tracks north of Gatlin. There had been a public outcry from the North Country, particularly from farming and business interests, but the drop in freight was significant and it appeared that ICC would have no choice but to grant the railroad the right to abandon.

In a bizarre twist, the governor of the state had stepped forward to support the abandonment, arguing personally that if the railroad's petition were granted, state government would acquire the right of way and build a new highway linking the distinctly different northern and southern portions of the state with a better transit route than that provided by the railroad.

The protestations of the Summit, Bolton and Quarry were dismissed and it seemed that there would be no way to save the line unless Shanahan Enterprises was willing to buy the tracks, improve them and offer its own brand of service. That option had been explored but Eastern set a price that even J.P. could not justify. It appeared that events had been set in motion that would lead to abandonment, and the end was but days away.

John shivered as a cold blast of wind swept across the ghostly freight yard and he stepped back to the station platform. The depot was a somber, soot-darkened building with telegraphers' bays facing *Seven Pines* on one side and the NEE mainline on the other. A telegraph operator who had been on duty when the *Sunbury Express* came in with the Shanahan business car apparently had gone home, as the train order signals were clear and the waiting room locked. A train arrival and departure board affixed to the station door had freshly-chalked notations that Train Sixteen from Sunbury, due at seven-fifteen a.m., was on time and that Number Twenty-Three, the same train, would leave for Gatlin and points north at seven-thirty a.m. Train Eight, from Gatlin, also the same train, was due back at Hill Junction at two p.m.

"What a ghastly place," John mumbled as he took a last look at the deserted station. It was already after seven o'clock. He noticed that the wind was shifting and that a cloudbank was building in the southwest. He limped back to the vestibule and re-boarded *Seven Pines* just as a pair of workers in greasy overalls and tattered sheepskin jackets appeared by the end of the car. They stood in the lee of the wind and John could pick up bits of their conversation.

"That must be Mr. Shanahan's boy," one commented. "Maybe he can get this railroad running again."

"They run a good company," the other suggested. "I thought the old man would come through. Just look at the SB&Q. Now that's some railroad."

A diesel horn sounded in the distance before the bewildered John could absorb what sounded like an abrupt change of direction by Shanahan Enterprises.

"Here comes Sixteen," one of the workmen announced. "They won't hang around here long. Good thing. We'd damn near freeze to death waiting out here this morning."

John stood in the vestibule for several minutes, still unable to grasp the significance of the car inspectors' remarks. "If Old Man Shanahan is going to fix this railroad, he's going to do it without his boy," he muttered angrily as he shoved open the interior door to *Seven Pines* and stepped into the warmth of the business car.

The car inspector was wrong when he predicted that New England Eastern's Train Sixteen, scheduled to depart as Train Twenty-Three would be out of Hill Junction without delay. The train was still at the depot an hour after the advertised departure time. First, there was a problem with a defective coupling between the passenger cars and *Seven Pines* could not be attached immediately to the train. Then the air-brake system malfunctioned and more workmen gathered to hammer at train lines. When some progress seemed apparent, the locomotive coughed, belched a cloud of smoke and died.

John drummed his fingers on the mahogany table in the dining room. "We're going to spend the rest of our lives in this God-forsaken place and die and nobody will ever know about it," he said as he got up and stumbled the length of the car in frustration. Then he settled in an easy chair and stared blankly out the nearest window. He needed a new direction, one that would lead him far from these railroads that had been the centerpiece of his life.

Chapter 2: Halfway to the North Pole

After the New England Eastern train crew swapped the disabled locomotive for a freight engine at the Hill Junction roundhouse and incorporated a steam heat car into Train Twenty-Three, it appeared that something might happen. The business car was placed behind an assembly of coaches and baggage cars of improbable age and the passenger train finally rattled out through the freight yard. It was nine forty-five. The train was already two hours and fifteen minutes late.

An odd clickety-clack startled John Shanahan after the train passed lines of freight cars that were redlined and apparently destined for scrapping. "What was that clickety-clack, Ramon?" he asked of his traveling companion.

"Diamond crossing," Ramon grunted, referring to a track structure that allowed one train to cross another."

"I see. There would be a reason for a diamond crossing in the middle of a freight yard?"

"Probably." Ramon was engrossed in a crossword puzzle and didn't look up.

"And now we're coming to a tower, although there doesn't appear to be anyone around," John noted.

"Probably not anyone around."

"The sign indicates the place is East Tower."

"Uh huh. Must be East Tower."

John grinned. "You're a font of knowledge, Ramon. Thank you for your insights."

"I always try to be of help to my friends. ... What's a seven-letter word for a fast passenger train, Boss?"

John shook his head. Although Ramon was several years older than the younger Shanahan, they had been close friends for years and he was with J.P. and Alicia at the station in downtown Chicago when John came home from the war. Ramon always addressed J.P. as "Boss," and on this trip, his and John's first together, the address seemed to be appropriate, at least to Ramon.

"A fast passenger train? Definitely N-O-T-O-U-R-S."

"That isn't how you do crossword puzzles. We're looking for one word here."

"You're right as usual." John yawned, pushed himself to his feet and wandered off to his tiny bedroom in the business car. He stared into a small mirror by the window. The image was certainly not that of the high school boy voted best looking in his senior class. His dark, curly hair definitely needed a trim and his complexion was sallow, accented by dark circles beneath his eyes.

God, you look a fright, Shanahan, he thought. John turned away sadly, realizing that the last year of his life—the most tumultuous one—had taken a toll. He was a strapping six-footer and once weighed almost two hundred pounds. He came back from Korea broken in body and spirit and at least thirty-five pounds lighter. He would probably regain some use of his injured leg, his doctors suggested, but not all, and recovery would be a long process. Now he was in New England, an unlikely place to recuperate, he thought, and he was quite unhappy. He wanted to go elsewhere, but he did not know where.

He was troubled by the possibility that his assignment had developed into more than picking up a few records and dismissing SB&Q's workers. He decided he would clarify that matter with his father in a collect long-distance phone call, if he ever arrived at Quarry. If J.P. had cooked up a new deal since he left Chicago and his assignment was to take on new dimensions, he would be on the next train out, he vowed.

Feeling confident that he could take a stand, John wandered back to the galley. Ramon was spinning his magical culinary talents with some kind of a creamy confection. John stuck a finger into the topping and was swatted abruptly with a spatula.

"Do I stick my fingers in your business, Boss?" Ramon demanded. "Go look out the window and think about your future. It will be a short one if you keep poking around in my kitchen. Pour yourself a cup of coffee. We don't have any hostesses on this train."

John poured coffee into a mug and slipped into a chair at the end of the mahogany table. "Where are we now?" he called to Ramon. "Doomsday Junction? Do we change here for Podunk Falls? Oh, I'm so sorry. I thought the train ran to Podunk today. It's next week? How foolish of me." He began whistling a country tune about a train ride through the South and about the magnolias and the sweet Southern breeze. From the galley, Ramon provided the words in a lilting melody.

The train slowed and then lurched to a stop. Storm clouds had moved in and it had become impossible to distinguish any features of the landscape. "So where are we now?" John asked again, almost absently.

"Hard to tell." Ramon joined John at the table and passed him a manila envelope. "The conductor gave me this for you while you were wandering around in a daze. He said something about train orders and some messages."

"Maybe we're going to turn around and go back. We could be so lucky." John shook out the contents on the tabletop. "Let's see. We have a train order announcing to God knows who cares that Train Twenty-Three will run two hours and fifteen minutes late from Hill Junction to Gatlin. Then we have one that instructs us to meet a freight train at 'Halfway' to somewhere.

"Oh, and here are some bulletins. This one says train speed is reduced to ten miles an hour between Milepost Fifteen and Milepost Twenty-Five because of rough track. I can see that we're going to be making hellishly slow progress today."

9

About then, *Seven Pines* lurched again and the papers skittered across the tabletop. John gathered the pieces and shuffled through more onionskins and pink message forms. "Here's an interesting one. 'All trains will use Track One at some place called Collier and will not exceed five miles per hour account of debris that fell on the main line track from a potato house fire.'"

Ramon nodded. "Must have been a big fire," he suggested.

"There's more. ... Oh, this one is neat: 'be prepared to stop on track foreman's signal at Milepost Eighty-One. Proceed only on his instruction, watching out for wrecked cars from Train Fifty-Six. Debris is scattered for approximately one-point-five miles. Do not exceed five miles per hour between Milepost Eighty-One and Milepost Eighty-Two, watching for possible obstructions on track.'"

"Hard times," Ramon observed.

"Here's one for us. 'Train Twenty-Three will proceed beyond wye at Gatlin Junction before turning. Disembark passengers at station. Run around train with locomotive, detach business car, placing it on rear of SB&Q Train One. Retain steam heat car. Car inspectors available. Reattach locomotive, board passengers for return to Sunbury, back train to wye and turn. Departure from Gatlin for Train Eight will be shown as time at west wye switch at Battle Brook Junction.'"

"The wye comes before the station," Ramon explained. "They usually turn first and back the train into the station. But if they did that, this car would be turned the wrong way around when we leave for Summit. That wouldn't be an orthodox way to run a train on a Shanahan line. And, as you know, we do our utmost to make sure we don't confuse the passengers because they might get angry and go out and buy expensive motor vehicles and never ride on our trains again."

"Uh huh. I see the logic in all of this. It makes sense. I guess." John remembered turning trains in Montana where the equipment was switched from the mainline and operated engine first along a sidetrack that veered sharply to the left until another switch was passed. Then that switch was turned and the train was backed along a similar sidetrack running to the right until it came to the mainline from the opposite direction.

But how would he explain that to someone who had never seen a wye? John wondered. Concluding that there was no way and that nobody really cared as long as the train showed up on time, he gathered up the papers.

"So we're going to get a ride on our own train after a while," John offered.

"After a while," Ramon said. "Right now, it looks like we're stopping to wait for that freight train, so we must be at Halfway."

"Does that name have any significance? Would that be halfway to civilization, by some remote chance?" John's voice dripped with sarcasm.

"No, halfway to the North Pole," Ramon responded. "It's some global thing that the people around here are excited about. The siding is at Latitude Forty-Five North. That's halfway between the equator and the top of the world, as I understand it."

10

"Well, top of the world to you, Ramon. I thought we were already there. I'd rather go back to the equator." Remembering events in his life last year, John looked seriously at his companion and asked, "Do you know where Latitude Forth-Five North crosses Asia?"

"I don't think it's near the Philippines," Ramon responded, as he picked up the unfinished crossword puzzle. "What's a six-letter word for the December solstice?"

"I'll tell you where," John explained, avoiding the question about the solstice. "It crosses Outer Mongolia and Manchuria and the northern Gobi Desert. Doesn't this place look like Mongolia to you, Genghis Khan?"

"Genghis Khan? Doesn't he play drums at that joint we used to go to on the South Side?" Ramon countered. "I never went to Manchuria and neither did you. Deserts are in warm places. You're all mixed up, Boss. Here, put your expensive education to work and do this crossword puzzle." Ramon tossed the newspaper to John and went back to his kitchen nook.

The passenger train finally began to move, almost imperceptibly at first and then, as the brakes released fully, with an abrupt surge forward. A rather dilapidated freight train came into view on the right side of John's train. A trainman bundled in a bulky sheepskin coat, railroad cap with earflaps turned down and scarf and mittens waved from the rear steps of the caboose and stepped quickly inside the car. It was only October, he remembered, but the train looked like something out of a film on winter railroading that John had seen many years earlier.

"I presume that would be the freight train," John said, as Ramon reappeared. "Gosh, I think they only had two or three cars. Business must be a bit slow."

"You presume correctly, Stanley," Ramon said. "That brakeman business in cold climates must be one heck of a way to make a living."

John nodded. "Too tough for me. I think I'll go to California and be a life-guard if we ever escape from this place. Want to jump off at the next station and see if we can buy a ticket on the first train to the West Coast?"

Ramon's eyes twinkled again and he smiled broadly. "Sure, Boss," he said as he wandered back to the galley.

Train Twenty-Three arrived at Carroll more than three hours late. The station appeared to be well maintained and located on what seemed to be the main street of a busy community. Several passengers got off and an equal number boarded for points to the north. The train creaked out of Carroll at twelve-ten p.m. It made another stop at Collier, at which passengers were let off and others climbed aboard. It crept by the overturned freight cars from Train Fifty-Six, several of which cleared the windows of the business car only by inches.

John limped over to a wall map that showed the territories served by New England Eastern and Summit, Bolton and Quarry railroads. He found Carroll and then traced the NEE line north to Gatlin. North of there, he found Mission, Blackwater, High Meadow, Camp Twelve, Hayshed, Camp Sixteen, South

Spanish, Spanish Junction and Summit. There was no indication of any highways linking the track beyond Gatlin.

He noticed that the only main road swung northeast from Gatlin and appeared to go toward the North Country. It was called the Hackmatack Highway. "Up in the boonies," he muttered as he turned away and slipped into an easy chair by a window.

At two forty-five p.m., four hours and fifteen minutes late, New England Eastern's Train Twenty-Three pulled up unceremoniously at Gatlin depot. Flakes of snow were flying in the air as passengers in the coaches ahead of the business car stepped quickly across the platform to claim seats on what was unmistakably J.P. Shanahan's *Northern Express*. Station clerks wheeled out baggage carts and made quick work of transferring luggage and express goods from one train to the other. Sacks containing the U.S. Mail were also exchanged between mail cars.

John studied what he could see of the *Northern Express* from the business car windows. He thought of the depiction of the train in the company's headquarters and realized that the artist failed to capture its stunning features. While the *Northern Express* was similar to the new transcontinental passenger trains that he had watched enter and exit the grand terminals in Chicago not long ago, John knew that in the world of gritty trains and grimy railroaders, this one was a gem.

Ramon appeared again, attired this time in the snappy white uniform of the private car attendant. He pulled a parka from the closet, donned it and tossed another to John. "Shape up, Boss," he said. "It's time to go out and meet some of the boys from the Shanahans' little railroad up in New England."

Chapter 3: Into the Snow and Cold

Ramon Martinez opened the vestibule's Dutch doors and cleared the traps covering *Seven Pines'* forward stairwell on the left side. He stepped smartly to the station platform at Gatlin and then stood at attention, hands clasped behind his back—much in the manner of a Pullman car porter—to let John Shanahan off.

"Fine day in the country, sir," Ramon announced mischievously. "Watch your step there." Then, leaning forward, he whispered, "Come on, grumpy, look smart. We have to impress the hired help on this railroad."

"You're getting to be a real pain, Ramon," John joked as the pair walked toward the train crew. "Remind me to fire you if I can't escape from this railroad prison and get stuck with taking over the Shanahan Empire someday."

"You're too lazy to try to escape. Besides, with your lack of personality and general absence of management skills, you couldn't even run a wind-up model train set," Ramon commented nonchalantly as they approached the four members of the SB&Q train crew. "Buck up, now. We're going to meet some real railroad men."

The conductor and rear brakeman sported immaculately-tailored dark blue uniforms accented by black vests into the pockets of which their watches were tucked. Both wore unbuttoned dark blue overcoats, trim zippered black overshoes and stylish uniform caps with "SB&Q Conductor" and "SB&Q Trainman" badges affixed to each to denote their positions. It occurred to John that the immediate setting, with the fancy passenger train in the background, could have been Grand Central Station in the heyday of the American passenger train.

The head brakeman, a gangling fellow with a closely-cropped dark beard, appeared to be in his early forties. He wore blue overalls, a sheepskin-lined jacket and a uniform cap that marked his place in the scheme of things as "Baggageman." He was engaged in an animated conversation with another crewmember, a considerably shorter man who also wore overalls, a well-worn sheepskin-lined jacket, oil-stained leather gloves, scuffed Army combat boots and a black winter railroader's cap with a badly-frayed visor. The cap was pulled down almost to eye level and he had to peer from beneath the visor to maintain eye contact with the brakeman.

Ramon went directly to the conductor. "Joe, it's good to see you again," he said. "I want you to meet J.P.'s son. This is John P. Shanahan III and he's come to see a great railroad." Turning to his traveling companion, Ramon said to John, "This is Joe Francis, conductor of the *Northern Express*, and the senior employee on this railroad."

John remembered his father's fondness for Joe, the Native American who came over from the New England Eastern in 1946 after years as a conductor on

13

that line. He was a stately man who had been a tribal chief once at the Penobscot reservation near Sunbury. "It's a pleasure to meet you, Joe," John said. "Father sends his regards."

Francis nodded. "A pleasure, John," he said as they shook hands.

The uniformed rear brakeman was introduced as John Kelly. He was a younger man, somewhat portly and distinguished mainly by an engaging smile. Then Ramon turned to the baggageman and said, "This is Carleton Ingraham Reardon, head brakeman and baggageman, potato farmer, poet, philosopher, college professor and teller of tall tales. He's said to be harmless, but we're never sure."

"That's me, Boss. C.I. Reardon," the tall man said, grinning ear to ear as he extended his hand. "The C.I. might stand for 'certifiably insane,' but nobody knows for sure. Now I want you to meet the man nobody can really figure out around here, our esteemed engineer of the day." Turning to the figure in the sheepskin jacket, C.I. bellowed, "Get out here, you little vagabond and make an effort to be nice to the man."

John extended his hand and looked straight into the eyes of a soldier from the not-too-distant past, a dark-eyed warrior whose act of courage in the hills of North Korea had saved his life. It was surely that soldier, he thought, that slight figure in a frozen moment in time whose features were so indelibly etched in his mind.

"William Sterling Travers," the engineer said, extending his hand. "Most everyone calls me Bill, except for Kook over here," he added, gesturing at Reardon.

John gripped Bill's hand tightly and could not let go. "You were in Korea, I think. In December 1950 ... before Christmas ... up on the road to Hagaru-ri. ... Weren't you?" John pleaded, searching the engineer's face and trying desperately to make the connection.

"Yeah, December seventh or the eighth. Hell of a fight, just below Koto-ri. We came in off the hills to the west. Almost missed the damned thing. ... You were there?" Travers squinted, and his dark eyes searched John's features.

"I was there. Smoke and fire everywhere and cold, so damned cold. I took some shrapnel and went down. You jumped a Chinese soldier who was about to do me in. Then you dragged me to an ammo truck and I passed out somewhere on the way to Hungnam."

"Son of a gun!" Bill's eyes burned brightly and there could be no mistake. "The lieutenant. Jeez, you were busted up pretty bad. My God, you got out." He pointed at John's cane. "The gimpy leg, you got that in the fight, didn't you?"

"Yes. Almost lost it. I looked for you ... for a long time when I got back stateside ... at the hospital in Texas. I just wanted to say ... thanks." John stepped forward unsteadily, embraced Travers quickly and stepped back. "Thanks," he said again, swiping at tears that started to trickle down his cheeks.

"You're welcome. Hey, man, that was a helleva fight. How long did your guys hold 'em off?"

14

"Ah, it seemed like forever. They kept coming and coming. We'd been fighting them—North Koreans and Chinese—off and on for a week or so, I guess ... day and night. I didn't think we were going to get out of that frozen hellhole. I really didn't. But we sure had it better than the guys up around the reservoir."

"Chosin Reservoir. Poor bastards. What a bunch of fighters. Those Marines dragged out their dead, bodies all frozen and busted up. They leave no one behind. Remember? ..."

John remembered and wiped his eyes.

"Hey, we gotta get out of here," Bill said, acknowledging a subtle signal from the conductor. "Why don't you ride to Summit in the cab with me? We'll talk over old times. We don't have a fireman today. They held him over to run a special section into Quarry for the school kids, in case we were late. Smart move, it turns out."

John frowned. "Ah, gosh. ... I'd sure like to ... ride the engine. ... But, well, I can't climb anymore. It's the leg, you know. It doesn't work like it used to, I'm sorry to say. But thanks ... anyway."

"C'mon," Bill insisted. "You look like you've got strong arms. Just grab on real tight and hoist yourself up. I'll come along behind and boost you, if you need it."

John took a deep breath. "Okay. ... Would it be okay with you, Joe?" he asked, in deference to the conductor, who in the railroad business was responsible for the train. Joe nodded. "Keep the engineer awake," he said and grinned.

"How about you, Ramon? Okay if I go up front?"

"Sure. Good riddance," Ramon said. "I've got some private business to talk over with the boys. See you up the line."

Travers escorted John Shanahan to the locomotive. "You know, I always wondered what happened after we got you aboard that ammo truck in Korea. You were hurt pretty bad."

"Yeah. Kind of brought my dreams crashing down. I used to be an engineer in Montana, before the war, steam and diesel. I wanted to go back but ... well ... I guess I need to figure out something else now. Anyway, bear with me and I'll try the climbing bit again," John responded as they reached the locomotive.

"You'll do fine. Hand me that walking stick and grip those climbing irons real tight. Piece of cake."

John negotiated the narrow ladder with its five steps methodically, and after reaching the top, pushed the door open and squeezed into the cabin. Once inside, he limped to the fireman's seat on the left side of the cab. It was always difficult to explain to his friends over the years that the engineer of a railroad locomotive operated the controls from the right-hand side of the cab, unlike the driver of a car or a truck. He learned later that British engine drivers sat on the left-hand side of their locomotives but drove home from the station after work on the right-hand side of their motor vehicles.

The railroad oddity was too complex to deal with so he avoided it in future conversations. "So this is the Five-Naught-One," he said to the engineer as Bill handed him the cane. "Sweet engine. Seems to be a match for the train."

"Yeah. This one's a beauty. It's got the whole works—steam generator for the coaches, nice view from the cab, a radio and lots of power. It's a prototype, you know, for shorter passenger trains like this one. The Eastern doesn't have anything like it. You saw what they used for power today—a beat-up freight engine geared for slow trains."

"I guess. Talk about slow trains. So what did all the delays do to your running time?"

"Blew it to hell," Bill said, pulling out his pocket watch. "We'll book out of here in a few minutes, probably about three-thirty p.m., four hours late. We should be in on the Quarry line now, half an hour before tying up, and we still have a hundred and twelve miles before we get there. The track is stove all to hell up at High Meadow, actually almost all the way to South Spanish, so we'll lose more time. We'll do well to get to Summit by seven. Then it's smooth sailing on the SB&Q. ... We ought to be into Quarry by eight o'clock."

Travers settled into the engineer's seat. "The Eastern is holding their local connecting trains at Summit, waiting for us. One runs up the branch to Eagle River and the other one covers the mainline through to Boundary. If anyone's on here for Boundary, they might be home by midnight. But probably not."

Bill's gaze shifted back to the train from the engineer's side window. Catching a hand signal, he waved his hand and slammed the window shut. "Joey's set on the rear. Let's roll." Bill released the brakes and notched the throttle forward. The wheels began to spin and he hit the sander control. "C'mon, girl. Just another cold New England day. You can do it." The locomotive gained its footing and inched forward.

The radio crackled. "Joe makes the departure at three-thirty p.m. How's that for you, Bill?" It was the voice of Carleton, the head brakeman.

"Works for me, Kook. What do we have for stops?"

"The Mission, Blackwater, High Meadow. Hay for the crew at Camp Twelve. Camp Sixteen, South Spanish and Spanish Junction. I've got a package in the baggage car for the operator at the Junction. Maybe we'll just slow down and I'll toss it off."

"Okay. I take it the padre from the mission was out shopping today."

"Yep. Father Mac."

"Tell him we need a prayer if we're gonna make Quarry tonight."

"The father says he prays for you all the time."

"Tell him that he's a fine man and I'd stop my train for him anytime, anywhere."

"He says, 'Bless you, my son.'"

Travers snapped on the running lights, scanned the control panels, fiddled with the air brake control and tapped the sander lever again. A spray of sand struck the rails ahead of the engine wheels, offering added traction. "Look's like everything's working," Bill said. "You comfortable over there?"

"Great," John responded. "My favorite place on a train. Sure beats riding back there. You're always looking for landmarks to figure out where you are. Up here, it's all out there ahead of you. … So, who's the priest and what's this 'mission' place?"

"The Reverend Bob McQuarrie. Nice old guy. The Catholic Church has an Indian mission there, about ten miles up the line. Some of the native people still live in the area. There's a road in from Pleasant Valley, but it's in tough shape and not always open, sometimes not for days at a time. The folks around the reservation use this train quite a lot and we appreciate their business."

Bill adjusted his seat, opened his window and looked back again. "Looks like everything's following us. I see the taillights on your fancy car. That's a good sign."

The engineer shifted his attention to the rails ahead. "I should tell you more about the priest. Years ago, an Eastern freight train got stuck in the snow six or eight miles above the mission and Father Mac got wind of it. He snow-shoed out in the night with a packsack of supplies for the crew. It was a helluva blizzard. Nobody knows how he made it. God's hand was on his shoulder, we know that. … I probably shouldn't tell you this but we've been giving the priest free rides ever since. We don't even record a stop at the Mission unless other people get on or off."

John leaned back in the fireman's seat. It's always comforting to have a priest on your side, he thought. As he watched ahead, he saw the first flakes of a storm that had been building all day. It was already getting dark. The engine's big head-light seemed to be searching frantically for landmarks, its powerful beam darting from the woodland on one side of the track to the woodland on the other as Train One, the northbound *Northern Express*, negotiated a series of S-curves north of Gatlin.

"So, Bill, it must be hard to know where you are when it gets stormy along here."

"A curve at a time. A signpost. A piece of rough track and God knows there's enough of that on this run. I catch a milepost now and then. Look up ahead on the right. We're coming up on Milepost Ninety-Six. The Mission is at Ninety-Nine. Gatlin was at Ninety and Summit is at One Seventy-Nine. Eagle River is ninety miles from Summit and so's Boundary. Makes it easy to do the bookkeeping."

The radio crackled again. It was a reminder from the conductor: "Passengers and mail at the Mission."

"Roger," the engineer responded and chuckled. "Joey always knows where we are. You watch on the right and you'll probably pick up the floodlights on the church. Somebody usually turns them on when we have passengers coming in or leaving after dark. There's no station there, just a shelter by the track and a mail crane that has a little light on top. We pick up a mailbag going both ways. I guess folks up here like to write letters."

Several minutes passed and then Travers notched the throttle back, pushed open the side window and peered out. "Come across and take a look." John hobbled across the cab and squeezed his head out the engineer's window. Ahead he spied the lighted church steeple and then the trackside shanty and a cluster of people on the platform. A green-and-white flag was mounted on a front corner of the shelter, signifying that passengers wished to board the train. Just beyond the structure, a tightly-bound mailbag fluttered in the mail crane very close to the track.

John looked back and could see the catcher arm extended from the mail car to retrieve the bag on the fly. The railway postal clerk was standing in the door-way, posed to drop a sack with inbound mail at the end of the platform.

The engineer waved as the engine slipped by the shanty and the mail crane clattered and collapsed as the catcher arm snagged the outbound bag. The sack with inbound mail that was tossed from the train landed on the platform twenty feet from the cluster of passengers as the train came to a stop.

"It's a better show when we don't have passengers here," Bill said. "We catch the bag at twenty miles an hour or so. Once in a while the one that goes off takes a crazy bounce and winds up out in the road or in a snow bank."

Travers continued talking about the mail service. "We've got more cranes up the line—at Blackwater, High Meadow, Camp Twelve, Camp Sixteen and South Spanish. Oh yeah, there's the one at Spanish Junction tower but just for railroad mail cause nobody except the telegraph operator lives there now. His name's Boomer and he is some kind of a pitching artist so he usually tosses the stuff right in through the baggage car door. We may have to stop tonight, so you probably won't get to see his routine."

"Boomer?"

"Andrew Johnson's his name. Comes north in the fall and settles into a camp he built at the Junction. The place is closed in the summer and he heads west. … He used to have a summer job at some tower on a mountain branch in West Virginia. The thing got knocked down by a runaway train."

John was still pondering the name because it seemed to stir memories of an operator he knew before the war. He was about to ask more about the man but Bill was continuing his discourse. " … God-awful good telegrapher. He's a boomer. You know, one of those Morse guys that drift from railroad to railroad with the seasons. Sort of a Pocatello yardmaster, you know the type, only he knows what he's doing."

John grinned and the memory was set aside. Instead, he remembered Poca-tello and the sprawling freight yard in the Northwest, where yardmasters came and went in rapid succession. It was a busy place, a yardmaster's nightmare, he recalled. The men would move on quickly to places where the pace was slower—places like this Spanish Junction, he supposed.

18

With its charges deposited safely at Mission, Train One pulled out into the teeth of a heavy flurry of snow. "This isn't going to be easy," Bill muttered as he opened the sanders. "Heavy rail. I hope to hell the dispatcher's thinking snow tonight."

As he reached for the radio, he said, "I tell you, this gadget is some handy. We have the only locomotive in these parts with a radio. I can only talk to the conductor, but it saves a lot of steps, especially in a storm. When I don't have a fireman, like tonight, I don't have to go across the cab to get a signal from the rear if the trainman has to be on that side."

The engineer clicked on the radio: "Hey, Joe. You there?"

"Right here."

"What do you hear about the snow? Getting a heavy rail up here."

"We figured. We'll stop at Blackwater and get Molly to find out what's going on."

"Good deal."

Before John could ask, the engineer said, "Molly McCaslin's the station agent at Blackwater. She lives there in the building—upstairs. Her husband was the track foreman until he died two or three years ago. Molly stayed on. God, she's too young to be a widow. I guess it's about the only home she's ever had but it's a hard place to get to. There's a logging road but it's not fit for a car, sometimes not even for a pulpwood truck. ... Blackwater is on the end of the power line, so it's about at the end of civilization as we know it."

Travers peered ahead. The snow was pelting against the windows and visibility was down to a few feet ahead of the engine.

"I'm beginning to think we're gonna have trouble making Summit," was his dour assessment. "It's a hard pull at best and this storm's getting worse even though it's too early to have any great amount of snow. Still, I'm not getting much traction. That's why we call it a heavy rail."

"I remember," John responded. Great, now we're going to be snowbound, he thought, remembering the stories his grandfather told about trains being stranded for days in the mountain passes of California. "How far is this Blackwater?" he asked, attempting to sound casual.

"About forty-five miles from Gatlin." The engine shuddered and the wheel-slip warnings came on repeatedly, sending red flashes across the cab. Bill looked worried. "Damned heavy rail," he muttered.

Travers hunkered down in the engineer's seat and the engine cab fell silent. The Five-Naught-One continued to slog along but the lack of visibility and frequent bursts of snow was making progress painfully slow. The speedometer flickered between fifteen and twenty miles an hour, sometimes falling to ten. Finally Bill caught sight of a milepost. More than fifty minutes had passed since he had spoken.

"Milepost One Thirty-Three. Keep your eyes peeled for some kind of lights ahead."

John stood up and squinted through the front windows into the swirling snow. Minutes passed. "There, up ahead, I think. On my side. Yes. Some kind of light." The engine clattered over a switch.

"Yep. We just bumped over south switch of Number Two track at Blackwater. Father Mac's been praying for us." The engineer was clearly relieved. Radio in hand, he called the conductor.

"Coming up on Blackwater, Joe. The station's lit up and the order board is out. We might need some help from here on unless this snow lets off real quick."

"Let's see what we can find out." Joe Francis was well acquainted with wintertime railroading and he knew that more snow could be a problem despite its unusually early arrival. The train ground to a stop in front of the rambling two-story wooden depot at Blackwater.

Bill turned to the VIP passenger in the fireman's seat. "Well, what do think, Mr. Shanahan? You really want to be associated with this railroad?"

John shook his head. "Not really. I was thinking about going somewhere warm when my old man sent me off on this expedition to close down the SB&Q. I get up here and hear this chatter about maybe he's planning something else. Do you know anything about it?"

Bill shook his head sadly. "No. We hear the stories, too. Sure, everybody wants that to happen. Hearing about this fancy car of yours coming up today probably gets people talking. Now and then there's speculation in the papers but it seems that the Eastern wants a lot of money for it. We figure that railroad would rather tear it up and give the roadbed to the governor. He thinks it would be a great idea to build a highway up through here. That shows you what kind of a nincompoop that fella is."

John was silent, realizing for the first time that the railroad really was needed. Finally he spoke. "All I know is that I was sent here to help close things down, I'm sorry to say. The last I heard was that Shanahan Enterprises wasn't about to pay the price the Eastern wanted. I wish I could be the bearer of good news but I can't do anything about it." He grimaced. One thing was for sure; he thought, he would be going back soon and would have to try to pick up his life somewhere else.

Chapter 4: Taking Stock at Blackwater

As quickly as the snowstorm blew into the wilderness north of Gatlin it dissipated. It would not be a blizzard. After all, it was still October in the North Country and while the region experienced snow at that time of year from time to time the weather anomaly was nothing more than an intense and lingering flurry that piled up several inches of snow in a highly localized area. The snow that fell iced the rails and that, coupled with the lack of visibility, had made the run from Gatlin to Blackwater long and difficult.

Engineer Bill Travers climbed down from the locomotive cab and met Conductor Joe Francis on the platform in front of the Blackwater depot. "Well, Joe, looks like the storm blew on by," Bill observed. "Now I'm wondering why the order board is out."

"Me too. Let's find out. Bring John along. I think Molly would like to say hello."

Travers nodded. "Hey, Shanahan, me and Joe gotta talk to the station agent. Toss me that cane and come on down and meet her. You'll like Molly. She's salt of the earth. Usually has something good to snack on and the best Irish tea on the line."

"Okay," John responded, not really wanting to grapple with the possibility that changes were in the wind and that he would be stuck in a place he wasn't sure he wanted to be. He dropped the cane to Travers and hobbled down the ladder.

The brightly-lit platform had been cleared of the new snow, apparently just before Train One's arrival, although the locomotive had pushed more off the track into a windrow along the edge of the passenger walkway. John Kelly, the rear brakeman was digging out the front steps of the coach *Bolton* so that several passengers could step off.

Up front, the postal clerk, Dan Stubbs, dragged a sack to the door of the mail car. Half a car length away, Carl Reardon struggled to place an express trunk destined for Blackwater on a snow-free portion of the platform.

"Let me give you a hand, Kook," Bill said as he grabbed the end of the trunk and helped set it on the platform. "Look, can I get you to baby-sit the engine for a few minutes while we get straightened out on what happens next?"

"Yep. I'll watch your engine. Take your time, buddy. Say hi to Molly." He peered down at the engineer, turned to John and whispered in a mysterious manner, "Engineer been okay? I worry about him."

Then the baggageman loped off to the locomotive.

"He worries about me?" Bill shook his head. "Nuts. Let's find someone sane to talk to."

John joined the conductor and engineer and the three went into the station together. The agent was hunched over her telegraph key, transmitting the combinations of dots and dashes that so fascinated John Shanahan as a boy. He had tried to learn to read the wire but could not unless a very patient telegrapher tapped out the code slowly. This was the real stuff—a blur of sound that made the railroads function, but a language that only the best in the business could transmit and translate.

Molly McCaslin looked up, smiled and beckoned for the men to step inside the telegrapher's office. John judged her to be in her mid- to late-thirties, an attractive woman with cropped reddish hair flecked by an occasional hint of gray. She was slight of stature and engaging, a quality sometimes lacking around railroad stations, John thought.

Her copying duties ended, Molly got up, gathered train order forms and messages for the conductor and engineer, and extended her hand to John. "You're Mr. Shanahan. I'm Molly McCaslin. Welcome to our little part of the world."

"I'm pleased to meet you, Molly." John shook her hand. "Just call me John."

"So, Molly, we were figuring back there that you'd have a change of orders because of the snowstorm, but that seems to have come and gone. Something else must be going on up the line," Travers speculated.

"Yes. Some unrelated trouble, I'm sorry to say. The Hayride derailed at Spanish Junction about an hour ago and blocked the main line. The dispatcher called a wreck train at Summit to try to pull a couple pulpwood cars off the track ahead of you." Molly checked the station clock. "I'd say they're out of Summit by now but I haven't heard for sure. ... Oh, here's an order, which basically tells me to hold you here until we figure out what to do next."

Joe and Bill read the order and then the messages.

"Um hum," Joe said. "I see that one plan could be for us to return to Gatlin and put the passengers up for the night, depending on the extent of the problem. One thing's for sure, it would be better to wait here and not gamble on running to the junction to find out there that we'd still have to backtrack to Gatlin."

"Yep," Bill responded. "That wouldn't be my idea of a fun way to end this escapade." He passed the order and messages to John. "So what would you do, chum, if it was your call?"

"Gee. Well, I don't know," he responded. "Fortunately, I don't have to make that decision. Thank goodness for that. ... What would I do? I definitely wouldn't go on because, well, then we might have to back up a longer distance ... but, on the other hand, we might luck out and they'd get the track fixed earlier and we could motor right along. However ... it's a dilemma, isn't it?"

Bill put his hand across his face and peered out between his fingers. "You, know, Joe, this guy is definitely supervisory material. I think he must have been a lieutenant in the Army in an earlier life."

"Don't pay any attention to Bill," Joe said. "And be thankful that Carleton isn't here to complicate this discussion. I'd sooner wait here as long as possible and then go back to Gatlin if we have to. Molly, you might remind the dispatcher that we have to be at some terminal by ten o'clock tonight because that's when our sixteen hours will be up."

"It's that federal rule," Travers added, "but you know all about that. On this line we call it the hog law. Our time will be up at ten, like Joe said. Ten tonight—kaput, it's over."

"The dispatching office is working on the time problem," Molly reassured the train crew. "And what time do you want to make your arrival here, Joe?"

The conductor and engineer pulled out their pocket watches together. "I'd say it was five-thirty." Joe answered and Bill nodded in agreement. "Two hours to go forty-five miles," he grumbled. "If I knew anything about math, I'd figure that to be pretty doggone slow. How are the passengers taking it?"

"They're good about it. Always good about it," Joe stole a look at John. "Our passengers are thankful for what we have. A lot of them are in the diner right now. Ramon pitched in and the crew is cooking up something he calls a blizzard stew."

John chuckled. "The same stew he served yesterday. That day it was mystery stew. The day before he called it New England stew. When we were going through upstate New York it was Yankee stew. But he's a great chef and a good traveling companion."

Molly went back to the telegraph key to report the passenger train's arrival time. Still confused about the train that had derailed, John addressed a question to Bill: "Molly said something about a train called the Hayride. Why is that?"

"Sorry, forgot to tell you. Each afternoon around two o'clock, the Eastern sends a local freight south from Summit with whatever freight is available there, plus any pickups along the way. They were late to start out, of course, and since they have to make their own meets with scheduled trains like ours by clearing the track ahead of us by twenty minutes, we don't know where they are most of the time. They'll be in a siding along the way and we'll just come up on them and pass without much fanfare."

"I see," John said. "So why is it called the Hayride?"

"Oh, you asked me about why that train is called the Hayride?" Bill asked absently.

"Well, I think so. But if I didn't ask and I think that's what I intended to do, why is that train called the Hayride?"

"Dunno. Hey, Joe, why's that train called the Hayride? You know, I wish Kook was in here right now. We could get into the real nitty-gritty of this question."

Molly came back from the key. "Billy's funning you, John." She smiled. "The train hauls hay in a couple of freight cars for the pulpwood camps north of here. The cars go back and forth all the time and when crews of woodsmen gather at trackside and flag them down, the train crew tosses off as many bales the woodsmen need. When the cars go into Summit on one trip and Gatlin on the other, local hay dealers restock the supply as needed. It's kind of a nice personal service. …"

She paused and then continued. "Now, there is tea or coffee and a little home cooking in the corner of the waiting room. Make yourselves at home."

The conductor poured coffee into a disposable cup, chose a molasses cookie and headed to the door. "I need to talk to the passengers, Molly. I'll send John Kelly in for a break, if you don't mind."

"And I need to relieve Kook," Bill said. "He might decide to take off with the train and leave us here. I'll send him in, Molly. He's fairly harmless today."

"Carleton's a fine gentleman, Billy. You know that. He's always welcome in my station. John Kelly, too."

"You're a lovely woman, Molly, but you're not a good judge of people. You holler if he gets that glazed look in his eyes." To John, Bill said, "You might want to stay here a while. It's a lot more comfortable. We'll get going by and by and I'd appreciate your company if you're up to it."

John nodded. After Molly completed business with the dispatcher, she came into the waiting room and sat down beside him. "I'm glad you came, but I have a feeling this wasn't high on your list of things to do right now." Her sparkly eyes searched his face.

"You are a good judge of people, Molly. No, it wasn't. I'm still looking for what I want to do with my life. I didn't even know how to get here when my father asked me to come. It was supposed to be for a little while and now from what I think I heard today, it could be a lot longer. I guess I wasn't planning on that possibility."

"I'd bet you'd find what you want right here if you looked at the possibilities with an open mind. There are some honest and hardworking people in these parts and once the economy picks up, you might be pleasantly surprised."

"You're an optimist, Molly, and I'm a pessimist. But your advice is well taken. Thanks. … Now tell me about that post office you have over in the corner. I noticed it coming in."

"Blackwater post office. I'm the postmistress. This is just a little village. Probably one hundred and fifty people year round at most. In the summer folks come up from as far away as Sunbury to stay in camps they have just down the street on Blackwater Pond. There's where the community gets its name. The pond is near the end of Blackwater Stream, which empties into the Spanish River through a thoroughfare just beyond the pond."

"Seems like a really pleasant place but I understand you don't have a year-round road out to civilization."

Molly laughed. "I suppose it depends on how you define civilization," she said. "You're right about the road. It's a rare occasion when anyone actually drives in here. That's why we're so dependent on the railroad … and why everyone is upset that the Eastern wants to leave."

The station agent went on to describe the village. "We have a little medical clinic here and a town hall that we also use for a grammar school. The children go to Summit and board there when they get to high school. My daughter, Annie, she's a senior this year, and she's there now. We try to get together when we can but it's hard in the winter."

"So, what do people do for a living here?"

"Most of the men cut wood for the timber companies. We have a sawmill but the Eastern, quite honestly, provides very poor service so the mill doesn't run anywhere near capacity. Good train service would mean a lot to this little village."

"I can't imagine why New England Eastern wouldn't want the freight," John offered. "My father's company is always scouting for business, all across the country. You should see the tracks and buildings they've constructed, mostly on speculation. I suppose that's one of the keys to his success."

"That's why everyone around here was hoping that he could do something for us. J.P. Shanahan is a big name in the railroad business. And if he could work out a deal, you should stay with us, at least for a little while." Molly smiled and put her hand on his shoulder. "Think about it. Please."

The station door swung open abruptly and Carleton bounded into the room, followed by John Kelly. "Molly, my love! How are you doing today?" the baggageman exclaimed, scooping up the agent in a bear hug.

"You're a sweetheart but put me down, you foolish man. Let me see your eyes. … John Kelly, are his eyes glazed over?"

"Hard to tell, Molly," the brakeman said. "I thought he was fairly normal today, but you never know." Then he burst out laughing. "Ah, he's harmless, you know that."

"Yes, I know. Now sit down, Mr. Reardon, and have a cup of Molly's Irish tea and crumpets. … Uh, oh. I hear the telegraph. Looks like I have more business on the wire."

Carleton finished his lunch and excused himself. "Well, now I have to go out and relieve Mr. Stubbs. I think Danny wants me to guard the U.S. mail for a few minutes." Carleton went to the door and peered out cautiously. "Looks like the coast is clear, John Kelly. You never know when the Dalton Gang or Jesse James will show up in this neck of the woods."

John Kelly followed Carleton to the door. "I'll guard the passengers, Carleton. You can't be too careful along this line. See you later, Molly."

John Shanahan soaked up the ambience of the half-century-old station with its highly varnished interior finish, perfectly arranged passenger settees and ruffled curtains. It was a classic rural depot with a charm greatly enhanced by its agent. Maybe this part of the country would do for a young man looking to get a new start in life, he thought.

A blast of wind rattled the windows, sending a chill up his spine. His leg was throbbing again and he stood up, leaned on his cane and peered out into the night. In the wake of the storm, the wind had picked up in intensity and was sending swirls of fine snow through the air. For a period of several minutes he had difficulty distinguishing the passenger train in front of the building, a mere twelve feet away.

"No, this is no place for me," he muttered. John would tell his father he needed to go far from here, and soon. He pulled on his flimsy parka, flipped up the hood and went to the station door. "See you next time, Molly," he called to the agent who was huddled against the telegraph instruments. Intent though she was on reading the wire, she waved. John shuddered involuntarily as he stepped out into the night air.

Once outside, he leaned against a station wall in the lee of the wind and lit a cigarette. He inhaled and coughed and stamped out the cigarette in disgust. If he could only get back to the business car, he'd get into the liquor cabinet and drown his demons, he thought, as he watched the snow swirl around the eaves of the trackside structure and form tiny windrows across the platform. *Seven Pines* was stopped beyond the wooden walkway and he decided the walk alongside the train would be too difficult in the dark, especially for a man with a crippled leg.

A downspout from a station gutter that had been jarred loose long ago creaked and clattered and the old wooden building that had supported it for so long groaned sporadically in a sort of feeble protest.

In front of him, only feet away, stood the train called the *Northern Express*, a mere toddler in the generational human endeavor known as railroading. It was a marvel of modern engineering, this train. Its stainless steel glistened even in the dull glow of the ancient platform lights. But the train seemed out of place in this backcountry village where life was still so intertwined with the past.

I'm out of place too, John thought. Born into wealth but lost and nowhere to turn. Stuck in northern New England when he ought to be where he wanted to be. But where was that? What was it that Molly McCaslin said—back there in the warmth of the Blackwater waiting room? "I'd bet you'd find what you want right here. ...Stay with us. ...You should stay with us ...for a little while. Please."

John held his hands to his head and shook his shoulders. He focused again on the train. Inside, coach lights had been dimmed and most passengers appeared to be snuggled in their seats. Only the diner was fully lighted. There the three attendants were gathered at a table with Ramon and seemed to be enjoying a lively conversation.

"I'll go and see Ramon," John said aloud. But the vestibule doors to the dining car were closed and were too difficult to open from the ground for a man so unsteady on his feet. He cursed, then shivered and coughed and went back into the waiting room. Molly was nowhere to be seen. He unzipped his parka and peeled it off and sat down on the long passengers' bench near the potbellied coal stove. The warmth was soothing to his troubled spirit and he closed his eyes.

Chapter 5: Running the Riffles

The agent at Blackwater station was kneeling by the long passengers' bench in the waiting room when John Shanahan opened his eyes. He tried to grasp where he was and couldn't place the woman who seemed to be trying to get his attention.

"It's time to go," she seemed to be saying, but he couldn't understand where he was supposed to be going. "Your train is cleared to head out," she said. "Billy's waiting."

"Oh, it's Mrs. McCaslin," John responded as he began to piece together his circumstance. "Molly, yes. … Well, I seem to be waking up … from a very long sleep. I was riding on a train somewhere, I think, and I got off at this delightful little station that was far away from where I started. … Billy, you say, is waiting … for me?"

Molly smiled. "Yes, and Billy can get a little impatient sometimes. The train you were riding on is ready to go to take you north to Summit."

John pushed himself to his feet. "Sorry, I guess I dozed off. It's been a long day. Please tell Bill I'm on the way." He pulled on the parka again and was about to walk away. Then he said, "You gave me some advice a while ago, and I appreciated that. I'm thinking on your advice, Molly. I'll see you again soon, I hope."

"You would like it here in the North Country, John Shanahan. I hope it works out so you can stay. If it does, I know that you'll never want to leave." Molly got up, took his hand and led John to the door. "God be with you wherever your travels lead."

"Thanks, Molly. God be with you, too." John stepped outside and limped along the platform to the passenger train's locomotive.

Engineer Bill Travers reached down for John's cane. "Have a little nap? You're looking sharp, good for another forty-five miles. That will get us to Summit for the night."

John climbed into the engine, took his cane from Bill and slid into the fireman's seat. The engineer released the brakes and nudged the throttle, hitting the sanders at the same time. The train inched away from the platform.

"We're moving. I make it out at seven-forty p.m." It was Joe Francis on the radio.

"Okay on seven-forty," Bill replied. "Hang on, back there. The Cannonball is rollin'." Then, still on the radio, he broke into song with several lines from a piece about a "Cannonball" of railroad legend. John noted that the engineer's musical ability was quite appealing. When Bill placed the radio receiver back in its cradle, John commented, "You're good. Ever sing out in the public?"

"Yep," Bill said. "I've got a little country and western band up in Summit. Bill Travers and the Northern Express. Sound familiar? We entertain about every Saturday night at a restaurant on the main drag. You ought to stop by sometime. I'd buy you a drink or two. If I'm a little short, I bet Kook would buy the drinks. He plays in the band—a big bass fiddle."

"If I'm there, I'll surely come calling," John promised. "The drinks will be on me."

John let the engine cab fall silent for a minute or so and then quipped, "By the way, I noticed a flagstaff sticking out of that gadget you're supposed to be keeping your feet on. Any significance to that?"

Bill grinned. "My, aren't you the observant cuss? I take it you guys in Montana used to trig the deadman?"

"Yep. And I was never able to explain to people who don't know about railroad engines exactly what the deadman is."

"I usually just tell 'em it's an emergency brake activator so that if I should pass out drunk and fall out of the seat the train will stop. If that happens, and I usually allow that it could, the device flips up and the brakes set. Then some smart aleck supposes that I'd probably fall flat on the deadman and hold it down while I was in a stupor or dead and the train would go racing off the end of the track. That's usually when I walk away."

John chuckled. "Best explanation I've ever heard."

Travers pushed the throttle ahead. "If we can make High Meadow in thirty minutes or so, I think we'll have it made," he said. "Stop there, get rid of the passengers quick and then tiptoe through the riffles almost to Camp Sixteen."

"What are riffles?" John asked.

"That's what we call that rough track up there. It all went to pieces in the rain a while ago and then it froze and thawed out and froze again unevenly. It's really rough. You'll see. It looks like riffles in a river or stream that sort of tumbles downhill. No falls, just a series of little rough spots. You know, riffles. I don't know what the hell you call 'em. Maybe railroad folks from away call them rips or rapids or something else."

John nodded. "Riffles sounds good enough for me."

Bill pulled out his pocket watch. "We'll reach High Meadow at eight-ten if I can make up a little time along here."

"I forgot to ask about what transpired while I was asleep. What did happen?"

Bill explained that the wreck train had reached Spanish Junction and expected to have the line open for the *Northern Express* by nine-fifteen p.m., barring any unforeseen delays. The train had brought along an extra locomotive to be used by the freight crew to return to Summit. The wrecking crew placed cars that were not directly involved in the derailment in another siding.

As for the *Northern Express*, Bill said they had a run-late order—six hours and twenty-five minutes—between Blackwater and Spanish Junction. "We were advised to be prepared to stop on a signal by the wreck crew about a half-mile south of the junction, in case they aren't into the clear before we get there. If everything works out okay, we'll get another run-late between the junction and Summit. This crew will be dismissed at Summit and the crew of the freight will take over and run the *Northern Express* through to Quarry later."

"I see. The bottom line is that Ramon and I will get to sleep in the mansion on the hill after all?"

"No doubt about it, Boss. You look like you need some real sleep. ... Say, what's this sleep thing with you? Something you caught when you were tramping around in that war zone in Never-Never Land?"

"Yeah, I guess so. That wasn't a real good place to sleep. And call me John. I've never been a boss, never will be. Well, maybe I was once for a very short time, in Korea, but you saw what that accomplished."

"That, Lieutenant Shanahan, sir, was a real accomplishment in the face of some incredible odds," Bill responded sharply. "I know. I was there. I saw the end of it and I figured out what happened after we cleaned up on those Red butchers. Anyway, I'll call you whatever you want, John."

Bill eased the throttle ahead another notch, checked various cab controls and indicators. Satisfied that things were going well, he settled back in the engineer's seat. "While we're on that topic, tell me about how you got dragged into the Grand Army of the Republic in the first place."

John nodded. "Not much to tell. I went to college and graduated in 1949. Didn't know what to do. I've never known what to do except to be an engineer. I knew I needed to serve my country for a while, so I did basic training and learned the military way to run locomotives, which I'm still trying to forget. Then I went to a short-term officers' school and got posted to Japan in the fall of 1950. That didn't last long because I came in on one plane and was ordered to cross the landing strip and board the next one out to Korea."

John paused and shook his head as if to shake the bad memories away. "We were behind the front for a while. Then they wanted us up front for bridges and transport. We wound up on the road to Hagaru-ri about the time the rest of the guys were trying to get out of there. Some people were calling it a retreat. ..."

"Retreat, hell. We were just attacking in another direction,'" Bill interjected, repeating a battle cry of some of the Allied forces there at the time.

"General O.P. Smith?"

"You bet. He made me proud of what we done up there. Yes, sir."

"Me, too. My unit kind of wound up mixed into a task force, I guess they called it. We tried to help cover the advance to the south so those poor devils who got shot up so bad could get out. ... I guess you know the rest of my story. Thanks to you there was more. I wound up in an Army hospital in Texas where the doctors patched me up. Last summer I got my orders to go home and be in a standby mode, whatever that meant for a guy that doesn't stand very well any more. ... How about you?"

"I quit high school in 1945 and went to work for the Eastern, first as an apprentice car inspector and later as a steam engine fireman. I went over to your father's railroad before I joined the service in '48 and became an Army Ranger

29

and went to Japan. Luck would have it that I was in the first unit dispatched to Korea. Worked around the docks at Pusan for a while, bringing in the gear. ..."

The radio crackled. "Passengers getting off at High Meadow."

"Yep. Got it on my agenda. Thanks, Joe," the engineer responded.

"Anyway, John, I volunteered for one of those task forces that went up the road to meet the North Koreans. We didn't have much for equipment and took a helluva hit when we tried to stop them near one of them cardboard box villages south of Seoul. We retreated, or shall we say we fought a reverse engagement, running like hell all the time, and wound up in the defenses of the Pusan Perimeter. That went on a long time.

"Eventually, after Inchon, we moved north and began to pound the livin' hell out of the North Koreans, right up onto their home turf. We were around Yudam-ni when the Chinese Reds popped up and changed things. We were sort of doing what you guys were doing below Hagaru-ri when our paths crossed. Anyway, we got down to Hungnam after a while, loaded on the last of the survivors and the refugees and then watched the Navy shell hell out of the port. You burn your bridges behind you, I suppose."

Bill coughed and then continued. "Morale was pretty bad when we got back to South Korea. General Ridgway came along and shaped us up and pointed us north again. We were slogging along when I got the word that my replacement was there and it was time to go home. I squawked about it but you know how that is. I got my sergeant's stripes just before that, and a commendation, for whatever that was worth, for the work we done on the Perimeter. That, for me, was the hardest fighting. Boy, hour by hour, day by day, and day after day. ... "

Bill's voice trailed off. "It was long ago," he added in a somber tone, staring out the side window.

John knew that Bill Travers had told him all he had to say about the war. "Yes, it was long ago. Long ago and far away."

The passenger train glided up to the boarded-up station at High Meadow. John Kelly stepped off the steps of the coach *Bolton*, set down the stepstool and guided an elderly couple to the safety of the platform. Then he placed a suitcase in their care, shook hands with the man and tipped his brakeman's hat to the woman. Snatching up the stepstool, he waved a highball with his lantern and scrambled aboard.

"High Meadow. In at eight-naught-nine. Out at eight-ten," Joe reported on the radio.

"Got it. Hang on, you guys. Now we tackle the riffles."

"Hanging on. Remember the hay at Camp Twelve and a trapper for Camp Sixteen."

"Roger on the fodder. Roger on the trapper. Frankie Farrington?"

"It is. He's going to his camp on Munsungan Bog to get ready to trap beaver."

"Wish him well, Joe."

Bill opened the throttle, but only a notch or two. He instructed John to watch ahead for the beginning of the rough track. Back in the coaches, Joe Francis and John Kelly began their rounds, securing suitcases, knapsacks and shopping bags in the luggage racks.

The passenger train came to what appeared to be an endless string of boxcars on what seemed to be a long siding. "I've seen a lot of those cars all the way up from Hill Junction," John said. "They all refrigerator cars?"

Bill nodded and explained that the cars were some of the famous New England reefers. There were several hundred cars in that string alone. "It's more than five miles long. They're used to haul the potato crop. At least they used to, when we had a crop. That's what really crippled this railroad—one bad harvest after another. Last year's was the worst. I figured most of the farmers were too far under financially to plant this year. They went ahead anyway, and damned if they didn't get the biggest yield in years. It was unbelievable."

John shook his head. "And now they're losing their railroad, so they get hit again."

"Yep. That's the sad story. When the railroad goes, well, I guess that will be just about the end of this part of the country."

John continued to watch the string of boxcars. "That's a long siding," he observed.

"Actually, it's not a siding," Bill said. He pointed out that it used to be the northbound side of double track between a point just above Blackwater station and Spanish Junction. It was almost thirty miles in length with several crossovers to the existing main track, which had been for southbound trains only. "In the last couple years," he said, "Eastern has taken out rails here and there for replacements, so it's kind of broken up. The freight train that derailed at the Junction was going in on the upper end of the northbound track."

John asked if Bill knew what had caused the derailment of the Hayride and the engineer said that he did not but Molly had heard something about an engine wheel breaking off. "That's a strange one. I never happened to be around where an engine wheel broke off but I suppose anything is possible, especially with the Eastern," Bill responded.

As they were pondering the incident, the engine's headlight illuminated a trackside sign with a pair of yellow lanterns hanging on its posts. The sign stated: "Slow Speed. 10 MPH." Beyond, the track bobbed in and out of the headlight's beam.

"Always looks worse at night," Bill muttered. "Some train's going to fall off here pretty soon and wind up in the Spanish River." He pointed to the dark void beyond the fireman's window.

The engine lurched abruptly and leaned and then straightened out. Travers eased the throttle back. "Damn," he said. "We're down to about eight miles an hour. We'll stall out if we have to go any slower. ..."

"Bad track," John observed.

"That's for sure. Worst I've ever seen."

Train One pulled up near the shanty at Camp Twelve where several woods-men were waiting with horses and a set of bobsleds designed to haul pieces of pulpwood over snow in the forest. Working under the dim lights of several kerosene lanterns, Carleton and Dan Stubbs, the mail clerk, appeared to be making quick work of tossing baled hay onto the bobsleds after Stubbs had retrieved a mailbag from the crane near the shanty. The passenger train occasionally handled hay when other service wasn't available.

As John watched he spotted the conductor talking on a telephone affixed to the side of the shanty. He knew that there was no electrical service along the railroad line north of Blackwater village but there was a railroad telephone system; one known as a composite line that could be used by railroad workers, shippers and passengers in the region. One section of the line ran twenty miles along the telegraph poles from Blackwater to Camp Sixteen. The other spanned the five miles from South Spanish to Spanish Junction. Electrical service reached the tower at the junction from the north, ending there. There was no voice link between Camp Sixteen and South Spanish, a distance of four miles.

"Looks like Joe's talking to someone on the phone," John remarked.

"Molly, back at Blackwater," Bill said. "Trying to get an update, I'd say."

A moment later the conductor stepped back aboard the train as the horses pulled their sled away. John Kelly swung his lantern in a high arc above his head and he, too, stepped aboard. "Let's roll," the engineer said as he released the brakes.

"Looks like eight-thirty on the departure, Bill," Joe Francis reported on the radio.

"Okay. ... Find out anything on the phone, Joe? We've got about thirty miles to go in ninety minutes. That's a guess, but with a stop at Camp Sixteen and South Spanish and God knows what at Spanish Junction, it's going to be tough. I think the track is a little better up ahead, so that could help, but it's going to be one hell of a scramble."

"Carl and John Kelly and I are having a conference. Hold on."

Several minutes passed. Then the radio crackled again.

"Okay, Bill. Frankie got off at Camp Twelve. He'll stay at the logging camp tonight and go from there with the boys tomorrow. So you can highball Camp Sixteen."

"That's good. We owe Frankie one. Anything else up the line?"

"Yes. The two passengers for South Spanish just decided to go through to Summit and come back down tomorrow. Nobody called in on the railroad phone to Spanish Junction so there'll be no passengers to get on. All you'll have is the mailbag."

"The news gets better all the time. Anything else from Boomer at the Junction?"

"Only that the wreck foreman promises a clear track about nine-fifteen."

"Well, I'd say things are looking much better, Joe. Thanks."

Train One shook violently and slatted hard against the outside rail on a curve as the engineer edged the speed up to about twenty-five. In a few minutes the shanty at Camp Sixteen, a boarded-up station, loomed in the headlight and then vanished in the gloom as the train glided on through the night. They were finally out of the slow-speed zone and headed downgrade, and the speed recorder edged by thirty-five.

"Getting close to South Spanish," Bill radioed to his conductor.

"Highball South Spanish."

The engineer gave the whistle cord two sharp tugs. "Look back to see if the mail clerk has the catcher out," he said to John.

"It's out."

"You're going to see a snap here," Bill said. Ahead, a solitary figure appeared in the headlight's beam near the corner of the station building. "That's the postman. He's come for the mail. The station's closed now, but the village has a little post office down by the river. Probably thirty people or so live here year-round. No kids, of course, just older folks and a few younger people with time on their hands. Lot more in the summer."

The engine was bearing down on the old depot at thirty-five miles an hour when John noticed that a semaphore signal atop the structure was lighted. "High green," he called to Bill.

"High Green?" Bill queried. "Yeah, that's right. That's what I used to call out when I was firing steam. The station's been closed for a while but the track crew still keeps the signal lanterns filled with kerosene and the wicks trimmed … for some strange reason."

With his window slightly ajar—just enough to peer back at the mail car—John watched in fascination for the catch. The snap was sharp and clean and the spring-loaded crane banged loudly as it collapsed. A mailbag, inbound for South Spanish, was kicked by the mail clerk, propelling it out into the darkness. It landed in a pile of snow the postman had heaped up near the station.

"Wow! Nice soft landing," John remarked.

"Dan always makes sure of that," Bill chuckled. "The post office folks have a system."

The track's riding quality was decidedly improved as the train headed up another grade and into a sweeping curve where the forest along both sides of the track seemed to plunge into a dark void. John guessed they were running across a deep fill when he caught the outline of a two-track, open-deck bridge ahead. He stood up for a better look.

"Spanish River Bridge," Bill called out. "Longest and highest on the Hill Division. I bet it's seventy feet above the river. Crack your window a bit and take a listen."

John inched the window open as the engine rolled out onto the decking. The sound of rushing water filled the cab. "Sounds like one wild river," he remarked.

"Yeah. There's a stretch along here that's pretty rough, considerably more than just riffles. We had some heavy rain the last week or two and the Spanish is running bank full. Great country if you like a lot of racket." Bill eased the throttle back and stood up as the train reached the north side of the bridge.

"We're closing in on the junction," he said. "Long straight ahead. Keep an eye out for some activity ... a flagman, if we're not so lucky. ..." The radio crackled.

"What do you see now, Bill?" It was Joe Francis.

"Nothing so far, Joe. ... Wait, now. ... Glow in the distance. I'm reining in the engine." Bill pulled the throttle back, sounded the air horns and made a short brake application. The speed indicator fell to fifteen.

A lantern appeared in the distance. Bill reduced the speed to ten miles an hour and the headlight picked up the dark figure of a man standing by the track. He stepped into the headlight's beam, signaled the train to stop and retreated to the engineer's side of the track. Travers sounded a stop signal and pressed the radio talk button.

"Dandy Dan Detweiler wants us to stop, Joe."

Joe chuckled. "Okay, Bill, you better stop."

The engine coasted up to the brakeman who clutched the locomotive's grab irons and swung onto the cabin ladder. "Okay, Bill," he yelled. "Go ahead real slow. We think we're just about ready." The brakeman entered the cab.

"So, Dan, what brings a hooligan like you out on a night when the girls are prowling at that dive down on Easy Street?"

The brakeman grinned. He was young, likely in his early twenties, and looked to John like a man who would spend his idle hours in a place such as Bill described.

"Yeah, that's where I was ... and just about to score good when the railroad tracked me down. Someday I'm gonna get a nine-to-five job so I can play my game on my terms."

"John, this is Daniel Detweiler," Bill offered. "Dan is a brakeman in his spare time and a rake when he's working on his game. It's a game in progress because he never scores. John is ... well I'm not sure, Dan. He's a Shanahan, if the name rings a bell. Old war acquaintance of mine, and a darn good soldier."

"A Shanahan, you say? One of the railroad Shanahans?" Dan extended his hand and grasped John's in a firm handshake.

"Pleased to meet you, Dan. Yep, I'm one of those Shanahans. ... The one that never scores either."

The passenger train crept forward and when the wreck scene came into clear view, Bill brought it to a full stop and set the brakes. The locomotive that had derailed was askew in the siding to the right of the passenger train, just clearing the main line. The front wheel set was missing and the diesel unit was resting nose down in some twisted siding rails. Workmen were hammering furiously at replacement rails that had been installed to restore the main track. To the left, two freight cars without wheels were setting upright on the ground, apparently

34

having been placed there by the Big Hook. The wreck train had been pulled back and moved into a siding to the left of the main line.

Detweiler checked his watch. It was nine-fifteen. He peered ahead through the windshield and noticed that the track workers were picking up their tools and tossing them clear of the track. Then a man who appeared to be in charge waved the all-clear sign and Bill sounded an acknowledgement. The brakeman climbed down from the cab and waved and Travers lifted the radio receiver from its cradle. "All clear, Joe," he said.

"That's good news. Let's pull up to the tower and see what Boomer's got for us."

"Roger." The train inched forward across the temporary track. "Watch on your side, John. We have some close clearances right along here. Yell if you think we're too close."

"Okay, Bill." John watched closely as the train eased through the wreckage with only inches to spare. A few rail lengths beyond the derailment, the telegraph operator stepped from the shadows and handed up the orders. The engineer waved and opened the throttle again. The final leg of John Shanahan's journey of discovery was about to begin.

Chapter 6: Warming an Irishman's Heart

In their final push to reach Summit, track builders of late nineteenth century New England faced their hardest challenge. They toiled into December 1894, working against a year-end deadline after which their contract would be declared void. The rails went down on green cedar ties hurriedly hewn from the forest. The sixteen miles from Spanish Junction were laid during a cold snap and, in the last day and night, in blizzard conditions. Summit was reached only hours ahead of the deadline.

The builders were Italian immigrants, hardy pioneers engaged in the final great track-laying venture in American history. Iron rails spanned the nation a generation earlier, and although the settling of the new land by Europeans began in places like New England, this backcountry was one of the last places to be reached by rail.

∞

John Shanahan knew from a general interest in railroads that this was a historic line, one that finally opened the Northeast's timber and agricultural interests to the American marketplace in 1894 and 1895. After this evening's run through Mission, Blackwater, High Meadow and the other remote flag stops along Spanish River—places seemingly frozen in time—he marveled at how little civilization had progressed in half a century.

He shifted in the fireman's seat to ease the ache in his leg and pressed his face against the side window. All he could see was a wall of trees; a demarcation line between the vast northern boreal forest and the track that penetrated, but only in a tentative way, that wilderness. Trains had run on this track for more than 50 years but on this late fall night the railroad seemed but a hesitant visitor to an empty land.

The *Northern Express* had pulled out of Spanish Junction at nine-twenty p.m., rumbling into the long grade to the north. The crew was advised that they would tie up at Summit for the night. The trainmen on the freight train that had derailed earlier had returned to that terminal and would take over the passenger train to Quarry with only the locomotive and the business car *Seven Pines*. A handful of passengers that were en route to destinations on the Eden Valley line would have accommodations in the private car.

"How are we doing, Bill?" he asked the engineer who had fallen silent after beginning the assault on the hill north of Spanish Junction.

"Good. We're coming over the top, just ahead. There's a siding at the top called Hillman. Then it's downhill again through a bunch of curves and pretty quick you'll see the lights of Summit."

"So Summit isn't at the top of a hill? I'd ask you why the place is called Summit but I know there is some illogical explanation and maybe I don't need to know."

"Probably not."

The passenger train clattered over the siding switches and tracked into an S-curve. Travers eased the throttle back. "We drift along here. Nice easy run now. We'll pull in at nine fifty-nine p.m., seven hours and fourteen minutes late. That's a record. ..."

Bill paused and peered ahead, apparently searching for something, perhaps a landmark, John thought. "I want to show you something up here, in the next curve. Maybe it'll connect a few things for you. You watch on your side. There'll be a couple of mounds out on the right of way, just before the tree line. ... See, right there!"

The headlight illuminated the mounds. They were distinct snowy hummocks that glistened in the powerful beam of light. "I see them," John said.

"I told you I quit high school in 1945?"

"You did, and you went to work for the Eastern."

"Yes. I was a state kid. I never knew my father, and my mother, bless her— she died young. I was put in an orphanage and Jim and Emma Cummings of Summit took me in. Jim was an engineer for the Eastern. Salt of the earth and so's Emma. I went to school there and made it into my third year of high school. God knows, I wasn't much of a student so I decided to stop wasting everybody's time and went to work for the railroad."

John listened intently as Travers told how he eventually became a steam-engine fireman and took jobs whenever a fill-in man was needed. "It was just before Christmas 1945, and the Eastern was running a second section of the afternoon passenger train from Summit to Hill Junction. I caught the job, firing for Jim Cummings. The regular passenger train went out first and we were about twenty minutes behind them with the mail cars and a couple of coaches."

Bill told how he was shoveling coal furiously into the firebox as the train labored over the grade south of Summit. "We were coming around this curve right here when Jim yelled, 'Bail out, Billy! Jump! Jump now!' I stuck my head out and this plow train was right in our face. I went out this side but Jim ... he didn't have time to get out."

The engineer coughed and cleared his throat. "Jim was a kind man, really good to me. I went into the rocks over here on this side, got a cut on my head and broke my arm. I saw the trains collide and our engine went over on your side. The plow on the other train came all to pieces, like someone set off dynamite under it. Pieces of iron and wood were flying everywhere. Their engine crumpled up and the tender came into the cab and tore it off and then rolled over. I didn't see anyone get out of the plow train. ..."

He paused again, momentarily overcome by the memories. "Oh, yeah. Those two mounds back there. That's the coal from the two tenders in the

37

wreck, just as it fell out when they went over. That second pile was ours, the coal I was shoveling for Jim."

The engineer told of how the trainmen came up from the mail cars and coaches and tried to find the missing men. "Jack Demers—the conductor on the freight that derailed tonight—was the flagman on our train and he helped me back to the rear coach and bandaged up my head. I was one hysterical kid, I remember."

"I can't even imagine, Bill. Did somebody mix up a train order or something?"

"No, it was just a bad time on the railroad back then. There were a lot of misfits, wanderers and drunks mostly, that came on board when the good railroaders were away in World War II. Most of them are gone now. ..."

"Anyway, that crew had been drinking all day in a bar down at Gatlin when they got called for the plow job. They had an order to come north with the understanding that they had to make their own meets on the passenger train schedule. They were in at Spanish Junction to clear the passenger train but pulled out right after the first section went by. The telegraph operator, an old guy who came before Boomer, tried to flag them down but he couldn't. He got the dispatcher on the wire, but it was too late."

"The first section must have been carrying green flags," John offered. "That would have made it clear that another section was right behind them."

"Damned right they were carrying green. I passed the green flags to the fireman at the station in Summit and watched him stick them in the holders on the front of their engine. Jim told me to do that because he wanted to be sure they were carrying green. Half a dozen guys around the station saw him put 'em up. I know the flags were up."

Bill pulled off a glove and put his hand to his face.

"It's hard to tell the story now. It shouldn't ever have happened. Anyway, the Interstate Commerce Commission held a hearing to investigate the accident and all that came out," Bill said as he slipped the throttle back a notch.

"The plowman and the head brakeman and the engineer and fireman on that job were all killed. The conductor was supposed to be in the caboose, so the story goes. The telegraph operator said he saw the flags but he didn't see the conductor at all because the head brakeman signed the register book. The crew was dead so they couldn't tell anything. ... The conductor was from out west somewhere, or so he claimed when he hired on, and he just disappeared. Nobody ever saw him again. I guess the general consensus was that he wasn't even on the train when it left Gatlin."

Travers went on. "The relief train took me and the mail clerk to the hospital in Summit. That was Danny, back in the next car—Dan Stubbs. He got banged around a little but he was okay. The doctors did some fancy stitching and set my arm. They found Jim's body the next day, under our tender. The other guys were all tangled up in the wreckage of their engine and the plow. When I got patched up, I went home and tried to help Emma.

"She's a good woman, that Emma. So was her sister Eva. Eva was married to Harold Boston who used to run the passenger train up to Boundary and back. Eva died just after their daughter was born and Emma helped raise her—Jennifer, she's a sweetheart, twenty, going on twenty-one, like a kid sister to me."

Bill told how Harold had died a few days after he retired in 1946 and about how his teenage daughter went to pieces over the loss. "Jen has a little girl now—Katie turned three last June—and they're on their own. They have Harold's home, right next door to Emma's. ... Emma's been like a mother to Jen and Katie. ... I still stay with Emma when I'm not running out of Quarry and I try to be around for all of them. Well, I'm rambling as usual. ... Guess that's enough family history. Watch for the lights at Summit."

John stood up and leaned on the console below the locomotive's front window. The skyline appeared lighter in the north and then lights began to twinkle through the trees. The passenger train rounded a curve and the first settlement of any substance in almost ninety miles came fully into view.

"Son of a gun," John commented. "That's quite a place. I'm surprised."

"Yeah, Summit's the county seat, business center and marketplace of the North Country."

Bill turned to the radio. "Hey, Joe. You there? Coming up on Summit."

"That's affirmative. Your watch keeping good time?" It was Carleton.

"Yep. It's nine fifty-six."

"Right on the money. That was a good piece of driving, my little man."

"Thanks. I hope that sentiment will be reflected in my next paycheck."

Travers cut the throttle back and Train One glided under the canopies that shielded the passenger platforms at the mammoth Summit station. He worked the air-brake handle gingerly and the passenger train coasted to a stop.

"I make it in at nine fifty-nine p.m." It was Joe on the radio. "Roger on nine fifty-nine," Bill answered.

"Good work in the engine," Joe said.

"Thanks. Good work back there."

The engineer leaned back in his seat. "Well, Mr. Shanahan, welcome to Summit and the end of the line for this crew tonight. What do you think, eh?"

"Jeez, Bill. It's pretty nice. My father said it was quite the place but I couldn't imagine anything like this up this far from anywhere. Look at all the people on the platform. I haven't seen that many people all in one place for days."

"Look over there, John," Bill said, pointing to a slim young woman and a little girl. "You see the one in the blue coat with the hood pulled up. ... The one with the little girl, right there by the waiting room door? That's Jenny and she's got Katie with her. When Jen's not working they come down in the evening if they know there's a train coming in. The girls love trains."

John opened the side window and looked. Then, trying not to appear to be staring, he looked quickly away. But his eyes were drawn back. Jennifer pulled back her hood and waved. Their eyes met. He waved back. She had dark hair and dark eyes and a smile to warm an Irishman's heart.

39

He remembered his father telling about his first meeting with Alicia McMahon many years earlier. It was a magical moment, his father had said, and this surely was a magical moment, too. Maybe I'm going to grow to like this place, he thought as he stared out the cab window, transfixed by the most beautiful young woman he had ever seen. He was warm again, he realized, even though a bitter wind blew through the open window on his side of the locomotive.

Bill picked up his traveling bag and crossed the cab to wave to Jenny and Katie and then turned to John. "Okay, we part company here. You might want to go back to the business car with Ramon. The engineer and two of the brakemen will ride up here and Jack Demers, the conductor, will be back with you and a few passengers for the branch. It's been a real pleasure, John. This was a reunion long overdue. Take care of yourself."

John nodded but his mind was elsewhere. He got up stiffly and limped to the door. After Bill descended the ladder, John passed his cane down. Jennifer Boston reached for it and cautioned him to be careful on the way down. He slipped awkwardly, of course, and caught himself and then clambered down the ladder. He turned, nearly stumbled and thanked her, retrieving the cane but not before almost knocking it from her hand. Tongue-tied, he simply said, "Thanks."

"You're welcome," she said and her dark eyes seemed to search his soul. She was incredibly beautiful, he thought, and so very gracious.

"You're Jennifer. ... And this is Katie. Bill told me about you on the trip up." John said, trying desperately to formulate another coherent sentence. He could not.

"Yes, I'm Jenny," she said, "and you're Mr. Shanahan. Katie and I are pleased to meet you." She pulled off a mitten and extended her hand. It was soft and warm. Her whole countenance radiated warmth and that seemed special on a cold night in a faraway place.

"Just call me John. I'm pleased to meet you, Jenny, and you, too, Katie." Before John could think of something else to say, Bill lifted Katie high above his head. "Hi, princess!" he yelled. "Come to see the train? Want to go and look at the fancy car on the rear?"

"Yes, Uncle Billy! Please take me up to see the fancy car." Travers tucked the squealing youngster under his arm and walked to the back of the train. "Wow! That is a fancy car," she exclaimed.

"She wants to be an engineer," Jennifer said to John. "My father was an engineer once and he took me in the engine a lot when he worked for the railroad."

"She's a beautiful little girl," John observed. "Bill said you two come to the station often. You must live nearby."

"Just down the street, third house on the left beyond the station. My father and my uncle built identical houses side by side and I have always lived there."

John nodded and wanted desperately to continue the conversation but he was at a loss for words.

Jenny smiled and looked up into his eyes. "I'm glad you have come here. This railroad situation is becoming desperate and everybody is still hoping that something will happen to save it. Do you suppose that is possible?"

"Well, gosh, I hope so, too, but, well, it didn't look too promising when I left Chicago ... whenever that was ... days ago, now. Honestly, I don't know. My father was trying but it seemed, at least when I left, that ... well, it seemed anyway ... that the possibility was ... slipping away. I'm really sorry, though, now that I'm here. ..."

"Be optimistic, John. We are." Jennifer was about to say more when a heavy-set and well-dressed but slightly disheveled man burst through the station door.

"John Shanahan!" he exclaimed. "We've been waiting for you." He shook John's hand. "I'm Henry Terrell of the Summit, Bolton and Quarry. Most people call me Hank."

"I'm delighted to meet you, Hank. My father speaks most highly of you and sends his good wishes. I know you talk often, so you've probably been in touch with him since I left Chicago. How is my dad?"

"He's fine, John. Concerned about your welfare mostly. He wants to talk to you but he's in some heavy negotiating and we have to move this train, or what will be left of it after the crew breaks it up, which they seem about ready to do." Hank pointed just as a whoosh of air from a parted brake line indicated that the switching move was under way.

The locomotive pulled the *Northern Express* cars away from *Seven Pines* and trundled them off to tracks leading to the shop. "We're doing the car cleaning here tonight, John. This relief crew from the Eastern will take your car on to Quarry so you and Ramon can settle in at the summer place. You'll also have five passengers on the way down. Okay?"

"Absolutely. After that long trip, they deserve a ride in a fancy car, Hank. So what do you hear about what's going on with the Eastern?"

Hank's face clouded. "Nothing, really. That meeting your father is in relates to that topic, but so far there has been no breakthrough. It doesn't look good. We thought the abandonment was decided a few days ago, and that's why you're here. Then Eastern came back to the table with another option. So far, it's nothing Shanahan Enterprises can accept, or should, for that matter. This meeting could be the last one, I'm sorry to say."

"Well, I'm sorry, too." John turned to Jennifer who was standing nearby. She appeared about ready to cry. John couldn't think of any words to console her. He patted her gently on the shoulder. "Something surely will work out, Jennifer," he said softly.

She looked up at him and managed a smile. "I'll pray about it. Now I must go home. Bill and Katie are waiting. I'd like to see you again ... before you go back home."

"Me, too. Perhaps I could call you sometime from Quarry?"

"Please. That would be very nice. Well, I'll just say goodbye … for now." She walked off to join Bill and Katie but kept stopping and looking back. Finally, she stepped inside the waiting room.

"She's a lovely young lady, John," Hank offered as Ramon came out through the same waiting room door. "Well, Hank, I guess it's time for me and Little John to climb aboard, Ramon announced. "Jack Demers has the passengers seated in the observation room and I have a little culinary surprise awaiting them."

"That would be stew, Hank," John chimed in. "It was blizzard stew back along, so what is it this time, Ramon? Oh, I know, homecoming stew. Right?"

"See what I've had to put up with, Hank? Imagine, a poor working-class stiff like me having such a polished brat around. It's enough to make a guy want to break into the Shanahan liquor cabinet and drown his sorrows in some high-class booze."

"Don't pay any attention to him, Hank," John said. "It's strange how that stuff has evaporated lately. Ramon has the only key to the stash, so draw your own conclusions."

"It looks like your train is ready to leave, and not a minute too soon. Thank goodness. Go now, please. Don't miss that train because old Hank's head is spinning. I'll talk to you guys later … much later." Hank turned on his heel and dashed into the station.

Train One left Summit at ten-ten, seven hours and ten minutes behind schedule. After realigning the main line switch at Quarry Junction, Conductor Demers checked on his passengers in the observation lounge and returned to the dining room area where John was seated. After placing the train's portable radio in an empty chair, the conductor sat down at the table.

"You're J.P.'s son, I understand," he said. "I'm Donald S. Demers, a train-man for the Canadian Eastern, New England Eastern and the Summit, Bolton and Quarry railroads. A little work here; a little work there." The conductor shrugged his shoulders. "No matter. A guy makes a living the best he can. It's nice to meet you, sir. … Just call me Jack."

John got up and shook the conductor's hand. "It's my pleasure, Jack. You seem to be quite the industrious fellow."

"Got a wife and half a dozen kids back home. Keeps a guy hopping to keep grub on the table. I'm an American but I live over the border across from Bound-ary. Mostly do spare work out of Sainte Anne on the CE or Boundary for the NEE. Gotta keep the family fed."

"Bless you, Jack. It's for a good cause."

"Thanks, Mr. Shanahan. Now tell me straight up and honest. What's going on with the Eastern deal? Go or no go? Lot of folks are just hanging on here, hoping it will go."

"Wish I could tell you but I don't know, honest and straight up. When I left Chicago, there was no deal. It was over. Since I got up here today, everyone's been asking the same thing. Hank told me there were negotiations going on.

That was news to me. I guess everybody knows about my mission. It was to attend to the closing down of the SB&Q. I didn't want the job. Still don't, but I owe my father plenty of favors. After that, God knows. A guy with a lame leg doesn't have many options."

"So what did you do before? Word around here was that you were in the war and got shot up. That so, Mr. Shanahan?"

"Just John. No mister stuff. I was a locomotive engineer on the South Montana Railroad when I wasn't in school somewhere. That's all I wanted to be, Jack. I used to be pretty good at it, but the war gummed up that possibility. Yeah, I was in Korea, up close and personal. I suppose I might get a pension from the Army someday. I don't know."

"You're a straight shooter, John Shanahan. So's your old man. That's why we were hoping something would come out of this talk about Shanahan Enterprises taking over the Eastern. We're still thinking positive … Well, I thank you for your time. Guess I need to get to work and find out where we are. I don't get down on this line very often."

Demers turned on the radio and depressed the mic button. "Calling Engineer Adams. You there, Asa?"

"Right here, Jack. We're going down into the valley. Message says we have a passenger for Johnson Farm. That's a couple flag stops ahead."

"Yeah. That's the one. Then Promised Land and Bolton. After that, highball to Quarry."

"Got it. With a short train like this we ought to be able to spot you right up close to the stations."

"Thanks, Asa. We'll drop the lace curtain at Quarry station, run down to the wye and turn. After that, it's a straight run to Summit where we leave the engine at the shop and head for home. … You got any work tomorrow?"

"Nothing in sight, Jack. Guess I'll drive up to the Terrell farm and see if there's any work in one of the potato houses. How about you?"

"Nothing here. I got a shot at the *Halifax Express* on the Canadian Eastern tomorrow night out of Sainte Anne's. Not a bad job, but it's only for one way. Then I get a day deadheading back. Maybe there'll be something here again in a few days. Plow job or something. You're right. Damn slim pickings."

"Good luck, Jack," John called as the conductor pulled on his coat in preparation for the first passenger drop. "Thanks, John. Good luck to you in whatever you wind up doing," the conductor responded as he entered the hallway leading to the observation lounge.

The *Northern Express* completed its run to Quarry at ten fifty-five p.m., almost seven hours behind schedule. Ramon and John got off on the platform and walked to a station wagon that was parked there with the keys in the ignition. They climbed in and Ramon drove up the hill to Seven Pines. John was struck by the grandeur of the place but was too tired to look around. He tumbled onto a sofa in the spacious living room and fell into a deep sleep. Ramon brought a heavy blanket and tossed it across his traveling companion.

43

"Sleep well, John," he said softly. "Tomorrow is the day that you start a new chapter in your life. God bless you, my friend. You deserve the very best. Maybe that young lady at Summit will fit into your future."

Part II: The Deal of the Century

Chapter 7: Happy Days Ahead

The mansion later named Seven Pines had been the corporate headquarters for the Black Hills Slate Company in Township Eleven, a remote site more than twenty miles northeast of Summit in the northernmost state in New England. The two-and-a-half story granite structure was constructed in 1890 atop a knoll that overlooked the Eden River valley to the south and east and meadowland bordered by the Black Hills to the north.

The imposing building provided offices for management and operations personnel on the first floor and residential space upstairs. One end of the second floor was dedicated to living quarters for the family of the principal owner; the other offered a similar arrangement for the family of the general manager. Above that was an attic of sorts with a series of dormer windows on both sides of the roof to let in light. It was a place to keep office records and supplies.

The first state highway from Sunbury to the North Country was a torturous earthen road that ran north to Gatlin before swinging east and north again to skirt the wilderness. It was called the Hackmatack Highway because of the extensive growth of juniper trees then predominant in the region. Local residents retained that name long after the state applied a gravel surface and designated the highway as Route Eleven.

The Hackmatack Highway entered the state's northernmost settlements from the southeast and connected with a north-south road at a farming village known as Four Corners. That public way ran from Boundary on the Canadian border through the heartland of the region's agricultural belt to a southern terminus at Summit. A side road turned to the east at a place called Siberia Crossing and extended nearly ten miles to the village of Bolton, where a box and barrel factory was constructed in the early 1890s.

The slate company built its own road in a northerly direction from Bolton for a distance of eight miles to gain access to places where slate was found in the Black Hills. That road and right of way remained the property of Black Hills Slate throughout its existence.

It turned out that the transporting of slate by oxcart over a series of rudimentary roads was difficult and expensive, and the operation was suspended to await the completion of a railroad line. That occurred in 1895 when a predecessor to the New England Eastern constructed track into Summit. A twenty-two mile branch line to the mining center was the next priority and its building was carried out the next spring and summer.

The slate company immediately recognized the railroad as an efficient way to move their product to market. To facilitate the handling of slate slabs from the quarries to the finishing sheds near the corporate headquarters, the firm built their own connecting line—one with an American standard gauge of four feet, eight-and-a-half inches between the rails—for a distance of almost eight miles along the front of the Black Hills range. Several spurs were built from the main track into valleys between the hills where quarrying operations were set up.

A company village took shape around the headquarters and the railroad built a switching yard there, along with a station, roundhouse and various support buildings. A coaling tower and a water tank were also constructed. The slate company built a huge steam plant to provide a local energy source. Steam was piped into several buildings, including the corporate office, to provide heat.

The place was called Black Hills Junction at first. That name was changed later to Quarry.

Black Hills Slate closed its operations in the North Country in 1944 and moved away. Some machinery was removed but the village remained intact, albeit empty. New England Eastern continued freight service on the branch line only as far as Bolton Box and Barrel in 1945 but soon afterward sought and received Interstate Commerce Commission to abandon the entire line.

∞

John P. Shanahan III found himself in the village called Quarry in late October 1951. He had been sent there to assist in the closing down of the railroad for a second time. He had arrived in the middle of the night and fallen asleep on a sofa in the large living room of what had been the slate company's corporate headquarters. When he awoke it took several minutes to adjust to his new surroundings, now a well-appointed summer home owned by his parents.

He sat up on the sofa and looked around. The great room was as his mother had described it, a large open space with an original granite fireplace that dominated the north wall. At the other end of the room French doors opened to a veranda that spanned the front of the building.

John picked up his cane and limped to the entryway for a look outside. The view to the southeast was of a pristine meadow bounding a river that meandered to the distant horizon. His mother had described that too, remarking that it was a piece of heaven on earth that God had been kind enough to bring to the attention of the Shanahan family. He remembered the stories of how his father had come there by chance to look at the abandoned railroad property and the possibilities of investing in a short-line operation to serve a limited rail freight base in the nearby village of Bolton.

∞

The railroad financier heard about the plight of the Bolton business place through Henry Terrell, who was the station agent there at the time of abandonment. Several Terrell brothers were partners in the business and worked relentlessly to save train service through representatives of outside railroad interests. J.P. was moved by Henry's direct appeal to him and decided to conduct a personal inspection to assess the prospects of reopening short-line service as a stopgap measure to keep the Bolton factory open. He and his wife, Alicia, traveled to Summit in their private railroad car so he could meet the business owners and look at existing railroad facilities.

During that trip, their first to the North Country, they rented a car and drove in on the Quarry Road from Bolton to see what was there. Their first stop was the abandoned corporate building on the hill. They walked hand in hand through the high grass and bushes that had overspread the lawn and lingered to admire the view beyond seven pine trees spaced equal distances apart in a line parallel to the road.

Alicia was enthralled. "This is such a beautiful place!" she exclaimed. "What a wonderful view out across that river valley. If I lived here, I would call this place Seven Pines."

"Would you like to live here some day?" J.P. asked. "Yes!" she exclaimed.

That was all it took. Through a series of contacts, J.P. found the slate company's site caretaker, a slate cutter-turned-farmer, who lived on Bolton Road. His name was Clement Morse and he had a key to the former headquarters. "Go in and take a look around, Mr. Shanahan," he said. "The company would love to get rid of the property. They told me they'd like to dump everything they own at Quarry, dirt cheap. They have other interests now."

The Shanahans returned to Quarry, went through the building and then explored the railroad yard. They walked along a dead-end street highlighted by a row of ten tiny quarrymen's houses, all of which were identical. When they returned to what had been the main road in the village center, Alicia spotted a street sign in the brambles. She pulled away the bushes. "Ten Commandments Street! I love it. Just think, with a little paint—some nice colors—how beautiful this little street could be."

The upshot of the visit was that Shanahan Enterprises bought all the slate company's holdings—almost a whole township's worth—along with the buildings and roads and the right to quarry slate if the occasion ever arose. Then the Chicago-based business bought the railroad branch in its entirety, a portion of the yard at Summit, the car shops there and, later, the massive Victorian-style station. J.P. had trains running again thirty days from the date of the sale and came back to Summit specifically to ride the first train into Quarry.

The Shanahans called their new seasonal home Seven Pines and the railroad was named Summit, Bolton and Quarry. The village proper was placed in the hands of a Shanahan-created nonprofit entity, the Quarry Village Community Association. Clem Morse was offered a position with Shanahan Enterprises as village supervisor, estate caretaker and engine house foreman at Quarry. He accepted the post gladly. Henry Terrell, who was then the station agent at Summit for New England Eastern, became manager of operations for the Summit, Bolton and Quarry Railroad.

John P. Shanahan III walked the grounds of Seven Pines that October day, stopping and leaning heavily on his cane from time to time to marvel at the transformation of Quarry from the way his parents described it at first to how it looked that morning.

It was a lovely little railroad town that had been brought back to life by his father, a visionary who didn't stop with a short-line railroad designed principally to serve Bolton Box and Barrel Company. He remembered that the senior Shanahan had contacts in the federal government, particularly branches of the military. The railroad financier had observed that the rolling hills and meadows to the west of Quarry village offered the kind of setting he had heard the Army was seeking to test new technological advances in train transportation. John remembered that J.P. went to Washington armed with charts and maps and data compiled by Shanahan Enterprises, and sold the Pentagon on his notion.

∞

Army engineers were on the scene within weeks of Shanahan's initial contacts in 1945. They came to design and lay out a year-round railroad facility where the testing would occur. It was to be a secure facility with access only through a guard post off Quarry Road. Shanahan's engineers were dispatched to Quarry to work with the Army to create a small interchange yard connecting the Summit, Bolton and Quarry main line with the entrance to the military installation. Unit trains containing rails, ties, construction equipment and supplies began arriving in Summit over the New England Eastern. Shanahan's SB&Q established a dedicated mixed freight and passenger service to bring in the equipment and personnel assigned to the task.

But only six years later, in the summer of 1951, New England Eastern, which offered the only connection for SB&Q with outside railroads, was almost bankrupt and was under the control of a holding company. NEE petitioned the federal Interstate Commerce Commission to abandon all track north of the mill at Gatlin. Although local opposition was widespread, the governor stepped forward to support the abandonment, with the understanding that the roadbed would be turned over to state government for the purpose of eventually building a new highway from Gatlin to Summit and beyond. Shanahan Enterprises was forced to declare that if abandonment were authorized, it would have no recourse but to close down as well.

The ICC reluctantly agreed that the abandonment was the only solution. Shanahan Enterprises made several offers to buy the property, none of which was acceptable to New England Eastern. With time running out near the end of October, NEE representatives made a surprise counter offer and negotiations were reopened. Even as John Shanahan III, representing Shanahan Enterprises, arrived by train in the North Country to participate in the shutting down of the Summit, Bolton and Quarry line, discussions were continuing.

∞

John went back inside and wandered throughout the house, peeking into the various rooms on the first floor. He was in a jovial mood when he found the kitchen where Ramon Martinez, his travel companion, appeared to be preparing a meal.

"Ahoy, there, Ramon, this sailor just dropped anchor and noted activity in the galley," he announced as he plunked down at the end of the kitchen table.

Ramon ignored him and continued to stir a pot on the sideboard. He added water on some occasions and a flour-like substance on others.

"I say there, Ramon, I see that you are preparing one of those elegant culinary specialties for which you are so well known in gourmet circles. And what would it be on this fine day?"

There was no answer. Ramon turned his back on John and continued stirring.

"C'mon, Ramon. John is hungry. Anything would do. How about a sandwich, say peanut butter on dark bread? Just some little tidbit to sooth a man's hunger pangs."

Ramon stopped stirring and turned around. "Oh, hi, John. Didn't hear you come in. Hunger pangs, you say? I see." He checked his watch. "Hmmm. Almost ten-thirty in the morning. How about a little warmed-over blizzard stew? I recall you expounding to Hank on that extraordinary culinary delight last night when we blew into Summit."

"Well, I was thinking more along the lines of some of those fabulous flapjacks that you can rustle up on a minute's notice, if you don't mind. ... Yeah, half a dozen of those special Ramon flapjacks floating in some of that Yankee maple syrup would do the trick. And I'd savor a cup of tea for a chaser. Irish tea, like Molly makes down at Blackwater."

"Uh huh. Tell you what. Here's a real specialty that even an oaf like you can prepare." Ramon went to the cupboard, perused the shelves and selected a jar of peanut butter, a loaf of white bread and a bottle of molasses. He placed each on the end of the table and slid them, one at a time, to John at the other end. A plate and eating utensils followed.

"There, my good man. We don't have dark bread in Ramon's kitchen because it's not meant for human consumption. Put a slice of white in your plate and slather it with the molasses. It doesn't taste the same, but the color is sort of close. Go easy on the peanut butter because that's the last jar we have. ... Will that satisfy your hunger pangs?"

"How about something to drink?"

"The glasses are in the cupboard and there's water in the tap, if the pump is running. If not, just tip the glass to your lips and pretend. The taste will be about the same."

Ramon went back to his stirring and John went to the cupboard for an empty glass, after which he attempted to create a peanut butter sandwich. When it was done, he took a bite. "Hmmm, Ramon, not half bad. And you'll notice that I'm really enjoying my glass of water." John raised the empty glass to his lips. "Wow! This invisible Quarry water is the best! Yes, sir, now John Shanahan the Third is finally enjoying the good life that he richly deserves. Wouldn't you say that is so, Ramon?"

"Without a shadow of a doubt."

With that contribution to the conversation completed, Ramon lifted the pot he was stirring and covered it. Then he plucked a cigar from his shirt pocket and unwrapped and examined it. Satisfied that it was genuine Cuban, he lit the cigar, inhaled and blew a smoke ring. He retrieved another cigar from a cache in the cupboard, along with a box of wooden matches, and shoved both along the table to John.

"Nothing like a good filched cigar to top off a fine breakfast in Ramon's kitchen. Wouldn't you say that is so, John?"

Ramon grinned first. Then John grinned back. Simultaneously, both burst into gales of laughter.

After regaining his composure, John suggested that he was still hungry. "So what's that concoction you were preparing when I so rudely interrupted you?"

"Wallpaper paste. Want to check it for flavor?" Both laughed uproariously. Then Ramon dumped the concoction into a garbage barrel. "I was going to do a little wallpapering, but I lost interest when you came bumbling in. ... You still hungry?"

John nodded.

"Me, too. What say we go down to your old man's garage, pick out the hottest looking vehicle in the Shanahan stable and motor off to Summit. I know a restaurant where the food's top notch, the prices aren't bad and the waitresses are the best part of the menu."

"Hey, I could do that. I don't have anything on my agenda that won't keep for another day. In fact, I don't even have an agenda. Let's do it."

An hour later, Ramon and John were sampling wines and eating T-bone steaks in a classy eatery on Railroad Street in downtown Summit. The food was great, the ambiance pleasing and the waitresses friendly and fetching. John was well into his dessert when he remembered the negotiations to determine the future of railroads in the North Country.

"Ramon, I forgot to ask about the railroad deal!" he exclaimed. "Did you find out anything before I fell out of bed this morning?"

Ramon shook his head. "No. I called Hank and all he could say was that negotiations recessed in the night but would continue this afternoon. He seemed more hopeful than when we saw him last. I'll tell you one thing, when J.P. sets his mind to something he makes it come out the way he wants if he has to work at it around the clock."

"So, you figure it might be a go?"

Ramon nodded. "There's a lot at stake, and that's when your father is at his best. I think this thing is going to happen, and if it happens to be something that appeals to you, I'd say you'd be around here for a long, long time. How does that notion wind your crank?"

50

"Well, twenty-four hours ago … as you probably remember … that was something that I would never consider. As we came up the line, the idea began to grow on me and …"

"And then you ran into a little lady who kind of caught your fancy?"

"Yeah." John scraped his pie plate clean and sat back in the booth. "Yes, that's right." He shrugged his shoulders. "I don't know. I came home from the war as, well, I'd guess like they say, a broken man. Hell, I just wanted to go back to Montana after my service time and operate locomotives again. Nothing more. …"

John stared sadly out the restaurant window. "But, with that option gone," he continued, "railroads didn't really appeal to me anymore. I definitely didn't want an office job, which I guess is what my father had in mind. So I agreed to come on this one job for him, after which I figured I'd go scouting around for something more suitable for a guy in … well, you know … in this condition."

"So, given your so-called 'condition,' what would you have wanted to try to do?"

"Well, truth is, I gave that a lot of thought when I was in the hospital in Texas and finally deduced that I wasn't qualified for anything. I used to sit in a wheelchair out in the hospital yard and watch people coming and going and feel sorry for myself. That stayed with me, even back in Chicago, as you recall. I was a nasty guy then—to you and my family. You set me straight, Ramon, one time when we went out to a bar on the South Side. Remember? What was the name of that band?"

Ramon laughed. "Genghis Khan and the Mongols. That was one wild night. You got whining about your condition right when I was getting into the music. So I grabbed you by the throat, called you some uncomplimentary names and gave you a good shaking."

"Yep. Scared the hell out of me. Best advice I ever had. Trouble is, I could never seem to come up with a job to last out my time on this earth."

"Let's just suppose the railroad thing goes and you hang around here. You discover one day, as I think you already did yesterday, that you can get up into an engine if you try hard enough and calculate your steps correctly, and then do the same thing coming down, which I saw you do. If that happens, you could operate a locomotive. Now if you worked two jobs, say like being some kind of an office lay-about one time and a locomotive engineer the next, how would that suit you?"

"That sounds like my kind of job," John admitted. "Yeah, I could do that."

"Good. Well, we need to get back to Quarry and do something constructive. I'll go out and start the car and you pay the checkout gal. Oh, and leave a nice tip for the waitress."

"I thought this fancy dinner was your idea and I was just going along for the ride."

"Look's like you thought wrong. I'll be waiting in the car."

51

Ramon made the return trip a leisurely outing, stopping often to point out interesting landmarks along the way. Although it was late in the year and the foliage was gone and patches of snow foretold the season to follow, the countryside had a genuine appeal, John thought. Farmland was the prevalent feature, broken here and there by fingers of forest seemingly intent on claiming back the open land.

After they reached Bolton village and turned in on Quarry Road the scene changed dramatically. From there the land was heavily forested and the softwood trees stood out against the deep blue sky. In the distance, the dark hills of Quarry rose from behind the unbroken evergreen forest.

Later, Ramon took John on a house tour and explained how the place had been remodeled into a fashionable getaway for J.P. and Alicia. Their wish was to retain as much of the original architecture as possible and yet convert the building from an office to a home. The sprawling "great room," central to the first-floor living space, was fashioned from an open office where upwards of twenty members of the slate company's clerical staff once attended to business records. A stone fireplace was upgraded and continued to be the centerpiece of the room. The room exited to a covered veranda that ran the entire length of the front of the structure.

A formal dining room and kitchen-pantry were created in the eastern end of Seven Pines where several offices for high-ranking officials had been before. An alcove next to the kitchen provided a place for a new spiral staircase that led to the former owner's living quarters on the second floor.

A hallway from the great room to a staircase providing access to the second story living quarters for the slate company's manager had divided the west end. Other offices and meeting rooms lined the hallway. That arrangement remained the same after renovation, except that the offices became bedrooms. One room, however, that of the company treasurer retained its original trappings, right down to a small bank vault. Books replaced corporate records on shelves that rimmed the room. The space became the family library.

The second floor layout remained the same. J.P. and Alicia made the owner's apartment theirs and kept the other for special guests. Both were refurnished and refurbished.

Ramon and John were standing by the windows in the guest apartment taking in the view of the village and railroad yard when they heard the distinctive sound of diesel air horns blatting in the distance. Ramon checked his watch. "Four-ten," he noted. "Looks like the Bill Travers gang is back in town."

The train reminded John of the matter of the railroad's future. "Seems like we ought to be hearing something pretty soon regarding the business in Chicago, wouldn't you say? You know, like where do we go from here. I'm thinking now that I'd like to hang around for a while."

"Me too. This place kind of grows on you."

The long-awaited call came at seven-thirty in the evening. Ramon answered. It was J.P. Shanahan. "Ramon, my friend, we just pulled off the deal of the century! It's ours, the whole doggone shooting match! I got it for a song. Hear me, Ramon? We got ourselves a real deal. It's a sure bet because it's worth more for scrap than what we paid for it."

"Fantastic, Boss! Hey, you want to talk to John? He got bundled up and went out on the veranda to take in the peace and quiet. I think he likes it here; I mean he really likes it."

"That's great news. Look, Ramon, I need to get some more calls out and fast. First to Hank, God bless him. I want this to be his announcement to the folks up there. I have press all over the place right now so I need to go. Tell John we'll have a long talk later. See you. Happy days ahead, my friend!"

Chapter 8: The Shanahan Team

Ramon Martinez stood quietly by the French doors in the great room at Seven Pines and watched his friend who was sitting on the top step of the veranda's staircase. John Shanahan was huddled in a blanket and appeared to be watching the stars that twinkled across the heavens. Maybe this place was the antidote John needed to put the tumult of the last year behind him, Ramon thought as he opened the door and stepped outside.

Ramon sat down next to John. "Nice evening," he offered.

"Yeah. I've been watching the stars come out. It's fantastic. I don't remember seeing the stars in Chicago. Too many streetlights, I guess."

"That's right. ... Oh, by the way, J. P. called."

"Really? So what's the rascal cooking up tonight?"

"Oh, nothing much. He bought a railroad today; dirt cheap, I guess."

"I see. Good for him. That's what a fellow can do with a lot of money."

"Right."

John returned his attention to the stars. "This is a fantastic place, Ramon. I can see why my mother loves it here. You know, I studied astronomy once but danged if I can identify any of these stars. You've been here before so why don't you give me a guided tour?"

"Well, I don't know. I'm more into making wallpaper paste these days."

"I'd make some smart remark and we could continue this conversation for hours. Give me a tour of the sky, please. Where's Polaris? Isn't that a logical starting point?"

Ramon got up and led John out into the front yard. Using the North Star as an axis, he pointed out the best-known constellations. John was struck by his friend's knowledge of the northern night sky. When he noticed a particularly bright celestial object in the west, one that stood out above the hills, John pointed in that direction.

"I bet that's a planet, Ramon. Probably Venus?"

Ramon shifted his attention to the object. "Ah, well, not quite," he responded. "What you see there is the beacon for the radio tower the Army uses over at the test site."

"Oh, so it is. I must be disoriented. ... What railroad did you say my father bought?"

"I didn't, but it's called the Hill Division of the New England Eastern. You ever hear of that one?"

"Sure. I think it's in New England, in the eastern part. Probably on a hill of sorts."

"Uh huh." Ramon rolled his eyes. "Well, it's been nice talking to you, buddy."

"Hold on, Ramon! That's the railroad that comes to Summit. The one he's been trying to save for the people up here. That's great news!"

"Well, I thought so until I got disoriented by the stars. Starlight, star bright, what star do I see tonight? Why, I believe it is Las Vegas in the constellation Nevada. Son of a gun, I'm one smart cat."

John peered skyward. "Definitely Las Vegas. Bright star. You took astronomy?"

"I don't know about you, Galileo, but I'm going to celebrate your father's success, beginning right now with the most potent drink I can find in his private stock."

"The seriousness of what you've been trying to tell me is just beginning to sink into my thick skull, Ramon," John said. "My father pulled off another deal of the century that could boost people's spirits around here, if nothing else. ... I wonder if you'd mind if I shared that information with a person ... ah ... that I met ... recently?"

"Sure. Know the telephone number?"

"No. But it must be listed."

"Never know, what's the name?"

"Ah, well, it's ... ah ... you know, Ramon. That person I met at Summit ... last night. ..."

"Of course. Come inside and I'll check. I know its Summit 5-2433, but let's be sure."

John wondered why Ramon would know Jenny Boston's telephone number as he watched his friend thumb through the pages of the telephone directory. Ramon nodded and then checked the calendar to ascertain that the person would be at that number on that day. Satisfied that would be the case, he said, "Yep. Dial the operator and ask for Summit 5-2433. I'll be out in the kitchen mixing some excellent drinks. I'll leave you to your conversation. Take your time. That bottle of liquor should last me a half hour or so."

John settled on the sofa and placed the call. The telephone rang several times and he was about to hang up when he heard a response. "Hello, this is the railroad roundhouse at Summit. Jennifer Boston speaking."

The voice was certainly Jenny's but why was she at the railroad roundhouse, John wondered. He was caught speechless.

"Hello, is someone there?" Jenny asked. "You have the Eastern's roundhouse at Summit. May I help you?"

"Ah ... yes. I was calling ... to let someone ... you know ... well, this is about something I learned."

"Hi, this sounds like Mr. Shanahan ... John Shanahan. Is that so?"

"Yes, and you're the Miss Boston, Miss Jennifer Boston, that I had a conversation with last night at the station ... in Summit."

55

"Of course. How kind of you to call! So, you had a good night's sleep, I hope, and now you're enjoying that lovely home in Quarry. How wonderful, John!"

"Well, yes. I just wanted to share some good news with you, in case you hadn't heard."

Jenny was puzzled. "Ah, no, I haven't heard about any particular thing today that struck me as unusually good news."

"How about the news that my father bought the Hill Division of New England Eastern?"

"Oh, my gosh! How wonderful, John, how absolutely wonderful! Our prayers have been answered. Thank God. I cannot believe this happened."

"Well, I just wanted you to know. It's really Hank's news to announce, so I'd appreciate it if you kept quiet about it until you hear from him."

"Of course. … As a matter of fact, I see him coming across the yard now on the dead run. I need to get back to work. I'm fixing an electrical problem on a road switcher that came in on the Eastern earlier today. Thanks, John. Please call me again, when you can."

John joined Ramon in the kitchen at Seven Pines after his telephone conversation with Jenny. The liquor bottle had taken a sizeable hit and Ramon appeared to be in high spirits. An ideal time, John figured, to find out more about the young woman with whom he had just spoken. But he had to approach the topic in a subtle manner.

"So, Ramon, it looks like you're well into the celebration of the rebirth of the golden age of railroading in the North Country. Think the poor Shanahan boy could have a tad before the booze evaporates completely?"

"Sure, buddy. Not to worry. There's plenty more where that comes from." Ramon pushed a glass and spoon across the table. John poured a man-sized portion of the whisky into the glass, added a splash of tonic and stirred the drink with the spoon. Then he sat down and stared at Ramon.

"How'd you happen to know the telephone number where Jenny works?" he asked pointedly.

"Jenny who?" Ramon squinted as if John were out of focus. "Oh, the young lady from Summit?"

"Yeah, apparently she works at the roundhouse."

"Sure, everybody knows that. That's why I knew the phone number. Anybody who's anybody in the railroad business knows the phone number at the Summit roundhouse."

John persisted. "She said she was doing some electrical work on an Eastern locomotive. I find that hard to believe."

"Why so? She's the best diesel electrician in these parts. Jen's really the second-shift hostler for the Eastern but she knows more about diesel-electric locomotives than anyone around here. When a problem pops up, she's the man to see."

John was stunned. Such an attractive and gracious woman should be working in an office or a store or even as a waitress, he supposed. Those were better workplaces for women, after all. Not only that, she was still in high school, according to Bill Travers.

"I understood she's still a student in high school. Isn't that so?"

"Sure," Ramon said. "But you must have noticed that she had a young daughter with her over at the station. She has no sugar daddy, my friend, and it's a cold, cruel world out there. Some people do what they have to do to get by. If they happen to be very good at what they do, they get by that much better. ... Considering that I'm a little tipsy and perhaps a little incoherent, I can't remember what I just said. But I think you agree?"

"Yes. I do, Ramon. You make a lot of sense, all the time, really. And I appreciate what you've told me. ... Still, I never knew of any women who worked for railroads, except office help and an occasional station agent or operator, like Molly, down the line."

"That's true. Well, actually, some railroads have female dining car attendants—waitresses, you might say—but not too many. The bottom line is this: Railroading is a tough, dirty and dangerous business and I suppose the big shots that run them figure those places aren't suitable for women, even if they try to get hired. Besides, you know what some men are like. A skirt goes by and they go absolutely ape. Follow me?"

"I do, and that kind of worries me, for Jenny's sake. ... You know what I'm saying?"

"I do, John, and that's one of your admirable qualities. You're a gentleman—a goofy one sometimes, but you really are a gentleman."

"Thank you. So are you. ... So, you say Jenny is a hostler? That must mean she not only services locomotives, she knows how to run them."

"Yes, I'm told she's one of the best in the business. Being a hostler at Summit, she had to qualify to run the diesels out into the yard. The unions have that clause in their contracts. In the process of qualifying for that type of work, she pulled a little sneaky and took the regular engineman's tests as well. She came out tops in the group that was qualifying and nobody caught on until it was too late. She's qualified on the whole system. Even down on this line, because SB&Q has only a handful of its own people and Hank has to go to Eastern and beg qualified help whenever he needs extra hands."

"I see."

"She learned the business from her father. He was an engineer. She rode with him and read a lot of books. Still reads them all the time to keep up with the latest technology. Sometime when you're sitting around trying to figure out what to say to her, just mention a type of diesel locomotive. Any type. She'll rattle off statistics that will set your head a spinning."

"I'm beginning to really like this girl, Ramon."

"Good. She'd be a fine catch. And what about her little girl? You understand that she comes with the package?"

57

"Of course. She's an adorable little girl. ... Obviously there was someone else in Jenny's life once. ..."

"Obviously. I've heard the stories that still go around. Supposedly it was pretty ugly and Jen was deeply hurt. But she pulled herself up and is making a life for herself and the little girl. That's why she's back in school, finishing up her high school education."

"Yes. I'd say she's quite the young lady." John poured another drink, heavy on the alcohol and light on the mix. "So, what's on the agenda for tomorrow?"

"Well, that's a good question. I've been kind of putting off unloading the business car. I suppose we could do that next. J.P wants it to go up to the shop for an inspection. And I imagine Hank wants us to get together and try to figure out how to get the new operation up and running. We're going to be busy beavers in the next few days."

John yawned. "Yep. Busy beavers. Hmmm. I'm tired already. Maybe I'll freshen up this drink a bit and toddle off to bed. Got a particular bedstead in mind?"

"Why don't you take the room on the right at the end of the hall? That one has a couple of windows that offer a great view of the train yard. I have the one across the hall on the left. It has about the same arrangement."

"Okay. Thanks again for the wise counsel tonight."

"You're welcome. Sleep soundly, my friend."

John slept soundly for the second night in a row. He awoke before the sunrise, bundled up in his winter gear and went out onto the veranda to watch the sun come up. The event was spectacular. The eastern skyline took on a faint glow at first and became brighter over a period of ten minutes or so. The sun peeked timidly over the horizon at first and then light streaked down into the Eden River valley. A few minutes later the transformation from night to day was complete. It appeared that the North Country would experience another pleasant late fall day.

After the *Northern Express* pulled away from the railroad yard at Quarry on its morning run to Summit and Gatlin, Ramon drove another of the estate's vehicles—a pickup truck—to the area near the roundhouse where the business car had been set for unloading. It took two trips to move the pair's personal belongings and another to transport boxes of company material that J.P. had decided should stay at Seven Pines even if the North Country railroad system were abandoned.

"Your father had this notion that he would keep Quarry as a permanent historic railroad settlement, sort of a museum, I guess," Ramon explained to John. "He's been gathering up old freight and passenger cars and locomotives for years and has them stashed on some back tracks behind Bolton Box and Barrel and up around the shop at Summit. There's some here, too, tucked out of sight. ..."

Ramon pointed toward the edge of the forest beyond the station. "Up in there, John, is what is left of the Black Hills Slate Company's railroad. I'd say there must be forty, maybe fifty, pieces of rolling stock, most dating back to the last century. He wants to restore the cars that can be fixed up and actually move them around for sightseers to ride and photograph. The other pieces will be painted up and used as a backdrop. He wants to add ... what's the word? ... ambiance, I think ... to the whole setting."

He paused and then continued. "If the railroad had been abandoned, the Army would have had to shut down the test site, and his idea was to incorporate all tracks in the township—including what the Army has—into an operating railroad museum. ... It's what you'd call a retirement project, I guess."

"Yeah. My mother used to talk about it quite a lot," John said. "She would always say, 'Quarry is your father's hobby, and every man needs a hobby.' ... You know ..." He was interrupted by the ringing of the telephone.

Ramon began whistling a tune. "Telephone, Ramon," John remarked.

"You Shanahans seem to think my huge salary obligates me to answer the telephone all the time. It does not. Let it ring, or answer it yourself." Ramon continued to whistle.

"All right, grumpy. I'll answer the damned telephone even if it is beneath my station in life." John pushed himself to his feet and limped across the room. He picked up the telephone but was at a loss to think of what to say.

"Hello. Is anybody there?" the caller asked. It was his father.

"Hello, Dad. It's me. John."

"Am I glad to reach you, son!" the senior Shanahan exclaimed. "Have a good trip? Hank kept me abreast of your progress. How do you like it up there? How's the house?"

"Yes. Everything you just said. All positive. ... Ah, so ... Well, I guess lots has happened since I left Chicago. ..."

J.P. cut him off. "Your mother wants to talk to you," he said. "Hold on. ... Alicia. Come to the phone. It's John."

It was a ruse, John thought. He knew his father well and the senior Shanahan was a master at diversion. He didn't want to plunge into the topic of a change of plans regarding trains in northern New England until he had carefully laid the groundwork.

"John, how are you?" It was his mother. "I was so worried. Did Ramon feed you well? How is your leg?"

"It was a fine trip, Mom. Ramon is a joy to be around. Yes, we ate like a couple of rich bankers on a holiday trip on the *Orient Express*. I am well. ... And you were so right about this place. It is a wonderful home."

"It is wonderful. Well, it seems that you have a lot of things to do now, according to your father. I love you, my son. Call me soon, won't you?"

"Love you, Mom. I'll call."

John's father returned to the telephone and began, in his circuitous way, to fill in his son on events that had transpired during the time John had been en route to New England.

59

"I was going to let the abandonment run its course," J.P. said. "Then I got a call from Eastern to see if we'd consider buying the railroad. I was getting calls from senators and representatives urging us to consider a purchase. We met with the Eastern and had some hard negotiations. All of a sudden after I made this ridiculously low final offer the wheels began to turn."

"I see." Sure, J.P. Shanahan, he thought, you pulled off the deal of the century.

"We pulled off the deal of the century, son. Shanahan Enterprises got the whole works—even the track from Hill Junction to the Gatlin mill—for less than scrap value. We also obtained track rights to run the *Northern Express* right into Sunbury. And we can still abandon our track after ninety days and make money. What do you think of that?"

"I think I'm finally beginning to appreciate what an extraordinary businessman you are, Dad. You seem to have made an exceptionally smart move, but then I couldn't imagine you making any other kind."

"Well, thanks. You're kind, John. You and I will make quite a team in time to come."

"Sure, Pop. We make a good team now. It can only get better."

"Good. Listen, like your mother, I love you, Son. Oh, and tell Ramon that Hank Terrell is going down to Quarry today to talk to you two about what has to be done. We're going to do this takeover quick."

"I love you, Dad. I'm mighty proud to be on your team." John hung up the telephone and turned to Ramon. "Hank Terrell is coming down to talk railroads with us."

"Good deal. I'd say the wheels are moving now. And it sounds like you're keen on this railroad thing. That so?"

"Yes, I am. For the first time, Ramon, in a long time I'm beginning to like the idea of being on the Shanahan team."

Chapter 9: 'Research and Development'

John Shanahan and Ramon Martinez were sprawled on the veranda in ragged dungarees and sweatshirts when Henry Terrell drove into the driveway at Seven Pines just after lunch. Ramon dashed down the walkway to help Hank with several boxes of papers he had brought along and John held the door open as the pair approached. "Welcome to Seven Pines, Hank," he said, and added with a sly smile: "The present inhabitants are a couple of wayfaring strangers but better times will bring a better clientele."

"Speak for yourself, John," Ramon grunted. "I tell you, Hank, working for Shanahan Enterprises can be a trial when this guy is wandering around the premises."

"I think you're both a little odd," Hank responded. "I come calling on official railroad business and expect to meet a couple of businessmen and what do I get? You look like a couple of drifters."

"Like John said, we're just a couple of wayfaring strangers," Ramon said sharply. "In this railroad game, you takes what you gets. You're stuck with us, unfortunately." Then he grinned at Hank.

"Well, I suppose that's something Hank will have to deal with as time goes on." The railroad manager winked as he passed John and entered the great room.

The railroad manager shuffled through a folder of papers and placed several pieces on the coffee table. Then he removed his topcoat, placed it over the back of a nearby chair and sat down on the sofa. Ramon pushed two overstuffed chairs across the room.

"So, Mr. Terrell, what are we drinking today?" Ramon asked. "You came to talk business and unless we hear that this business will be conducted on our terms, Mr. Shanahan and I will boycott this meeting. That's correct, is it not, Mr. Shanahan?"

"Absolutely correct, Mr. Martinez. I'm not into business talk when a liquor cabinet so adequately stocked as ours remains off-limits when serious policy matters are at issue."

Hank looked at his watch and checked it against the grandfather clock in the great room. "Looks like your timepiece is running six seconds slow, Mr. Martinez. I won't report this infraction to management if you trot out the good stuff real quick. Once the matters are settled, however, the fun and games end."

John's eyes lit up. "I say, Mr. Martinez, the longer we drag out this meeting, the longer it will take to reach an understanding and, therefore, the longer the bar is open. How much booze do we have stashed away?"

"Lots." Ramon grinned. "This could be a most interesting policy meeting."

"Enough!" Hank screamed. "Ramon, please fetch the drinks; and you, John Shanahan, zip your lip."

Ramon brought in the refreshments and Hank declared the meeting in session. First, he produced morning editions of the Summit Sentinel for John and Ramon. "We received some excellent coverage," he said. "I should point out, John, in case you didn't know, the managing editor of the paper is Nolan Terrell, who happens to be my brother."

"The Terrell family is quite well known around here, John," Ramon added. "I hesitate to say this but it is true. They are all upright citizens and good people, even Hank. Nolan runs the paper; Angus has the big potato farm at Siberia Crossing; Steve runs a jewelry store in Summit and is the state senator from this district. The other two brothers—Jim and Bill—operate Bolton Box and Barrel. … Oh, yeah, then there's Maurice—he's Nolan's son and he's the manager of the pulp and paper mill in Gatlin."

"Thanks, Ramon. Yes, I'm quite proud of my family," Hank said. "Now, go ahead and read the papers, boys, and then we'll get on with the meeting."

John picked up his copy. He didn't have to go far to find what he wanted for it was emblazoned across the front page in about the biggest newspaper headline he had ever seen: "Shanahan Buys Eastern's Hill Division." The subheads added: "Shippers Laud Acquisition by SB&Q Owner" and "Railroad Financier Plans Rapid Railroad Transition." A stock photo of J.P. and a stunning shot of the *Northern Express* entering Summit yard from the Quarry line accompanied the article.

The story appeared to be factual and well written. His father had been working the telephones, John mused, as he read the numerous quotes attributed to J.P. Several paragraphs down in the article, the senior Shanahan stated that during the transition period all day-to-day operations of the line would be handled by Henry Terrell, general manager of the Summit, Bolton and Quarry.

He read on, stumbling upon references to his place in the scheme of things.

John P. Shanahan III arrived in Summit late Monday night aboard the Northern Express the day before officers from New England Eastern and Shanahan Enterprises completed final negotiations leading to the sale. He is a 24-year-old university graduate and a Korean War veteran decorated for valor in combat in early December 1950. Seriously wounded there, Shanahan is recovering well, his father stated.

The younger Shanahan is a qualified locomotive engineer, according to his father, and was reported by sources at the station in Summit to have arrived aboard Train Number One's locomotive in the company of SB&Q engineer William S. Travers. Travers returned recently from Korea, where he, too, served with highest distinction as an Army Ranger and was decorated for heroism.

Terrell said the younger Shanahan and Ramon Martinez, superintendent of passenger train operations for Shanahan Enterprises, are expected to be involved in planning the merger of the operations of New England Eastern's Hill Division and the Summit, Bolton and Quarry. In addition to acquiring the entire division, some 435 miles of track, John P.

Shanahan Jr. said operating rights for one passenger train round trip a day between Sunbury and Hill Junction were granted to Shanahan Enterprises by the Eastern.

"This means that we can ensure a timely daily schedule for passengers between the North Country and Sunbury, a destination of choice for many residents of the northern part of this state," J.P. Shanahan said. "As we speak, excellent equipment is en route from Wisconsin to supplement our top-of-the-line passenger train," the business tycoon added in the exclusive interview with the Sentinel.

Quite the showman, my father, John thought. The article told about how the company would use its Summit shops to refurbish freight cars for potato shipments. It would also aggressively pursue new business and be of assistance to persons interested in shipping. "This could apply to a trapper sending out his annual catch of furs in our passenger train express cars or to a timberland manager interested in moving hundreds of cars of wood products by freight train each year," J.P. was quoted as saying. Topping the freight train priorities, of course, would be the transportation of the potato crop to marketplaces.

John was about to wonder who was going to conduct the aggressive marketing when he found the answer in the article. "Just call Mr. Terrell or my aides at the Summit station with any questions about our plans to revive railroad service in the North Country," Shanahan said.

I guess I know what I'm going to be doing for a while, John thought as he read to find specifics of the timing of the transition. Near the bottom of the story the Sentinel reported that the New England Eastern would cease operations on the Hill Division on or about 11:59 p.m. on the fourteenth of November 1951, at which time the Summit, Bolton and Quarry would take over all train service in the region. It will be a seamless transition, Shanahan promises, the Sentinel reported.

John placed his copy of the newspaper on the coffee table. Ramon followed suit. "So, gentlemen, any questions?" Hank asked.

Both shook their heads. "It looks like we'll be busy for a while," John observed.

"We will be busy," Hank acknowledged. "We have about two weeks to have everything in place." He shuddered visibly and held a hand to his head. Then he grinned. "But we can do it because we're all smart railroad men."

Then the railroad manager laid out the challenges that he anticipated. There would be the matter of determining how many employees on New England Eastern's Hill Division rosters would exercise seniority rights and move to other divisions of that railroad. There would be no attempt to solicit those employees to stay with the Summit, Bolton and Quarry, although they would be welcomed if they chose to join the new railroad. Union agreements, which were similar for both NEE and SB&Q, would be adhered to by the new management. Hank made it clear that Shanahan Enterprises intended to treat employees from both railroads in an equitable fashion with respect to their rights spelled out in labor contracts.

"It is my opinion that a contented workforce makes for a smooth operation and that's what we intend to have," he emphasized.

Equipment needs were a major concern because the sale agreement covered property, track, structures and all of the refrigerator cars on the system as of the date of the sale. Smaller pieces, such as track-maintenance motorcars and tools would be left for SB&Q but all locomotives, most freight and all passenger cars and train-mounted maintenance equipment would be moved off line at the earliest date possible. "As a matter of fact, Eastern will begin taking out some of its unused rolling stock as early as tomorrow," Hank said. "They plan to vacate the premises by the fifteenth of November. That means we have to have equipment in place then to make this 'seamless transition' that J.P. talked about in the newspaper story. ...."

Hank rolled his eyes. "This is going to be tough, particularly so because—and this is really confidential—I have it from very good sources that the potato market is about to really explode. There have been reports of potato crop failures in several major shipping areas across the country so the locals expect to cash in big time this year. You fellows probably don't know what the North Country is like when the potatoes are moving, it's been so damned long, but let me tell you, it can be one frantic scramble when it starts."

Hank shuffled his papers and looked up. "Any questions, so far?"

Ramon looked at John. "You, buddy?" John shook his head. "Not so far."

"Okay, then, let's continue," Hank said. "One of our priorities—like tomorrow—is to get the business car into the shop for an inspection. Then, perhaps as early as tomorrow afternoon, I want to head out over the line. That's the whole system—from one end to the other—to see what we need to do immediately. Basically, this trip will be for the three of us and Fred Wilson from the shop. I want us to be conversant with every aspect of this railroad. We'll run a special train with one of our locomotives, the business car and the dome car that we'll take off the *Northern Express* at Summit this afternoon. I figure that's the best place from which to view the line as we roll along. J.P has cleared this with the Eastern, so I'll want you two guys to come up on the passenger train in the morning and be prepared for as long as it takes to do what we need to do."

The manager said that over the years the senior Shanahan had assembled groups comprising management personnel and workers with specific skills in various aspects of railroading. They came from several railroads controlled by Shanahan Enterprises and would be dispatched to newly-acquired lines to set up management systems. The first transition teams would arrive within days to create an accounting and business department to be headquartered in Summit station. Accompanying that group would be a team involved in dispatching and crew assignments. There was a lot of unoccupied space in the station and that included an intact dispatching office that the Eastern had used before transferring that aspect to the terminal in Sunbury.

"There are still a lot of unknowns," Hank added. "We are running an advertisement in tomorrow's Summit Sentinel for several temporary clerical positions, basically to answer telephones and take messages as they come in to the switchboard at Summit. I think those people can be assured of full-time work,

64

depending on their skills, once we get going. Larry Smith, Eastern's agent at Summit, plans to stay with us, and I've put him in charge of getting basic office furniture together and making sure the telephone system is adequate for the time being."

Hank pulled a folded map from one of the boxes he had brought to Quarry. After clearing the coffee table of papers, he laid out the system diagram of Eastern's Hill Division. It covered the top of the table and John noticed that it was quite detailed.

"I'm leaving each of you one of these maps and I'd like you to study them carefully, particularly you, John, since this is your first trip into the North Country. You'll notice that the Hill Division starts at Hill Junction. We now own about two thirds of the yard there, along with the engine house, an old shop and a tower-station at East Junction. The Hill Junction station remains the property of Eastern."

Hank traced the main line from Hill Junction to Gatlin and pointed out a twelve-mile branch that led to the east at a point about two miles south of Gatlin station. "This line has been closed for a couple of years but J.P. wants to reactivate it immediately. There are a number of farmers in a village called Battle Brook who have been after him for years to acquire the branch as a short line because Eastern's service had been so bad. That's a matter we also have to attend to right away."

The main line from Gatlin to Summit was also discussed and Hank pointed out something that John remembered from his trip over the route in the locomotive of the passenger train. "Parts of the present mainline that used to be the southbound side of a thirty-mile section of double track are in horrible shape. There are also several hundred refrigerator cars stored there on the northbound track that we have to start moving into the shop for repairs. By moving the cars immediately, we figure we can divert trains over to the other track and speed up our train service on the main line. I want to look at that situation closely when we make our inspection trip."

Hank made a passing reference to the Quarry line, which he said would become a branch under the new arrangement. "It will be the best branch line in the Northeast, there's no doubt about that, and the *Northern Express* will continue to originate and terminate in Quarry. By gaining access to Sunbury on a daily basis, we intend to institute a new section of our passenger train, one that will have a crew originating in Sunbury. A crew will continue to come out of Quarry, and where the two trains meet, the crews will switch trains so that both will be in their terminals at the end of the day."

The mainline from Summit to Boundary was also traced, with Hank pointing out that the route ran through the heart of the region's agricultural belt. He also drew attention to a spur line that originated at Aroostook and ran twenty miles in a northeast direction to a place called Heartland. This branch had originated up to thirty-five percent of Eastern's potato traffic for many years.

A large terminal yard existed at Boundary and several businesses were dependent on the railroad. Hank pointed to an international bridge and an interchange with the Canadian Eastern Railroad at a place called Ste. Anne. "I have a lot to tell you about this one, but I need confirmation from J.P. about a really innovative deal he's working on."

Then Terrell traced the line that swung to the west from Summit before turning north to run through a land of forests and lakes, occasionally breaking out into farmland that extended from the east. At the terminal in Eagle River, a branch line led to the east and was apparently serviceable for ten miles or so. Beyond that, Hank said, the line was intact but out of service for several miles. The other end of the line was in service for about twelve miles and switched on a call basis from Boundary.

"So that's what we're looking at, gentlemen," Hank concluded. "If we can get the equipment we need it appears we could make a success of this venture. Damn! I need to call the agent at Boundary." The railroad manager picked up a nearby extension telephone and called the operator. "I'd like BO5-1234, please," he said.

The connection was made immediately. "Hello, Adrian. This is Henry Terrell. ... Yes, I'm fine. How about you? ... Yes, we're quite excited about the change. You're signing on with us? Are you sure that's what you want? ... Great! It will be a pleasure to work with you again. ... Uh huh. ... Look, we're going to run a special train up your way in the next day or so to look around. We can talk over old times. ... You bet. ... Tell me, Adrian, have you heard anything from Canadian Eastern about some passenger cars coming in from Wisconsin? ... Fantastic! ... I'd say there should be a number of pieces coming in shortly. ... Well, we'll get together soon. Thanks. See you later. ..."

Hank turned to Ramon and John, his face wreathed in a smile. "The wheels are turning, guys. The equipment for the second side of the *Northern Express* is coming into Boundary sometime tomorrow night. It's supposed to be a near duplicate of what we have now. I think we'll move the business car and dome up to Boundary tomorrow afternoon on the regular Eastern passenger and have it coupled onto the new cars and show off the equipment on the way back down over the next few days. How about that?"

"Exciting!" Ramon exclaimed. "That calls for another round of drinks, assuming, of course, that you haven't recessed our meeting yet."

"Absolutely not! Let's have a toast and then we'll recess the meeting, after which I'll try to drive back to Summit. We have more to talk about, but that will be tomorrow."

Hank left Quarry after four o'clock. Two hours later John and Ramon were still perusing printed materials that the railroad manager had given them. John was drawn to a file containing track diagrams and gradient charts for the entire Hill Division, and he studied the information intently. Ramon was preoccupied with booklets describing passenger train equipment that Shanahan Enterprises was thinking of acquiring to upgrade its services in the North Country.

John was jotting down notes about the Battle Brook Branch when the telephone rang. Ramon picked up the phone. "Hello, this is the research and development branch of the Summit, Bolton and Quarry Railroad," he said. "Do you have any research that needs developing?" John buried his face in his hands to suppress a sudden burst of laughter.

"You wish to speak with our head researcher? And you say his name is John Shanahan? ... I'm sorry, madam, that name does not ring a bell. ... He's the tall, good-looking gentleman? ... That would be me, but my name is not John Shanahan. ... Heaven forbid. ... The Shanahans of Quarry are a worthless lot. ... Well, if you insist. Hang on and I'll try to rouse the loafer." Ramon put the telephone down and walked to the kitchen. "John Shanahan," he yelled. "Get out of the liquor cabinet and answer the telephone!"

Ramon closed the door but John could still hear his peals of laughter. In reaching for the telephone, John dropped his track diagram book and then misjudged his distance from the phone. Groping for the receiver, his elbow hit it and knocked the phone under the sofa. He slid to the floor from his chair, grasped the receiver again and struggled to say something. "Hello" was the best he could do.

"I hesitate to ask at this point, but is this John Shanahan and, if so, is he coherent enough to talk for a minute?" The voice sounded like that of Jennifer Boston, the night hostler at Summit engine house.

"Ah, yes. This is John and I apologize for all the confusion. I'd like to explain it ... "

"But you can't!" It still sounded like Jenny and it seemed that she had taken the shenanigans in stride. "So, just what kind of research were you two characters involved in today?" Then she giggled and John knew it was Jenny.

"Oh, a little of this and some of that. Nothing earthshaking. ... Well, maybe when I dropped the telephone on the floor it sounded like a small earthquake to you. I truly apologize for that. I'm a bit of a clumsy oaf sometimes ... but I really mean no harm."

"No apology is necessary. We're good friends ... ah, acquaintances. ... I just, well, wanted to call ... to see how you spent your day. ... Not to be nosy. ... I'm not that kind of person. ... Really not at all."

"It was a very good day for me. How about you; you know, classes and work? Did everything go well for you?"

"Yes, very well. ... Well, I really didn't want to disturb you, so I'll just ..."

"No, no. Don't go! I'm delighted that you called, Jenny. Really delighted. Let's see now, tomorrow must be Thursday, I think, so I suppose you'll be doing your usual thing ... school and work and all."

"Yes. That is pretty much my agenda for tomorrow. Just so you'll know, I work at the engine house from four to midnight Tuesday through Saturday. I have Sundays and Mondays off. There are only two of us here—the day man and me—so once in a while one or the other gets called in if there's some emergency. I don't know how things will be after SB&Q takes over. I hope the same. ... I really need the work right now."

"Gee, I'd think there should be plenty of work once the new railroad gets going. Oh, I guess I started to say something about when you'd be around ... you know, not working or going to school, because Hank and Ramon and I will be in Summit tomorrow to take a tour of the system. Everything is kind of tentative. Maybe, if you'd like ... I don't mean to be forward about this. ... I just thought ..."

"I'd love to see you again, John. ... Drat! It appears that I have a locomotive coming in now, so I really have to go. Call me when you can. And take good care of yourself."

John placed the telephone receiver back in its cradle and picked up his track diagram book. He stared at the book for a while but couldn't focus, so he put it down. He really liked this young woman—Jenny—and she seemed interested in him. Then he tried to figure out the business train schedule but didn't have enough information to figure much of anything. Oh, well, sooner or later he would get to Summit again when Jenny would be off work and out of school. Then, maybe, he could sit somewhere, perhaps at a coffee shop, and have a pleasant conversation and get to know her better.

Chapter 10: The Speaking Engagement

John and Ramon arose early after their third night at Seven Pines. After a hearty breakfast they were ready for Clem Morse, the estate caretaker, who came by to help move their luggage to the business car. Both had been instructed by Henry Terrell to dress up because they would be representing management and needed to put on a better appearance than when they greeted the manager at the estate a day earlier.

The business car had been turned and coupled into the *Northern Express* behind the last coach, a spot usually occupied by the dome car, *Aurora Borealis*. That car was already at Summit to be readied for Henry Terrell's inspection tour.

The passenger train to Summit and points south was on the mainline at Quarry when the crew gathered in the station. John and Ramon joined them—Bill Travers, Joe Francis, Carl Reardon and John Kelly, along with Jim McDermott, the regular fireman, who had been on another run when the group had met earlier in the week.

Joe approached Ramon and John and shook their hands. "I've been asked by this crew to express our gratitude to Mr. Shanahan in regard to the purchase of the railroad," he said. "I'm just a railroad conductor and not a speech maker. We want you to know that J.P. has been a good friend to people around here and has come to their assistance again. Ramon, and you, John, please tell J.P. thanks on behalf of the employees."

As the others continued talking, Bill pulled John aside. "Understand you've been talking to Jenny. That so?"

John was embarrassed. "Ah, yeah. A couple of times, I guess."

"So, what's on your mind in that regard?"

"Nothing really, Bill. I just find her ... very pleasant ... and very gracious. ..."

"And you're not troubled that she works for the railroad?"

John shook his head. "I'm kind of a traditionalist, protective of women but ... well, she seems to have a handle on what's she's doing. It's not for me to interfere in that."

"Damned good engineman, you need to know. Got it from her dad." Bill squinted at John. "So your motives are just to make her acquaintance? You're not just taking stock of what North Country women have to offer? You know what I mean."

"Sure, I know what you mean. ... And I just enjoy talking to her ... nothing more. I'd like to talk to her, now and then ... and well, maybe see her, occasionally. Later. ... You know, down the line ... sometime," John stammered. "Now you listen, Bill. ... I'm not some Casanova out for a good time. I respect her a great deal. ....."

Bill gripped John's hand. "You're an okay guy, Shanahan. Emma, my foster mom, she'd like to meet you. She's like a mother to Jenny, too, and to Katie. You come over sometime. Impress Emma and you'll be in good in the Cummings-Boston-Travers clan."

"Thanks. If Mrs. Cummings wants to meet me, it would be my pleasure."

"Good. That'll give me a chance to keep an eye on you. I can be a mean cat to deal with if you cross the line. Get my drift?"

"Yeah. I remember one day last December. Glad I wasn't fighting for the other side."

"Okay, we see eye to eye. ... Looks like the students are climbing aboard so it's time to rev up the school bus. Remember our little talk today. See you down the line, buddy."

The passenger train left Quarry at six fifty-five and John settled in for the first leg of a trip that would likely run through the weekend. He would have preferred to ride in the engine where he could get a closer look at the unique "school-bus" operation on the branch but that would have to wait for another day. He was aware of the frequent stops and the slow speed of the train but being at the rear he could see little so he plunged into the track diagrams he had been studying the night before. The *Northern Express* pulled up at the school stops outside Summit yard, discharged student passengers at each and then moved forward through Quarry Junction and into the main passenger terminal.

A New England Eastern passenger train that had come in from Boundary stood on the track closest to the station. It was headed by a 2,000-horsepower diesel-electric locomotive and carried a mail and express car, a baggage car and three coaches. Engineer Travers brought the *Northern Express* alongside the NEE train so that mail and express could be transferred while passengers getting off at Summit disembarked from both. Those from Boundary and other points north of Summit who were going on to destinations to the south clambered aboard the *Northern Express*.

A mixed train that came down from Eagle River earlier had discharged its mail, express and passengers over the branch line's platform on the southwest side of the station. The two Eastern trains would switch their passenger cars into designated coach tracks near the SB&Q's shop and both crews would take freight trains back to their points of origin.

Later fresh crews would start out from Eagle River and Boundary with local freight trains. Upon arrival, one would take the passenger train connecting with the afternoon arrival of the northbound *Northern Express* back to Boundary, while the other would return to Eagle River on a passenger run.

John knew that NEE mail and passenger operations north of Summit were created clumsily when that railroad had been denied permission to end all passenger service on those two parts of the line. He expected that Shanahan Enterprises would fashion something better in the weeks to come although he was unsure if there was any appreciable passenger base on the largely wilderness Eagle River branch.

Ramon and John stepped off the business car at seven fifty-five in the morning just as Brakeman John Kelly and a car inspector went about disconnecting the car from the *Northern Express*. They made quick work of the setoff. Kelly signaled a highball from the rear steps of the coach and climbed aboard as the passenger train pulled away. He waved to Ramon and John from the vestibule before stepping inside to help Conductor Joe Francis collect tickets.

"Well, let's go find Hank," Ramon suggested. "Maybe we'll learn something new today." They were about to step into the station concourse when Henry Terrell came to the door and pushed it open. "Good morning, gentlemen," he said. "Don't you fellows look dapper today? I'm pleasantly surprised."

The railroad manager motioned for Ramon and John to follow him up the stairway to his second-floor office. The telephone was ringing as the trio entered the room. Hank picked up the receiver and slid into his office chair. "Good morning, SB&Q Railroad," he said. "Henry Terrell speaking. ... Mr. Roberts from the high school, of course! ... Oh, that was today, wasn't it? Honest to God, I've been so pushed up the last few days ... "

Hank covered his face with his hand and peered through his fingers. "Yes, I know the assembly is at eight thirty." Hank focused on John and appeared to be seized by an idea. "Hold on just a moment, Mr. Roberts. I need to talk to one of my colleagues. Thank you."

Hank covered the receiver. "John, would you be up to doing old Hank a tremendous favor, one for which he would be eternally grateful?"

"Ah ha," Ramon piped in. "Sounds like old Hank is in a bit of a bind. You might want to take him up on this favor thing. It would be a bargaining chip for down the road."

John grinned. "Sure, Hank, what did you have in mind? Ramon and I are here to make your life so much better. I'm sure that if I'm not up to the task, Ramon will be, so ask us. We can always say no." John chuckled.

"Very well, smart guy. How would you like to address an assembly at Summit High School at eight-thirty? The topic is, well, careers for high school graduates, more or less. We need to emphasize the railroad industry, of course."

John paled. "Ah, well, I'm not really up to snuff on railroad stuff, you know. ... Been away, you know, doing that military thing in a far and distant land. Yeah, far away ..."

Ramon leaned over and whispered: "Good opportunity for you, buddy. I understand the gal of your dreams is the class president so it's pretty likely that she will be around. ...."

"Uh huh. Well now ... Okay, Hank, I'll take on this challenge as a personal favor to you. It will be costly, I would say, in time to come, but ..."

Hank put his fingers to his lips. "Hush, Shanahan. I'll tell you when to talk." Then he turned his attention to the caller. "Mr. Roberts? How would it be if my friend, John Shanahan, would represent the railroad at your assembly? ... Yes, he's the son of J.P. and quite knowledgeable about our industry. ... Uh huh. Yes, he's the soldier just returned from Korea. He's a fine, fine young man. ... That would be swell! I have somebody here to bring him right over. Thank you again."

Hank sat back in his chair and clasped his hands behind his head. "Ramon, how about you take the company car and deliver Mr. Shanahan to the wolves?" Then the railroad manager chucked. "Ah, strike that. These kids are top-notch students, very well behaved and usually interested in things of an educational nature. I have a box of public information material that you can pass out in case you get lost for words."

Ramon delivered John to the school and scanned the premises. "There, buddy, the coast is clear. I notice that an attractive young lady is headed this way to lead you to the wolves." He pointed to the entryway where Jennifer Boston was pulling on her coat.

John's companion went around to John's side of the car and helped him out. "You go with Jenny and I'll take the box of goodies in. Good luck." Ramon dashed on ahead.

Jenny approached John and extended her hand. "Thanks for coming on short notice, Mr. Shanahan ... John," she said. "I really appreciate this." He grasped her hand and held it. "I'm pleased that I can be of assistance ... especially to you. ... Ah ... now what exactly should I be talking about? I'm a little rusty when it comes to public appearances."

"Oh, you'll be great! You've been the talk of the town ever since the newspaper article came out. Just be yourself and talk about railroads and trains and locomotives and different kinds of railroad jobs. I'm really looking forward to this. You'll do fine." Jenny squeezed his hand and led him up the walkway.

The pair followed a corridor to the side door to the auditorium's stage. Principal Roberts was at the door and shook John's hand. "It was very kind of you to come on short notice, Mr. Shanahan," he said. "You have met Miss Boston and she's prepared to introduce you to our students. We were thinking about a twenty-minute presentation, more or less, and then kind of an open discussion between you and the students. The individual packets that were prepared by the railroad are available, so if you'd like we will distribute them before the presentation. I have one here for you, which you might like to peruse again before you go in."

John nodded. "Yes. That would be fine. Just a quick run-through, if you don't mind." The principal nodded and pulled up three chairs by the entrance to the auditorium. John spent several minutes skimming the materials and then acknowledged that he was ready. Mr. Roberts excused himself and joined the audience. Jenny led John inside and across the stage. The audience stood and began clapping and cheering. It was a sustained applause that continued for several minutes.

Then Jenny began her introduction. "My fellow classmates, this is Mr. John P. Shanahan the third, the son of the owner of Shanahan Enterprises in Chicago, the company that has acquired New England Eastern's holdings in the North

Country. He has come to talk to us about the railroad industry from the perspective of both management and railroad workers because he is a qualified engineer on steam and diesel-electric locomotives."

She went on to tell about how John had attended high school and college in Chicago and worked summers and vacations on the South Montana Railway out of Helena where he learned about locomotive operations. Jenny also touched on his military career, his service in Korea and the fact that he had been commended in the support of the evacuation from Chosin in December 1950.

"And now, John and his colleague, Mr. Ramon Martinez, have come to Summit to help Mr. Henry Terrell organize the new railroad that we all look forward to having in place very soon. John will talk to you about the new railroad, I think, and will entertain your questions later on. ... Please welcome our speaker, John P. Shanahan."

John got up and limped to the podium. Realizing that it would be uncomfortable to stand there very long, he turned to Jenny and beckoned for her to come forward. "Jen, how about if you and I sit up near the front of the stage and talk from there," he whispered. "I get a little off balance when I stand still for a while."

"Of course, John. You stay right here and I'll fix things." She pulled two chairs to the front and stood by as he approached. John held her chair for her to sit first. She blushed and several male students whistled as she seated herself and John sat down beside her.

John scanned the audience. "I really don't know where to start," he said. "I came here on behalf of my father with the understanding that the trip would be to help Mr. Terrell go about discontinuing our little railroad down to Quarry. We wouldn't have been able to continue it without the connection that New England Eastern had offered up until then. After I arrived earlier this week, I learned that Shanahan Enterprises had made an acceptable offer to Eastern. I had never been here in my life. Miss Boston has told you about me, more than I knew that she knew. She was kind with her remarks. ...

"I learned about railroading from my father and my grandfather. Then I worked my way through college by taking railroad work in Montana when I could. I understand this assembly is about you and your aspirations and dreams for your futures. I had a dream once, and it was to be a locomotive engineer. But I didn't want anything given to me by my family, who as you probably know, are people of ... I guess you'd say people of means. I went to work as a steam engine fireman ... and that was, well, quite hard work. I imagine most of you, especially those from farm families or perhaps the children of railroad workers around here, really know all about hard work."

John paused. "Ah, well, let's see now, if you're a young man, you probably are thinking about military service. You have difficult decisions to make. I guess most young men understand they have an obligation to serve their country either before or after they have set a course for their life's work. It's not my place to advise you as to when, where or how you go about fulfilling that obligation. I went through college and graduated and had a job as an engineer when I decided to join the service. I went to officers' school and was a second lieutenant when I was assigned to Korea ... in 1950, last year. That was a difficult time and, well ... I did the best I could. ..." His voiced faltered and he looked away. "Anyway, whatever you do, always do your best. ... And that applies to everything you do with your life."

The students stood and applauded loudly. Jenny reached over and touched his hand. John could see tears welling in her eyes.

"Anyway, I'm really here to tell you about opportunities that may be presented to you by the railroad," John continued. "Everything is a little tentative right now but I know the wheels are turning. I'd bet by Christmas we'll be up and running full-bore and that could make the world of difference to the local economy. I understand you've had some down years around here but that surely will change. I know that from my experience out West. When I went there everything was, well, flat ... down and out. The railroad made some wise investments, and so did the business community and it wasn't long before we couldn't get enough workers to carry the load. The last I knew, everything was still booming."

John pointed out particular instances of how the region's economy flourished in conjunction with that railroad's growth. The line's owner invested in track improvements that resulted in more efficient train operations and more local employment. New industries came to the area, used railroad service and also offered more jobs. "It really was American capitalism at its best, because everyone gained from it," he explained. "I believe you will find the same thing happen here as time goes on."

Then he talked about jobs, saying, "I should caution you that outside jobs around the trains and tracks, are dirty and dangerous and that's the reason we talk about safety all the time. I know it gets tiresome, but if you work for us, our ranting is something you'll have to accept." Then he went through a litany of job descriptions. The students appeared to be interested, particularly when he disclosed wage scales and benefits.

Finally, John directed the students to the packets and went through the profusely illustrated contents with them. "Gosh!" he exclaimed. "I'm really reading some of this for the first time, and I'm excited already. If I were a little younger, I think I'd go to work for the railroad." Laughter broke out across the auditorium. He grinned and continued, "This stuff about opportunities at the car shop is quite impressive. I'll have to remember to tell my dad that Shanahan Enterprises has quite the sales pitch."

Laughter filled the room again. "Yeah, that Shanahan fellow is quite the promoter!" one young man called out.

"He is," John responded. "Take that from someone who really knows the guy." There was more laughter.

John looked at Jenny and smiled. "Want to give your classmates a little rundown on your experiences on the railroad?" he whispered. She nodded.

John stood up and leaned on his cane. "I should have my friend here add a few words. As you probably know, Miss Boston is a railroad man, too. ... Ah, well, a young woman, really, but a very good railroad man, so to speak—a railroad woman, if you wish. She can tell you a lot about working on the railroad."

The students arose again and chanted, "Jen-nie! Jen-nie! Jen-nie!"

Jenny stood up and talked for several minutes, beginning with her connection to the railroad through her father. "I read all his books about engines and asked him lots of questions," she said. "Later, I was able to get more literature on railroads and enrolled in a correspondence course on diesel-electric locomotive operations." Jenny described her employment as a journeyman locomotive electrician and night hostler at the shop. "It's important when you decide to pursue a career that you know particulars about the work so that you won't be disillusioned later," she added.

The assembly went well, John concluded, as he walked down the school corridor with Jenny after the event. They lingered in an alcove near the entrance and watched for Ramon to re-appear. "You were marvelous, John," she said. "I thank you for your time."

"You're welcome, Jenny," he said. "You were marvelous, too. I wish we had longer—just you and I—to talk about railroads and ... well, anything else that interests you."

"I wish there were more time," she responded wistfully. "Maybe when you get back from the trip, or perhaps if you happen to be here overnight during the trip? Aunt Emma would like to meet you, and so would Katie ... again. ... Oh, there's Ramon coming!"

"Yes, so he is. Well, I'll see you later ... for sure." John looked into her eyes and smiled. Then he squeezed her hand and walked away slowly. After a few steps, he turned around and waved. "See you ... as soon as I can," he said, and then trudged on.

Chapter 11: Welcome to Canada

One building dominated Summit. It was the imposing stone and wood complex that served as the railroad station in the small northern New England city. Constructed largely of granite in the last years of the 19th century, the building was designed to be a railroad terminal of magnificent proportions, far greater, in fact, than the region's train business would ever warrant.

The station stood at the junction of New England Eastern's mainline from Hill Junction to Boundary and a branch line to Eagle River, deep in the state's northwestern wilderness. Another shorter branch to Quarry, a slate production center of considerable importance at the turn of the century, veered off to the east at a point about a half-mile north of Summit station. In the beginning, the station was a bustling business center around which the community of Summit grew and prospered. In time, however, the railroad's business declined, more recently because of a succession of potato crop failures, and the structure saw less use.

The station's unique V-shaped configuration was created to fit the junction between the mainline and the Eagle River branch. The ticket and telegraph offices were located on the first floor in the turret at the base of the V and faced out across platforms on both railroad lines. The second floor provided space for the railroad to conduct its freight business. In later years, J.P. Shanahan had a round third-floor office created in empty space in the turret that rose above the rest of the station and supported the giant four-faced clock, the city's best-known landmark. The clock was visible throughout the community and its elaborate works sounded each hour of the day and night.

The long two-story wings of the building extended in northeasterly and northwesterly directions and contained a variety of railroad-support facilities, most of which were unoccupied by mid-century. But that would change in the coming weeks, as the Summit, Bolton and Quarry took over what had been New England Eastern's Hill Division.

The huge concourse and passenger waiting room utilized first-floor space from portions of both wings along with a newer one-story, largely glass addition that was constructed across the inside of the V where the two wings came together. The addition faced a parking lot at the end of the city's business district on Railroad Avenue. The glass was a J.P. Shanahan innovation to bring light into the cavernous concourse and it worked brilliantly.

∞

It was almost train time again at Summit station and a surprising number of passengers for a late fall day were gathered in the waiting room. New England Eastern's passenger trains to Eagle River and Boundary were assembled and

76

awaiting the arrival of the *Northern Express* from the south. Fred Wilson, super-intendent of the Summit Car Shop, had been invited to join Henry Terrell, John Shanahan and Ramon Martinez on the inspection tour. His first mission would be to inspect passenger equipment that was expected to arrive in a Canadian Eastern train that evening, after which he would affix new stainless steel name-plates to the cars after their placement in the yard at Boundary.

John was intrigued by the names: *Northern Mail, Spanish River, Sunbury, Carroll* and *Gatlin*. "So, what's with the names?" he asked Hank.

"Your father's idea," the railroad manager answered. "Those cars match the ones we use on the *Northern Express*. You see, with the new arrangement of run-ning through to Sunbury, we'll need two train sets of our own, instead of one. So he thought we'd name them in a similar way, using other important commu-nities on the route."

Hank went on to explain that *Northern Mail* was for a mail and baggage car similar to *Rural Delivery*. The dining car would be *Spanish River*, a car that was comparable to *Eden Valley*. The three coaches would be named for the three principal passenger points on the southern section of the new system.

"I see," John said. "That's neat, but you obviously don't have another dome car to bring up the rear. Not that you need a dome car on every train, I suppose."

"Well, not yet. But I hear rumblings from headquarters. In the meantime, this string of cars that are coming in has a matching lounge-observation car, so we'll go with that for the time being. It's already named something that we can use. ..." Hank pulled a sheaf of papers from his traveling case. "Let's see, these cars came from a Shanahan line in Wisconsin. Technically, they are owned by Shanahan Enterprises and are on loan to us. The mail car wasn't named on the previous line; the diner was *Chippewa River* and the coaches were *Douglas, Prince* and *Sawyer*. ... And the observation-lounge car was ... let's see. ... *Polaris*. We figured that would sort of go along with *Aurora Borealis*."

"Okay, so what about a locomotive, something that would sort of go along with the Five-Naught-One?"

Hank chuckled. "Got it already. Perfect match. It's our backup engine for the *Northern Express*. Let's go out on the platform, I want to show you." He led John toward the head of the train that would soon leave for Boundary. The lead-ing diesel unit was the same one that had arrived from there earlier. The trailing engine was SB&Q Five-Naught-Two.

"My gosh, it's a ringer!" John exclaimed. "I had no idea there were two of them."

"It's all about your father's management skills," Hank responded. "He al-ways arranges to have backup equipment. Everything is planned in a way that most emergencies can be handled with a minimum of effort. I learned a lot from him. He's a great railroad man."

The pair returned to the back of the train and climbed aboard the business car, which was coupled ahead of SB&Q's dome. The NEE conductor checked the platform for stragglers and seeing none, climbed on the rear coach and waved a highball to the engineer.

The four SB&Q officials gathered in the observation section of *Seven Pines* and Hank passed out the excursion's itinerary. The crew of the northbound Eastern passenger train on which they were passengers would make routine station stops through to Boundary where the last paying customers on the trip would be discharged. Then the cars would be placed on the service track near the engine house.

After that, the SB&Q locomotive would take the business and dome cars across the international railroad bridge to Ste. Anne, where they would await the arrival of a special Canadian Eastern train from Montreal that would be carrying the new cars. Representatives of the media would go along to record the interchange and would be permitted to accompany the excursion in the days that followed, if they wished. Once the interchange was completed and American and Canadian Customs cleared, the equipment would be moved across the bridge to the yard at Boundary.

John knew that Fred Wilson was a key member of the Shanahan management team even before their first meeting on the inspection trip. He remembered that his father often talked about the young mechanical engineer he had met when he first went to the North Country and how he had convinced the Summit native to work for Shanahan Enterprises. Fred's first assignment was to re-design the rambling locomotive and freight car facility that J.P. had purchased from New England Eastern. It had been a masterful accomplishment and the facility became the central rebuild shop for Shanahan Enterprises in the eastern United States despite its long distance from many of the company's holdings.

When railroad business was slow, the shop was adapted to handle outside contracts from other railroads, but perhaps more importantly for logging and forest product contractors and farming interests in the region. It was not uncommon to find a shop crew working on the power plant of a logging company's pulpwood towboat on one track in the facility while a boxcar or locomotive was being repaired on the adjoining track. The shop crew even designed and serviced truck hoists to pluck barrels of potatoes from the fields during the annual harvests. Customers were always required to seek service at local businesses first so that the shop would not be competing with enterprises in the region.

Because of its ability to diversify under Fred's unique management, the train repair facility was able, even in the hardest times, to retain its status as the largest employer in the North Country. An arrangement was made with the unions so that a number of workers from New England Eastern and Summit, Bolton and Quarry were allowed to hold seniority rights in primary jobs on the railroads and secondary positions at the shop or vice versa.

John was also aware that if the newly created North Country railroad system were to meet the challenge of handling a bumper crop of potatoes in the coming months, the Summit shop would be pressed to upgrade the refrigerator car fleet and keep the equipment in operating order. That duty would fall to Fred Wilson.

Hank was thumbing through his sheaf of papers when Ramon interrupted him. "I think you were going to tell us more about the trip itinerary. John and I need to know more about the nightlife we can expect along the way."

Hank squinted at Ramon. "I'd say the nightlife would amount to a few moose and deer that you might notice as we rumble on through the night. That's not the answer you wanted, of course. The schedule is quite flexible. The primary mission will be to see what we have, especially what we have to fix up. The second objective will be to show off some new passenger cars, so the station stops will take up some time."

The manager said he wanted to go south from Boundary the next day. "We'll definitely stop at Lyndon and Aroostook at mid-day. I want to leave most of the train on display there and take the locomotive and the dome and business cars down over the Heartland Branch and then back to Aroostook. We want to make a stop at Siberia Crossing and then try to get into Summit tomorrow night. ... It gets sketchy after that. Probably we'll go to Gatlin on Saturday and into Sunbury on Sunday afternoon. We'll work our way back on Monday and go north on the Eagle River Branch on Tuesday."

The New England Eastern passenger train made regular station stops at Siberia Crossing, Aroostook and Lyndon, along with numerous flag stops between Summit and Boundary, arriving at the latter terminal at five-fifty p.m. After the passengers got off and the mail, baggage and express was unloaded, the regular passenger cars were switched to the service track. The Eastern's locomotive was taken to the roundhouse for servicing and the head-end crew transferred to the SB&Q locomotive.

The next move was to retrieve the dome and business cars and turn them on the wye in Boundary freight yard. After the turning maneuver, the locomotive pushed the dome and business cars across the bridge to the interchange with Canadian Eastern near the station at St. Anne. There, the two cars were placed on a siding and the locomotive proceeded to the main interchange switch to await the arrival of the Canadian train.

The SB&Q officials were inside the station talking to the agent when the special train sounded an approach signal and came into view. It was headed by a regular passenger diesel unit and the cars were lined up in reverse order so that the observation car was at the front and the mail car at the rear, as requested by Shanahan Enterprises. John stepped outside the waiting room door to see the train pull in.

The conductor was standing in the rear stairwell of the diner *Chippewa River* as the train rolled in from the west. When he saw John, the man hopped off and sprinted up to the station door. He was a slight, energetic fellow and wore a standard Canadian Eastern black passenger train uniform trimmed in red. His pillbox hat was part of the traditional early 20th century conductor's uniform.

"Mon ami, J'acceuille vous au Canada!" the man exclaimed, extending his hand. "Welcome to Canada."

"Jack Demers! What a pleasant surprise. You really get around." John gripped Jack's hand firmly.

"Like I told you a few days ago, John, a man's gotta keep grubbin' for a livin'. Job here, job there. Hey, this one was a piece of cake. Hopped on up at the end of the Canadian Eastern division in La Belle Province this morning and here I am, back home again. Man, this is some train you folks picked up. I've been riding in the fancy diner. That's one fine piece of equipment."

"It's certainly good to see you again, Jack. So, are you going to be down our way again anytime soon?"

Jack chuckled. "Bright and early tomorrow morning. I understand from New England Eastern that Hank's got this fancy train running around your new system for a few days. They needed a conductor and since I had nothing in sight over here, I signed on."

"Ah, come on, Jack. You fell in love with this train and you figured you'd just follow it around for a while. That about right?"

Demers nodded. "You bet. Besides, it beats lying around the house. ... Well, I need to get inside and sign the register book. This job ends here after we put the engine in the roundhouse. Then I walk about around the corner and I'm home. It doesn't get any better than that. I live right over there." He pointed to a row of small houses on a quiet side street leading to the station.

The Canadian Eastern locomotive pulled the string of coaches beyond the east interchange switch and a brakeman aligned the switch so the SB&Q locomotive could pull out onto the mainline and retrieve the cars. After that, the engine was moved back by the station and eased the observation-lounge *Polaris* to a gentle coupling with *Seven Pines* and *Aurora Borealis*. Customs formalities were completed and the train rattled back across the international border into the North Country.

Townspeople were gathering on the station platform at Boundary even as the train approached. Boundary was a bustling border town of more than 6,000 inhabitants and was a marketplace for farming interests along the river valley that marked the border between the northeastern United States and eastern Canada. The station was adjacent to the main street that led to the international highway bridge. Residential streets extended to the east and the railroad yard and support facilities were to the west of the main line.

The Boundary wye also led to the west and marked the beginning of the New England Eastern branch line that ran some thirty miles along the river and back into the wilderness to the frontier town of Eagle River. A portion of the line had been out of service for at least two years, leaving stubs on each end that were serviced periodically by freight trains from the main line and the Eagle River branch.

The evening was taken up with guiding visitors on walk-through tours of the new train. Adrian Lajoie, the longtime agent at Boundary, assisted Hank, Fred and Ramon with the tours and John was designated as the official greeter and assigned to the dome car. A staircase was set up at the rear exit to the car and volunteers from the local Chamber of Commerce assisted visitors onto the train.

More than eight hundred people took the tour. As the event was winding down, Jack Demers, his wife, Jeannette, and their six children entered the dome car. "I just wanted you to meet my family, Mr. Shanahan," he said. "Jeannette, especially, wanted to say hello."

"It's a pleasure to meet you, Jeannette," John said, extending his hand.

"I'm pleased to meet you, too, sir," she said shyly. "Donald speaks highly of you. ... We really just wanted to say thanks for buying this railroad and for trying to make things better ... for everyone around here. There have been some hard times."

"I know," John responded. "My father is an optimist and he usually invests in things that pay off. You folks around here certainly deserve a break. I believe this will be the year that things start to change."

John watched as Jack and his wife and children explored the dome car and then moved on through the train. They were good, hardworking people, he thought.

Fred began affixing the new car nameplates from a stepladder after the visitors departed. John followed him around the train and helped by retrieving the old plates as Fred took them off and by passing up the new ones. When they were done, the night switcher shuttled the cars off to the service track when a crew of car cleaners descended on the train. The pair rejoined Ramon and Hank and walked to the nearby International Hotel for supper and their first lodgings on the trip.

Chapter 12: A Day in Potato Country

Henry Terrell and John Shanahan sat together in the waiting room at Boundary station on the second day of the Hill Division inspection tour. Their discussion touched on changes that would likely occur under the new management. Hank urged John to keep track of running conditions in particular. "I've been talking to your father often this past week, and he knows you want to be an engineer again so you'll need to have a handle on the track layout."

John was taken aback. "Really? You're not spoofing me, Hank? This is serious stuff. My dream was to be an engineer, but, well, you know ... I don't get around all that well."

"Bill Travers told me you've developed a way to get up and down from the cab units. He figures that if you keep working on that technique, you'd be a valuable asset to the railroad, especially as we make the transition. I figure you can do some things around the office from time to time and you can be an engineer on the spare board as well. Down the road your father has bigger things in mind, but this should do for a start."

John beamed. "You've made my day, Hank. I'd hop up and click my heels right now but I'd probably fall flat on my face, so I'll get right to taking notes."

When the train crew appeared Station Agent Adrian Lajoie made the introductions although most knew each other from earlier meetings. Asa Adams of Summit was a spare board engineer for the Eastern and had worked freight between Boundary and Aroostook the previous day. His fireman was Andy Anderson, who had driven from his home in Eagle River early that morning. Donald "Jack" Demers of Ste. Anne was conductor and was attired for the occasion in his New England Eastern uniform, after his previous day's work on the Canadian Eastern. The head brakeman was Dandy Dan Detweiler of Summit, who had been working on a freight train out of Eagle River and had accompanied Anderson on the way over. The rear brakeman was Stan Larrabee, also of Summit, who had been working on the Boundary day switcher. Stan was a spare board employee of New England Eastern and the Summit, Bolton and Quarry and wore his SB&Q trainman's uniform.

Hank outlined the day's plan for his colleagues and the crew. As a passenger extra, they would be allowed to run at passenger train speed but there would be places along the way where the officials would want to proceed slowly or stop for ground inspections. Jack Demers would ride with Hank's party in the dome car and would have a portable radio to communicate with the engine crew. Station stops were scheduled at Lyndon, Aroostook, Heartland, Four Corners and Siberia Crossing, and there might be others as time permitted. The plan was to tie up at Summit and have the train on display in the evening.

The train departed Boundary at eight o'clock in the morning with a number of passengers. John worked his way up the narrow stairwell to the dome in *Aurora Borealis* and was directed by Hank to take a double seat at the front of the dome compartment. There were twelve such sets of seats to accommodate twenty-four passengers per sitting when the car was in regular service. Ramon brought along a stepstool used by car attendants and positioned it in a way so John could prop up his left leg. "I was thinking that your leg might cramp up a bit so give this a try," he said, and sat down in the double seat behind John.

John nodded. "Thanks, Ramon. You know, I go around telling people about dome cars and how great they are and I can't remember ever riding in one. The view's fantastic."

After ascending a slight grade through a wooded area south of Boundary the track broke out onto a broad rolling plain that was clearly farming country. Sidings leading to potato storage buildings were passed but no attendant railroad cars were in evidence. Hank had said only that morning that he wouldn't be surprised if potato brokers started calling in car orders within days. John's father had alerted Hank that some of his contacts in the financial world sensed North Country potatoes would be in high demand soon.

Because of an anticipated need for cars, Fred Wilson had moved his entire shop crew onto potato car inspections and repair that morning. In the meantime, the independent North Country Heater Car Service had leased track at a railroad pit near Summit to equip cars with standard alcohol-fired heaters that it owned or leased. The heating units were traditionally set up in end bunkers of the railroad cars, an area accessible only through hatches in car rooftops. Those were the parts of the cars where ice was packed when the equipment was used in summer refrigeration service.

John was acquainted with that summer service and remembered the great fleets of West Coast refrigerator cars that were used to handle perishable commodities in transit across America. He was also vaguely familiar with the wintertime use of the same cars that were needed to keep perishable commodities, such as potatoes, from freezing while en route from farmers' warehouses to marketplaces. Just the night before, Hank had shown him a typical North Country waybill that detailed heating instructions for each car shipped. A lot of science had gone into that 1940s-era technology, he supposed, but what really impressed him was the work involved by scores of men along the railroad lines who were responsible for getting the goods to market in marketable condition.

There were a total of fourteen sidings, all lined with potato houses and public loading sites, in the twenty-two miles between the northern terminus of the mainline and Lyndon, the first sizeable community south of Boundary. There were also two flag stops, North Road and Marysville. A closed station still stood at the latter, and Hank said it likely would be re-opened when potato shipments started in earnest.

Lyndon appeared to be a pleasant market town with giant maples and elms lining its streets. The downtown district was near the railroad yard and station, a rambling and dilapidated wood frame structure. According to Hank, J.P. already had been in touch with local officials and proposed to make temporary repairs for winter and construct a new facility come spring. Lyndon was home to various milling facilities and a creamery, but the latter had been in danger of closing because New England Eastern could not provide milk car service on a regular basis. The milk was being trucked south over the Hackmatack Highway but that service was abysmal, the railroad manager said.

"We'll be hauling milk cars on our passenger trains from Lyndon to Hill Junction beginning on November fifteenth," Hank emphasized. "We have another creamery at Carroll that is trucking but we'll get that as soon as we get our schedules worked out."

John remembered the odd arrangement of passenger trains Eastern provided north of Summit by the Eastern. "If we're going to have better service up this way, I'd say we need more cars and engines."

"Correct. I can't tell you, because I don't know yet, but there are certain plans in the works. I can tell you one thing, the equipment is already on the way, so I'd say the outcome must be a sure thing."

More than four hundred people toured the passenger train at Lyndon and it was ten-thirty when the conductor waved a highball to the engineer. Another dozen sidings were passed over the next twenty-three miles. Three were flag stop shelters: Dryden, Benson and Walker Settlement, and at each upwards of twenty people were gathered to wave as the train pulled by.

The train reached Aroostook, the second largest community in the North Country, at eleven-fifteen. Probably the best-planned community in the region, its main street was unusually wide and sizeable parking areas were abundant. A number of large retail outlets were in evidence and the place throbbed with shoppers. Unlike Summit, which was largely a railroad town, Aroostook had a small railroad yard and appeared to be more highway-oriented when it came to transportation needs. It was the first sizeable community reached in the North Country by the Hackmatack Highway, which merged with the Boundary-Summit Road at Four Corners, about ten miles to the south.

Still, Aroostook provided a strong base for passenger train service and it was the intent of J.P. Shanahan to build on that potential, Hank said. "There's no money in passengers, of course, and we all know that," he added. "It's really all about public relations, and there isn't a better way to a shipper's heart than to provide an opportunity to load the wife and kids on a train every now and again."

The exhibition train was spotted alongside the platform at Aroostook, where at least one hundred people were already assembled. The station was an almost new brick structure that provided a variety of railroad services. An earlier wooden building had burned in a fire in 1948, at which time Eastern applied for permission to discontinue all station service in the city.

But residents, even those who rarely used train service, complained loudly and the Interstate Commerce Commission ruled that the railroad would have to replace the depot with what it described as a "substantial" multifunctional passenger and freight agency. That need was based on the volume of railroad freight traffic through the community several years earlier, which happened to be a boom year in the potato industry. The regulatory commission based its findings not only on inbound and outbound shipments at the station but added in all freight to and from the Heartland Branch.

And that was the reason, Hank said, for the side trip down the branch. "We're going to have a couple dozen shippers aboard, so we're taking the business car and the dome," he said as the train crew switched out the cars. "We want to hear from them because they are the ones who can make or break this new railroad in the end."

The railroad manager placed Ramon and Fred Wilson in charge of train tours at Aroostook and a number of volunteers solicited by the local Chamber of Commerce were on hand to assist. After the business and dome cars were cut from the train and assembled behind Engine Five-Naught-Two, Hank and John invited the Heartland shippers aboard and the train was moved to the junction switch to await an outbound freight.

The extra left the junction at eleven-thirty and in order to meet the shippers, John set aside his note taking for the return trip. The line was twenty miles in length, ending at Heartland village. There were eighteen sidings on the line, and each was lined with potato storage houses. There was an open station at Travis Farm, six miles south of Heartland. More than one hundred refrigerators cars were on storage tracks along the line. Those were part of the sale by Eastern and would have to be inspected by the new owners.

During conversations with the shippers, Hank and John were made to understand that while they were pleased with the transition in ownership, they fully expected Shanahan Enterprises to deliver improved service. Shipper Harry Travis of Travis Farms, who seemed to be the spokesman for the group, was blunt: "We're putting you Shanahans on notice that we expect prompt service all the time no matter the weather. When we need cars, we'll expect to have cars and when we want the potatoes moved, we'll expect a train here to move them."

Hank said he understood the shippers' needs but the railroad also had needs. Travis turned to John. "And you, young Mr. Shanahan, what do you understand?"

John cleared his throat. Then he stared directly into the shipper's eyes. "I understand a lot of things about railroads and very little about potatoes. I believe I understand your needs, Mr. Travis. I don't speak for Shanahan Enterprises because I'm just an employee here. ... You may not like this, but I'll tell you straight out what I think."

He paused, surveyed his audience, and continued. "In this transporter-shipper game there's a little give and take of which you may not be aware. We will set up a time that is mutually advantageous to both of us as to when we will expect our trains to arrive at your potato house door to do the switching. If you're not ready for us at such an agreed-to time you may rest assured that you would be dropped to the bottom of our priority list. ...

"There are a few rules we play by. Yes, we want your business. And apparently, you want our service or you wouldn't be on this free ride. We'll provide you cars when we have them and when we don't, we won't. We can't manufacture specific cars overnight. You've been burned by Eastern over the years, but that is no fault of ours."

John looked out the window of the dome car and noticed a long-haul trailer truck straddling a siding in order to reach the trackside door of a potato house. He directed attention to the truck. "There's also a matter of who owns the track where your potato storage houses are located. My understanding is that we own that track and will be using it after midnight on the fifteenth of November for railroad purposes. Let me tell all of you something specific about track under the control of Shanahan Enterprises: We don't share it with competitors from the trucking industry." John's eyes narrowed to slits. "You do follow me, don't you, Mr. Travis?"

Travis stared at his colleagues. "Well," he said. "Perhaps we've been told a thing or two about the shipper-transporter game. I'd say this straight-talking young fellow knocked the wind out of our sails. I believe he's dead right. How about you, gentlemen?"

The response came in nods and murmurs of approval. Travis extended his hand to John who clasped it in a firm handshake. "I like you, John Shanahan. You tell it like it is. You folks give us the best you can for service and we'll be available to lend a helping hand any time in any way. And yes, we'll make sure that no trucks drive on your property."

"Very good, Harry. We seem to have an understanding. I may be an engineer once in a while on a train that comes down this branch. I'm told that I'm fairly good at what I do and I would have no qualms—none at all—about pushing a truck trailer off our tracks if it were in our way when we were doing our switching thing. I'd probably stop even if we had no occasion to do so, and push a truck trailer off our sidetracks just for the hell of it."

After the passenger extra stopped at Heartland, reconnected to the rest of the train at Aroostook and made additional stops at Four Corners, a staffed flag station, and Siberia crossing, an open agency, Hank slipped into a seat in the dome car across from John. They hadn't had an opportunity to talk since Heartland and both were weary and sat in silence for several miles. Hank was about to speak when John noticed a spur leading to the west.

"So where does that track go?" he blurted out suddenly. Then he noticed the sign. "I see. The sign says Esker. What's there?"

"Oh, there's a railroad gravel pit in there a mile or so," Hank answered. "Several tracks in all. Some of them get moved around as the gravel is taken out. Eastern hasn't used it for a while and the heating car service sets up shop there in the winter. It's about five or six miles by road in from Summit. And there's still a spur line off that track that leads to the old Air Force base just above town. The base has been closed for years."

"I see," John responded. "I guess I interrupted something you wanted to say when I asked you about Esker. Did you have something in mind?"

"I did." Hank seemed uneasy at first. "When you addressed Mr. Travis earlier today, I thought, 'Oh, boy, we're in for it now.' Harry isn't a fellow who takes any backtalk when he sets his mind to something. So, yeah, I was worried as to where that was going."

"How do you feel about it now?"

Hank grinned. "Harry's okay about it and so am I. I was all along. We talked on the way back and he thinks you're the cat's meow in the railroad business. He said he likes blunt-talking people."

"Well, let's hope we keep talking blunt and purring like a bunch of hungry kittens."

Chapter 13: A Night to Remember

The passenger extra pulled into Summit yard and was directed to stop on Track One next to the station. Henry Terrell was about to step off the observation car when he turned to John Shanahan.

"There will be a dinner break at any restaurant of your choosing and it's on the railroad tab," Hank said. "Then we hold an open house on the train from seven-thirty to whenever. Anything specific on your agenda now that you'll be in the big town on a Friday night, young Mr. Shanahan?"

"Ah, no, guess not. Food; work, if you call it that, and sleep. Start out again tomorrow. That suits me. ... Well, actually, I might place a local phone call ..."

"Really? And whom do you know in Summit?"

"Ah ... well, just someone I ... ah, met ... a few days ago. It's not important, really."

Hank nodded. "Okay. But if that someone happens to be the night hostler at Summit, that person has been recruited for the evening to serve as a tour guide on the train and we're paying for a replacement to fill that person's shoes over at the engine house."

The railroad manager squinted at John. "Perhaps I've assumed something, my friend John. If I might be nosy, who was this person you wished to call?"

"Ah, Hank, be nosy, what the heck. You know more about me than I do. Since we're both talking about Miss Boston, yes, that's the person I thought I might call. You're obviously way ahead of me. I guess I just like to talk to her once in a while."

"Very good," Hank responded. "So I'd advise you to freshen up a bit in your business car, after which you should don your topcoat, hat and gloves, walk through the waiting room, exit onto the street and go to Five Railroad Avenue. That would be the third house beyond the station. Be a gentleman and tap at the front door. I'm sure someone inside will be ready to walk you down to a restaurant that she picked out earlier."

John grinned. "Henry Terrell, you're the gentleman. Thanks."

"And a bit of fatherly advice, my son," Hank said in his most serious tone. "Be nice to her. She's a fine young lady who had a terrible time after her father died a few years ago. She's back on track now, finishing school with top grades and working and raising a fine young daughter. Jen's a real gem, remember that."

John stepped out of the concourse at Summit and turned up the collar of his topcoat. With night approaching the air had a distinctive chill. The streetlights were on and John could see that city traffic was heavy. Then he remembered that it was a Friday evening, a busy time for most market towns across the country. He could see the row of small, similarly structured houses beyond the station on the left and figured that he should follow the sidewalk from the station along that side of the street to avoid having to cross the wide thoroughfare.

He was almost to the third house, Five Railroad Avenue, when the door opened. A little girl stepped out. "Hello, is that you, Mister John?"

"Yes," he said. "You must be Miss Katie Boston who lives at Five Railroad Avenue."

The little girl giggled. "Yes. Please come in. Mama is expecting you." She ran out the walkway and took his hand. "Come with me, Mister John. Mama is waiting."

John almost stumbled on the first step and caught his balance. "Are you okay, Mister John?" Katie queried.

"Yes. I guess I'm just a little clumsy sometimes. I have to be careful when I climb stairs. I'm fine now. And thank you for being concerned."

"You are welcome," Katie said as she pushed open the door and took John inside. "Mama! Mister John is here," she called up the stairway that led to the second floor.

"I'll be right down, sweetheart. Please invite Mister John into the living room."

Katie led John into the living room and asked if he would like to sit on the sofa or have the easy chair, which tilted back. "I think the sofa would be best, Katie," he said. "If I sit in that lovely easy chair I'd have a hard time getting back to my feet."

"I know. Mama said you were hurt in the war. You are better now and that is good."

"Yes. I'm better and I'm glad to be back home ... back here. ..." John paused and looked up when he heard footsteps on the stairway. He grasped his cane and pushed himself to his feet just as Jenny came into the room. It was then that he realized she was truly a stunning young woman, petite and poised and remarkably beautiful. She wore a fashionable evening dress that accented her good looks and John was at a loss for words. He reached for her hand and clasped it in his. They looked into each other's eyes and he knew that it was a special moment for both of them.

"How nice to see you again, John," she said softly.

"It's truly my pleasure ... really ... It is nice to see you again," he stammered, and was trying to say something else when the doorbell rang loudly.

"I think that's Uncle Billy, Katie," Jenny said. "Would you get the door, please?"

Katie scampered to the door and opened it. "It is Uncle Billy!" she exclaimed.

"It's my princess!" Bill Travers yelped as he picked up the little girl and plunked his railroad cap atop her head. "There, folks, meet Katie Boston, engineer of the *Northern Express*, the best express train in the whole doggone world."

"Best train in the world, Uncle Billy?" Katie squealed.

"Best, fastest, most class and it has the best engineer of all of them!" Bill responded and winked at John. He sat Katie in the easy chair and pulled off his sheepskin jacket, which he tossed over an arm of the sofa.

"So, Jennifer Boston, you little twit, all dressed up fancy to go out for the evening? And you, John P. Shanahan, aren't you quite the dresser, too. I imagine you met most of the up and coming folks up north today."

John nodded. "Yeah, quite a few. One fellow on the Heartland Branch came on a little strong but I think ..."

Bill cut him off. "I know, Hank told me you ran smack-dab into Huffy Harry, The Big Potato, and put the loudmouth in his place." He laughed gleefully. "Man, don't I wish I'd been there to see that. You're okay, Shanahan." Bill grasped John's hand in a vise-like handshake.

"You weren't unkind to Mr. Travis, were you?" Jenny asked. "That doesn't seem to be your nature."

"No, not really," John said. "He made some comments about what the shippers expected of the railroad, and I basically said what the railroad expected of the shippers."

"Tell Jen what you said about bulldozing the damned highway trucks off the sidings when we come to do their switching," Bill interjected. "C'mon, Shanahan, spice it up."

"Yeah, I guess that's the gist of it. It ticked me off to think that Eastern crews have to sit around waiting for the trucks to get loaded so they'll get off the track."

John recalled a story about an engineer who had worked the farm sidings in Idaho. He was on long hours and pretty much had it with tiptoeing around the truckers. So he pulled the locomotive up against a tractor-trailer that was sitting on the track he was supposed to switch. He bumped it gently and touched off a series of blats with the air horns. "Then he revved up the engine, honked to beat heck again, released his brakes and shoved the throttle ahead."

John paused and eyed Jenny. "Should I continue?" he asked.

"Certainly, John. I'm beginning to like this engineer."

"Well, he pushed the truck right along down the track and smashed the conveyor from the potato house to the truck and the pieces wound up stripping the siding off the building. Anyway, he pushed the rig about two hundred feet until the roof of the trailer collapsed and it rolled over and down an embankment, spilling spuds all over the place. Then he backed out of the siding and along the mainline to the station. He stopped there, shut the engine down, got in his car and drove away."

John fell silent and waited for a response.

"All right, Shanahan, I'll bite," Bill said. "There's more to the story, isn't there?"

John nodded and told how the engineer moved to California and hired on with a railroad that handled produce out of the Salinas Valley. It wasn't long before a similar situation arose regarding a truck on the track, only that time it was on the main line. Once the engineer ascertained that the driver had jumped clear of the open-body rig, he touched up the throttle a bit and slammed into the vehicle, reducing it to a pile of rubble. It was loaded with garden produce and when the authorities arrived, the engineer was sitting in the cab surrounded by piles of lettuce and making a salad to go with his lunch.

"An investigation ensued, of course, but, surprisingly, he was cleared of any wrongdoing and the trucking company was required to pay the railroad for equipment damage and fined for being on the track. "From what I heard, the engineer went on to be a division superintendent," John concluded.

"I love it!" Bill yelped. "That's the way to handle trespassers."

Jenny shook her head in disbelief and tugged at John's arm. "I think it's time for us to get on our way," she said. "Billy has agreed to sit with Katie until Aunt Emma gets back from her church group meeting. They're all planning to tour the train later."

The pair walked down Railroad Avenue to the heart of the business district. Not long into the walk, Jenny slipped her arm through his and looked up at him. "So now that you've been here a few days, do you think you might want to stay … for a while?"

"I'm beginning to like it here, especially now," he said and smiled at her. "Yes, I think I'll stay a while."

"I hope so," Jenny murmured.

Her response warmed John's heart. Then he told her how Hank had alluded to the possibilities that he might do some office work from time to time and likely get a chance to run as a spare board engineer. "I put a lot of attention today to the track and I've been studying the grade and curve charts and trying to get a handle on where everything is. But I need to compile a personal notebook to keep track of particular operating conditions along the different routes."

"That's a great idea, John," Jenny said. "I have notes that might come in handy if you'd like to look at them. I guess you know that when I qualified as a hostler I took the engineer's written exam and road tests so I can run anywhere on the Hill Division."

"I heard about that from Ramon, Jenny. I think you have an unusual interest for a young woman and I applaud you on your success. You're a remarkable person."

"You're a very kind man," Jenny responded. "So would you like to get to-gether sometime and study up on what an engineer needs to know about this railroad?"

"Let's do it the first time that you and I have some free time. I'll probably be back in Summit again after this whirlwind tour of the latest conquest by the Shanahan Empire."

Jenny's eyes twinkled. "Oh, it's an empire, is it? It is your ambition to be an emperor?"

"Emperor John P. Shanahan the Third? Hmmm. That has a nice ring. I could take over the place down at Quarry, fortify it and build a moat and make it my castle. Let's see, I'd need to …"

Jenny elbowed him in the ribs. "Cut it out, Shanahan!" she exclaimed.

"Okay. No, Jenny, I never wanted anything more than a chance to make a decent living doing what I really wanted to do. That was to be an engineer. I had big ambitions once. I was going to be the engineer of the fastest express train in the world. … At this point, well, I'd settle for a local freight train on some back-woods branch line."

The couple turned at the intersection of Railroad Avenue and County Road and walked by several retail stores. "The restaurant is just ahead," Jenny said. "It's called Cedars and it's really the best place in town. Hank made the reservations and I think you'll like it."

Upon entering, it was clear to John that the restaurant was a first-class establishment. It was quiet inside and the labyrinth of serving rooms offered a degree of privacy rarely found in most dining places. A doorman took their coats and the table attendant led the couple to a secluded corner booth for two from which no other diners could be seen. Soft lighting added to the intimacy and classical music offered a soothing backdrop.

John was about to seat Jenny when he remembered something. "How do we arrange this seating thing, Jen? I'm left-handed and usually wind up poking the person next to me with my elbow … or worse, if I happen to be into serious slashing with a knife."

She giggled. "Oh, the Emperor is a slasher! I see. Well, aside from me sitting at a table in the next room, why don't you slide over to the left and I'll follow you in?"

"Ah, well, I suppose but that doesn't seem quite proper. Maybe, I could sort of push the table your way and …"

"Don't be difficult, John! Sit now, and don't be a klutz, please." Jenny giggled again.

"Well, I don't know about that. Perhaps I could pretend I'm right-handed and we could do this properly."

"Perhaps I could call the manager and have you removed from the building. That might be proper. Would that solve our problem?"

"Not really, because I'd still be left-handed, and that means …"

"Mr. Shanahan, you have ten seconds to seat yourself or I will seat you."

"Really, Miss Boston? Somehow, I don't think a little gal like you could push around a big lug like me. Do you?"

Jenny grabbed his left arm and pinned it behind his back. "Sit," she commanded. He slipped quietly into the booth and rubbed his forearm. "That hurt, you know." Then he grinned and she giggled.

"I believe I'm really going to enjoy your company, John," she said sweetly. "How about you?"

"Yes, I believe you are … ah, I mean, me …I'm going to enjoy your company. Very much. Often, I hope, even when I get a little dippy." He squeezed her hand gently.

John walked Jenny back to the railroad station after the dinner date. Hank was waiting at the concourse door and ushered them through the crowd that had gathered to tour the new train. She would be the official greeter in the observation lounge of the dome car and John would be in the dome section to point out the amenities of such a service on the expanded Summit-to-Sudbury service. Several of Jenny's classmates had volunteered to lead groups through the cars and railroad personnel were in each to describe the accommodations and pass out brochures prepared by Shanahan Enterprises.

After the last of the more than twelve hundred visitors left, Jenny climbed into the dome and sat down next to John. "Well, Jenny, what did you think of that?" he asked.

Her reaction was that of a schoolgirl. Jenny beamed and blurted out, "It was wonderful! Did you see all the children? They loved the train. … This was the best thing the railroad could have done. I'm so excited … for all of us! … And you met Aunt Emma, just for a minute. … And she told me afterward that you were the nicest gentleman, and Katie was excited … and even Billy. … It was a grand tour, John, and a night for me to cherish."

"It was, Jenny," he said. "For me, this was truly a night to remember, and sharing it with you was the best part of all."

Part III: The Transition Starts

Chapter 14: A Prospect for an Engineer

When John Shanahan went to the door of the Summit Heights Hotel where he had spent the night he realized that the weather had changed abruptly and a cold northwest wind was sweeping the North Country. He stood in the foyer awaiting his taxi to the railroad station and knew this was the beginning of the winter to come. It was November now, and he was no stranger to November winds. In Chicago, where he had grown up, the winds had chilled him often, and in Montana, where he learned his trade, the wind and snow were factors of everyday life. And then there was Korea, where everything was bleak and bitter and cold and windy.

John shook his head to make Korea go away. He was starting a new life now and there was a young woman who was often on his mind. He knew so little about her, having met Jennifer Boston only days before, and yet it seemed they were destined to be together one day when he found his place in life. Maybe that place was here in the North Country but it was so cold this November morning.

The taxi pulled up at the foyer. John gripped his traveling bag in one hand and his cane in the other and stepped into the wind. He was caught off balance immediately and dropped the bag and leaned heavily on the cane for support. Seeing that his fare was having trouble, the taxi driver hopped out and came to his aid. "Dirty day in the country, sir," he said, grasping the bag and taking John's arm.

"I thank you," John said. "I wasn't expecting the wind to be that strong. I'm from away and not tuned into your kind of November weather. I should be, though. It seems like I've been in this kind of climate before."

The driver looked back at John after they were both in the car. "Say, you must be that young Mr. Shanahan fellow, the soldier home from Korea. It's an honor, sir, to be your driver this morning."

"Yes, I'm John Shanahan. Back home again," John responded, and quickly changed the subject. "I guess I didn't catch your name."

"It's Richard Smith," he said, extending his hand.

"I'm pleased to make your acquaintance, Richard. I suppose being in the taxi business takes you to the station quite a lot."

"I'd say eighty percent of my trade is either to the station or from the station. It fell off a lot when the Eastern began cutting back, but with the *Northern Express* running through to Gatlin, it has bounced back better than ever. Now, with the new direct service to Sunbury, things are really looking good."

94

The taxi driver pulled up at the concourse at seven-thirty and carried John's bag to the door. Hank was there, took the bag and pressed several bills into Smith's hand. "Thanks, Dick," he said. "We always appreciate the special service you give us at the railroad."

"Call anytime, Hank, and thanks for the business."

Once inside, Hank led John to the express office. "We received a couple of packages for you yesterday afternoon on the *Northern Express*. They're from your mother. I apologize for not getting them to you sooner but I got taken up with all the excitement."

"Oh, that's quite all right, Hank. I can't imagine what my Mom would be sending. Maybe homemade cookies? Let's take a look. I'm hungry for cookies already."

"Don't bother. The boxes contain work gear; you know, your engineer's rigging. The stuff you brought back from Montana before you went overseas. She thought you might make use of it when we get things up and running around here."

"I see. Perhaps someone from this railroad called her recently and tipped her off that maybe her son would be doing a little engine driving again. Would that be a possibility?"

"Possibly."

John laughed. "You crafty old fox. You knew just exactly what I wanted. A couple pairs of overalls, a lined Whitefield frock jacket, my summer and winter caps, my oiled boots, bandannas, boot straps, some woolies and ... ah ... let's see ..."

"Your leather gloves with the tie backs, the long-gantlet pair you used on steam, your sheepskin jacket and time book and the trucker's wallet with the chain attachment to your belt. You already have your watch," Hank stopped abruptly, stared into John's eyes and squinted. "So, tell me, young Shanahan, why the hell did you have a trucker's wallet with a chain? I can't imagine a railroad man wanting to look like a truck driver."

"Hank, you're a jewel. I mean that. Thank you. As for the wallet, well, I experimented with several kinds but that one just seemed to work. I'd get fumbling around trying to stuff the standard billfold into my back pocket of my pants under my overalls but it would tumble down the leg, which was okay because of the leg straps, so it was safe."

John paused, attempting to judge Hank's reaction. There was none, and he continued. "Trouble was, when I went into a restaurant and needed to get my money out, there I'd be bent down, pulling at my pants legs and some waitress with particularly good looking legs and a skimpy skirt would be standing over me and ..."

"Enough, Shanahan! I get the picture. Yes, indeed. Oh, and speaking of women in general, how'd things go with you and Miss Boston last night?"

"It was wonderful." John grinned. "What did Jenny say? I'm sure you already asked."

"It was wonderful, that's what she said. Did you guys rehearse that line?"

"It was really wonderful, and I thank you for arranging it."

"Hank's here to help the hired help be happy. ... I'll get your gear over to the business car so you'll have it handy when you want it. Why don't you hustle along and find a good seat. We're going to follow the *Northern Express* and make some important stops today."

Hank added that several car inspectors from Fred Wilson's shop crew would ride to a place where the string of refrigerator cars were located on the old northbound mainline. "We'll let them off there and they'll work down to the string to see how many cars we can move right away. The *Northern Express* will pick up the inspectors for the trip back."

"So the wheels are really turning on the takeover. That's encouraging."

John went to the platform and stepped outside where a sizeable crowd was gathered. The *Northern Express* was loading passengers on Track One, with the exhibition train behind it on Track Three. He stepped back against the station wall to escape the wind and was attempting to adjust a scarf around his throat when he felt a steely grip on his arm.

"You had a good time last night?" It was Bill Travers, who squinted up at him from beneath the ragged visor of his trademark railroad cap.

"Morning, Bill," he offered. "Ah, yes. I had a very pleasant evening."

"So I heard. I believe the word was 'wonderful,' at least from my source." Bill grinned. "Hey, you're an okay guy. So you're off to the big city today?"

"Yep."

"Staying overnight?"

"Uh huh."

"Lotta nightlife down there. You know, wild bars and loose women."

"I see. ... Well, I could make some dumb remark, but truth is, I'm trying to absorb a lot of information in a short time and I kind of need to keep focused."

"Good, pal. Keep absorbing and focusing. You're okay. ... Well, I see Joey over there checking his timepiece. You know what that means. See you next time." Bill sprinted across the platform, bounded up the cabin ladder and slammed the door. Conductor Joe Francis waved a highball and Bill sounded an acknowledgement on the air horns.

John watched the gleaming silver cars glide by: *Rural Delivery, Eden Valley, Summit, Bolton* and *Quarry* ... and then one more, a superb creation with large windows and a sweeping curved rear observation section. It was *Polaris,* which had been on the exhibition train and it appeared to be carrying a full load of passengers. The regular train pulled away and accelerated quickly as it swept into the grade south of Summit station.

Hank came by. "That observation car looks quite nice," he noted.

"Yeah. But why would you give it up for a few honest-to-goodness paying customers?"

"We need to make a buck when we can. We had a bunch of first-class tickets that some folks were dying to use, so we figured we'd put our assets to work. ...

Now we've lollygagged around long enough. Hop on, we have places to go, people to meet."

John climbed into the dome and got back to his note taking. This was his second trip over the mainline and already it was becoming familiar. He paid attention to the Summit Grade, as it was called, and the leveling off point near Hillman, a passing track. He also remembered Bill's story about the train collision near there and watched for the two mounds on the embankment where the locomotive tenders had spilled their coal. It was the place where the man who was Jenny's uncle and Bill's foster father had died.

John paid close attention as the train slowed down on the approach to Spanish Junction. He hoped to see the telegraph operator, but he was not on duty that morning. The extra continued at regular speed by the site of the derailment of the Hayride earlier in the week. Two wrecked cars had been removed and the track repaired.

Just south of a crossover near South Spanish the first string of stored refrigerator cars came into view. Engineer Asa Adams signaled the train's approach and stopped.

Brakeman Stan Larrabee dropped a stepstool to the ground and stood by as the workers stepped off. It appeared that the men would work in teams and each team leader would list the car numbers on a conductor's tally sheet in their order from north to south. Team members would check each car, paying attention to brakes, couplers and air hoses, and, especially, the condition of packing in the journal boxes.

John knew it was there, where the ends of the freight cars' axles turned in the steel cases that were part of each four-wheel set that the greatest potential for disaster lurked. Many a railroad accident over the years was traced almost immediately to a "hot box," or defective journal that ran hotter and hotter without appropriate lubricant until the end of the axle burned and broke off, if not detected soon enough to stop.

It was his experience that most railroad train crews were always alert to the possibility of hot boxes, particularly on heavily loaded long-distance freight trains. In the daytime, smoke was a telltale sign. At night, a red glow near the bottom of a freight car was reason to stop quickly and inspect the train.

As for the work at South Spanish, it was John's understanding that the car repairmen would mark each reefer with red or blue chalk as each was assessed. The cars marked in red mean that they exhibited serious defects. When it came time to move the potato cars to the shop at Summit, the train crew would have to switch out the cars with blue chalk, assemble them into trains and leave the others on the storage track, pending further inspection. That would be an interesting detail for some train crew in the near future.

After the train resumed its normal speed, Fred Wilson sat down next to John. "You probably know what we are doing," he said. "The plan is to make a quick inspection to see if the cars can be moved in a train of twenty cars or so from here back to the shop."

"Yes, I thought so," John said. "So how soon will you start moving them? Not until the fifteenth of November, I suppose."

"No, actually if we can come up with a few trainmen, we could start as soon as tomorrow or Monday. We have an agreement now with Eastern that we can start the car-moving project anytime with our own crew even though we'll still run on their train orders and by their rules. Our rules are identical anyway, so that will be no problem."

John nodded absently. "That should work out okay."

"But we've got to find a qualified engineer and conductor before then. That will be the problem." Fred peered intently at John.

"That could be a problem. The original SB&Q doesn't have that many train crews."

"No, not many and anyone employed by Eastern now is required to stay with them until the fifteenth. They'll need to do a lot of car moving of their own, so they'll all be busy until then. The crew on this train is still working for them."

"Gosh. I don't know what to say. I guess our project will have to wait."

"John, I know you're a qualified engineer. When was the last time you actually ran a diesel-electric locomotive?"

"Ah, gee, quite a while. I went into the service in the summer of 1950 after my last run on the South Montana. Then there was some Army transportation school stuff where I had a choice of learning how to drive a truck or run a train. I never wanted to drive a truck, so I opted to play around with switcher engines. That would have been in the fall, just before I got shipped off to Japan and Korea. That mission came to an end quickly, but I was in a couple of hospitals a long time so it's been more than a year."

Fred got up quickly, apparently seized with an idea. "I need to talk to Hank. I think he's down in the lounge. Stay right here. We'll get back to you." John watched as the shop foreman bounded down the narrow stairwell to the lounge section of the *Aurora Borealis*.

John slouched in his seat, trying to will the ever-present ache out of his lame leg. It seemed like the opportunity of a lifetime was dangling before his eyes but it was just beyond his grasp. He knew he could operate a locomotive about as well as any of his peers. "But I walk with a cane," he muttered to himself. "I'm crippled for all practical purposes. I should apply for an Army pension now and go to an old soldier's home. Why am I thinking I can ever do this engineer thing again?"

He blinked back tears that welled in his eyes. Then he thought of Jenny who had so taken his fancy of late. She was confident that he could do anything he wanted and it was clear that she supported his desire to run trains again. Maybe he could, he thought, if he paid attention to his footing and kept his stout cane handy. He remembered an older engineer in Montana who got around really well and he had lost a foot in a terrible train wreck. He was fitted with a prosthesis and except for a bit of a limp no one knew the extent of his injury. He didn't even use a cane.

Fifteen minutes passed before Fred appeared at the head of the stairwell with Hank behind him. They came to the front and sat down in the double seat across from John.

"So, Fred's been talking to you about an interesting prospect for a young engineer," Hank began. "What do you think of that notion?"

"It's been my dream all my life, but given my condition, Hank, I ... well, I just don't know." John looked away but continued to talk. "It really all comes down to whether I can navigate in and out of the locomotive. I think I can." He turned back to his two colleagues across the aisle. "Damn it, I know I can. Other than the bum leg, my reflexes are good, I know the operating rules and I'm really a pretty good engineer."

"That's what I wanted to hear, son!" Hank exclaimed. "Now let's talk about logistics. I'm going to propose that you get your gear together and get off when we stop at Blackwater. We're going to be there for a while to show off this train before the *Northern Express* gets back from Gatlin. When it gets there, I want you to ride back to Summit in the locomotive with Bill and Jim McDermott. Soak up all the operating techniques you can."

The railroad manager went on to spell out John's agenda for the rest of Saturday. "There is always shop switching to do and we have a locomotive for that purpose. We'll find a brakeman somewhere and try to get another qualified engineer to get you back into the routine of moving cars around. Would that work for you?"

John nodded. "I need to do that."

"The rules, Hank," Fred interjected.

"Yeah. That's right. I'll need you to write up the rules and that will take a while. Let's say you do that after the engine workout. Check in with Larry Smith, the agent, when you get there. He's also our rules examiner. I'll be talking with him later today and arrange that end of it. You'll stay at Summit for a few days, so I'll see that you have a room in the crew quarters at the station. When we get to Blackwater station I'll be in touch with Summit and talk this thing out. This will be a work in progress, subject to revisions as we go along. Okay?"

"Okay. I'll do my best to make it work."

Hank peered out the windows of the dome car. "We've been bouncing over the riffles and now I see we're passing High Meadow. I'd suggest you go up to the business car, get your gear together and be ready to change trains after we get to Blackwater."

John pushed himself to his feet, grasped his cane and stepped into the aisle. "There isn't much I can say, Hank ... and Fred ... except to thank you from the bottom of my heart." He shook hands with both men and limped to the stairwell, tucked his cane under his arm and eased himself down the stairs. He walked through the car, crossed the enclosed vestibule between *Aurora Borealis* and *Seven*

Pines, which had been turned at Summit and was being hauled in reverse, and entered the business car.

Ramon was in the galley when he entered the dining area. He looked up when John plunked down at the table. "You came to snoop around Ramon's territory?" he asked.

"I was hoping you'd be kind enough to fix a little snack for the both of us, seeing as the lunch hour is looming, my good friend Ramon," John answered.

"How little can you stand, chum?"

"Oh, just a bowl of soup and some crackers would do the trick, I think."

"I'm glad you thought of that. Just what I had on the menu. Soup, crackers and coffee on a cold day." Ramon rustled around the galley and emerged with a tray. "So you're jumping ship here and getting a chance to do something you really want to do. That means Ramon won't have to chaperone you around Sunbury on a Saturday night."

"That's true. But who's going to be chaperoning Ramon in the big city where I'm told a lot of loose women hang out?"

"I expect Ramon will behave. Hank will figure ways to keep Ramon out of trouble."

"Well, that's a relief. I can get off here and embark on a new career and not have to worry about Ramon's well-being," John joked. "But I expect we'll be involved in more memorable adventures."

"No doubt about that. Adventuring with John Shanahan the Third is one of the great highlights of my life. I wouldn't want it any other way, my friend."

Chapter 15: At the Throttle Again

Most of the villagers at Blackwater had toured the passenger extra before it pulled into Track Two to clear the *Northern Express*. John Shanahan's traveling bag and boxes of engineman's gear were stacked on an express cart for quick transfer to the northbound train. As he stood alone on the platform to await the train's arrival he was certain that this was the first time that his presence in the scheme of things had a definite and positive purpose. It seemed right that this new chapter in his life would begin in this remote place—one that had been unknown to him only days earlier when he came to the North Country for the first time to help close down his family's business interests in the area.

John had met Station Agent Molly McCaslin on his first stop at Blackwater and she had been a factor in his decision not to demand of his father that he should return to Chicago immediately and find something else to do. He would always remember her advice: "You would like it here in the North Country, John Shanahan. I hope it works out so you can stay, at least for a while. ... If it does, I know that you'll never want to leave."

Molly stepped out of the station just as the headlight of the *Northern Express* appeared in the distance. She passed John a message that had been wired from the railroad headquarters at Summit: "J.P. Shanahan III report for engineer re-fresher training at Summit on arrival of Train One this date. Agent L.R. Smith has details. Expect to need you Sunday as engineer on work extra to retrieve stored reefer cars near South Spanish as specified by shop crew. W.L. Westfield, Acting Chief Dispatcher, SB&Q RR."

John pulled his South Montana time book from its traditional chest pocket of the lined railroad jacket that he had taken from one of the packages his mother shipped. Then he folded his message carefully, inserted it inside the front cover of the book and returned the book to the pocket. His freshly washed and ironed working gear still fit reasonably well and that surprised him, considering the weight loss he had suffered during hospitalization for his war wounds. He felt good again in baggy work clothes, and particularly fancied the oiled boots that afforded the kind of protection for his lower extremities that dress shoes failed to offer. His black winter railroad cap was fairly new and for that reason lacked the character of the one worn by Bill Travers. Each railroader's work cap had its style, it seemed, and his would, too, in time, he guessed.

"You look mighty fine in your work gear, John," Molly offered as she reached up to adjust the wooly bandanna scarf that he hadn't tucked completely inside his jacket collar. "Remember that it gets cold around here this time of year, so always bundle up," she added as the train pulled to a stop near where they stood. "Climb aboard now. God bless you in your new calling." She smiled, patted John on the arm and hurried down the platform to greet the incoming passengers.

Head Brakeman Carleton Reardon was placing John's luggage in the baggage compartment of the mail and baggage car *Rural Delivery* before John could get there to help. "All taken care of, John," he yelled from the doorway. "Looks like you and me and young Robbie Rankin will be working together tomorrow. Hank asked me if I'd take the conductor's job on the work extra with you."

"That's great, Carl," John responded. "I hope you understand that I'll be rusty for a while, so be real careful around the cars when we get to switching."

"We take our time and do things right, John. Slow and careful is the only way to go."

The cabin door on the fireman's side was open when John reached the locomotive. He was pondering how to deal with his cane when Fireman Jim McDermott reached down. "I'll take that, Boss," he said. "Just concentrate on the steps. It'll be a piece of cake before you know it."

John gripped the grab irons tightly and pulled himself up the ladder a rung at a time, placing his weight principally on his right leg. Pull hard, concentrate on the footing and drag the bum leg along, he thought as he inched up the ladder. He knew a vise-like grip on the grab irons would make the difference between success and failure because, in his mind, entering and exiting the cab was the only questionable aspect of his being a locomotive engineer again.

He stepped inside the cab and Jim returned his cane and took his seat on the fireman's side of the cab. John was about to sit on the narrow bench at the back of the cab when Engineer Bill Travers stood up and grabbed John's arm. "Here," he said. "Sit right here. Me and Jim are along for the ride for a ways. I want to see just what the engineers on the South Montana taught you about locomotive driving."

"Ah, gosh, Bill, I don't know ..." John stammered. "It's been a while and this is a passenger train. ... I ... ah ... I think maybe I'd better ..."

"Hey, pal, you're talking to the commander of this here locomotive. What would you say, Jim? That would be like a lieutenant in the Army, wouldn't you say?"

"More like the general, I'd say, or an admiral in the Navy, maybe. Engineer on the *Northern Express* is a mighty important position."

"Okay, guys, I'm outranked. I was just a lowly lieutenant once and not good at that, but that was long ago." John grinned as he scrunched around in Bill's seat to get comfortable. He looked down at the deadman control, noting that it was trigged so he wouldn't accidentally activate the emergency brakes in a sudden lapse of concentration. After that, he sat up straight, reached over to the control console and closed his eyes. Without looking, he grasped each lever cleanly with his left hand and called off the designation for each, after which he grasped the radio receiver and brought it to his ear.

Then he reached up with his right hand and touched and identified each of a series of switches located about the engineer's side window. Jim and Bill looked at each other in disbelief. "That son of a gun knows where all the controls are without looking!" Bill exclaimed. "God, I have to search every time I need to adjust something. That's unreal!"

The radio crackled. "Okay, John, we're all set back here. I make it one-fifteen out of Blackwater." It was Conductor Joe Francis and he had identified the engineer as "John." He looked at Bill, who checked his watch and nodded. "Yep, one-fifteen," the engineer responded. "I cleared it with Joe to let you do some running on the way up to Summit."

John released the brakes, nudged the throttle and spoke into the radio mike. "Okay, Joe. One-fifteen out. What's next up the line?"

"Passengers for High Meadow first and a mailbag will be in the crane. Then we tackle the riffles; you know, the rough track that goes on up to Camp Sixteen. You'll want to check the bulletins on that. Then a stop at Camp Twelve to drop supplies from the baggage car. There'll be a mailbag at Sixteen and one at South Spanish and we need to stop there to pick up the shop crew at the station. We'll talk more as we go along."

"Okay. We copy that. Thank you."

John marveled at the ease with which the locomotive handled the six-car train. He was up to maximum mainline passenger speed after tinkering briefly with the throttle to find the notch best suited for track conditions. Then he settled in for the ride, remembering from earlier experience that the best place from which to observe the terrain and track was right where he was sitting. When he felt confident at the controls and the track appeared clear ahead, he pulled out his time book, went to the first blank page and penciled a notation stating that he had been allowed by Engineer William S. Travers on November 1, 1951, to run the *Northern Express*, SB&Q's Train One, north of Blackwater on the New England Eastern Railroad. He added the departure time of one-fifteen p.m.

Then he flipped the page back to his last entry, which was on the last day of July in 1950. It ended with his arrival time in Helena as engineer of South Montana Train Four Forty-Two, a local passenger that ran a daily round trip between the state capital and a Canadian border connection with transcontinental service from Montreal to Vancouver.

His final notation caught his attention. It read: "It is with great sadness and no little trepidation that I leave this wonderful job at eight-ten this evening to enter the Army and fulfill an obligation to my country. I do not know where this will lead with all the trouble in Asia but I earnestly hope I will be able to come back here some day and continue my railroad career. JPS III."

He closed the book and looked back at Bill. The engineer appeared to be asleep and John remembered being in a similar situation when he was riding in new diesel locomotives as they replaced steam on Shanahan's mountain line. The hum in the electrical panel was guaranteed to induce sleep quickly in even the most alert engineman.

"It's the hum back there," Fireman Jim McDermott offered, pointing at Bill and leading John to assume that Bill had indeed dozed off. "The worse place to be in an engine when you have absolutely nothing to do. I used to hate to sit there when I was learning the road. I always fell asleep."

"I guess I did most of my riding time in steam engines. We had them longer out West, so I qualified on steam. I had to do a lot of studying about diesels but only had a few riding assignments in them. Retirements were coming fast and furious and I only made about a dozen trips as a fireman before I was set up as an engineer."

"I noticed your time book when you were making notations a while ago. Forgive me for being nosy, but I think you read something that stirred some strong memories."

John nodded. "Yeah. My last trip before Korea." He held the book at arm's length. "Here, Jim, take a look if you'd like, and overlook the fact that I'm a sloppy writer."

The fireman stepped across the cab and took the time book. "Thanks. I'm always interested in how other enginemen keep their notes. Especially the left-handed ones like me. I have an awful time when I'm running a job somewhere because I'm always banging my elbow against something in the cab when I try to make notes."

John savored his time at the controls of the *Northern Express*. Never in his wildest dreams when he used to stop by his father's office and view the artist's rendition of the special train in faraway New England did he expect to ride the train let alone sit in the engineer's seat and actually direct its movement. The locomotive was purring along at close to forty-five miles an hour as the railroad track broke from the forest into a large clearing with a spectacular vista of a wilderness river and wooded hills in the distance.

Jim closed John's time book, stepped across the cab and returned it and noted that the train was traversing the high meadow for which the next station stop was named. "You'll want to cut it back a little here, John," he said. "Our stop is about a mile ahead at what used to be the station. It's been closed a long time but we make a stop about every time we go by."

John eased the throttle back and responded: "I think I remember it from my first trip up this way in the night. Kind of a shabby, boarded-up place on the east side of the track?"

"Yep. There's still a year-round settlement back at the edge of the forest. Apparently, a number of old-time railroaders and woodsmen still live here, especially in summer. There isn't a road for miles. Just a few trails and tote roads left from the heavy logging days. Local folks plant gardens around the meadow and what's left is still hayed each year for the lumber companies that have horses in back of Camp Twelve and Camp Sixteen. ... If you look off to the west you'll see the highest mountain in this state. It's a ways off, but it shows up well this time of year because of the snow cover on the peak."

John looked across the cab. "I see it. It's beautiful but it makes me shiver. Probably cold up there on a day like this."

"No place I want to go this time of year." Quickly changing the subject, Jim added: "That last entry in your time book, John, that's a beautiful piece of writing. You really like this line of work, don't you?"

"Sure do. Ever since I was a kid. I know my dad wants me to learn the business end of railroading, and I suppose I should someday but what you see right now sitting here, well, this is the real me. … Ah, there's High Meadow up ahead." John sounded the air horns and Joe responded on the radio. "Okay, John, try to spot us just by the station. You'll see a pathway that leads back to the settlement. We call it High Meadow Main Street. John Kelly will wave you along to our usual stopping place at the end of the path."

"Okay. I'll be watching." John opened his window, looked forward to observe the position of the mail crane and then peered back alongside the train. Brakeman Kelly stepped into view from the stairwell of the coach Bolton and waved a slow-down signal. John slipped the throttle back gently and tapped the brakes. It was a smooth stopping procedure designed for the comfort of passengers who might be moving around in the coaches. He heard the loud clatter of the mail crane when the catcher device on the side of *Rural Delivery* snatched the mailbag.

Several elderly passengers were assisted off the coach by the brakeman who helped to carry their bags to the beginning of the path beyond what appeared to be a siding. It was only then that John remembered it was really the former northbound running track and apparently would be the main line again in the Shanahan scheme of things.

After John Kelly's highball John sounded the air horns again and eased the train forward. He glanced quickly at the track bulletin clipboard and saw that the beginning of the restricted speed zone was just ahead. Joe reminded him of that by radio: "Nice smooth stop back there, John. That was good. … I make it in at one forty-four and out at one forty-seven. Keep a sharp eye ahead. We'll be coming up on the riffles real soon."

"Thanks, Joe. I'm watching." John accelerated slightly but kept the speed near twenty miles an hour. After rounding a curve, the first of the longest string of stored refrigerator cars came into view. It was then that Bill appeared to wake up. He yawned loudly and stood up. "Ah ha, I see we're still on the track, Jim," he said, addressing the fireman. "Must have dozed off back there for a bit. So, where are we now?"

"C'mon, Mr. Engineer. You were dead to the world," Jim chided. "You missed all the excitement along Main Street on the high meadow."

"Really? Did that skunk walk down the path again and scare the passengers off into the bushes? You remember that time, don't you, Jim?"

"I guess! John Kelly was out there with a broom trying to shoo the critter out of the way. Finally Joe let out an Indian holler and the poor little rascal went slinking off into the pucker brush."

John smiled. He knew it wasn't just the engineer's work that attracted him to this profession. It was the camaraderie and the funny events like the skunk on

Main Street in that delightful little village he had just passed in the North Country of New England.

Bill came to his side and placed his hand on John's shoulder. "You're a crackerjack engineer, my friend, no doubt about that. Jim thinks I was sleeping back there, but I was watching you like a hawk. You do your job well. Now I think we'll give Jim a crack at running this beast and I'd like you to sit over in the fireman's seat. I'm going to stand up by the windshield and point out some peculiarities in the track up ahead. We're going into the riffles and since you're going to be doing some hauling along here for a while, there's a few quirks I need to fill you in on. You might want to take some notes."

"Yeah, that would be a big help," John said. He relinquished his seat to Jim and limped across the cab to the fireman's side as the regular fireman took over the controls. Bill stationed himself near the center of the cab next to the windshield and gave John a mile-by-mile analysis of gradients and curves, operable and inoperable crossover tracks, and pointed out places where the northbound track had been broken when rails were needed on the existing running track.

Bill was in the engineer's seat again when the passenger train crested the grade at Hillman and began its descent into Summit yard. "You'll notice that the semaphore is clear up ahead, John. Actually there are trains around the passenger platforms waiting for us but since we're the only train running at the moment between Gatlin and Summit we can proceed, under caution, of course, on our running schedule and go right up to the station on Track One. If you're out here on a freight job, always be prepared to stop at the semaphore and call in for a clearance before entering the yard. Got that?"

"Got it, Bill."

The *Northern Express* arrived at Summit at two forty-five p.m. John eased himself down the side ladder and took his cane from the outstretched hand of Bill Travers. "Good luck on your new assignment this afternoon and tomorrow," he said. "Behave yourself," he added with a sly grin. "I'll be keeping tabs on you."

John pondered Bill's closing remark as he made his way around clusters of passengers on the platforms. As he was about to enter the station a stranger approached him. He was blond-headed, tall and tanned and struck John as a man who had spent considerable time on a beach in California. The parka that he wore was not enough to disguise his true identity.

"You must be John Shanahan," the man said pleasantly and extended his hand. "I'm Bill Westfield and I'm heading up the team to set up a dispatching office and crew calling center for the railroad. In real life I dispatch trains on a Shanahan line out West."

"I'd have guessed that, although I was thinking you looked more like a surfer or a lifeguard on one of those California beaches where all the good-looking gals hang out," John said as he shook Westfield's hand. "It's nice to meet you. I thought nobody would know me in these trainman's duds. ... Ah, of course, the cane—my trademark."

106

"Not really. You just look like your old man. Hey, let's get inside where it's warm." He opened the door and held it for John. "You're right, I do a lot of surfing and girl-watching when I'm not tied up in the mundane work of moving trains around."

John headed for the stairway that led to the second floor of the station. "Hold it," Bill said. "I discovered something unique for an old station around this corner behind the stairwell. Follow me." Puzzled, John limped along behind the dispatcher. There, in an alcove was an entrance to an elevator, which led to the upper stories of the building.

"Doggone, I learn something new every day around here," John muttered.

"I tell you, John, this station, the freight yard, the shops over there with the old coaling tower and the water tank, man, this is a living museum," Westfield quipped. "You know, if this railroad doesn't make it this time, there ought to be a bundle to be made, say forty years from now when the tourists come looking for links to their past. They'll probably be flying in here in jet planes just to take a look-see."

John grinned. "Sounds kind of far-fetched, Bill, but you could be right. What do they call those people these days? There was some term I read in the newspaper just the other day. You know, those idle rich folks who fly to exotic places for vacation."

"The jet set. That's my goal in life. But I'm not rich and this place isn't exotic enough."

Chapter 16: A Touch of Impertinence

The office in Summit station that was to become the train-dispatching center for the new Summit, Bolton and Quarry Railroad was jammed with temporary desks and telephones for Bill Westfield's transition team. Several filing cabinets had been pushed into a corner in a helter-skelter fashion and stacks of files were scattered about the room. It appeared that carpenters had been building consoles adjacent to the front windows for the installation of telegraph instruments but that project seemed far from completion.

"I'd like to say that we're making progress, but that would be stretching the truth beyond reason," Bill remarked after finding a clear space on a long table that was designed for some future use. He rolled an office chair in that direction and invited John Shanahan to sit down while he searched for another chair for himself. "So far, it has been utter chaos. Hank told us to call it a day early this afternoon and start over tomorrow."

"I can't imagine what goes into setting up a headquarters for a railroad that started as a twenty-two-mile branch line and suddenly became four hundred and twenty-five miles long," John offered. "When I left Chicago with Ramon the plan was for us to help Hank close down the SB&Q. We expected to be here about a month, no more."

"I know. The news gets around the Shanahan network at the speed of light. We figured this line was a goner when the Eastern made their case for abandonment. From what I hear now, the potatoes are apt to start moving soon and we're not even remotely ready."

Westfield said his team would start planning a freight-car dispatching operation the next day. "That's one of the reasons we need you tomorrow to start moving those stored reefers into the shop," he said. "The best we can count on for serviceable cars right now are the one hundred that SB&Q owned before the takeover. This has the makings of an operational nightmare. ..."

Bill grimaced and continued. "I understand Shanahan Lines has another three hundred cars under lease that are on the way and should be at Hill Junction by now. We have to move them up the line quick. Eastern wants to get out of here before the fifteenth."

"Hope they don't know something that we don't know," John said. "I never heard of a railroad so gung ho to get out of town as that one."

"Me neither. I hope the answer isn't in those reefers in storage. If we find very many defective cars, it will be impossible to pull this thing off this late in the season."

While Bill and John were still pondering potential pitfalls facing the transition planners Larry Smith bounded up the stairway and entered the office. He dropped a sheaf of papers on the table and introduced himself to John.

"I think we can make this bookwork short and sweet," he said. "We checked your work record through the South Montana headquarters in Helena and you're squeaky clean. Top marks from all your colleagues, unblemished record as an engineman and several commendations for running passenger trains. That one for the rescue at Snowshed Seven—my God, man—that was incredible! Bill Travers and Jim McDowell figure you're a first-class engineer who is ready to run on this line. What do you think?"

"I've got a lot to learn about running conditions but I'm up to that challenge."

"Good. We're going to forgo you writing up the rules because we use the same general rulebook as most of the Shanahan Lines, including the South Montana, and you've already written those up. There are copies of the SB&Q and Eastern rulebooks and the timetables here. You'll need to fill out some forms but first we need to get you out in the yard to do a little practice switching so you'll have a handle on the layout of this terminal. We've got a couple of people coming in to assist. Sit tight and I'll round them up." Smith dashed out of the dispatching office and down the stairs two at a time.

"That guy is a whirlwind," Bill Westfield observed. "You know, this station has an old public address system that hasn't worked since after the big war. He's been trying to rebuild it and figures he'll have it done by Christmas if he can find enough parts."

"Ah, Christmas," John said wistfully. "After my last one ... well, anyway, I kind of fancied a beach scene this year, probably sort of like where you came from."

Bill walked to the windows that overlooked the yard. "Yeah. Me too. Only it looks like we'll still be flat-out trying to make this line a go again. I'll bet come Christmas Eve, I'll be stuck in here and you out there, God knows where, pounding through the snow, maybe trying to get some stranded passengers home for the holiday."

Larry Smith came rushing back up the stairs. "Got your colleagues in tow," he said, as he stepped into the office. "Step lively, you guys," he yelled over his shoulder. "This is John Shanahan, the son of the owner, and he seems like an ordinary kind of fellow."

John pushed himself to his feet to greet the pair and nearly tripped over his cane when the first person appeared. The guy was a she, a tiny woman attired in railroad gear but as beautiful as she had been when she was dressed up fancy at the Cedars the night before.

"Hello, John, It's wonderful to see you again," Jenny Boston said as she removed a leather glove from her right hand and clasped his. Her dark eyes searched his face and she smiled when she detected his bewilderment. Then she blushed slightly, turned quickly and motioned her companion forward. "John, this is Rob Rankin, a new brakeman for the SB&Q and a classmate of mine. Rob, this is John Shanahan."

"I'm very pleased to meet you ... both of you ... and thank you for trying to help a badly out-of-practice engineer get ... well ... back on his feet ... so to speak." John stammered as he shook the hand of the young brakeman.

"I'm pleased to meet you, sir," Rob said and stepped back quickly.

Larry noticed that daylight was fleeting and called the shop to instruct the watchman there to turn on the yard lights, a duty that would fall to a yardmaster once that office was re-established. "There, gang, I'd say it's time for you three to get your engine out of the roundhouse, tour the yard and then attend to some shop switching that needs to be done. Bill and I guessed we'd have you work a regular shift, so that would take you through to about ten, maybe. Based on when you book off tonight we'll plan for tomorrow. We're hoping for at least two round trips between here and South Spanish. Any questions?"

There were none. "Okay, Jenny has a schedule worked out for the exercise. Plan your moves; work slowly and with a great deal of care. I'll be the acting yardmaster in this office, and I'd like you to call in from the telephone contact points around the yard. I seriously doubt that many of them work, so let me know where you are when you can. We have no other trains running tonight, as far as we know now. That might change, so call in often and get permission first if you plan to go out on the main line. Some day we hope to have a radio base station, but that won't happen for a while."

The three trainmen rode the elevator down to the concourse and exited the station through the passenger doors leading to Track One. Then they crossed the tracks because it was the shortest route to the round house, which was just west of the shop complex. Jenny stopped often to point out different parts of the freight yard as they went along.

John had studied the yard charts and as Jenny described the surroundings everything seemed familiar to him. Almost all the yard tracks were on the east side of the main line, or Track One, as it was known in the vicinity of the station. There were only two tracks on the west side north of Summit station: Number Two, a siding that served businesses on Railroad Avenue, and Spur A that ran back to the commissary in the east wing of the station. It was a track where dining cars were placed for re-stocking.

Tracks one, three and five were for passenger trains and Track Seven was a run-around track that separated passenger trains from freight. Beyond that were at least twenty freight sidings that were reached from ladder tracks off the main line. The south ladder was the main route to the roundhouse and shop. It ran on by the shop buildings where parallel tracks were used for passenger train servicing, and then swung northeast along a residential street called Shop Road to a junction with the Quarry Line at Summit Heights.

The shop yard was a sprawling affair to the southeast of the south ladder track. Several tracks entered buildings and others looped around the shop to form the so-called "Back Shop Yard." Running alongside the ladder was storage space for maintenance equipment such as snowplows, spreaders and a wreck outfit complete with a wrecking crane.

Beyond their range of view was the north ladder track that swung back to join Track Three near Country Road Crossing. North of the highway crossing was Quarry Junction, which was the beginning of the Quarry Line. Tracks one and three finally merged and became the main line again about two miles north of the station. On the Quarry Line, there were passenger train stops with platforms and canopies at Summit High School and Summit Grammar School. Both were between the junction switch and Summit Heights.

The beginning of the Quarry Line was actually the south leg of a wye used by both railroads. West of the second County Road crossing at Summit Heights, the north leg diverged across an open plain and joined the mainline north of Quarry Junction. Several miles beyond, the mainline passed Esker gravel pit and the former Air Force base.

South of Summit station the branch leading to Eagle River diverged to the west. A short three-track yard converged at the junction switch. Spurs and sidings served several Summit industries from the branch line within the city limits. The business places included a metal fabrication plant, a starch factory and a large sawmill. In West Summit, six miles out on the line, two sidings provided rail access to long rows of potato houses.

When the three arrived at the round house, Jenny unlatched the big doors to the first stall and pushed them open. Rob helped her secure the doors in the open position. After ascertaining that the turntable was set and secured to permit passage of a locomotive onto the engine terminal entry track, she led her co-workers to the diesel that would be used.

John had seen the artist's rendition of Summit, Bolton and Quarry's yard switcher but could not understand why a lowly switch engine should be depicted so superbly. It was a basic yard goat of the time, a rectangular box-like affair with what seemed to be an oversized cab at the rear. The locomotive was painted white with the classic Shanahan cerulean trim and was lettered in red. The railroad name "Summit, Bolton and Quarry" extended the length of the engine housing and the letters "SB&Q" fit nicely under the engineer's and fireman's windows with the locomotive number "1" centered beneath that. A catwalk extended from the cab's front-facing door on the fireman's side alongside the engine housing to a platform across the front with stairwells on each side. A similar walkway came back along the engineer's side but there was no access to the cab. Stairwells and a platform provided a way to the back door of the cab from the ground. The view was best from the back of the cab, which was entirely glassed in.

"Wow!" John exclaimed in awe. "That is some classy. Looks like some hostler around here keeps the equipment looking good. I wonder who that would be. If I'm not mistaken, I'd say that somebody applied a extra heavy coat of automobile wax to that beauty."

Jenny blushed. "Oh, once in a while I have a little time on my hands so I … well … I work on it quite a lot … really. You really do like it?"

"Yes, I really do. I've seen pictures of it but I never imagined it looked this sharp. This was my Dad's first SB&Q locomotive, I think."

"It was. My father told me it was coming here brand new so we made a special trip to the shop when it came in. It's always been my favorite locomotive. We mostly use it around the shop. Well, let's hop aboard and talk about what we have to do."

Inside the cab she produced conductor's tally sheets listing cars on all tracks outside the shop proper. Except for stored equipment, the terminal was largely devoid of freight cars, attesting, he knew, to the dearth of commodities traffic on the Eastern of late.

Jenny and Rob took seats on the fireman's side as John settled into the engineer's seat. She leaned forward and whispered, "Watch him, Rob. Billy told me he does something unique before he moves the engine."

Oblivious to the others in the cab, John tested his reach from the seat to the controls and went through his eyes-closed check of the location of each. His companions sat in awe as he completed his routine. His earliest training on diesel locomotive operations had been in similar units in the terminal at Helena, Montana, so he was no stranger to this one. Then he nosed the engine out onto the turntable where he stopped while Jenny and Rob closed the engine house doors. Next, they moved onto the south ladder track and proceeded to the vicinity of the mainline, where Jenny stepped into the switchman's shanty and reported their whereabouts to Larry Smith at the dispatching office.

Then John moved the locomotive onto Track Seven, passing the station and running the length of the yard to the north ladder. The next move was down the ladder to Track Fifteen where Jenny directed him to stop. Producing her copy of the conductor's tally, she went over scheduled work—the classifying or "blocking" of a dozen loaded cars from the Quarry Line that would go south on the next Eastern freight train.

"Shuffling the deck," John observed.

Jenny chuckled. "That's right and the jokers are on the top. Those are the freight cars destined for Gatlin mill and they go in the first block, followed by cars for Hill Junction and Sunbury. The third cut is for Eastern's mainline points to the west and the last is for other destinations beyond that railroad's most distant interchange." John supposed that one car loaded with pallets produced by Bolton Box and Barrel would be switched another six or eight times before reaching its destination in the Southwest.

John found the switching maneuver easy. Rob appeared to be an alert brakeman who knew where to place himself safely and provide distinct signals to the engineer. Jenny joined the brakeman and attended to the setting and reversing of the switch.

After the crew completed the switching, the locomotive was moved back up the ladder track to the connection with Track Three. Rob called in from the switchman's shanty and received permission for SB&Q Engine One to run down the Quarry mainline to Summit Heights and the connection with the shop track. There, he called in again to report their movement along Shop Road to the vicinity of the shop complex.

Jenny directed John to stop near the highway entrance to the shop grounds. "We're going to enter Spur BS just ahead," she said. The purpose was to go around the administrative offices and the paint shop and then enter the Back Shop yard. "There are several pedestrian crossings, so train speed around the buildings is restricted to five miles an hour. There isn't enough space to sound out a full crossing approach signal on the horns, so we just make a couple of short, impertinent blasts when we come up on each."

Jenny expected a response. She looked across the cab and saw that John had his left hand up alongside the cord that activated the air horns. He appeared to be imitating a maneuver to strike a certain chord with the horns. "What are you doing?" she queried.

"I don't know," he answered. "What is an impertinent blast? All I know about diesel air horns are that there are long blasts and short blasts. Now on a steam engine whistle, a clever, musically-inclined engineer can actually play a tune … Anyway, I don't understand 'impertinent' in this context."

"I think you're being difficult, John. You know exactly what I mean."

"Au contraire, fair lady. I understand impertinent to be not pertinent or, in another word, irrelevant. I was brought up to believe that all soundings of whistles or air horns were indeed pertinent, or relevant."

"If I jumped up and screamed and stamped my feet, would you say I was impertinent?"

"Why don't you do that and I'll decide whether you're being impertinent or downright eccentric." John continued to study the activating cord leading to the air horns.

A smile played around Rob's lips but he offered no comment and looked away quickly. Jenny persisted, however. "C'mon, John. You know what I mean. Impertinent! Snappy! Sharp! Meant to bring attention to … well, to a train that is about to pass."

"I suggest that impertinent could also mean officious or intrusive."

"Okay, I agree!" Jenny exclaimed. "So, if we are a bit officious or intrusive and we succeed in keeping people off the track, aren't we doing the right thing?"

"I see your point," John said. "I got it! Listen to this." He sounded two snappy blats on the horns and several shop employees in the parking lot looked up and waved. "Oh, look out your window and wave to your fan club, Jenny," he added and burst out laughing.

Jenny smiled and waved and then turned back to John. "I still think impertinent is the right word in this case." Then she giggled and winked at the engineer.

"Actually, now that I think about it, I like snappy or sharp better, but you're a good sport, Jen, and a great instructor, so forever after I shall sound the air horns impertinently when I go trucking down Spur BS at Summit."

The trio conducted several more switching moves in the shop, the last of which was to pull two repaired former Eastern refrigerator cars from the paint shop. The cars bore a fresh coat of yellow paint with black trim and new lettering: SB&Q 1105 and SB&Q 1106. The cars were to be set on Track Seventeen where the service contractor would hold them until movement to Esker pit for the installation of heating units.

After eating a lunch that Jenny had prepared for the occasion, the train crew completed its work detail by making up the train that John would move to South Spanish the next day. There were several supply and personnel cars, along with a wheel derrick and several flat cars containing spare freight car wheel sets. A caboose was added to the rear before the engine was moved back to the service center to have the fuel tanks topped off. Jenny handled the refueling and made a brief inspection of the engine before they returned to the station's ticket office at ten o'clock.

Larry Smith passed John several employment forms that needed to be filled out. "Why don't you take these to your room and fill them out after you get settled. I've got to beat it out of here for a while, so just leave the papers with whoever is on duty in the morning."

Smith handed John a key to Room One in the trainmen's quarters that were at the end of the west wing of the station. "One of our express handlers put your gear that came in on the *Northern Express* in your room," he said. "It's not the Ritz but the place is clean and comfortable. We're planning on a seven o'clock reporting time for tomorrow. The night telephone operator will tap on your door at six if you're not up by then. The restaurant will be open so you can get breakfast and a bag lunch before you head out."

To John's amazement, Larry was writing out messages from the telegraph wire as he talked. After he was finished, John posed the obvious question: "So, Larry, how do you carry on a conversation, read the wire and write down the words all at the same time?"

Smith shrugged his shoulders. "I don't know. Never had time to really think about it. Funny thing about this place is that as dead as it looks, it isn't dead at all." The telephone rang. "See what I mean? Good luck, John. You're a real asset to this railroad."

John walked with Jenny across the concourse to the street side exit. They lingered in an alcove near the door and talked about the day's events. "You're a fine engineer, John," she said. "And a real asset to the railroad," she added, repeating Larry's remark.

"Thanks, Jenny. You were kind to tolerate my nonsense, or should I say, my impertinent behavior. It's just that ... well, I enjoy your company ... a lot ... and sort of forgot that we were on duty out there."

"I enjoy your company, too, John," she said and grasped his hand tightly. "Perhaps ... well ... I'd really like to see you again ... if you'd like. You know, when we're both off duty. Perhaps a dinner or a movie or something like that."

"Let's do that ... a dinner or a movie ... or something together ... soon."

Chapter 17: A Piece of Cake

John Shanahan walked down a long corridor and found his room on the second floor in the west wing of the cavernous station at Summit. It was Spartan in appearance and the furnishings simple and utilitarian: Cot, dresser, mirror, chair and portable wardrobe closet. A barracks-type common washroom served the needs of the occupants of the several rooms at the far end of the wing. This wing was empty on this night and apparently had been unoccupied for some time.

The room's one undraped window offered only a blackout shade for privacy. John pulled the shade to cut the glare of a streetlight near the window. A Summit, Bolton and Quarry publicity calendar hung askew on an otherwise bare wall. He went over to straighten it and take a closer look.

The winter photo of the *Northern Express* exiting a rock cut near Promised Land was spectacular, as were most photographs produced for Shanahan Enterprises. The calendar was dusty and as he blew on it, he realized that the page was for December 1950, a month that changed his life forever. He placed the calendar on the cot and sat on the chair, resting his head in his hands. "Dear God, thank you for letting me live through that time, and thank you for leading me to this place," he prayed aloud. "Help me make the best of this opportunity to make worthwhile contributions where I can. Amen."

John placed the calendar atop a box of his belongings so he would remember to take it along when he moved on. He knew that the lodgings in the station would be eliminated soon as the space was needed for offices for the expanded railroad operation.

He took off his work clothes, folded each piece carefully and stacked the gear on the dresser, placing his cap and leather gloves atop the pile. He smiled when he remembered that was his end-of-the-workday ritual in Montana. Those were good times, he recalled, as he donned the new flannel pajamas with depictions of trains that his mother had forwarded with his workingman's gear. He remembered that he needed to wind his pocket watch before retiring because that was part of the routine of a good railroad man.

His business suit that had been stuffed into his traveling bag earlier was hung in the wardrobe closet because he expected to be staying in the room for a few days. He would be working in this building when he wasn't filling in as an engineman so he knew he would likely have to find a place to live in Summit after the crew quarters were closed.

John decided he would take each day in its time. His thoughts wandered to Jenny and he wondered how she would figure in his future. But it was too soon to dwell on that prospect so he turned his attention to the employment forms

116

that needed to be filled out. He made an earnest effort to print legibly and place the information in the correct spaces although that was not a skill he had ever developed. After several erasures he completed the task and was surprised that he could read his writing when he reviewed his work.

Satisfied that he had done his best, John shuffled through the railroad gradient charts and siding diagrams to review the Summit to Blackwater segment. This time he compared the documents to Eastern's timetable. He assumed that the timetable would be updated and reprinted by the SB&Q when that railroad assumed operations.

He confirmed the location of all stations and sidings between Summit at Milepost 180 and Blackwater at Milepost 135. In the first segment, the locations were listed as Mile 178, Hillman (Milepost 175), Mile 169 and Spanish Junction (Milepost 164).

What had been designated as double track from Spanish Junction to Blackwater, a distance of twenty-nine miles, was now a one-track mainline with the former northbound track and its several crossovers generally referred to as "unused storage track."

Spanish Bridge (Milepost 162) on the southbound track had no sidings. The next place with a siding and a closed station was South Spanish (Milepost 159.) Then it was four miles to Camp 16, a location with sidings and a closed station (Milepost 155). A place that no longer existed and had no sidings was called Hayshed and was at Milepost 154. Camp 12 (Milepost 153) had a station building that was closed and one siding on the west side of the existing mainline. Two miles south of Camp 12 was High Meadow, with a closed station and two sidings and was the south end of the rough track dubbed "the Riffles." There was one more siding at Mile 143, eight miles north of Blackwater.

The sidings at miles 178, 169 and 143 were short four-car tracks reserved as emergency setoffs for defective cars that could not be moved immediately to another location. The rest were available for public loading and/or switching moves that needed to be made. Sidetracks at Hillman, Spanish Junction and High Meadow were specifically for the meeting of trains running in opposing directions.

Finally satisfied that he knew the route and engine-operating restrictions by rote, John put his papers away, turned out the light and crawled into bed. It had been a fulfilling day, albeit tiring, and by the time the station clock had completed tolling the midnight hour he was fast asleep.

John arose before the crew caller's tap at his door, polished off a breakfast of bacon and eggs and was picking up a takeout order at the cashier's desk in the station restaurant when Carleton Reardon appeared in the entry. After a brief exchange of pleasantries he motioned for John to follow him upstairs to the dispatcher's office. "Little change of plans, I'm afraid," the conductor offered as they rode up on the elevator. "Bill Westfield is in and he can explain it."

The pair joined Brakeman Rob Rankin and Roger Nickerson who Bill introduced to John as the assistant shop superintendent and crew director for the refrigerator-retrieval project. It was obvious that neither Roger nor Bill were happy about what had transpired.

"The Eastern called me at four this morning to let us know that they decided to report a work train at Aroostook at eight o'clock to take spare equipment to Sunbury," Bill lamented. "So we don't get exclusive use of the mainline until later than we planned."

John nodded. "That eliminates at least one round trip for us, I suppose."

"Yeah. And it screws up our schedule at the shop," Roger interjected. "I have a crew called for nine o'clock to set up equipment to go over the cars as you bring them in. I also have the crew that is supposed to go with you and they are standing by in the shop. They're decent, understanding fellows and agreed to do some housekeeping while they wait. ... As for the Eastern, they have no regard for the rest of us in this game."

Bill looked at Carl Reardon who was perusing his New England Eastern timetable. "Got any ideas, Carl?" he asked.

"Yes. Matter of fact, I do. I have it from good sources that the heater service has some Eastern reefers at Esker Pit set up with alcohol heaters and they'd like to move them to the shop for final inspection and anything else you need to do to get them rolling. I was thinking if Bill here could work something out with Eastern, we could dash up there and get that part of the process ..."

Westfield jumped to his feet. "By Jove, that's it! Roger, how about that for a starter?"

"Son of a gun! Works for me. Yes. That would really help."

The dispatcher grabbed the nearest telephone and asked the switchboard operator to place a call to the Eastern's dispatching office at Sunbury. The call went through quickly and Bill laid out the alternate plan. The conversation went on for several minutes and shifted from heated rhetoric to caustic sniping and finally to a somewhat jovial exchange.

"Okay, pal," he told the Eastern representative. "You guys hold up your end of this deal and we'll hold up ours. ... It's really great working with you, and, oh, by the way, if any of your crew needs a good dispatching job when the Eastern goes bankrupt, give us a call. ... Uh huh. ... Sure. Yes, and you too, have an extraordinarily fine day. I'll be sitting here by my telegraph key watching the clock and waiting for that train order. ... You betcha. ... So long for now."

Bill flipped the telephone into the air, caught it deftly behind his back and dropped it into the cradle. "Kiss my grits, you Eastern lackey," he muttered as he turned to his colleagues.

"So it appears you have charmed the Eastern's dispatcher into a compromise," Carl said, his face wreathed in a broad grin. "Give us a hint as to what's up."

"Yep, I charmed 'em. Remind me never to apply for dispatching work on the Eastern. Anyway, here's the plan. You fellows take the engine and caboose off the work train and pick up those two reefers on Track Seventeen that John switched out last night. I'll call the heater guys to let 'em know you're coming.

118

By then, I should have an order to get you to Esker. Go in, drop the reefers on the inbound track where the heater service is set up and pull whatever cars they're prepared to release. Okay so far?"

The three trainmen and the shop supervisor nodded in unison.

"Dandy. The Eastern plans to have that equipment train rolling at nine with no stops. They're restricted to twenty miles per hour, so that's a running time of two hours and fifteen minutes, more no doubt, from there to here, making it an expected arrival time at Summit of eleven-fifteen. If they keep on going without any dallying around here ..."

The sounder at the one telegraph console Westfield and a lineman had connected sometime in the night began to rattle off a series of dots and dashes. "That's for me!" he yelped and bounded across the room to the key. "Carl, get your engine and caboose and those two reefers and pull up here on Track Seven. I'll have some paper for you by then."

The crew climbed into the locomotive outside the shop at seven-fifteen. "I think we can gain some time at Esker if we go to the rear of this train with our locomotive, nab the caboose and run up the north ladder to Track Fifteen. We push the caboose in on the reefers, couple it on and leave it there. Then we bring the locomotive back down the north ladder and around to the other end of Track Fifteen. We go in with the engine, pick up the cars and the caboose and pull through the south ladder to Track Seven. Okay?"

Rob nodded. "Okay with me," John responded. "Steer me in the right direction."

"If I have it figured right, we'll arrive at the station caboose first, followed by the two spud cars and then the engine," Carl went on. "You okay with pushing the train to Esker, John? That pit yard is a tangle and if we do it this way, we save switching time there."

"Sounds like a good move," John said. "And you'll be in the caboose to sound the backup air signal for the crossing at County Road?"

"That's right."

"Definitely a good move. Let's do it."

Westfield was standing alongside Track Seven at seven-thirty when the work train reached the station area. Carl stepped off the caboose where the dispatcher was standing and signaled for John to move ahead to that location. Bill and Carl climbed into the engine and went over the order with John and Rob. Issued at Sunbury, it permitted SB&Q Engine One to work extra from seven-thirty to ten-ten a.m. between Summit and Esker, not protecting against other extra trains. Extra Seven-Five-Naught-Six, the Eastern's equipment train, would receive a copy of the order at Aroostook.

After reading the order aloud in the presence of the dispatcher and the train's brakeman, John and Carl signed it. Bill and Carl returned to the dispatching office, where the dispatcher, in the role of telegrapher, advised the Sunbury dispatcher that Engineer Shanahan and Conductor Reardon had read and signed the order. Bill received a clearance to deliver the order to the trainmen and the bookwork was completed at seven thirty-five. Bill advised Carl that he had called the heater service office at Esker to explain the move and was told that workers there would be ready for the train by eight o'clock. He also issued the conductor a portable radio that would provide communication between the engine and caboose, along with Eastern switch keys for each member of the train crew. The work extra left Summit at seven-forty.

The backup move went without incident and the train backed into the pit complex at about eight o'clock. The caboose was dropped on the main spur and the two cars needing heaters were spotted on a short service track near the office. Then the crew took the engine to the area where the cars with newly-installed but unlit heaters were stored. There were thirty-two cars in the string.

Carl sat in the engine with John and Rob and calculated the tonnage: Thirty-two cars weighing thirty-one tons apiece produced a total load of 1,052 tons. The caboose added another 30 tons, making the total 1,082. Although the site was referred to as a pit, it was a place where gravel was mined from an esker and the ground was level, allowing a maximum trainload for the diesel switcher of 1,080 tons.

"Want to quibble over two tons, John?" Carl asked, pretending to be serious.

"Well, I don't know," the engineer responded in his most serious tone. "Two tons, you say? I suppose we could throw off our lunches and some of our gear and the bunks and cook stove in the caboose and maybe struggle out of here. You and Rob could walk along beside the train and that would lighten the load by another three hundred pounds or so. If you were inclined to push, that would help. You interested in any of those options?"

Carl burst out laughing. "Ah, you're a joy to work with, John Shanahan. Now I'm thinking there's a bit of a tailwind out there in the open on the mainline. I'd imagine a tailwind would help compensate for a slight overload. How about you?"

John opened his window and peered out. Then he licked a finger and held it up. "Appears to me that your meteorological observations are correct. I calculate the wind at about six knots, nautically speaking. Coupled with a high-pressure system to the west and a low somewhere to the east, the wind will continue to blow in this fashion for at least thirty minutes. So barring any unfortunate events during that time we could reach Summit before the wind shifts and we could do it in record time with a record load."

"That we could," the conductor observed. "On the other hand, that cloudbank to the south had the definite appearance of an impending thunderstorm. That could produce heavy winds, hail and lightning. Once in a blue moon a funnel cloud appears in conjunction with such a cloudbank, and, golly, we might be talking tornado here."

"Uh huh. And that could be trouble. Of course, if the tornado were to take a southerly course, it might pick us up and carry us right into Summit. ... On the other hand, it might take us to Aroostook and deposit us in front of Eastern's fast freight to the junkyard."

Rob appeared to be trying to follow the conversation but seemed bewildered as Carl continued: "That would be tough for Bill Westfield to explain to the Sunbury dispatcher. Maybe we better just stick to the traditional way of doing things around here by bumbling along and hoping everything comes out right."

"Good idea." John said. "Let's take 'em all in one trip. Piece of cake, Carl."

The return to Summit went well and the exercise gave John an opportunity to experience the handling of a string of empty potato cars. Handling loaded cars interspersed with empties—a more traditional train—provided different dynamics, he knew, but he was confident that he remembered the necessary operating techniques from his earlier days in locomotives in Montana.

Rob stayed with the train while Carl and John took care of the bookwork with the dispatcher. With their mission on the mainline accomplished, the work order was canceled without the extra train at Aroostook having to receive a copy. The bad news was that the Eastern train had been delayed at least an hour because of a power failure on one of the two assigned locomotives.

Westfield stood by the dispatching office windows, his hands jammed into his pockets. "So, Carl, I guess you guys need to trundle your train over to the shop and set up the cars for Roger's crew," he said. "After that, well, that beats the hell out of me. Maybe you can line the cars up in numerical order. Or maybe you can push them off the end of a spur track somewhere over there and we'll set fire to the whole damned lot."

A half hour later the refrigerator cars were in place on tracks outside the shop. Carl was climbing into the engine when he spotted Bill Westfield loping across the freight yard. "Looks like something's happening, John," Carl observed.

"Finally some good news, gang," Bill commented when he climbed into the cab. "Both of Eastern's engines failed, so they've canceled the extra for today. I'm getting an inkling that they're about ready to fold this operation. Anyway, here's your work order for today. Go down to South Spanish and start pulling the reefers. You have exclusive use of the track until four o'clock. We'll play it by ear after that. ... "

Westfield paused, remembering another matter. "Oh, yeah, I almost forgot, Carl. There's supposed to be a locked window in the station at South Spanish that opens from the outside. Inside, there's one of those composite telephones with instructions on how to reach the operator at Spanish Junction. Eastern's going to have him on duty for a while. Call there with your arrival time at South Spanish. Looks like we're going to put a telegraph operator in there, maybe tomorrow."

John and Carl signed the work order, coupled onto the work train and waited for the shop crew to board the riding coach. The conductor gave his brakeman the radio, assigned him to the caboose and took the fireman's seat in the engine. Rob Rankin stepped off, checked with Roger Nickerson as to the status of his crew and signaled a go-ahead. John pulled the train forward and watched for Rob's signal that the caboose was in his vicinity, at which time he stopped the train. When he was aboard, Rob activated the radio and radioed that the air-brake indicator in the caboose showed sixty pounds of pressure.

"Good, Rob," Carl answered. "Sit back and enjoy the ride." John sounded two blasts of the air horns and set the train in motion. Westfield was at the main-line switch with a hoop that contained the order and a clearance form. John reached down and snatched it as the train moved onto the main track. "Tell Rob I'll line the switch back, so you guys can beat it out of town," Bill yelled. "I'll make your time out at nine forty-five."

"Gotcha. Nine forty-five out," John yelled back. Carl radioed Rob in the caboose and advised him of the time out and the fact that he would not have to step off to realign the mainline switch. "Yes, sir, Mr. Reardon," the brakeman responded. "I have that. I'll go up in the cupola and keep an eye on the train from here."

"That's one sharp young brakeman, John," Carl said to the engineer as he settled in. "Alert, polite, very cooperative, quiet and a genuine nice guy."

John nodded. "I agree. He seems like a fine young man. I hope he's got aspirations for the future; you know, education, whatever."

Carl shook his head. "Tough situation. His father died a couple years ago and his mom has several young children. She works at the starch factory at night but it's not enough. They're really hard up so Hank hired Rob on real young to help. He's college material, but ... I don't know. A bunch of us—Billy, Joe, me, Hank, most of the SB&Q guys—have a secret college fund going for Rob but that isn't going to help the family. Delores—Mrs. Rankin—and her kids are special people, the kind you only meet once in a lifetime."

Chapter 18: The South Spanish Shuttle

The Summit, Bolton and Quarry's work extra pulled up at South Spanish station at ten-fifty in the morning on the second day of November 1951. Conductor Carl Reardon stepped from the locomotive, opened the station's access window to the composite telephone and cranked the ringer for Spanish Junction. Operator Boomer Johnson answered, took the train arrival time at South Spanish and wired the information to SB&Q's headquarters at Summit and the New England Eastern's dispatcher in Sunbury.

After a brief conversation with Boomer, Carl returned to the locomotive and advised Engineer John Shanahan that some of the shop men would get off there to continue inspecting cars for major defects while others would congregate near the first crossover north of the station to assist in the movement of inspected cars onto the mainline.

"It's going to be a one-car-at-a-time pull, John," the conductor cautioned. "We want to do it slow and easy because we really don't know much about the condition of any of the cars. We've got the track crew from South Spanish on duty to check the storage track as we pull the cars out. Roger Nickerson's men will be there to stop us if they spot something wrong. This needs to be a slow-and-easy operation."

John nodded. "How long do you suppose those cars have been sitting there, anyway?"

"Nobody seems to know exactly. I'd say the ones on the ends of each string are the newest additions. When we get into the string, I'd guess we'll find cars that have been here five years, probably more."

"Long time for a freight car to be sitting around in all kinds of weather," John observed. "Do we really know if all the cars are on the track?"

Carl grimaced. "No," he said. "And we don't know about the condition of the track under them. There could be washouts that nobody has noticed. I imagine some of the cars have broken couplers and drawbars." The conductor added that they would have to develop a plan to set out the defective cars as they came to them, probably by placing them on the track behind the station. "First, though, we need to set this train in on the south end of that track. Then we have to pull our caboose off from the north end and set it on the mainline so we can build our salvage train ahead of it."

"I'm ready when you are."

After setting the equipment cars behind the station and placing the caboose on the main track, John moved the locomotive to the crossover. The track crew had removed the spikes holding the switch closed, oiled the switch and pronounced it safe to use. A shop worker had set up a tripod and was taking pictures when Carl lifted the switch handle and aligned the locomotive into the siding. The conductor waved a hand signal to move slowly through the crossover and walked ahead to the first car in the string.

John noted that it was eleven-fourteen when the undertaking began. He inched the locomotive forward and listened to the squeal of the wheels as an accumulation of surface rust on the rails yielded to the switcher's weight. As he nosed the engine closer to the first freight car John detected hardwood trigs that had been placed under the reefer's two first wheels as a precaution against an unlikely movement of the cars.

Carl guided John to a point about five feet from the end of the freight car and motioned for him to stop. John leaned out the window for further instructions but Carl came around the cab and climbed in. "The boys are going to knock out those wooden trigs," he said. "It'll go better after that because we'll work everything on the hand brakes."

"Okay." John stood up and tried to see over the nose of the locomotive. "You know, I think we made a fundamental flaw when we planned this operation," he suggested.

"That would be we work for a railroad when we could have found a job elsewhere?"

John grinned. "Well, that's true, of course. ... No, I was thinking that we needed to turn the engine around." He pointed to the expanse of windows at the back of the cab.

Carl got up and looked. "Absolutely. Why didn't we think of that? Okay, when we take this first string back to Summit we'll turn this crate around. ... That's a far better plan."

After applying hand brakes on some of the cars, it took the shop crew several minutes to hammer the trigs free. Then Carl signaled a slow movement toward the first car. John edged up to the reefer, felt a slight bump and set the engine brakes. The hand brake on the first car was released. At Rob's signal from the rear of the car, one confirmed by Carl, John reversed the locomotive, released the brake and nudged the throttle. The freight car came away from the string cleanly and rolled through the crossover. The switch was re-aligned for the main track and the car was pushed back and coupled to the caboose. Hand brakes were set on both and the process was repeated until ten cars were assembled.

Roger Nickerson suggested an air-brake test at that point and the train crew complied. There were no problems. The hand brakes were released and the air-brakes set on the cars in the train and members of the shop crew made a detailed inspection of each.

The process was repeated until twenty refrigerator cars were coupled against the caboose and the shop supervisor pronounced the train fit to move at twenty miles per hour back to Summit. Carl calculated train weight at 651 tons, well under the 940-ton maximum authorized for the switcher locomotive on the long grade north of Spanish Junction. Roger assigned several car inspectors to ride in the caboose with Carl on the trip back and he joined Rob and John in the locomotive. The rest of the crew was dismissed for a lunch in their boarding car before returning to inspection duties.

Carl advised Boomer Johnson by telephone that SB&Q Work Extra One was leaving South Spanish at one-thirty p.m. The conductor stepped back to trackside and signaled for John to move ahead until the caboose reached the station. After boarding, checking the air-brake indicator and seeing that the car inspectors were seated, he radioed the engine. "All aboard, Work Extra One. I make it out at one-thirty. Keep an eye out for Boomer at the Junction. He'll have some paperwork for us."

"Gotcha, Carl. One-thirty out. This historic mission continues." John scribbled a notation in his time book, twisted his seat around and nudged the throttle forward. It was not the most comfortable position for an engineer with a lame leg, he realized, and he looked around the cab for a leg rest. Rob sensed the reason for his discomfort and got up.

"How about if I push that flag box over your way, Mr. Shanahan?"

"By golly! Yes, let's try that." Rob and Roger placed the box near John's seat and pushed it under his leg. "Ah, that's just right. Thanks, guys. I really appreciate that."

Fifteen minutes later Rob spotted the train order board at Spanish Junction. "Red board," he called across the cab. "I see the operator on the platform with an order hoop."

John pressed the portable radio microphone in the cab. "Red board at the Junction."

"Okay. The boys back here wonder if Roger wants to take a look-see at the train. Those old journals have had a bit of a workout by now." John passed the mike to Roger. "Let's do it to be on the safe side," Roger said. "A quick look wouldn't hurt."

The train coasted to the place where Boomer Johnson was standing. The shop supervisor and the brakeman stepped off and began walking along the train to check for defects. John got up and motioned for the operator to climb aboard.

"Hi, Boomer," the engineer said, extending his hand to the telegraph operator. Johnson was fifty years old, perhaps older, a man with an engaging smile and a thatch of silver hair that spilled from beneath a battered fedora. Then it struck John that he was a familiar figure from the past. "I ... I remember you, I think. You're Operator A.W. Johnson, from that little station up north of Helena on the Alberta Branch ... out west. ..."

Boomer grinned. "Yep, Buffalo Creek," he responded. "And you're Engineer J.P. Shanahan the Third. You were running the *Bootlegger* in Montana before you went off to the war. I passed you your last train order on the last day of July 1950 on the southbound run. It was account of some livestock on the track at Mile Sixty-Three."

"My last order. I remember! Better still; let me look at my time book. Come in and sit down, please." John fished the book from his frock and remembered a pocket that was attached inside the back cover. He reached inside and retrieved a carefully folded onionskin. The train order, issued by a dispatcher for the South Montana Railway, was dated July 31, 1950, and delivered by Operator A.W. Johnson. It read: "To Engineer and Conductor, Train 442, Engine 6405 at Buffalo Creek. Do not exceed five miles per hour approaching Milepost 63 account livestock may be on track."

John looked at Boomer and blinked back tears. He had difficulty speaking as he passed the order to the operator. "It seems so long ago ... a different lifetime," he finally managed. "I loved the *Bootlegger* run; damn, I loved that train ... but I had something to do ... another commitment ... and, well, I wasn't able to go back after that."

Boomer perused the order, nodded and passed it back to John. "Good keepsake, laddie," he said, and continued in the style of old-time telegraphers, speaking in short, clipped sentences. "Good times out there. Good times for all of us. Now they don't even call it the *Bootlegger* anymore. You remember that they nicknamed that train for the rum certain folks used to smuggle back across the border during Prohibition? New people came later. More sophisticated types. Now it's the *Alberta Flyer.*"

"You still go west in the summer, Boomer?"

Yep. Used to go south. North Carolina. Tower job at the foot of a hard grade. Sort of like here. They had a runaway some years back when I was away. Wrecked the train and stove the tower to hell. They never rebuilt it. I never went back. ..."

Boomer stood up abruptly. "Gotta run and talk to the dispatcher. Been a pleasure to meet again." The operator gripped John's elbow. "You were a damn good engineer out there, young man. That surprised some of the brass that figured you were just a plant, being the son of the owner. But the working men knew you had the right kind of stuff."

"Thanks," John said. "I'm glad we met again. I look forward to working with you."

John perused the messages that Boomer left for him as the operator darted back to the tower. His train was instructed to call in from the south semaphore at Summit yard and to drop the refrigerator cars on a specific siding near the shop. They would return immediately to South Spanish for a second run. Another message stated that Eastern did not expect to call any more trains until at least six p.m.

The next message came as a surprise. It stated that the special train being run for the SB&Q and initially scheduled to leave Sunbury on Sunday afternoon had been canceled. There was no explanation. And the last message had a particularly disconcerting tone: "All Eastern train crews operating on Hill Division advised to call dispatcher at Sunbury by 6 p.m. this date regarding work tomorrow. SB&Q crews operating on Hill Division may wish to call their dispatcher at Summit regarding possible changes in scheduling."

Roger and Rob returned to the cab after the inspection at Spanish Junction and the shop supervisor assured John that the reefer cars were suitable for transit. Carl echoed the assessment by radio and advised John to resume the run.

"Okay, Carl," John said. "Boomer's going to be on the platform with messages. Let us know what you think after you check them over. Looks like something big is cooking."

After the train began to roll forward, the engineer passed the message clipboard to Roger and Rob. "Some interesting reading here, guys. Take a look."

The radio crackled shortly after the caboose cleared the order board at Spanish Junction. "I made our time into SJ at one forty-five and out at two p.m.," he said. "How's that jive with your timepiece?"

John pulled out his watch again and studied the dial. "Yep. Out at two o'clock. So, read your mail yet? Any comments?'

"You called it, John. Something big is cooking. We're about to become the prime hauler in these parts or the Eastern is kicking us off the property and buying it back."

The locomotive took the hill in stride, passing Hillman at two thirty-three p.m. John eased the throttle back so that when the semaphore board came into view, he was able to coast to a stop. "You're one smooth engineer, John," Roger offered. "Last time I was on a work job, it was crash and bang all day long."

"I guess the stuff I learned is coming back. I'm a little off on my timing but I think I can fix that. ... Now, Mr. Rankin, my brakeman buddy, I'll pull up to the semaphore and maybe you'd be kind enough to do the honors and check in with the station."

Rob stepped off seconds after the train stopped and made the call quickly. Then he bounded back into the cab. "Mr. Westfield says to come in as per the message we got. The switch is open to the south ladder so we don't have to stop. He said to drop these cars on the second siding in front of the shop, turn the locomotive on the table and he'll be at the roundhouse for important updates. Mr. Nickerson should come along, he said."

"I think we all need to be there, Rob. If you'd be kind enough to call Carl on the radio and fill him in, I'll get us in there as fast as possible."

The train pulled into Summit yard at two forty-eight p.m. The cars were dropped quickly, after which the caboose was retrieved and the train moved to the roundhouse. Several shop workers employed as gang leaders were on hand when the train crew entered the stall reserved for the locomotive used on the work train. Westfield climbed atop a workbench and addressed the assembly. He was terse, mincing no words.

"We have some changes that affect all of us here and I've been asked by Henry Terrell to advise you of them. Eastern wants to skedaddle quicker than planned. It is imperative that any of you here who have primary employment on that railroad but might be working for us at the moment need to report to the station waiting room immediately and Larry Smith will fill you in on details. All others are being notified directly at home."

Bill paused and then continued. "We can't solicit you to come to work for us—that's an agreement by both companies—but if you should choose that course, Hank assures you that there will be work here. To protect any rights you have with Eastern, Hank suggests that you exercise those rights and if things don't work out, the door is always open at SB&Q. Now if this is all right with Roger Nickerson, I'd like a number of gang leaders to canvas the shop and inform anyone in there about the urgency of this matter."

Roger designated several employees to spread the word among shop workers and go with them to the station. After they had left, Bill continued. "What we have, gents, is a major dilemma. The return of the passenger extra that was on display on Sunbury today has been canceled. Eastern also scratched all of its passenger trains on the Hill Division as of tonight. Early tomorrow they plan to make a sweep of the system with as few employees as possible to gather the rest of its equipment and shuffle it to Hill Junction.

"Shanahan Enterprises has been working with the Eastern continuously since last evening to work out some kind of passenger schedule. The plan now is for us to institute through Sunbury-to-Quarry service in the morning. We will use that display train on the northbound leg tomorrow and since the Eastern crew that's on it has already committed to work for us, they'll bring it through to Quarry. Our crew reporting at Quarry will run through to Sunbury tomorrow and return the next day. They're agreeable to that. That brings us to Carl Reardon, conductor on this work extra. You here, Carl?"

Westfield scanned the audience. "Right over here," Carl called from amid the crowd.

"Carl, you hold the baggageman's position on the original *Northern Express,* so that will continue to be your regular job along with that engine crew and Joe Francis and John Kelly. We'd appreciate it if you'd stay on this work extra as conductor for a couple of days until we can figure out how to crew the trains we'll need. Is that acceptable to you?"

"Sure. I might even take it full time if you want to make that offer."

Westfield laughed. "Well, you never know," he said. "It isn't going to be an overnight venture. ... John, we'd like to keep you on as engineer on this work extra. That okay?"

Picking up on Carl's comment, John began: "I might even take it full time if you ..."

Westfield cut in. "Do I hear an echo in this building? I'll take that as a yes. And Rob Rankin, you have classes tomorrow but we'll have something for you after school."

"I'd appreciate that, Mr. Westfield. Anything you'd have would be good for me."

Then the SB&Q dispatcher answered several questions posed by the workmen. He said there would be no immediate resumption of passenger service between Boundary and Summit or on the Eagle River Branch until manpower and equipment needs were met. The Hayride between Summit and Gatlin was canceled indefinitely and only limited freight service would be available. And there still were no orders for refrigerator cars to start moving fresh potatoes to markets.

"Obviously we are not going to be able to make the 'seamless transition' that Mr. Shanahan promised, but it's no fault of ours," Westfield added. "Anyway, that's it, guys. Get back to your work and we'll make a go of things somehow. If the crew of the South Spanish Shuttle will hold on a minute, I have some goodies for them."

The four principals—John, Carl, Rob and Roger—gathered at the workbench. "I have a new work order for you," Bill said. "What we have here gives you exclusive use of the mainline between here and South Spanish station until eleven p.m. After that, you'll be afoul of the federal hog law anyway and you know what that means."

"I always wondered what that meant, Bill," John piped in. "What actually would happen if we just kept right on working through the night and into the day tomorrow? Would the feds come and handcuff us and take us away? What would they do if we resisted and attempted to run them down with the locomotive? I always wanted to ..."

"Damn it, John the Third of the House of Shanahan, I don't know and I don't care. Period. Go ahead, try it and find out. Only I won't know you when you call for bail money to get out of Alcatraz." Bill attempted to stare daggers at John but he couldn't keep a straight face and finally burst out laughing. "Ah, let's all go to work. I'm booking you out of Summit at, let's say, ten minutes from now. That should be three forty-five p.m., more or less.

"Oh, one more thing," he added. "We authorized Boomer Johnson to take the section crew's motorcar to run down to South Spanish and open the station there. He called just before I came over here to advise that he's there, off the track, and running the station. We're going to keep him at South Spanish while you're pulling cars, so that should be a help."

"Great help," Carl said. "Wise move. Okay, we'll turn the locomotive and highball at twenty miles an hour in the general direction of the Spanish River valley. If you don't hear from us in a couple of days, you can assume that we went to work for Eastern. Now we'll bid you a fond adieu, friend Bill, and frolic on down the Yellow Brick Road once again. Maybe we'll find the Wizard of Oz this time. I think he works for the Eastern."

"Beat it, you clowns!" Bill screamed. "God help me. If there were a train leaving today for the West Coast, I'd be on it."

"For the price of a first-class ticket, we could give you a ride as far as South Spanish," John offered. "It's a short hop instead of a long jump, but success is often measured in short hops. ... Or is it long hops and short jumps?"

Bill clamped his hands over his ears. "Good grief, I've been assigned to an asylum!" he yelped as he raced out of the building and across the freight yard.

Chapter 19: A Change of Plans

The South Spanish Shuttle ran around its caboose at Spanish Junction on its second trip and pushed the crew car ahead of the engine over the five miles of track to the work site. After checking in with Operator Boomer Johnson at four-fifty p.m. the crew plunged into the switching routine and the train was ready to leave thirty-five minutes later. It was back at Summit at six-thirty p.m. and began the third trip south at six-fifty p.m. Larry Smith was on duty at headquarters but had nothing new on changes in operations.

After arriving at South Spanish, Roger Nickerson said lack of time precluded a fourth trip but the crew might take more cars on trip three to conclude the day's work. After a discussion by telegraph with headquarters, an agreement was reached that the train could take its maximum nine hundred and forty tons or thirty empty reefers and the caboose over the grade to Summit. The engine responded well, although the drag was heavier.

Most of the shop workers opted to stay overnight in the crew cars at South Spanish so they could begin work at five a.m. It appeared the car-retrieval project had reached a place where a number of defective cars had been identified so Nickerson decided to move the workers south to the next crossover where the long string of cars was separated.

It was eight-fifty p.m. when the train entered Summit to end its final pull. Routine switching followed and the train crew returned to the station to sign off at nine-thirty. They had been on duty fifteen hours, traveled one hundred and twenty-six miles and had moved seventy refrigerator cars from long-time storage to the shop tracks and the beginning of rehabilitation for anticipated use by potato shippers.

Larry Smith congratulated the crew for its work and advised John Shanahan and Carl Reardon that they were being counted on for the same duty at five-thirty in the morning. Rob Rankin had classes to attend but was asked to report at four in the afternoon for some yet undefined trainman's role. "We'll use you somewhere, Rob, that's guaranteed."

Carl offered to drive Rob home, he accepted and they departed quickly. "Mind if I sit for a minute, Larry?" John asked of the agent. "Seems like I've been on my feet all day."

He squinted at John. "Really? Do you drive an engine standing up? Come on, Shanahan, I'd think you'd be tickled to stand around, maybe lean against the wall and harass the agent a bit. I thought all of you engineers did that."

John grinned. "It's part of our union contract. Get an agent when he's out straight selling tickets, pecking at the telegraph, making switching lists, answering the phone ..."

The telephone rang and Larry exploded in laughter. "Well, if you'll excuse me, my good man, it's in my union contract to answer the phone." He picked up the receiver as John waved goodbye and shuffled toward the door. "SB&Q Railroad. Larry Smith speaking. ... Oh, good evening, ma'am. This guy's name is Shanahan, you say? Gee, I'm sorry, the name doesn't seem to register. A lot of railroad men come and go here. Could you describe this individual about whom you are inquiring?"

John had stopped in his tracks and inched back into the room.

"Uh huh," Larry continued. "Tall fellow, you say? Bloodshot eyes. Could stand a shave. Looks a bit unkempt. ... You'd describe his appearance as seedy? I'd say seedy sums it up pretty well. I figured he was a hobo panhandling a meal off the railroad."

John sat down across from Larry's desk, folded his arms and glared at the agent. "What's all this about?" he demanded.

"Excuse me, ma'am," Larry said. "The seedy fellow is being persistent. Hold on. I'll have the night watchman boot him out and then we can get down to a serious discussion."

Larry peered slyly at John and passed him the telephone. "This is for you, Shanahan."

"Okay, Larry," John said. "I'll play your game. That phone line is dead and you and I know it. Nobody around here knows anybody named Shanahan or cares a whit." He took the phone, held it near his mouth and continued. "Why would anybody concoct a weird name like Shanahan? Now Smith I could understand. I'm sorry, caller, but the name Shanahan doesn't exist anywhere in our ..."

"John Shanahan, you and Larry Smith are positive buffoons! I have half a mind to report you two directly to Mr. J.P. Shanahan Jr. in Chicago. I'd bet he doesn't take kindly to such shenanigans. Explain yourself now or ... well, I'll stamp my feet and scream."

The caller was Jennifer Boston. John grimaced and Larry roared with laughter. "Ah, gee, Jenny. ... Gosh. Well, I was just funning here with Larry and I ... well, I honestly didn't think a person was really on the ... you know, the phone call, I didn't know ..."

It was Jenny's turn to laugh only it came out as a suppressed giggle. "I was just calling to find out if you had supper yet? There's a luncheonette just down Railroad Avenue and I thought, well, I'd treat if you'd want to go there. I hope I'm not being too forward ..."

"I could be the absolute buffoon that I am most of the time without even trying and make some absurd comment but I don't want to mess up what sounds like a really nice way to end a long day," John said. "Yes, I'd like that and if I can borrow a few bucks from Larry here, I'll head right out. Hold on, please." Still holding the telephone receiver, he continued. "Oh, Larry, my good man, I see here in your union contract that you are obligated to provide itinerant trainmen, specifically engineers, with the wherewithal to purchase a lunch when they are

131

short between paydays. It also states that the courtesy should be extended to the engineer's guest, especially if the guest is another engineer, so I'd take a ten-spot and enter that amount on my next expense account. ...

Larry snatched the telephone from John's hand, held it to his mouth and continued the conversation. "Why, yes, Mr. Shanahan, I would be more than tickled to pay for your lunch and that of Engineer Boston at any establishment that will let the likes of you on the premises. Since there are none, I will give you this ten-spot, of which I have the serial number and will expect it returned promptly at five-thirty tomorrow morning. ... Oh, gee, I seem to be talking into the telephone again. ... Well, Miss Boston, if you're still there, I'll route this ne'er-do-well out the Railroad Avenue exit and trust you'll be watching for him so he doesn't wander off into the night never to be seen again. Good night, ma'am. It's surely been a pleasure conversing with you."

Larry hung up the telephone, leaned back in his chair and clasped his hands behind his head. "You know, John, I really love my job. Where else could a diligent working stiff like me have an opportunity to sit in the middle of a vaudeville show every day he reports for duty? Now why don't you get the hell out of here so I can go back to sleep."

John stepped outside as a gust of wind swirled down around the concourse doors. It was a cold November wind and he shivered as he pulled his jacket collar tight and snapped the top clasp. He limped along the side of the west wing of the building, which was in the lee of the wind, and followed the structure toward the cluster of small homes sandwiched between the station and the downtown business blocks.

Summit had an appeal that grew on John each time he walked its sidewalks. He thought of what it would be like to settle there one day, perhaps in a modest home near the freight yard where he could hear the trains at night. That would be a priority. But would he really settle there? Certainly not, if this railroad venture failed. He would have to move on—back to Chicago probably—and accept his predestined role as heir to Shanahan Enterprises. But not for a lifetime, he thought. He would dissolve the business some day and move on, but where? Lost in thought, he suddenly realized that he was standing in front of a business place—a small hardware store that had closed for the night.

Perplexed, he turned and almost bumped into a person who must have been following him in the shadows. "You lost, sir?" she asked and stepped into the light. It was Jenny.

"Ah, oh, it's Miss Boston ... Jennifer, that is," he stammered. "Why no. I don't think I'm lost. ... Just lost in thought ... and seem to have forgotten where I was going. ..."

Jenny giggled. "You were wandering off into the night, just like Larry said you would do. I've been instructed to direct you to the Summit Luncheonette where you're supposed to treat a friend to an evening snack."

"I see." A smile played at the corners of John's mouth. "Okay, if you'd remind me who this friend is and point me in the right direction, you will have completed your mission and I will thank you for it."

"Uh huh. I'll disregard that remark. My mission is to see that you have a decent meal at the end of a long workday. Then I will see that you return promptly to your quarters where you will get some sleep and be useful to the railroad tomorrow. Is that clear?"

Jenny waited for a response. "No smart response?" she asked and peered at John.

"Response? I'm sorry, I was thinking about something else."

"Really? And what was that?"

"I think you know a lot about switching freight cars in really confined situations with not a lot of tracks to work on."

"Yes. And this is leading to what, specifically?"

"Well, I've been thinking about those old reefers down at South Spanish. There's not a lot of available sidetrack and we're going to have to pull out some cripples sooner or later, and ..." John paused and looked intently at Jenny. "You know, I believe you're the prettiest young lady I ever met. I'd like to take you to dinner or a midnight snack as the case may be. I happened to notice this luncheonette just ahead and, well, I think ..."

"I think you should take me to lunch now and while we're eating we could diagram this switching maneuver, analyze the situation and design a definite strategy to resolve the problem." She smiled, slipped her arm into his and walked John toward the diner.

It was still dark the next morning when John had breakfast in the station restaurant and rode the elevator to the second-floor, soon-to-be dispatching office. Bill Westfield appeared to be engaged in an animated telephone conversation.

"Okay, that's settled. ... Yeah. ... That should work. Nothing else has worked so far so let's give it a try. Uh huh. John just came in. Okay, hold on. Hey, John. Hank says great job with the reefers, he's coming up this afternoon on the *Northern Express*, thank God, and Ramon's the cook on the train, and things are falling into place. ... All right, Hank. Message conveyed. Good to hear from you. Bon voyage."

Westfield got up, strode to the windows overlooking the freight yard and shoved his hands into the back pockets of his pants. He stared out the windows for several minutes before turning to John. "Oh, good morning. Didn't see you come in. Working today?"

"Well, I thought so. Maybe not?"

"You really want to work?" Westfield asked as he returned to his cluttered desk. "I don't but, heck, I can't think of anything else to do. It's too cold to go fishing. What do people do around here anyway, except work or complain about the train service?"

"Gee. I don't know. Haven't been around here that long. I'd have to ask someone who knows. ... So, what's on the menu today? Any new news to report?"

Bill squinted at John, grinned and then laughed uproariously. The engineer tapped his fingers on the desk impatiently. "You could answer, 'Yes, I have news,' and not tell me about it, or you could say, 'No, I have no news,' but offer a hint as to what the heck is going on," John said. "Instead you just sit there grinning like a Cheshire cat and laughing like a hyena. It's not like I'm offended—not in the least—but I always like to share in a good laugh if there is something funny going on."

"Ah, I apologize, buddy. It was your question: 'Any new news to report?' and I remembered this old coot we had for a telegrapher back home on one of the coastline branches. Every morning he'd sign in on the telegraph at six sharp and I'd tap out: 'Any new news to report?' He'd always respond: 'Haven't been out today.'"

Bill noticed that John appeared bewildered. "I know that doesn't seem funny if you don't know the circumstances," he continued. "This old guy lived by the end of the freight yard and knew exactly when every train went by around the clock. He'd get up about three a.m., walk the entire yard, track by track, check the docks, crossing signals, sniff out defective boxcars ... man, he was on top of everything. So, when I asked him the routine question first thing when he came in, he'd respond the way I told you. Then every few minutes, I'd get these little bursts on the wire: 'pearls of wisdom,' my colleagues called them. It took about an hour to get all the updates and it was all pertinent stuff. He was a good man and we really missed him when he retired."

John nodded. "It takes special people like that to make a railroad work."

"Sure does. ... Anyway, you asked for info. A lot of things happened in the night. Let me explain what we're up against."

Westfield reiterated that the Summit, Bolton and Quarry would initiate through passenger service between Sunbury and Quarry at eight a.m. by using the cars on last week's exhibition train and the crew that had been assigned to it. All of the crewmen on that train provided by Eastern had decided to transfer to SB&Q service and agreed to stay on the train for as long as it took for the new owners to provide work near their terminals.

The longtime SB&Q crew on the original *Northern Express* would continue to staff the other side of the train, running from Quarry on Monday, Wednesday and Friday, and returning from Sunbury on Tuesday, Thursday and Saturday. As soon as a workable schedule was adopted, the plan was for a crew change at the meeting point and a return to their home terminals on a daily basis.

As the Eastern intended to retain all of its locomotives and remove them from the Hill Division, SB&Q was virtually helpless to offer any other service that morning. However, the dispatcher added, a block of ten new Shanahan locomotives bearing likeness to the Quarry Line's passenger equipment would arrive at Hill Junction during the day. Some were steam generator-equipped for passenger service; others were strictly for freight.

There were also two hundred almost-new refrigerator cars already at Hill Junction. The Eastern had refused to move the cars or the locomotives north because they had been billed only to the interchange point. In the next few hours, Westfield said, he hoped to pull together enough of a crew to move the equipment to Summit.

"Oh, and we've got another string of passenger cars awaiting pickup over the border at Ste. Anne's," he said. "The Canadian railroad is complaining because the cars are jamming up the transfer yard and New England Eastern is too busy to help. ... We have word of snowplows en route, snow spreaders and a Big Hook because Eastern is taking the one they own out of Hill Junction. There are a hundred new pulpwood cars coming just over the horizon ... and more locomotives—used, from other Shanahan lines. ..."

"Uh huh," John observed. "Looks like we're going to be busy. ... By the way, did you guys find a brakeman to replace Rob Rankin today?"

They had, Bill said. Two volunteers from the shop crew—Elmer Knowlton and Roland Evers—were both qualified Eastern conductors but had not worked on trains for years and now had full-time work as gang leaders. "Elmer will go with you and Carl, and Roland will fill Carl's job on the passenger train for a few days. There are some others over there but Eastern burned them once and they're not crazy about going back on the trains. Perhaps we can provide incentives to make such a move worth their while."

John nodded. "Sometimes money talks. I guess I'd weigh the pros and cons. Shop work seems to be steady, a lot of it is out of the weather and I understand the pay is pretty good. And if they have families, I'd think it would be nice to walk down the street at quitting time to a nice home-cooked meal. When's the last time you had a home-cooked meal, Bill, aside from your own home cooking?"

Bill pondered the question for a minute or more. "I'm no cook," he said. "I'd say it was my mother's cooking. That had to be in my high school days or maybe an occasional meal on college break. ... Ah, home cooking. Wow. You know, John, some day when all the dust is settled here, we need to hire a lady from the community to put on a real home-cooked meal for a few of us transients. Just for old time's sake."

Roger Nickerson, Conductor Carl Reardon and trainman-for-a-day Elmer Knowlton arrived a few minutes after five and were filled in on the work schedule and advised of the latest happenings, as John had been earlier. They boarded their locomotive and caboose and departed at five-thirty a.m. The object would be to switch out at least one twenty-car train and spot it at Spanish Junction and begin blocking another at South Spanish prior to the arrival there of Train Two, the southbound *Northern Express*.

The first twenty cars were placed at Spanish Junction and Work Extra One was within sight of South Spanish when the station's order board was suddenly displayed. John eased the locomotive to a stop and Operator Boomer Johnson climbed aboard. He carried a message for the train crew and the shop supervisor. "Change of plans," he said as he distributed copies.

Each read: "Conductor and Engineer Extra One, Supervisor Nickerson and Operator Johnson. Train crew set loco and caboose into clear at South Spanish. Relief crew includes Engineer Boston and Brakeman Rankin, arriving on Train Two from Summit.

"Engineer Shanahan and Conductor Reardon deadhead to Hill Junction on Train Two to make up northbound extra with Shanahan Lines East Engines Five-Thirty through Five Thirty-Four. Train will consist of two hundred reefers and caboose NEE Four Six One Four. Freight cars on tracks one, three, five and seven. Engines on Track Two. Caboose could be anywhere. We're still looking. We have hostler to serve as fireman and two qualified former Eastern brakemen who will be at HJ on your arrival.

"Train load estimated at six thousand two hundred tons plus six hundred and fifty tons of locomotives, more or less. Eastern's rating on ruling grade HJ to SU is seven thousand tons at 20 degrees or warmer for this class of engines. Watch the temperature. Think you can make Summit on the hog law? We'll play it by ear after Gatlin.

"Brakeman Knowlton is qualified as Eastern conductor and will relieve Reardon. Engineer Boston is qualified Eastern engineer, taking over for Shanahan. Rankin becomes brakeman on work extra at South Spanish. Acknowledge this message. Good luck. —W.L. Westfield, Acting Chief Dispatcher."

Carl was the first to speak. "Looks like we're off on a new adventure, John. What's your take on this?"

John shrugged his shoulders. "I guess one takes what one can get. I was just getting to like this shuttle service. But, you know, I'm glad I'm here. I could be in the office at Summit with Bill and Larry and Hank, I suppose, trying to figure out what the heck we're doing. That's not very appealing at the moment. ..."

Part IV: Reassembling the Pieces

Chapter 20: In the Game to Stay

Carl Reardon and John Shanahan were standing on the platform when Train Two arrived at South Spanish station at eight forty-five in the morning. Jenny Boston climbed down from the engine and met John at the bottom step. "Skipping school, young lady?" he asked and winked.

"Authorized absence," she responded and winked back. "It's called a work-study exercise. You never know when you grow up what your calling will be. ... You will take care of yourself on that big train, won't you?"

"I will. Maybe we'll both wind up in Summit about the same time and somebody will spring for a lunch for a couple of engineers at the Summit Luncheonette."

"That would be great. ... Uh, oh. Better get on quick. I see that my grumpy cousin is getting edgy." John climbed into the cab and she passed up his cane. Engineer Bill Travers slammed the door and stuck his head out the window. "Get to work, you little twit," he yelled. "You waste everybody's time, like every other woman I ever knew."

After resuming a normal running speed, Bill turned to John who had taken a place on the rider's bench in the passenger locomotive. "Well, buddy, looks like you knocked off a bunch of those old reefers yesterday. How'd everything go?"

"Good. Thanks to a great crew on the train and on the ground and a lot of backup support. ... It was a small start, really, but for me it felt good running out on the line."

"And now you're gonna tackle the big stuff," Bill observed. "Westfield told me you'll have five locomotives and a couple hundred cars out of Hill. Feel comfortable with that?"

John smiled. "Hadn't really thought about it. I guess I just kind of take each situation as it comes up and try to remember how I handled it before, if I ever did. I hauled a few heavy trains in Montana and we had some stiff grades in the foothills. The high country had its quirks, too, and the tunnels were kind of scary at first. The old snowsheds were downright ugly."

Bill shuddered. "I never ran a tunnel or a snowshed but I rode through a few when I went in the service. The idea of being in the engine didn't strike me as being a big thrill."

John nodded. "You're right, it wasn't, at least with the steam engines. Doggone smoke used to roll back and settle in the cab. We had one long tunnel where I used to pull my bandanna up over my face. When we'd get off at the end of the run, the agent used to laugh and say something about he didn't know which of us was the fireman."

"So, did you get a decent night's rest after yesterday's workout? I understand you ran into my cousin who schemed a lunch off the railroad. That so?"

"Well, I guess one might look at it that way. I enjoyed it and paid for it. And you know, Bill, she diagramed a neat switching move on those reefers."

"She's a pretty smart switchman. So what's the move?"

John explained, saying that he couldn't understand at first how the crew could switch out crippled cars quickly because of the dearth of sidetracks at South Spanish.

"But it made sense after she pointed out how we could use both crossover tracks. We'd pull a cripple out through the south-facing crossover onto the main and then back through the north-facing crossover to the other siding switch, towing the car. After that, we'd nose it into the piece of siding between the crossovers. Those pieces can handle four cars at a time. So that could save a lot of transit time that we would have had to use up to get those cars to a real siding, say up at Spanish Junction. Besides, the train we were building on the main would be in the way if we had to move the cripples to another place."

Bill pulled a scrap of paper from his time book and drew a diagram. Fireman Jim McDermott came over to take a look. "Piece of cake!" he exclaimed." The engineer continued to study the diagram. "The little twerp is right," he agreed. "Smart kid."

Bill was seized with an idea. "John, you'll be running through here later. Want to do a little test run to Gatlin? After that, I'll have to sit here and try to figure out where I am. Haven't been below Gatlin since before the war and it'll take some serious attention."

John got up and changed seats with Bill, who pressed the radio mike. "You there, Joe?" he called. "Yes, you want to give John some running time?" Joe asked. "Good idea. Stops at Camp Sixteen and Twelve and High Meadow. Remember the riffles."

"Got that. Thanks for the opportunity," John answered. "We'll tip-toe through the riffles." He reduced the throttle, made a gentle brake application and then touched each of the cabin controls within his reach.

"Everything where it should be?" Bill asked. "I haven't moved anything lately."

John grinned. "I know. It's just my routine. Remember the steam engines? The wizards at the shop used to move the gauges around every time the locomotives went in. You'd look for your boiler pressure gauge and it would be where cylinder pressure used to be. Sometimes you couldn't see a gauge and have to get information from the fireman."

"All the more reason for a fireman," Jim chortled. "Maybe if we had more levers and dials a fireman's job would be more secure. I suppose the day will come when you fellows will be riding up here all alone."

"That's a sad reality, Jim," Bill interjected. "Even worse, some genius will create a locomotive that can be run like a model train set and the dispatcher will be the engineer."

John made the appointed stops en route to Blackwater, eased up to the station there and waved to Molly McCaslin as the train rolled to a stop. About a dozen passengers boarded and fill-in baggageman Roland Evers shuffled baggage and express between the carts and the baggage car. At his signal, Joe Francis waved a highball and stepped aboard. The engineer acknowledged the signal, released the brakes and edged the throttle ahead.

The routine was repeated at Mission and the train moved on down the line, arriving at Gatlin on time. Just as Train Two coasted to a stop on Track One the headlight of its counterpart, the newly refurbished northbound *Northern Express* appeared on the running track south of the station and crept up alongside the southbound. It was an historic moment for the Summit, Bolton and Quarry, John thought, as he noted the trains' arrivals in his time book. He realized that a new schedule would have to be devised, however, because both trains lingered at the station to waste away time that would have been used to turn both on the wye at Battle Brook Junction. But each event in its time, he thought.

Bill took over the controls when it was time for Train Two to commence its first run-through to Sunbury and John moved to the rear bench. A pilot engineer employed by the Eastern but paid by SB&Q went along in the locomotive at the insistence of Henry Terrell because of this crew's lack of familiarity with the run to Sunbury.

John watched intently and kept his gradient and siding guide handy as he took note of running conditions south of Gatlin. There were scheduled station stops at Collier and Carroll and a flag stop at Crawford. The train passed the sidings at Halfway and picked up speed over what Bill referred to as "the racetrack" leading into Hill Junction yard. There, the stop was at the odd station-tower complex known as East Yard Tower. It was at the beginning of a wye, the east leg of which led to Eastern's mainline to Sunbury. John climbed to the ground from the engineer's side behind the station and Jim passed down his traveling bag and cane.

"Good luck, John," Bill called from the engineer's window as he awaited a go-ahead signal from the conductor. "Hey, just a sec. I damned near forgot the radio Westfield put on for your caboose crew." The engineer passed it down to John and waved as he acknowledged Joe's signal. It was almost two p.m. when the train departed and Carl Reardon loped up the platform to join his engineer.

"I've got the radio, Carl," John said and passed it to his conductor. "So where do we go from here? I think our destination is the other end of the yard?"

"Yep. All that planning and the railroad delivered us a mile short of our destination. I'm not up to walking that far to work. How about you?"

"Not a chance. Maybe somebody around here has a wheelbarrow and you could take me and our gear ..."

"Maybe you could wish upon a star," Carl responded and laughed. "Let's call on the agent and see what he knows."

"I'd imagine an agent around this place is ancient history. But you never know."

Carl stepped to the station door and reached for the handle when he saw the notice taped to a window: "Station closed permanently." He turned to John. "You're right. Ancient history. Now what?"

The pair spied a settee on the platform facing the running track into Hill Junction yard and was about to sit down when a motorcar appeared in the distance. It pulled up and the operator stepped off. "You fellas must be the engine crew for the SB&Q. I'm Andrew Rogers, the hostler for the Eastern down at the engine house. There doesn't seem to be anybody around here except for the car repairmen at the shop and me. We're all that's left and I guess that's because we're going with the SB&Q."

Carl introduced John and himself. "Well, I'm glad you're with us. You must be the guy that offered to be a fireman on this run."

"That's right. I put in a call to Summit from home to find out what was going on. Your brakemen, Bobby Hollis and Jack Burnham, are out in the yard trying to find the caboose that we're supposed to have. Those guys have been working as car-knockers the last year or so, so they inspected the train. We don't seem to have an agent anymore and the station at Hill Junction is locked up, like this one, so I figured you could come over to my house, up back of the shop, and get your orders."

"That would be much appreciated, Andrew," Carl said. "If John here wants to look over what we have to work with, I'd go with you and get the paperwork over your telephone."

"Dandy. Hop on the motorcar. I borrowed it from the lineman's car house and I'll take you to downtown Hill Junction. Keep an eye out for trains because I don't know anything about the Eastern's schedule today. I really don't know how to run this gadget either but I got up here, so I guess I can get back."

The three men climbed aboard the motorcar and ran down the mainline to the vicinity of Hill Junction station. John noted in his time book the unusual way his southbound run had been concluded. When they reached the station, he tapped Carl on the shoulder. "Since you're the conductor on this expedition, I'll have to rely on you to give me our arrival time," he said and grinned broadly.

"Absolutely," Carl said. He pulled out his pocket watch, checked the time and announced officiously: "I make it into Hill Junction at two-twenty aboard an Eastern motorcar borrowed by SB&Q Fireman Andrew Rogers. How's that with you, Andrew?"

"Fine," he said, beaming. "My first assignment with the new railroad. I like it."

Carl went with Andrew to report their arrival to the headquarters at Summit and to receive any further instructions. John met brakemen Hollis and Burnham who had found the caboose on an obscure spur near the station. The locomotives were on a lead to the engine house and he ascertained that the units to be moved were on the north end of the string. It would be a simple matter of uncoupling the five passenger engines and firing up the five freight engines at the front.

The brakemen-car repairmen knew the routine and handled the uncoupling. John set up the controls in the leading unit, Number Five Thirty-Four and checked each of the training units to determine that the control levers were removed and that all were working in multiple with the leading engine's control system. Satisfied that they were, he asked the brakemen to observe an engine brake test. Everything worked and he flashed an okay sign to the men on the ground.

Carl appeared a few minutes later and climbed into the engine with John and Andrew and the two brakemen. "You won't believe this, guys. The Eastern has suspended all of its train service on this division for the rest of the week. That means we have the whole line to ourselves except that SB&Q's work extra is hauling reefers out of South Spanish. Our two passenger trains are out of range now so they'll be no problem."

"What about open stations between here and Summit?" John asked.

"Only Blackwater and South Spanish and they're on our tab now. The only trackmen we have are at the work site with our car-retrieval crews. ... Now, John, we have a running order from here to Blackwater, where it runs out, so we'll need more paper there. Engines look good, sound good."

"Brand new, Carl. All tanked up and the sanders are filled. Yeah, they sound okay."

Carl nodded. "Okay, gang, let's get that caboose out onto the main and then we'll start building the train. I'd say let's just take them as they come, from tracks one, three, five and seven. I don't have any tally available, which is really unfortunate ..."

"Excuse me, Mr. Reardon," Jack Burnham interrupted. "The car-knockers went over the cars yesterday for the Eastern and I found copies of the report this morning. I thought something like this was in the wind, so I ... well, sort of took one of them." He reached into his overall jacket pocket and pulled out a sheaf of folded papers. "It's not a real car tally but it lists the cars from east to west according to Eastern's directions. If we change that to from north to south, I think we have a listing." He passed the sheets to Carl.

"Fantastic! You're a lifesaver, Jack. Well, let's go switching."

The switching was completed at three-forty and a successful brake test was run. Carl assigned Burnham, the senior brakeman to the head end to ride with John and Andrew Rogers. The conductor stepped to one side of the track and Bob Hollis went to the other and signaled for John to move the train forward. The train was a mile and three-quarters long and the locomotives were well into the grade north of East Yard Tower when the call came from the caboose: "We're on back here, John. Gun her when you're ready. I make it out at three-fifty p.m. I don't know about the hog law. You and I outlaw at nine-thirty. Unless we can make up half an hour on running time ... you know the numbers."

"Yep. A hundred and eighty miles. Top freight train speed is forty-five in some places, forty and thirty-five in others. And there's the slow order in the Riffles. We'll see what we can do. If worse comes to worse, maybe we can hitch a ride home with the extra."

"That's what I was thinking. They go off at midnight. We'll give it our best shot."

John worked the throttle forward and applied sand liberally. The diesels, totaling eight thousand horsepower, were performing magnificently. Despite his limited knowledge of the line, he felt that if he could anticipate troublesome places and plan accordingly, the run could be made in the time allotted.

Andrew was alert to track conditions and often reminded John of what was ahead. His interest in locomotives from the perspective of a hostler came in handy and he had made two internal inspections of all five units by the time they approached Gatlin.

"Coming up on Gatlin, Carl," John radioed. He snapped on an engine light and noted that it was six-twenty. The train had run ninety miles in two and a half hours for an average forward speed of thirty-six miles an hour. They passed the dark station at Gatlin under a high green at thirty-two miles an hour and accelerated into the grade leading to Mission. John's mind drifted back to Jenny and he wondered how her work was going.

In the approach to Blackwater, the engineer cut the throttle and instructed his fireman to observe if the station agent was on the platform. "There will be a red signal but if she's there with an order hoop, she'll signal for us to either stop or roll through. We need an order of some kind, but if it's a Form 31, we have to stop and sign it. I hope not."

Andrew stood up against the front window and peered ahead. Then he yelled, "It's a highball, John. The lady is coming out to the side of the train with the order hoops."

"Okay, Andrew, if you'd change places with me quick, I'll grab the order and I'll yell out 'highball' when I get it and you jam the throttle ahead about three notches."

"I'll do it." He stepped aside as John struggled into the fireman's seat. Then Andrew bolted for the engineer's position and grasped the throttle. John pushed the fireman's window open and waved to get Molly's attention. She aligned the hoop with his outstretched arm and gripped the staff tightly. The catch was clean and John waved before pulling his arm inside.

"Highball, Andrew!" he yelled. "Three notches." The power plants surged and the train lunged forward. John grabbed the radio. "Molly's on the platform with a Form 19, Carl. "We're up to thirty-five miles an hour, so hang on back there."

"Like a chimpanzee, my friend."

142

The order authorized a straight run to Summit with provisions that they not exceed fifteen miles an hour in the Riffles. John's train was to proceed with caution at South Spanish, where Work Extra One would be in the clear on the car-storage track. They would also forgo calling in from the south semaphore at Summit but the engineer would sound the air horns continuously on the approach to Summit station.

I'll give them a serenade when we get to town, John thought. The train would run through the station yard on Track One and continue north until the conductor reported that the caboose was clear of County Road Crossing. John would stop the train there and leave it on the main line. The crew would be picked up with a highway vehicle.

A separate message from Hank Terrell congratulated the trainmen on their progress to that point. Each man would be needed the next day after eight hours' rest, it also stated.

The radio crackled in the cab. "I make it by Blackwater at seven twenty-five. Good time, my man. You guys in the engine understand the order?"

"Yep. Okay by me." He turned to his cab companions, Jack Burnham and Andrew Rogers. They both nodded. "Jack and Andrew are okay," John said. "And it looks like we all have jobs tomorrow. Where do you think we're going?"

"Dunno. Jen and Rob go back to school for sure. That leaves Elmer Knowlton on the work job and the five of us. Two enginemen and four trainmen for two trains because I figure Hank will want to keep this train going north in the morning."

"Roger. Well, back to the present. Two hours and five minutes to make forty-five miles with some slow speeds. It's going to be touch and go, Carl."

"That's true."

John returned to the controls and pushed the train a little harder. He was up to almost fifty miles an hour south of High Meadow and then began backing it off. They rolled into the Riffles at twenty miles an hour and were down to fifteen just beyond the slow order sign. After passing Camp Sixteen, he picked it up to thirty when he thought of something he wanted to do.

He found a South Montana message sheet in his time book and wrote on the back: "Dear Jenny. Hope your day is going well. I'm scribbling this before we reach South Spanish. We're scratching to make Summit before nine-thirty. I was thinking I'd hang around the station and walk you home. It will be late but I'd like to see you. If I can figure out how to toss this off when we go by, I will. I think of you often. John."

He inserted the note in a South Montana Railroad envelope, addressed the envelope to Engineer J.L. Boston, Work Extra One at South Spanish and rummaged for an old newspaper in his traveling bag. After rolling the paper tightly, he bound the envelope to it with the string that came off the train order he picked up on the fly at Blackwater. The key would be to drop it near Jenny's engine where it could be seen and retrieved.

"High green at South Spanish," Andrew announced. "Operator is waving a highball."

"Okay, Andrew, I'll watch on this side for the work job on the siding." He spotted the caboose lights first and then a string of reefers where his train had pulled cars the night before. Finally the locomotive came into view and he spied several workmen standing on the siding in the engine's headlight. As his train rolled by, John reached out and waved the rolled newspaper to attract attention before tossing it into the middle of the sidetrack.

The smallest member of the crew stepped out of the shadows and picked it up and waved to him. It was Jenny. He waved back and closed the window. After shifting to a more comfortable position in the seat, he snapped the throttle forward and watched ahead. The slow speed signs had been removed at Spanish Junction and he asked for more from the diesel power plants. The train went into the hill north of the junction at thirty-eight miles an hour and he was able to hold it above thirty all the way to the top.

The radio crackled as the train rolled by the semaphore. "Look at your watch lately?" Carl asked.

"Don't dare to. How close are we?"

"It's nine-twenty. Good job. You might want to serenade the boys in the station along about now. Remember your message. They asked for it."

"Yeah," John responded fiendishly and began a discordant series of blasts—a long, a short and two longs, the reverse of a crossing approach signal—and then five short blasts, followed by two longs and three shorts, three longs and two shorts; four longs and one short; and finally a dying wail. Hank and Bill Westfield were on the platform with their hands over their ears so he sounded several impertinent blasts for their specific benefit.

Later, when Hank picked up the engine crew from a dirt road that paralleled the main line more than two miles north of the station he stared at John sternly at first and then burst out laughing. "I need to remember never to advise you to sound the air horns more than the prescribed series of blasts. We started getting calls from people wondering if a circus train was coming to town. ... But all clowning aside, I say the lot of you did us proud this day. We picked it up and showed the Eastern that we're in this game to stay."

Chapter 21: Improvising on the Fly

The crew of Extra Five Thirty-Four North gathered in the waiting room of Summit station after their run from Hill Junction and Henry Terrell laid out the plan of work for the next day. The South Spanish Shuttle was expected in at eleven p.m. with the last of one hundred and fifty reefers that were moved over the two-day operation. The shop tracks were jammed with cars and a decision was made to suspend the work until the inspectors and car repairmen could catch up. Jenny Boston, Elmer Knowlton and Rob Rankin would report again at four p.m. as a shop switcher crew to move the cars around at the direction of the shop foreman. Knowlton had been dismissed at South Spanish at the end of sixteen hours of duty and chose to ride back to Summit with the Shuttle.

The others on the Five Thirty-Four run would report at five-thirty a.m. and take the two hundred reefers north to Aroostook for storage and inspection by a mobile shop crew. After that, another highway unit run by the heating service would travel to Aroostook to begin installing alcohol heaters. The five diesel units would be operated through to Boundary where three would be set out at the engine house for future use at that terminal.

At that point, Hank said, the crew would run across the border to St. Anne and try to clear the Canadian Eastern interchange of passenger equipment that had accumulated there. "We're sending along a shop crew to inspect the cars and locomotives and have it ready for train service as soon as possible," he said. "What we're really interested in, gentlemen, is to get a few cars together and run a passenger train from Boundary to Summit so we can provide a northbound connection with the *Northern Express* tomorrow afternoon. ... It's the first step to getting regular service back in place."

When the manager noticed that Carl Reardon had a notebook and appeared to be doing some calculating, he said, "You're figuring out the time. How does it look?"

"Tight but it should work," the conductor responded. "If we get out of here by five forty-five, and allow an hour-and-a-half of running time to Aroostook, another 20 minutes there if we can drop everything including the caboose on the long siding—I think it's Track Eight—then another hour-and-a half will get us into Boundary. It would be a little after nine by that point. Then we'd need thirty minutes to set out the engines and turn one of them and touch up the fuel and scoot for St. Anne by nine-thirty. If we grab everything as it comes and drag it back across and sort some of it, we'll be pushing eleven and that would be about time to think about heading south. ... Uh, oh."

Hank grinned. "And you're thinking, doggone it, no heat for the passenger train. These are freight locomotives we're dealing with. Right?"

"Yes, I was going there but then I remembered something." Carl returned Hank's grin. "It was that steam heat car we loaned the Eastern a few months ago for some strange reason. We won't embarrass you and ask about that maneuver. Anyway, if we could have that in operating order we could put together some kind of a passenger train. Maybe. ..."

"Ah, but Carl, you're really thinking that there's nobody at the Eastern roundhouse today to fire up the heat car. That's right, isn't it?"

"We're going to have our shop crew on hand, so I don't see a problem. However ..."

Hank scowled. "There is always a 'however.' Go ahead, Carl, rain on my parade."

"However, since it seems that while we have been exploring the hypothetical stuff, the guys who have to do the leg work have been quiet. I'd like to hear from them."

"So would I. Any observations? We should hear from the fellows from Hill Junction."

Fireman Andrew Rogers looked at his colleagues—Jack Burnham and Bob Hollis. "Bob and I are okay," Burnham said. "We just appreciate the work. Times were getting tough for us." Andrew nodded his head. "That goes for me, too."

"We appreciate having you on board," Hank said. "So that leaves John Shanahan. I hesitate to ask, but what's on your mind?"

John was staring at the ceiling, apparently oblivious to the conversation. "I was thinking about a box of chocolates. Any stores open this late that would sell chocolates?"

In a pose that was becoming familiar to John, Hank put his hands to his head and peered through his fingers. He started to make a comment but bit his tongue. "Sure, son. Summit Variety at the corner of Railroad Avenue and Easy Street. Just down from the station. They're open all night. ... But why chocolates?"

"Oh, ah ... well, I guess ... I just got a craving for chocolates. ... Yeah, I'd say that's a good reason. Really. I like chocolates."

"Hey, if this engineer wants chocolates, by golly, he gets chocolates," Carl interjected. "I know you're a little short these days, John, considering the low wage scale around here, so here's a fiver," he added, pulling out his wallet. "Pick out something nice in a fancy wrapped box. I think she'd ... I mean you ... you'd enjoy one of those variety packs with the nougats and the white chocolate and the peanut butter and ... Heck, I think I'll get myself a box so why don't you ride over with me, we'll get stocked up and I'll bring you back before heading out for the farmstead."

After the shopping expedition, about which Carl asked no questions, John took a seat in the darkened waiting room and placed the box of chocolates on the settee. He had intended to change clothes but the arrival of the South Spanish Shuttle was imminent so he watched for a headlight from a front window. Hank had gone home and Bill Westfield was upstairs where contractors were at work

146

in several rooms being redesigned for office space. John shuffled around to get comfortable on the wooden bench and pulled his cap visor down over his eyes.

He dozed off and did not hear Work Extra One pull down the south ladder of Summit yard and leave its train on the only track still available near the rambling complex. The crew trekked across the freight yard and climbed the stairway to the dispatching office, where they signed off and received their assignments for the next outing.

Jenny Boston lingered and peered around the office. Westfield looked up. "Misplaced something, Miss?" he asked.

"No. I was just looking at your office and imagining how it will look when it's done."

"We're all imagining," Bill said. "I expect we'll still be imagining come Christmas. ... Oh, yeah, on your way out you might look in the waiting room. There's a tall fellow sleeping in there that you might recognize."

"Oh, Bill," she said and blushed. "I've been a little obvious lately, I guess ... so I'll run along now." She turned in the doorway and added: "Thanks for the information."

"Information is my business. Have a pleasant evening, pretty lady."

Jenny entered the waiting room quietly and spotted John slumped down by the window. She crossed the room, sat down next to him and spotted the box of chocolates that had a railroad shipping label attached by a piece of string used by telegraphers to deliver train orders. In his best penmanship, John had written: "For Jenny, about whom I think often these days when I'm out on the line. Affectionately, John."

Tears trickled down her cheeks. "Oh, John," she murmured. "You precious man. Thank you from the bottom of my heart." She reached over and pushed up the visor of his cap. He stirred and opened one eye and then the other and squinted to focus on the fuzzy image seemingly that of a person hovering nearby. "Hello, I'm John Shanahan," he said. "I'm with the railroad and when I regain consciousness I should ask your name."

"My name is Jennifer Boston and I'm looking for a companion to walk me home. The person has to be reliable and of good character. Are you such a person?"

"Well, yes. I think so. Now that I'm reorienting to the real world, I think I'd fit your criteria for a companion to walk you home. When I'm asleep, I don't know what kind of a companion I would be because ... well, when I'm asleep I'm really not awake to describe what I'm like. ... In fact, I'm not sure I'm making any sense right now, so perhaps I should just say good night and go back to sleep."

John pulled his visor back down and slumped over on the waiting room settee.

"If you don't get up right now, John Shanahan, and formally present that gift that you so kindly purchased, I will stamp my feet and scream!" Jenny exclaimed.

John bolted upright. "Really, would you do that in this lovely but vastly over-sized railroad waiting room? Do you realize how the echo of a scream would bounce around in here? It would be deafening and someone would call the police and an ambulance and absolute pandemonium would occur."

"I see your point. So after you make your presentation, I shall thank you in an appropriate manner and we will quietly exit the premises. Wouldn't that be an appropriate thing to do?"

John nodded, picked up the box of chocolates and clasped her hand. "This is for you, Jenny, and it is but a token of how I feel about you. You have been on my mind a lot of late and … well … gosh, besides, I really like you … a lot."

"And I like you a lot, John." Jenny leaned forward, kissed him on the cheek and squeezed his hand. "I was taken by the note you dropped off going by South Spanish and the way you did it." She reached inside her overall jacket and produced the rolled-up newspaper and the note enclosed in the South Montana Railroad envelope. She removed the note and turned it over. "Did you look at what was on the other side before you wrote those precious words for me?"

"Naw. I was just rummaging around in my time book kind of in the shadows and pulled out this folded piece of paper. We used to get a lot of those messages from different stations. I didn't have any blanks and I wanted to write the words before it was too late."

"May I read it to you? It made me cry when I read it the first time."

"Oh, I see. I can't remember much about the messages. I had several folded up in the back of my book, all from my last trip. Go ahead and read it if you really want to."

Jenny read the message: "Engineer J. P. Shanahan III, Train Four Forty-Two at Foothills Station: Your request for a leave of absence to serve in the U.S. Army has been approved this date, July 31, 1950.

"Your service to the South Montana Railroad has been exemplary. I have in my files in Helena unsolicited letters from thirty-one of our engineers—several who were employees from this railroad's beginning—and they all state that you have skills with a locomotive like no other engineman they have ever known. For example, Engineer W.A. Terwilliger wrote that you have extraordinary eye-hand coordination, a sixth sense in that you anticipate events before they unfold, and an understanding of the mechanics of steam and diesel-electric locomotives that baffles anyone who has worked …"

"Hold on a second, Jen," John interrupted. "That was just a message I got near the end of my last run. I certainly don't want you to think for a minute that I pulled that one out special to impress you … or whatever. … It's just a form letter, really. No big deal."

"I think I know you by now, John Shanahan. You never try to impress anyone. Quite the contrary, you put yourself down most of the time. May I continue, please?"

"Well, if you insist."

"Engineers Skylar, Lightfoot, Hiller, Price, Andreasen and O.T. Adams—all legends in South Montana history—remarked in their letters that your ability to size up unexpected situations and react correctly every time is a gift that few enginemen possess. They say to a man that you have the smoothest hand on the throttle of any of our engineers. You hauled my business train once and I can certainly attest to that fact."

Jenny paused and wiped away tears that flowed freely. "This is so precious. ...What a wonderful, wonderful tribute."

"I'd forgotten. After Korea, I definitely tried to forget. There was no ... no going back ... not after that, and I wanted so much to go back ... again."

"But you brought your talent to us instead. ... I'd like to read on, John." He nodded.

"Your father sent you to us as a young teenager and asked that we afford opportunities for you to observe our locomotive operations. We agreed with some trepidation because we had never done anything like that before. Yet, at age eighteen you were a qualified fireman on steam, a most demanding occupation; and six months later you were running the line regularly as an engineer. You made that risky pull in the Bitterroots after the snowshed collapse at Christmas time and people are alive today for your effort.

"Retired engineer Albert Goodine told me personally that what you and your crew did at Snowshed Seven was something he had never seen in forty-eight years of railroading."

Jenny choked up, whipped her cheeks and continued hoarsely. "I personally salute you, Engineer Shanahan, for your service to this railroad. I salute you for your desire to serve your country in these troubling times ... and I offer my personal prayers for your safety while you are away. I am directing that this message be transmitted by telegraph to all employees of the South Montana Railroad because they all know and admire you. Most sincerely yours, R.J. Vandergrift, President, SMRR Co."

Jenny cried and clutched John's hands. "I wish I had known you then. I would have been so proud."

"Ah, Jen, really. That's just stuff. I don't know. You go out and do your work the best way you can. I think sometimes because I'm a Shanahan, folks single me out and that's not right because on the railroad every person has a hand in its success, if it is successful."

"I would like to keep this paper because of your note to me. But you should keep it because of that wonderful message to you. Really, John, you should."

"How about if you keep it for us? It will be a lot safer in your hands. ... Actually my mind is wandering here and I'm thinking about how good those chocolates would taste. How about sampling a couple just to make sure they are okay. Okay?"

"Okay. Just one. And then we have a quick walk to take because I need to get home soon and you, even though you've been snoozing, have a really long day tomorrow."

John had difficulty arising the next morning and the switchboard operator tapped on his door in the crew dormitory before he was up. He groped for his work clothes and threw a change of gear into his traveling bag as an afterthought. It occurred that he might be in Boundary that night and maybe longer.

Extra Five Thirty-Four was dispatched from Summit on an order written by Larry Smith. Several other members of the Shanahan Transition Team were on hand that morning and the crew received their instructions in the second-floor hallway. The engine crew was delivered to the head of the train by taxi.

John had the train rolling at five forty-five a.m. He attached his gradient and siding guide to a hook from the radio console and consulted it frequently as he accelerated into territory he had traversed only once in the dome of a Shanahan passenger car. Still, everything seemed to be where it should be, at least according to the guidebook. The heavy train rolled remarkably easy and the new locomotives functioned well.

The setoff was made on Track Eight at Aroostook as planned and John re-entered the mainline, reversed the locomotives and rolled alongside the caboose to pick up the rest of his crew and the shop gang. Carl Reardon and Bob Hollis placed the caboose marker lights on the rear locomotive, Engine Five-Thirty, and climbed into the cab for the forty-five mile run to Boundary. The shop workers clambered aboard the other four engines.

The locomotives left Aroostook at seven-thirty and arrived at Boundary station fifty-nine minutes later. Although the station was closed, Agent Adrian Lajoie was sitting in his car adjacent to the station platform. He waved, exited his vehicle and stepped onto the platform. John pulled up alongside and stopped. "Come on up and see our fancy engine, Adrian, and don't construe this invitation as an incentive to join our railroad because we can't coax you to switch over, you know."

The agent stepped into the cab and shook hands with the crew. "Actually, John, I'm working for the SB&Q now and the Eastern has locked me out of the station. It's that way all along the line this morning. Hank and I made an arrangement by which I will keep track of things here and do all of my communications from home by telephone."

"Well, at least, the way it seems to work is that the SB&Q has a right to use the tracks as long as Eastern isn't running any trains," John offered.

"That's true, but we have no rights inside the buildings. There are exceptions but most Eastern employees who plan to go with Shanahan are locked out. Those who are staying with Eastern aren't working because nothing is moving at this point."

Adrian checked his watch. It was coming on eight-forty. "Listen, men, the local radio station has an interview with Hank coming on in a few minutes. We can hear it on my car radio." The station agent descended the cabin ladder and the engine crew followed. Carl and the other workers also gathered around the automobile.

150

Before a commercial was aired for an auto dealership, the announcer advised listeners to stay tuned for an update on the "railroad situation." Two minutes later, Henry Terrell was introduced and spoke via a telephone link from Summit. The trainmen cheered.

"I just want to let your listeners know that the Summit, Bolton and Quarry is working feverously to restore service to the Hill Division," he said. "We were left in the lurch when New England Eastern shut down this week more than ten days before the purchase agreement we negotiated in good faith was to go into effect. We're working around the clock and just moved two hundred new potato cars to Aroostook this morning.

"As I speak, we are assembling a train to re-commence passenger connections between Boundary and Summit. Since Eastern has barred our use of stations along the line, we invite travelers to assemble on public land as near to the stations as possible and we will stop there to board and discharge riders. I should add that we hope to provide several coaches and offer this service on a donation basis because we have no ticket agents on duty north of Summit. Our receipts will go to local college scholarship funds."

Hank provided a tentative schedule, saying the train would leave Boundary at twelve-fifteen and Aroostook at one-thirty and arrive at Summit at two forty-five to connect with the northbound *Northern Express*. The train would return to Boundary on the same schedule as that provided by Eastern before it suspended service. The train crew would also make flag stops at other locations served by Eastern earlier.

"Gee, I think that's the first time I ever got my orders over a commercial radio station," John observed. "I guess we're improvising on the fly," Carl joked. "Looks like we better rustle up a train and make this thing work."

The makeshift train that was the Summit, Bolton and Quarry's first scheduled passenger service from Boundary on November fourth attracted a sellout crowd and throngs of onlookers. It was an odd combination: two freight units, two dining cars, three standard coaches, a parlor car, another coach, a mail-baggage car and the steam generating unit on the rear. Brakeman-car inspector Bob Hollis attended to the heat car. The same crew worked together through November fourteenth and covered most of the railroad system. Late on the fourteenth, towing eighteen old reefers destined for the repair shop, they entered Summit yard for what was promised to be a weekend break.

Chapter 22: There's Always Tomorrow

John Shanahan was surprised to find that his gear left in the crew quarters at Summit station was stacked neatly in his room at the Summit Heights Hotel. A note from Larry Smith explained that the crew quarters had been gutted and replaced by new accounting offices. The note was attached to the 1950 calendar that he had wanted as a memento.

John fell into a deep sleep that lasted many hours. When he awoke about ten in the morning and sat up the telephone was ringing. He picked it up and listened. No one spoke until the caller finally said, "Hello. I hope I have Mr. Shanahan's room. If not, I'm sorry for inconveniencing you."

"Jenny? Is this Jenny?" he responded.

"Yes," she answered. "It's you! I hope I didn't wake you."

"Oh, no. I was just sitting here trying to figure out where I was. Now I think I know and I'm so very glad you called. It's been so long. ... Where I was I couldn't call you. It was always in the middle of the night and I didn't want to disturb you at those awful hours."

"I understand. It's so good to hear your voice. ... I really missed you. Katie did, too."

"I missed you both. Look, Jen, I'm off for, well, it looks like a while. Gosh, I'd ..."

"Would you like to come to dinner with us?" she interrupted. "Aunt Emma, Katie and me? Billy's working today, or he'd be here, too."

"I would, I'll get a cab and go to the station to check in. I should do that just to confirm that they don't need me anytime soon. Then, I could walk over when you're ready."

"That would be grand. Then I'll see you in a little while?"

"Absolutely. I'll make this quick."

John found his suit hanging in the closet. It had been dry cleaned along with a white shirt and trousers, and his dress shoes were buffed. He was torn between the casual look—a pair of raggedy denims and a sweatshirt—or the suit, and the latter seemed right for the occasion.

The taxi came by at ten and whisked John to the railroad terminal. The place was still a beehive of activity and many office workers were on duty even though it was a Saturday. He rode the elevator to the second floor but everything seemed different. The dingy rooms that lined the corridor had become modern office spaces. He spied a door marked "Dispatching Office" when Bill Westfield came bounding out. He charged by and was at the stairway when he stopped short and came back to where John stood.

"Don't I know you from somewhere before?" he asked. "We don't get many fancy dressers around the railroads now. But you could pass for a railroad engineer that I used to know. ... Ah, but he wandered off into the North Country many moons ago and has never been heard from again."

"Well, he wandered back. It's great to see you again, Bill."

"You, too, buddy." They shook hands. "Now, before I get engaged in a conversation with you—something that could drag on for hours—get downstairs to the front door, pronto. A young lady will be waiting. We know where you'll be. Enjoy yourself."

Jenny was there and they stood silently and held hands for several minutes. "The dinner's almost ready," she said, finally breaking the silence. Having anticipated that he might not have the right outerwear for a bitter New England morning, Jenny had tucked some woolen mittens into her pockets before leaving home. "It's cold out, John. Perhaps you should try these," she said, and passed the mittens to him.

"If I were out here on my own, I'd freeze to death," he said. "You're very thoughtful." He stuffed his flimsy dress gloves into a coat pocket and donned the mittens. She was an adorable personality, he thought as he pushed the door open for Jenny and then stepped outside behind her. It was cold but warmth coursed through his body.

"Aunt Emma's going to be ready for us about the time we get there," Jenny said as the couple walked along the sidewalk bordering the station's west wing. "I think you know about the three houses up ahead," she said and told John of how three railroad engineers built them at the same time and in the same way. The first one belonged to Harry and Geneva Ryan, Jim and Emma Cummings had the second one and her father and mother had the third. Mr. and Mrs. Ryan had moved away and their place was still vacant.

John eyed the first house as they walked by. "This one's vacant, you say?"

"Yes. It's a nice place, really, but it needs someone to keep it up. Maybe a small railroad family. Anyone with any money in these times builds out in Summit Heights, which is really what they call an upscale neighborhood."

"This Ryan place, is it for sale? I don't see any signs around."

"It is for sale but nobody has been buying with all the uncertainty about the railroad."

John and Jenny turned into the walkway leading to Emma's front door. John was still looking back at the Ryan house when Emma's door swung open and Katie appeared. Like her mother, she was a dark-haired, dark-eyed bouncing bundle of joy, John thought.

"Hi, Mama. Hi, Mister John. Auntie Emma said to come right now. Dinner is almost ready." She took John's hand from her mother's and led him up the steps. "You are our special guest today, Mister John," she said. "Isn't that right, Mama? Come. Hurry."

Emma Cummings emerged from the kitchen. He had met her earlier during the running of the special passenger train, and still marveled at her youthful appearance and pleasant demeanor. She was tall and slim and exuded the same friendliness so evident in her niece. This was a 60-year-old woman, he remembered, one who had known the harshest of tragedies but seemed to carry on with fortitude and grace.

"Welcome to our home, Mr. Shanahan," she said, extending her hand. "Jenny and Billy have been talking about you ever since you arrived. If you'll wait in the living room a few more minutes, we'll be ready to eat. Jenny has a dessert that needs attention and Katie wants to talk to you about trains, so why don't you two sit in the living room."

Katie tugged at John's hand. "Come, Mister John. Tell me about trains."

John took off his jacket, folded and placed it with his cap and mittens on an overstuffed chair and limped across the room to the living room sofa. Katie took his cane, placed it by the chair and crawled into his lap. "Do you like my Mama?" she asked, apparently having forgotten about trains. She looked directly into his eyes.

"Well … yes, I do," he answered, slightly taken aback by the little girl's question.

"That's good," she said. "Now, please tell me about trains."

She was so alert, such a precocious little girl, he thought. "Well, Katie, I'm learning as I go along. I used to be an engineer before I went off to the war. Now I'm trying to get over it and learn about trains again and help my father with this railroad."

"Uncle Billy said your father owns this railroad," Katie asked.

"Yes, Katie. He's a very busy businessman and he owns a lot of railroads."

"Can he fix this railroad?" Katie pointed toward the back of the house.

"He can, Katie, and he wants to fix it up so that it will be better than it was."

"I'm glad. Uncle Billy said it needs to be fixed up. Do you like my Uncle Billy?"

"I like your Uncle Billy. Do you know that we met in the war a while ago?"

"You did? Did you run trains?"

"Well, no, we didn't. We were kind of busy doing other things."

Katie slid off John's lap and scampered across the room. "Come, see this, Mister John. It's about my Uncle Billy."

John pushed himself up from the sofa and walked gingerly across the room. Katie was pointing at a framed newspaper clipping that hung above the mantle of a tiny fireplace. The headlines read: "Summit Soldier Receives Medal of Honor" and "Sgt. William Travers Gets Highest Award for Heroism in Korea."

"The Medal of Honor! Nobody deserved it more," John said as he scanned the story and remembered how Bill had said something about the intense fighting near Pusan. "Sgt. Travers was singled out for heroic action in the defense of freedom in the Taegu sector of the Pusan Perimeter in August 1950," he read from the newspaper clipping.

"Your Uncle Billy was a very brave man," he said as he leaned down and gathered Katie in his arms. "I bet he didn't tell you that he saved my life once, later on in the war," he said, wiping away tears that began to trickle down his cheeks.

"You're crying, Mister John. Are you all right?"

"He's just remembering the war, Katie." It was Jenny, who had slipped quietly into the room. She took Katie and held her hand. Then she gripped John's arm with her free hand and said, "Billy didn't tell us. He never talks about the war. He wouldn't even tell us about the medal until the story came out in the newspaper. Were you with him at Pusan?"

"No, it was up in North Korea a few months later. His unit saved mine, and Bill ... got to me when I was sure I was a goner. ... I didn't know it was Bill until we met at Gatlin station when I came up here. ... I had tried to find him for a long time."

"Will you tell me about it sometime?"

"Yes, of course. He deserved a medal for that too, the way he fought his way into that battle. He came running across the battlefield in front of us ... under heavy fire, awful fire. It was a terrible place. Koto-ri. ... We were pinned against the rocks and ..." John stopped and wiped his eyes again. ... "A bunch of us made it out of there because of him and his unit," John said, his voice breaking.

"You should know that when I came here," he continued, "I really didn't want to come. I wanted to go... well ... I don't know where. Somewhere away from the railroad because I didn't think I could handle trains, not for a while. ..."

"Don't go away, Mister John," Katie said. "Mama would miss you."

"Shush, Katie. Now let's get to dinner and not keep Aunt Emma waiting any longer." Jenny turned away, blushing noticeably.

The dinner was elegant, as John knew it would be. Pot roast, fresh string beans, potatoes and gravy and a garden salad, the kind of meal that sticks to your ribs, as his mother used to say. And Jenny's blueberry pie was scrumptious. "This is wonderful," he told the hostesses as the group finished their dessert.

"Now Aunt Emma is going to sit in the living room and the rest of us will do the dishes," Jenny announced. "Out, out, Emma. Come on, John Shanahan and Katie Boston, we have work to do," she added, gathering plates and silverware. "I hope you're not a klutz around the kitchen, Mr. Shanahan."

"Don't trust me with anything valuable, Jenny," John warned. "I'm okay as long as I concentrate on just one thing at a time." To Katie, he whispered, "Imagine, a lieutenant on kitchen cleanup duty. Don't tell your Uncle Billy, will you, Katie? It's our secret, yours and mine."

"I won't. We have a secret that nobody will know. Don't you tell Uncle Billy, Mama."

The dishwashing detail was carried out quickly and John, Jenny and Katie joined Mrs. Cummings who was reading the newspaper. Jenny sat down next to her aunt and Katie crawled up into John's lap when he settled into an easy chair.

Emma looked at John and smiled. "I understand that you were an engineer once before, Mr. Shanahan, and a very good one, according to the reports I'm getting."

"Yes, I was an engineer but the jury is out as to my value. I was always interested in locomotives from the time I was a little boy. My father has railroads here and there and when it became clear to him that I didn't have any interest in managing railroad money he suggested that I work on one of his lines in the summers in engine service. I think he figured that once I got a taste of hard work I'd come back to the office."

"It sounds like he learned about his son from that experience," Emma offered.

"I guess so. I kept going back each summer and winter vacations and qualified as an engineman quite young. I liked it a lot and would have stayed, but I knew I should serve my country for a while in some way. And that's how I wound up in Korea."

"And you won an award for bravery," Jenny interjected. "Your father and mother must have been proud of you."

"Ah, yes, I think so," John shifted uncomfortably in his chair. "But I wouldn't have lived to talk about it if Bill's unit hadn't shown up when they did. I was just one of a lucky bunch of guys, those of us who got out. A lot of my friends didn't and a lot of Bill's …didn't get out either."

"When you're up to it, John, would you tell me more about how you met Billy over there?" Then, sensing his discomfort, Emma quickly changed the topic of conversation. "So what do you think of your father's plans for this railroad?" she asked.

"He'll invest a lot of money in it and try everything he can to make it work," John answered. "He's that kind of guy. Now my grandfather, John Patrick, would have steered clear of this railroad because he invested only when he knew for sure there would be plenty of money to be made. Father bought this on speculation because he believes the potato business will rebound and the passenger trains he buys will attract riders. I hope he's right. He's the optimist and I guess I'm more of a pessimist, like my grandfather."

"Your father's right about up here," Emma said. "Mark my words, young man, this is going to be a banner year for the farmers, and for all of us. This railroad will prosper and people will use the passenger trains."

"I certainly hope things pick up, for all of us," John said wistfully. Then he noticed Jenny pointing at Katie. He looked down and the little girl was nestled against his arm, fast asleep. He grinned. "She's a little princess, just like her uncle said."

Jenny picked up her daughter gently and placed her on the sofa beside Emma. "She's tuckered out," the aunt observed. "Why don't you young people take a walk around the neighborhood while she's sleeping, if you're up to it, Mr. Shanahan."

"I'd like that," John said. "You, Jenny?"

"Yes, let's go for a walk. … I want to stop at my house, Aunt Emma, and then I should show him around town. If he's going to be working here, at least for a while, he should know his way around, don't you think?"

"Yes. Take your time. Katie will sleep for hours. Go and enjoy yourselves."

Jenny handed John his coat, cap and mittens and cane and retrieved her jacket from the closet. He noticed for the first time that Jenny's eyes were sad and her face troubled.

John opened the door and they stepped outside. She closed the door gently behind them. "I want to talk to you alone and I have to do it now before I lose my nerve," she said, looking into John's eyes.

"Sure. I hope I didn't say something out of place in front of Emma and Katie."

"No, you did not. You're the only real gentleman I've ever met, except for Billy and Uncle Jim Cummings and my father. I need to talk to you about me and Katie and school and a whole lot of things, but I'm going to cry first, so please bear with me."

Jenny groped in her coat pockets for a tissue and, finding none, she wiped her eyes with her sleeve. John pulled a handkerchief from his shirt pocket and passed it to her and slipped his arm around her waist. She led him to her house and opened the front door.

"You don't have to tell me anything unless you really want to," he said.

"I need to tell you," she sobbed. "I need to tell you now because I don't want to lead you to a place you wouldn't want to be. Come sit in the living room and listen. … When I'm done you can walk away. I'll still have a lifetime of pleasant memories of this day."

With that, Jenny told her story, sparing no details.

Her father, Harold Boston, had been home only a few days after he retired in the summer of 1946 when she found him dead from a heart attack in their garden. She was devastated and cried for days. Emma and Billy were there to help but her world had collapsed. She was only sixteen and tried to put things together again by entering her junior year of high school. It didn't work and her focus on family values faltered. She began seeing a drifter who showed up to take part in the potato harvest, or so he said.

Jenny, overcome by her loss, was adrift and sought solace in the wrong places. There was drinking and there was more. She wanted to say no to his advances but she didn't want to lose him. He controlled her every move and she left school at his insistence. Not long afterward, Jenny learned she was pregnant and begged the young man to marry her.

"He laughed at me and slapped me around," she related through her tears and her shoulders shook. "Then he pushed me out of his car out on the County Road and took off. A sheriff's deputy found me by the road and brought me in to the hospital. I gave the officers a description and they put out an all-points bulletin but he got away."

John put his arm around her shoulder and squeezed her hand. She continued her story, telling him how Emma supported and sheltered her through a difficult pregnancy and was by her side when Katie was born. "She was a precious baby. I love her so," she sobbed.

"And the man, did you find out what happened to him?" John asked.

"Billy found out that he was running with a bad crowd out west about a year later. They were involved in armed robberies and some shootings. They killed a policeman and then he was killed in a shootout. ... I didn't even know his real name. That's how mixed up and foolish I was then. ..."

John held her closely. "It's over now. It's over, Jenny. And you're back in school and you have people who care deeply for you. ..."

"Yes. My life has changed, thanks to Emma and Billy and Katie. I go to church as often as I can and I thank God every day for my blessings. I'll graduate from high school this spring and I'll keep working so I can stay with Emma, as she gets older. ..."

Jenny continued after fighting back more tears. "Maybe I'll go to the community college here in Summit and take a few courses and get some kind of a degree. Right now, I'm happy with my work but I need more time with my daughter."

They sat in silence for several minutes as Jenny struggled to regain her composure. Then she looked up at him, wiping at her eyes. "So, John Shanahan, you can walk away now and I won't complain." She broke down again and sobbed convulsively. "Walk away ... and pick up your life ... and remember me for good times that we had."

Jenny struggled to get up but John still held her firmly.

"Jenny Boston, listen to me now," he said. "I've grown fond of you this bit of time we've been together. I would like this friendship to grow more as time goes on. I'm going to be around here for a while, maybe a long time, and I'd like to spend more time with you ... that is, if you would like ... and take things as they come along. Understand?"

Jenny sobbed. "I'm not trying to take you where you don't want to go. Please, you understand, don't you? I have a child. Don't you know what that means?"

"I know that you have a lovely daughter and a fine family," John said. "The past is the past. Thank you for sharing it with me. Let's turn the page now and get on with today and tomorrow and the day after that. I hope you will be a part of my life for a long time to come. A long time ... I care for you very deeply. I hope you know that."

"And I care for you, John. You're kind and you're a gentleman. And you like my daughter and my aunt and my cousin, Billy. Thank you. ... If you really want to, I'll work on today and tomorrow and the day after that." Jenny smiled bravely through the tears and wiped her eyes again.

"Let's get hiking, then," John said, squeezing her tightly. "I need to get oriented if I'm going to find my way around this place. I need you to lead the way, my dear friend."

"Very well, my dear friend, but I need to do one more thing." Jenny stood up and kissed John gently on the cheek. Her tears were warm against his face. "Thank you, John Shanahan, for the very best day of my life. Now if you'll let me fix my face, we will go and see the sights."

They were at the end of the walkway about to turn down Railroad Avenue when Emma emerged from her house. "John, the railroad called," she said. "They need you right away." He looked at Jenny and shook his head sadly. She smiled and squeezed his hand. "There's always tomorrow, John, and the day after that. I'll be here when you get back."

Chapter 23: Highballing on the High Iron

When John Shanahan reported to work at Summit on the afternoon of November 15, shorthanded crews the length of the railroad were scrambling to handle urgent calls from potato shippers for refrigerator cars. His assignment in the company of Conductor Carl Reardon was to move one hundred heated reefers north to Aroostook and begin setting them in sidings between there and Boundary. His former crewmates from Hill Junction had deadheaded south earlier to take assignments in their home terminal. In their stead, brakemen Stan Larrabee and Rob Rankin of Summit joined Carl and John.

The run to Aroostook was made quickly and by four p.m. the crew was placing cars for potato shippers on the fourteen sidings between there and Boundary. The first substantial delay came when they had to clear the mainline for the northbound afternoon passenger train from Summit. The move was made at Marysville station and required the use of several sidings. In addition, what was supposed to be a snow squall had blown in by then and visibility was extremely limited. Two obstacles were apparent before long: The squall might be more than that and the train was handling too many cars to switch effectively in the small mainline freight yards along the way.

After the passenger train had passed, Carl loped across the yard from the caboose and climbed into the cab. "Getting nasty out there," he offered as he pulled off his jacket and shook it through the open door to knock off the snow. "I think we're in for a first-class storm and I don't like the way we're all tangled up in cars."

John nodded. "Me neither. I know the shippers need the cars but it seems like it would have been quicker to drop off empties at each place and then go back to set up the doors."

"Absolutely. Well, we do what we're told and keep plodding along." Carl wolfed a sandwich as he talked. Then he pulled on his jacket again and went back to work.

Four hours later, the train pulled up at Boundary station with fourteen cars destined for the long yard spur into Last Chance. After a quick lunch in the passenger station and a conversation with Agent Adrian Lajoie, they headed in on the spur. Adrian agreed that the crew should drop enough cars for each siding inbound and set the cars on the way out.

The crew was back at Boundary at midnight after more than six inches of snow had fallen. They were then directed to return along the mainline to Aroostook, picking up twenty-six cars set earlier that had already been loaded on the sidings along the route. The train arrived at Aroostook at four-forty in the morning. Four more reefers were set for loading at a public platform in the yard before the crew booked off at five-ten, more than fifteen hours after reporting for duty. The night operator advised the men to return at one-ten p.m. for an assignment still to be determined.

The Summit, Bolton and Quarry Railroad owned the line at that point although it had been running trains exclusively for several days. Management requested and union officials agreed that freight train crews would work on a "first-into-a-terminal, first-out" basis until specific schedules could be worked out. Passenger train operations would be bid off to ensure that personnel would be available at the right places at all times. Enough NEE employees had transferred to the new railroad to run most operations although there would be a dearth of train and enginemen if business expanded as expected.

Another message stated that SB&Q also had the task of moving designated New England Eastern equipment to Hill Junction as time permitted. The equipment had been marshaled at Eagle River, Aroostook, Summit and Gatlin. There were still more than four hundred reefer cars on the former northbound track in the area of Camp Sixteen and a considerable number taking up valuable track space at Hill Junction, Halfway, Collier, Bolton and Esker. Passenger service had not been restored to the Eagle River Branch but the transition team was working to establish a branch line connection with the *Northern Express*, along with a link to "a proposed second daily passenger run between Hill Junction and the Canadian Eastern connection at St. Anne."

John looked at Carl. "I keep hearing about a proposed second daily passenger run that's always imminent but never seems to get here," he said. "You know anything about that?"

Carl threw up his hands. "Beat's me. I hear about it too. Say, isn't your name Shanahan? You happen to know any Shanahans who might be in the know?"

John appeared to be in deep thought. Carl tapped him on the shoulder. "Hello," he said. "Anybody home?"

John shook his head. "How can you get a 'hello' response if nobody's home? I suppose if you enunciated the 'hello' in a certain way, an echo might respond 'hello.' But how would you be able to strike up a conversation with an echo?"

"Hmmm. Interesting. It's a conundrum. Now if I were back in the field of academia, surely I could get a handsome grant to study the phenomena of echoes and how one might, from a strictly scientific point of view, carry on a conversation in that medium."

"Indeed. You might even be endowed with oodles of foundation money and ... "

"Ah, but I'm really only a lowly railroad conductor," Carl interrupted. "And I'm dog-tired and would like to stagger over to the nearest inn and collapse from exhaustion."

"Me, too, Maestro Conductor. Let me pick up the baton and lead you and Stan and Rob because I'm more adept at staggering than the lot of you." He thumped his cane on the waiting room floor for emphasis.

The train crew was back at the station at one in the afternoon to face a new challenge. The task was to take a train consisting of derelict Eastern equipment south to Hill Junction at a maximum speed of twenty miles an hour. Two SB&Q car inspectors were assigned to ride along and see to safety issues. A freight train coming off the Heartland Branch that should have been in Aroostook by one o'clock was still switching reefers on the line and one of its two locomotives was needed for the run.

The train arrived at two-thirty and the locomotive facing south was set off at the station. It was a Shanahan West Lines' general-purpose road unit classified as a GP-7, and one with which John was familiar. It had stairwells both front and back with narrow catwalks leading to the cab. John knew it was the most accessible diesel around for a workman with limited mobility.

Extra Twenty-One Forty-Five moved out of Aroostook yard at three-fifteen with the strangest array of equipment the engineer had ever hauled. There were four passenger coaches directly behind the engine, followed by eight flat cars loaded with scrap rails, ten old hoppers, sixteen faded box cars of improbable age and the NEE caboose the crew was using. All, including the caboose, were billed to Hill Junction for the Eastern. At only twenty miles an hour, John calculated, the trip would take more than twelve hours if no stops were made. He looked back at the derelict train and dismissed that likelihood.

The first incident occurred just six miles south of Aroostook after a vestibule door on one of the coaches rattled loose and tumbled into a ravine. As John eased the throttle back, Stan Larrabee, who was riding in the cab, picked up the radio and called the caboose. "Vestibule door fell off one of the coaches, Carl," he reported. "Looks like it landed in that little brook we just crossed."

"Uh huh," Carl responded. "Well, I'd imagine it would be too heavy to lug back up the bank. It's wooden, so it should float. That little brook leads to a bigger brook, a couple of streams and the Eden River, which eventually enters the Spanish. We'll send a message to the Eastern that if they want their wayward door they should send somebody down to the river in Sunbury in the spring and they can fish it out. I'd say we just boogie along and hope the rest of the car doesn't fall apart. The car inspectors agree."

Stan grinned at John, who nodded. Then the brakeman depressed the mike button: "Engineer says, 'Roger on the wayward door, Carl. Let's keep boogy-ing.'"

A stop was made at Siberia Crossing station. It was there that the car inspectors found a cracked wooden beam in the underframe of the coach, which had caused it to sag. In the process of setting the car on a back track, the beam let go and the coach caved in on the rails. After going over the remaining coaches, the inspectors decided that all of the cars had defects not reported by Eastern and should be left behind. After that, a defective journal was found on the first flat car and that was also shuttled to a siding. The inspection and switching consumed the better part of an hour and it was after six p.m. before the train was under way again.

John slowed the train to a stop at Summit station where the order board was displayed. "Red signal, Carl," John radioed. "Nobody's on the platform, so I guess they want us to hop off and yell, "Is anyone home?""

Carl chuckled. "But who will answer if nobody is home?"

"Speak a little louder, Carl, I think I hear an echo. … Ah, now I see that rascally Larry Smith donning his windbreaker at the door. Hold on, Stan's going down so Larry won't have to come out in the cold."

"Good man, that Stan."

John watched as the two men conversed in the station door. Then the brakeman came back to the side of the engine and advised the engineer that there was a change of plans. "Call Carl, will you?" he said. "He and Rob need to come up to the station. Looks like some of us have a new assignment."

John relayed the message and then stepped out onto the catwalk leading to the nearest stairwell. I like this engine, he thought as he eased himself down to the station platform. Then he stepped into the lee of the wind to await the arrival of Carl and Rob.

The group gathered in the waiting room to hear what the agent had to say. "We have a Hill Junction train crew reporting in a few minutes," Larry said. "That's just a train crew—Conductor Mark Littlefield and brakemen Warren Stanley and Howard Chapman, and we want to get them back to the other end of the line. No engineer. So we want John to continue on as engineer of this train, after we inspect it again. We also need to get back to pulling those reefer cars near Camp Sixteen, so we're reporting a job out of here in about half an hour. Jenny Boston will be engineer, Carl conductor and Stan and Rob will be brakemen. You guys came on at one-ten this afternoon, so we'd like to run you the full sixteen hours, or until five-ten tomorrow morning, if necessary. I know that's demanding, especially for the students, but we're really desperate for those cars. You okay with that?"

"Sure," Carl said after getting nods from Stan and Rob.

"As for you, John, five-ten's the deadline, too. How far would you expect to be down the line by then? We're going to rip out anything left in that train that's not fit to move and cut it up for scrap. What do you think?"

John appeared to be sizing up a damaged closet door in the waiting room. "You know, Larry, I saw a door flying through the air up the line today that I'd bet would fit your closet over there."

"Really? Wouldn't happen to have some mahogany paneling in it?"

"I'd think so. It sailed pretty good."

"Thanks, I'll look into that. … Now what did I ask you, anyway?"

"Dunno. But it must have been important."

"Well, it will keep. We're sending you along to Hill Junction with the relief crew."

"I see. What's at Hill Junction?"

"Nothing that I know of. You?"

"No, but I'll go, if that's what you're asking. Don't beat around the bush, Larry."

John met the Hill Junction crew for the first time. All were experienced railroaders and Conductor Littlefield had forty years of service. Brakeman Stanley was a qualified conductor who preferred to take braking jobs when available and replaced Stan Larrabee in the cab. Just as the inspection was completed and the train was judged safe to move again, Jenny came through the station door and dashed to the side of the engine.

John reached down and clutched her upraised hand. "I was hoping you'd get here before we had to leave … which I guess we have to do right now. Take care of yourself out there."

"You, too, John," she said. "I'll be thinking of you."

"And me, of you," he said. "I'll try to call from somewhere soon. …"

John sounded the air horns in response to the conductor's lantern signal from the rear. Apparently Littlefield hadn't realized a radio was on hand in the caboose. He checked his watch and jotted a notation in his time book that Extra Twenty-One Forty-Five left Summit at seven-ten p.m., six hours after the original crew's reporting time at Aroostook. He would have ten hours to reach Hill Junction before running afoul of the hours-of-service deadline. At the mandatory twenty miles per hour, the train should be able to make the one hundred and eighty mile run with an hour to spare, barring any delays. A meet with a northbound train at Gatlin would likely narrow the time window.

The trip went remarkably well. The northbound freight was in a siding at Gatlin per train order and no time was lost. From time to time, he crowded the speed limit and cut back the running time by a few minutes. Only one ten-minute inspection stop was made at Collier and the train pulled into the yard at Hill Junction at four-thirty in the morning. Brakeman Stanley gave John a lift to the Railroad Motel about a quarter mile from the station on his way to his home just outside the village.

John pulled down the blackout shades and sprawled on the bed, too tired to completely undress. He slept soundly and awoke just before noon to a ringing telephone. The caller was Henry Terrell.

"Hank! How nice to hear your voice," John said. "What's going on?"

"We have an interesting assignment if you don't mind running alone. There's a new industrial switcher at Hill Junction that belongs to Gatlin Mill. They are paying us a hefty price to move it," Hank said. "Bill Westfield figures a departure time from Hill of three-thirty p.m. Without a train, that forty-four ton diesel is restricted to twenty miles per hour so you'd be in Gatlin at about eight p.m."

"What happens if I get lonesome along the way?" John asked.

"Sing to yourself," Hank responded. "So we can sign you up for this prestigious run?"

John took the job and sang a few songs to pass the time. He enjoyed the run.

In the weeks that followed, Summit, Bolton and Quarry train crews cleared the northbound track between Spanish Junction and Blackwater of stored refrigerator cars. Maintenance forces repaired the track and made it the mainline, thus eliminated the rough section of southbound track known as the riffles. Train speeds were increased accordingly, prompting J.P. Shanahan to send a telegram to the state's governor that the railroad was "highballing on the high iron" instead of tearing up track to build a new highway that would be an onerous burden on taxpayers for decades to come.

The governor did not respond, even after the state's leading newspapers carried feature stories about the railroad's remarkable comeback.

By mid-December, Operations Manager Henry Terrell was able to announce that a new train called the *North Country Night Express* would begin through passenger service over three New England railroads and the Canadian Eastern between New York City and Halifax, Nova Scotia. Several top-ranking federal officials from Canada and the United States were on hand for the first run, along with leaders from the maritime provinces. No state officials participated. The train was designed to carry local traffic to and from principal points on the Summit, Bolton and Quarry, and sleeping and coach cars that ran the whole distance were featured. Connections between Summit and Eagle River were also restored and the train was named the *Wilderness Flyer*. The daily round-trip connection between Boundary and the *Northern Express* trains at Summit was called the *Potatoland Connector*.

The potato business boomed and additional refrigerator cars were leased to supplement SB&Q's growing fleet. Pulpwood shipments increased dramatically and the startup of a long-planned paper machine at the mill in Gatlin swelled traffic between that point and Hill Junction. Full-time freight services were opened on the Quarry Line and the branch from Gatlin to Battle Brook Farm. Several long-closed railroad stations along the former Hill Division of New England Eastern were hastily refurbished and pressed into service.

The station at Summit was upgraded so that all SB&Q operations formerly conducted from the headquarters of Shanahan Enterprises in Chicago were transferred to the stately building. The transition teams continued to function as advisers and new workers were trained in the different departments. The freight crews continued to work on a first-in, first-out basis because of the rapid expansion of business and a dearth of experienced train workers. Hotshot, nonstop potato freight service was established between Boundary and Hill Junction, and crews routinely were on duty twelve hours or more at a time, often seven days a week.

John made several of the hotshot runs and handled a number of trains that contained more than one hundred and thirty cars. He also operated pulpwood trains on the Eagle River branch, moving wood from yards at Skagrock Stream and North Branch to the mill at Gatlin. Substantial snow held off but temperatures plummeted in December and train air-brake systems froze. On one run out of Eagle River, it took John eight hours to pump air through a long train consisting of mixed freight before the crew could depart. The ninety-mile segment of the run from Eagle River to Summit required another four hours and the crew was hard pressed to make Gatlin before running out of time.

Jenny Boston bid in the engineer's job on the four p.m. to midnight switcher at Summit because it fit into her school schedule. She saw John only occasionally after that because he was running in the engineer's pool system-wide. He had not had a day off since the second week of November and not seen Jenny for almost a month when he was forced to tie up on the morning of December 24, 1951, in Gatlin with only minutes to spare on the hours-of-service law. He and Brakeman Rob Rankin planned to deadhead back to Summit aboard the *North Country Night Express* on Christmas Eve to begin a two-day holiday break that Henry Terrell had worked tirelessly for days to try to fashion for the railroad's exhausted work force.

But a philanthropic effort by Shanahan Enterprise to provide a group of students at Summit High School an opportunity to attend a rare national symposium on railroad transportation went awry when a bus connecting with the trains broke down that day. It fell to John Shanahan, the most overworked engineer on the line, to fetch them at Hill Junction and get them home for Christmas even as the most furious snowstorm in years swept across the North Country.

Part V: The Christmas Train

Chapter 24: A Missed Connection

A telephone was ringing insistently somewhere but John Shanahan couldn't seem to track the source. It must be in the darkened room, he thought, but he couldn't remember where even though he had been in the same unit at the same motel many times since his arrival in the North Country. He bolted upright at last, just as the phone stopped ringing.

He groped for his cane, found it and pushed himself to his feet. Only then did he realize that he was still dressed in his trousers and work shirt. His railroad overalls, greased-stained from his last long outing on a train, were in a heap on the floor, along with boots and outerwear. He must have tumbled onto the bed in the early stages of undressing and fallen asleep.

John found the light switch, snapped it on and reached for the nearest window shade. He stumbled, caught himself and yanked at the shade. It slipped from his hand, whirred loudly on its roller and slapped hard against the windowpane. A burst of light from the setting sun streaked across the floor, illuminating the dark recesses of the room. He squinted and turned away.

∞

Ninety miles to the north, Henry Terrell studied the crew board in the dispatching office of the Summit, Bolton and Quarry Railroad and knew there was only one possibility. John Shanahan would be the only engineer available for the emergency and he was still on rest after a tortuous 16-hour run that ended less than five-and-a-half hours earlier. Hank would have to rouse him from the sleep the man needed so desperately and ask him to take on an improbable mission: A run from Gatlin to Hill Junction with a spare locomotive, a quick transfer to a passenger train already being assembled there, and then a 180-mile odyssey on a winter night to Summit.

Why did this have to happen? Why on this day before Christmas would a bus break down and strand forty-two students and their chaperones at a forsaken crossroads far from the railroad system? Would they have been there had the railroad not provided financial support for the outing? Why were the weather forecasters calling for a severe snowstorm—a blizzard, really—in the coming night that would surely ensnarl the entire North Country transportation network? Would the replacement bus, only then en route to the scene of the breakdown, make it through the storm to reach the special train?

Why would this happen on the day when the owner of Shanahan Enterprises and his wife were in the North Country for a surprise visit with their son, the only engineer available for the mission? Their visit was to be a secret, so carefully guarded up to now, and one that he vowed to keep from even his closest associates. Ramon Martinez had met the Shanahans at the airport the day before and whisked them off to the estate at Quarry. So far, he had no reason to trouble them with details of the difficulties that had been encountered, but that would have to be attended to as the day wore on.

His plan to shut down the railroad for a Christmas weekend, so carefully choreographed to get everyone home for the holiday, had been torn asunder. Now he had to rouse this weary engineer from a deep sleep and try to convince him to take on a mission that would test the mettle of the most rested railroad man. Vowing that he would retire after this night, Terrell gritted his teeth, called the station's switchboard operator and asked if he would place another call to Room 14 of the Starlight Motel in Pleasant Valley.

∞

John found his pocket watch on the bedside table and studied the dial, trying to focus on the numbers. It was three-fifteen, and there was daylight, so it must be afternoon. But what day was it, he pondered? And where was he on this afternoon in what appeared to be the dead of winter? He shook his head to clear the cobwebs, could not, and was about to tumble back onto the bed when the telephone started ringing again.

He tried again to trace the source of the sound. Then he remembered that it was a wall phone, adjacent to the door. "How handy," he muttered as he arose and shuffled across the room.

"Who's this?" he queried sharply after he maneuvered the receiver to his ear.

"Hello, is this John?" The voice was strangely familiar but he couldn't connect it with a name.

"It depends on who this is," he answered, still trying to identify the caller. "Perhaps you have a wrong number."

"John, as tired as I know you are—God bless you, son—we've got a difficult situation on our hands and we need your help ... again," the caller responded. It was Henry Terrell, general manager of the Summit, Bolton and Quarry Railroad.

"Hank, it's you!" John exclaimed as he hooked the rung of a table chair with his cane and dragged it to the phone. After seating himself, he added, "Gee, it's been a long time. Since yesterday, I'd guess, whenever that was. What the heck day is it, anyway?"

"Coming on Christmas Eve and things aren't going quite as planned," Hank answered wearily and John knew from his tone that the man was near wit's end. John remembered how the manager had planned for weeks to shut down the railroad over the Christmas weekend and have all employees at their home terminals on Christmas Eve.

"Sorry about that," John said. "Sure, I'd be glad to help, but where am I? Honest to God, I can't seem to remember."

"I'm not surprised, son. We've run you the gamut these last few weeks. It's going to get better, I promise you, if we can just get through this problem. You do understand? I hope."

"Ah. ... Sure. I think so. But, damn it. I don't know where I am. ..."

"Oh, yeah ... forgot that. You're at the motel in Pleasant Valley, if I called the right number. You've had about five hours of sleep and you're the closest to rested of any engineer on the system. We'll have people straggling home half into the night the way it looks and nobody will be rested again until well into tomorrow."

"Ummm. I remember now." John yawned. "Okay. So what were we talking about, Hank? You know, before you kindly told me where I am."

"Remember the students who were coming back from that conference today? Coming back on Train Three?"

"Sure. Hey, that all fell into place pretty well. I thought that was a great idea."

"I thought so ... then. ..." Hank paused. "But something came up. They'll miss the connection with Train Three because their bus is broken down up in the williwaws and we can't hold Number Three, not tonight because we have to protect the connection with Canadian Eastern. ... Not tonight, for sure. ... I don't know where we're going here but we have to do something. ..." Hank's tired voice faded and the line went silent.

But John was fully awake, his adrenalin pumping. "Aha, I see the problem," he responded. "We need to get a train together and pick them up somewhere and bring them home. Piece of cake. I'll be available, according to the federal hours of service folks, at six-o'clock—of course what the weasels there don't know won't hurt them—and we'll round up a crew and head out. That seems simple enough. Really."

"I admire your youthful exuberance, my boy," Hank chuckled. It was the old Hank again, the one John liked a great deal. "You've summed it up pretty well. We definitely won't mess with the hours of service, so I'd expect you to report for duty at six, not a minute before then, and we'll go from there. Now I need to know if Robbie Rankin is up and around. I imagine he's pretty worn out, too, but we need him for a brakeman. I haven't got anybody else ..." Hank's voice trailed off again.

"Robbie? Sure, it'll be a pleasure to have him on board. He's a good man, you know. Hold on, Hank, I'll get him." John put down the receiver, shuffled across the room and banged his cane against the wall. "Robert Rankin!" he yelled. "Arise, my young friend and hustle over here. The chief has an important assignment for you. Hurry now!"

There was a tap at the door almost immediately. "It's me, Mr. Shanahan. Rob. May I come in?"

John pulled the door open and peered at the sleepy-eyed and disheveled young brakeman. "Well, don't you look like a night on the town," he joked loudly. "Perk up now and speak to the man on the phone. Be on your best behavior and don't tell him about the capers we've been cutting in our spare time."

169

Rob grimaced and took the phone. "This is Robert Rankin, sir," he said tentatively.

John hovered nearby. "Tell the man that he needs to be talking about a raise if he expects us to go out on Christmas Eve."

Rob pretended not to hear. He turned away from John, huddled over the telephone and spoke quietly, nodding his head often. "Yes. ... I will do that. ... I'm glad to be of help. ... Certainly, sir, I will. ... Yes, that's right. ... Thank you. ... Yes, I understand. Thank you for calling, Mr. Terrell."

The brakeman hung up the phone and turned to John. His face was clouded. "Those are the students from Summit High School ... my classmates," he said, choosing his words deliberately. "Their bus broke down ... and they'll be late to the junction. I know they planned to be home for Christmas. It's a big thing up home. ... We can do this, can't we? The weather guy on the radio says there's a snowstorm coming this way ... tonight, I guess."

John went to the window, leaned against the sash and peered into the south-western sky. A cloudbank was clearly visible against the skyline even as the sun-light faded behind a wooded ridge. An ominous sky, he thought, and he remembered his experiences in winter railroad service in the mountains of Mon-tana. Hauling freight in a storm was routine; transporting passengers was another matter. He glanced at his watch, noting that it was pushing past three-thirty, and then he turned back to the brakeman.

"Sure, we can do it, Rob," he said. "It might get a little messy, but we can do it. Right now, let's get our gear together, grab some eats and beat it over to the station. We need to get tuned in to what's happening up and down the line."

The Gatlin station clock was sounding five-thirty when John Shanahan put down the sheaf of salmon-colored message forms, rubbed his eyes and leaned back in the stationmaster's swivel chair. He was tired already. It was dark outside, and an occasional flake of snow danced tantalizingly beneath the platform lights. The wind was quartering in the northeast, he noticed, and strengthening with each passing gust.

This mission wasn't going to be a piece of cake, he realized, as he pondered the probabilities of what was ahead. The messages issued by the dispatching of-fice over the signature of Henry Terrell during the last two hours, superseded by updates, one after another, suggested an increasing degree of difficulty. Hank avoided mention of the impending snowstorm but John knew that was his major concern.

As the minutes ticked away, forty-two high school students and three adult chaperones were supposedly en route by bus from a northwestern state college campus to Hill Junction where this train crew would pick them up with a make-shift passenger train and take them home for Christmas. John and his brakeman would climb into a locomotive shortly and hightail it for the junction, 90 miles away. There, they would leave their temporary means of transportation and board a train consisting of a standard passenger engine and a streamlined coach car and head north again, all the way to Summit. John knew it could work, but

170

the weather reports were not favorable, and weather in the North Country, he had learned, always made the difference between success and failure.

The engineer had not seen his assigned locomotive. He shuffled through the messages again, but there was no number listed. He turned to the longtime night telegrapher at Gatlin, Ken Wiley, who was hovered by his instruments, and asked, almost absently, "What are we going to have for an engine, Ken?"

"I dunno," Wiley responded. "Funny number. I didn't recognize it. SB&Q fifty-something. Apparently it came in earlier on the local from Hill." He stepped to the bay window and peered out. "We'll know in a minute. The hostler, Sheldon Sims, is bringing her over right now."

John was puzzled. He was unaware of any locomotives on the property bearing numbers in the fifties although Shanahan Enterprises was ferrying in new and used diesels on a regular basis. He got up awkwardly, tucked his cane under his arm and limped to the window. The big engine was being backed in on Track One, adjacent to the main passenger platform. It was different than any he had seen before. It appeared to be gray in color with few visible markings except for red lettering under the engineer's side windows indicating ownership and number: SB&Q 53.

Then he remembered a trade magazine he had perused weeks earlier. "Well, son of a gun!" John exclaimed. "Ken, it's one of those new branch-liners! Just like our standard Class F3s, you know, the freight engines. Only in a different car body. Sixteen-hundred horsepower, two-hundred and forty thousand pounds, interchangeable parts with the Fs and picture windows for a windshield."

Wiley squinted at John from beneath his traditional telegrapher's green eyeshade. "Picture windows, eh? You might recommend that the railroad put a couple of those in the front of this station. Then I wouldn't have to get up to wave to you guys when you go ripping through town." The telegrapher grinned and winked at Rob who was standing nearby.

John smiled. "How about a couple of portholes, you know, like on the ships you used to sail in the service. Then you can stick your head out so that the enginemen will know you're not sleeping on the job."

Wiley laughed and went back to his telegraph instruments. "I sailed in a submarine. No windows. Makes me seasick to think about it," he said as he cut in his key and responded to an insistent station call. Outside, the hostler scrambled down the side ladder, sprinted across the platform and stepped inside the waiting room.

"Got your wheels, Mr. Shanahan," he announced. "She's a Jim-dandy, brand new and all juiced up for a good night's work. Handles real good. I topped off the tanks, gave her a heavy dose of sand and fixed your markers on the rear and the white flags on the nose. There's snow shovels and switch brooms stashed inside, just in case."

"Thanks, Sheldon." John shook the hostler's hand. "I think I'm going to have to learn how to run it on pretty short order."

"Ah, she's a jewel, just like the standard freight engines," Sheldon said.

John nodded. It seemed that everyone was caught up in the changes that were coming to the railroad and he knew that was a good thing. Then the telegraph clattered loudly in the background. "Ken's taking our order, I think," he whispered.

When he was done the telegrapher passed the order and several more messages to John, with copies of each for Rob Rankin. Hank Terrell hinted that he might have someone he called "a senior employee" available at Hill Junction for the trip north. John hoped so because a two-man crew on a passenger train would be a tall order, especially in a snowstorm.

John read the order aloud: "Engine Fifty-Three run passenger extra Gatlin to Hill Junction and meet Number Three, Engine Five-One-One at Carroll. Passenger Extra Fifty-Three South takes siding from north switch of Number One track at Carroll. Number Three takes this order at Hill Junction."

Then Rob read the order and said he understood. John signed the order as engineer and passed it back to Ken. The signature was acknowledged by telegraph and the order was completed with copies returned to John and Rob. Then the engineer clasped the brakeman's shoulder and said, "Okay, let's get our gear aboard and get it done."

∞

Henry Terrell sat next to Dispatcher Bill Westfield. It was five fifty-nine and the telegraph wire was silent. Then the clock struck six and the signal came. The pair in the Summit dispatching office deciphered the dots and dashes and spoke the words together: "Passenger Extra Fifty-Three South left Gatlin six-naught-naught p.m. Engineer Shanahan, Brakeman Rankin. Running light. Nose south. Wiley, Operator."

The pair flashed thumbs-up signs simultaneously and the dispatcher clicked out the response: "Got that. Fifty-three out GT [Gatlin] at six on the button."

∞

The odyssey of the Christmas train, one destined to become legend in the annals of railroading in the North Country, had begun.

Chapter 25: 'Bon Soir, Cinquante-Trois'

John Shanahan was still stealing glances around his new surroundings in the cab of Engine Fifty-Three when the floodlights of the tower on the south leg of the wye at Battle Brook Junction appeared. Rob Rankin, riding in the fireman's seat, spotted the order board first, and yelled across the cab: "High green at the tower, Mr. Shanahan!"

"Okay, Rob, let's see what this engine's got," John responded as he notched the throttle forward. "Keep an eye out for the flashers at the County Road crossing, about eight miles or so ahead. ... Boy, this beauty's got some pick up. Feel that surge!" he added as the locomotive accelerated rapidly. He checked his watch, pulled out his personal time book and scrawled "By BBJ 6:05 p.m. southbound," tucked the book into a crevice on the engine's console and cracked the throttle ahead another notch. Three miles south of Gatlin he had the locomotive in a cruise mode of forty-two miles an hour when snow began to swirl noticeably in the beam of the powerful headlight.

With visibility worsening his better judgment prevailed and he eased off on the throttle. A few minutes later he caught a glimpse of the whistle post denoting the northern approach to County Road and pulled the first long blast of the air horns. The crossing flashers appeared and he stood up for a panoramic view through the windshield windows, the largest he had ever encountered in a locomotive.

The brakeman stepped up to the windows, also, and peered into the worsening storm as John pulled the second long blast of the horns. Like the good trainman that he was, Rob's focus was the highway on both sides of the track and he detected flashing lights approaching rapidly from the left. "Snowplow truck!" he yelled. "He's not stopping!"

John yanked the whistle cord with one hand to sound a series of short sharp blasts of the air horns. With his other hand he activated the engine bell. Then he cut the throttle hard and locked the engine brakes. His heart raced as the snowplow disappeared from view directly in front of the locomotive. "Please, God, help us," he muttered as the engine skidded along the rails, and he braced for a crash. "Grab something and hang on!" he yelled to his brakeman.

The plow truck burst into view suddenly and a wall of snow raked the engineer's side of the locomotive, striking the windows with a resounding series of thuds. John closed his eyes instinctively and then opened them. He looked down from the cab and saw the truck's taillights disappear in the swirling snow. The locomotive slid to a stop south of the highway crossing.

John mouthed a silent prayer and turned to his companion. "Thanks, Rob," he said in a solemn tone. "I couldn't ask for a better man to work with. You okay?"

"Yes, sir. I'm fine. That was kind of close, wasn't it?"

"Yeah. Close. Too damned close," John responded as he adjusted the operating controls. "What in the world do you suppose that guy was thinking?"

Rob shook his head. "I don't know. If we saw him, he must have seen us. The crossing lights were flashing ... and our lights were on ... and the air horns ..."

The engineer resettled in his seat, and jotted a notation in his time book: "Near miss, County Road crossing south of Gatlin, 6:17 p.m."

After the locomotive was humming along again, John pulled a message form, a piece of carbon paper to make a copy in his time book, and a pencil from his jacket pocket. Then he flicked on an overhead light and wrote: "Agent, Collier. Denny, please advise dispatcher of 'near miss,' County Road crossing, Mile 84.9, at 6:17 p.m. this date. Southbound highway snowplow truck failed to yield to flashers. Engine bell and horn in operation. Set brakes at 26 mph. Truck cleared engine by approx. two feet, no more, and continued without stopping. Engine 53 stopped south of crossing, engine checked over and run resumed at 6:21 p.m. Signed/ J.P. Shanahan III, Engineer."

He held up the paper and pencil and turned to Rob. "We have to let the dispatcher know about what happened," he said. "Please read this, and if you agree, sign your name at the bottom. We'll drop it off at Collier station."

Rob read the message, nodded his head and signed the paper while John fetched a fusee from the locomotive's storage box. He inserted the message in a red railroad envelope to indicate its urgency, rolled the envelope around the flare and bound it with string. "I'll toss this off when we get to Collier."

John propped his left leg over a convenient cross member in the radio console stand and refocused his attention to the chore at hand. The wind would abate periodically and the view ahead would improve. Then it would blast in again and visibility would be reduced to a few rail lengths at most. The engine passed several sidings where refrigerator and pulpwood cars were set to await loading. The evidence that business was booming again on the railroad was everywhere and that was heartening.

Just over a half-hour into the run, John picked up the station lights at Collier and spied the signal atop the bay window. "High green at Collier," he announced.

"I see it. High green," Rob answered.

John slowed the engine, picked up the fusee with the message attached and opened his side window. Holding the unlit flare at arm's length he waved it up and down. Agent Dennis Chambers, bundled in a sheepskin jacket and winter cap, stepped outside the station and acknowledged the engineer's signal.

Certain that the agent knew what John was doing, the engineer lobbed the fusee out from the engine and it dropped harmlessly in the snow. Chambers picked it up and yelled, "Godspeed!" John waved again, pushed the throttle forward and slammed the window shut but not before the wind sent snow streaking through the cab. "Dirty night in the country," he muttered.

∞

Dennis Chambers re-entered the station at Collier and went directly to his telegraph set in the agent's office. After tossing his coat aside, he opened the line to make his report: "Passenger Extra Fifty-Three South by Collier at six-thirty-nine p.m. Message from engineer follows."

The dispatcher responded: "OK on the Fifty-Three, Denny. Three's out of Hill at six-naught-five. Heavy load. Passengers for CR [Crawford], CA [Carroll] and CO [Collier]. We'd like to keep you on duty until the Fifty-Three gets by on the return. OK?"

"OK. Ready for the message?"

∞

John notched the locomotive to passenger train speed after crossing the last switch at Collier yard. He knew the track was well maintained and that was a plus, but the storm was making visibility increasingly difficult. They had only logged twenty-five miles, so there were sixty-five to go, and then there was the return run to Summit, totaling another one hundred and eighty. Unless the weather improved dramatically it would be a long and difficult trip. John knew that the depth of the snow would become the principal factor in the success or failure of the mission.

∞

Hank Terrell hovered over Dispatcher Bill Westfield as the message came through about the near miss at County Road. "Mother of God," Terrell muttered. "I didn't need to hear that. Well, they're safe, at least for now." He went to a telephone across the room and called the state's public safety building at Carroll. The telephone rang several times before a sleepy voice responded. The railroad manager identified himself and explained the incident at the crossing. Then he read the telegram in its entirety.

"Really?" The person at the end of the line let out an audible yawn. "We have a report here that a train operating with limited illumination nearly ran into a highway snowplow on a crossing near Collier. The train did not whistle and the crossing signals were not working. I assume that would be the train to which you refer?"

"Just where the hell did you get that kind of information?" Hank screamed into the telephone.

"Keep your cool, please," the office attendant said. "I have passed the information I received nearer the time of the incident to an officer. An investigation will be conducted at the earliest possible time. Apparently you are not aware that highways are closed in this area because of the storm. We suggest that you park your trains immediately to avoid any further problems."

"I don't believe I'm hearing this," Hank screamed. "I'd suggest that you are a jackass and that I will speak to someone higher up the endless chain of command at your establishment. Go back to sleep, you useless drone, where you'll

175

do the most good. This discussion has been most enlightening." He slammed down the telephone and crashed his fist on the desk.

The dispatcher eyed Hank quizzically. "What's up, Boss?" he asked.

"Just another bureaucrat wallowing in the public trough. He says he has a report that our train tried to run down a highway snowplow and that information will provide the basis for an investigation that will be carried out in due course. He suggests that we 'park' our trains and stopping running down innocent plow trucks on railroad crossings. That's about it."

"I see." Westfield chuckled. "Park your train, eh?" The dispatcher made an obscene gesture. "Park this, Bureau of Public Safety," he added.

∞

The 25-mile sprint from Collier to the next station went without incident. The wind seemed to subside and the visibility was much better. The trainmen in Engine Fifty-Three picked up the lights of the bustling market center of Carroll from a distance of more than a mile, prompting John to remark, "It seems sort of like a hurricane, Rob. The front end slams through and then there's a lull in the action when the eye ...." He paused and stole a glance at Rob, who pursued the thought.

"Ah ... but doesn't the storm pick up on the back side of the eye?" he asked.

"So it does. I guess we're not quite out of the woods yet. ... Probably not by a long shot."

∞

Agent Darrell Woodward of Carroll had placed his chair in such a way that he could look to the north and then to the south through the station's bay windows without moving about the office. Two trains were coming—one from each direction—and both required priority handling. Railroad management needed this meet to occur with precision if the rest of the night's events were to occur in any semblance of order. Trackmen were standing by to help turn switches in the yard, if needed, and Woodward was asked to report to the dispatcher immediately when he saw the first headlight. The planning of the night's work was "a work in progress," according to Henry Terrell, with whom the agent had spoken several times that day.

The headlight of Engine Fifty-Three appeared first and the agent cut in his telegraph key immediately. "Headlight north of Carroll at seven-naught-nine," he wired. The agent turned and looked south to see a second light, and continued: "Headlight to the south. Make that seven-ten."

"Bingo, Carroll." It was Dispatcher Westfield, who added another line to his transmission for all the operators on the circuit who were listening in. "Hot damn. We're getting there, gang."

∞

John Shanahan picked up the headlight of Train Three as he eased into Carroll yard. He notched the throttle back and his locomotive slipped quietly up to the station. The north switch of Track One was just beyond the platform and he noted that Train Three was creeping up to the switch from the south. A couple of trackmen came into view and they, too, approached the switch.

"We're getting close, Rob," he told his companion. "The switch stand is on this side, so you might want to hop off through my door. Looks like you've got some help there if the switch gives you any trouble."

Rob nodded as he pulled up the hood of his parka and climbed down the side ladder. John coasted to a stop about six feet from the switch. As Rob approached the stand, one of the trackmen unlocked it and yanked the handle into the siding position. The brakeman nodded his appreciation, restored the switch lock and signaled a "go-ahead" to John as the northbound passenger train pulled to a stop on the main line.

Shanahan moved the locomotive through the switch and was trying to estimate the place where he would clear the main track when a crash of static and then a voice came over the engine radio. It was the first time he had heard the radio that evening. Since the Gatlin station didn't have a spare handset for his brakeman, he hadn't given radio transmissions a second thought.

"Bon soir, Cinquante-Trois! We'll holler when you're in the clear." It was the distinctive voice of a friend from earlier outings on the railroad.

"Good God, I think I made a wrong turn at the last junction and I'm pulling into Gare St. Lazare in gay Paree. So what is Jack Demers doing out on a night like this?"

"Playing Santa Claus, mon ami. ... Okay, you're looking good. Stop right there. My engineer's going to pull up by the station and let you out from the north end 'cause there's a lot of snow piled ahead of you. He wants to know how you like your new engine."

"I like it, guys, so far. We've got a few miles to go so I'll have to give you all a report later. We almost nailed a highway plow at County Road. Ran us on the flashers."

"Bastard. You can't teach them highway-hoggin' hotshots nothing. ..." The northbound train began to pull away, its two big passenger engines rumbling in the dark. "See you next time. Joyeux Noel!"

"Merry Christmas to you, Jack, and the missus and the kids, and the rest of you guys in the engine."

John got up and stretched and then limped across the cab to watch Number Three's cars go by. There were nine this night; the diner and the coaches lighted and most of the Pullman's quarters darkened for the night. When the observation car of the northbound pulled sufficiently by the switch, Train Three's rear brakeman signaled an "all-clear" to his engineer. Rob reversed the switch again and stepped across the track to signal back up to John, who answered with a couple of short blasts on the air horns. Then he radioed the northbound train.

"We're coming back now, Number Three. When we leave would you be kind enough to give the agent our departure time?"

"We'll take care of it. Good luck, Mr. Shanahan. ... You're doing a good thing, you know." It was the veteran engineer Sam Wibberly of Boundary whose retirement at age sixty-five had been postponed until spring so he could help with the transition.

"You're doing a good thing, too, Sam. Everybody on the railroad appreciates your help right now. I thank you for myself and for my dad, in particular. I hope you guys get in before the weather gets any worse."

"Thanks. You, too. It's a dirty night out there."

Extra Fifty-Three South left Carroll at seven-twenty p.m. and Number Three departed six minutes later. At seven-thirty, the storm roared back with a vengeance, often cutting visibility to scant feet from the locomotives. "I guess the eye has passed, Rob," John said to his brakeman. "Now we get the other side. Heaven help us."

∞

First Trick Operator Harry Hopkins, who had been held over after his regular stint, was seated in the tower at East Junction when he detected the distinctive sound of a train. Bolting from his seat, he pressed his face against a windowpane. "What the hell is going on now?" he said aloud. It was seven-thirty, Number Three was gone and all that was left was the arrival of a locomotive from the north, after which a relief passenger train would depart from the station at the far end of Hill Junction yard. The locomotive was expected in at about eight forty-five and the relief train would leave a short time later. Then he would walk up the hill to his longtime home in the village, forget about the railroad and help arrange last minute details for his family's Christmas.

The storm had abated. He cracked a window and the roar of diesel engines was unmistakable. Suddenly the mystery train bolted into the floodlights that illuminated the east end of the yard when SB&Q trains were soon to arrive and leave. It was a New England Eastern freight and it was backing over the diamond crossing less than five hundred feet from his vantage point. He remembered then that the Eastern had retained rights to some storage tracks behind the main freight yard that were accessible only over the diamond. There were cars in there but they were redlined and were to be scrapped at the site.

According to the sales agreement, he remembered, Eastern was to obtain clearance from the SB&Q tower operator before crossing the diamond. There had been no such request. At a loss as what to do, Hopkins set the north semaphore on the approach to the junction in the stop position and displayed a red signal at the tower. Then he picked up the telephone and called the NEE telegraph operator at Hill station. The phone rang a dozen times but there was no answer.

Instinctively, Harry fumbled for the radio and was about to call an alert when he heard the locomotives rev up. Then he remembered that the Eastern's radio channel was different than SB&Qs. The train was apparently pulling cars from the track, one that had not been plowed at any time in the winter, as he recalled. He leaned over his telegraph instrument and was about to address a query to the dispatcher at Summit when the locomotives burst back across the diamond with a string of freight cars.

Hopkins watched in disbelief as the old cars rocked wildly. Then somewhere deep in the string there was a shrill cracking of metal and a shower of sparks, and the cars began to leave the track. Some rolled over under the yard lights and the crashing of metal against metal was deafening. Other cars vanished beyond the lights' range of illumination but the gut-wrenching sounds continued. A sudden gust of wind shook the old wooden tower, rattling the windowpanes, and his view of the disaster was obliterated in a swirl of snow. The storm was back.

He shook his head as to erase the violent image. Only then did the enormity of the problem sink in. The only entrance to the freight yard by SB&Q was cut off, and the relief train was assembled beyond the wreckage. Hopkins cut in his telegraph key and pecked out the dispatcher's call letters.

The response was immediate. It was Dispatcher Westfield and he was in his usual jovial mood: "Well, if it isn't East Junction Tower. Getting bored, Harry? Relax. We're gonna have some activity for you in just a bit."

Oh boy, Hopkins thought, how do I do this? He tapped his fingers in Morse code on the desktop, framed a message in his mind and hoped Henry Terrell would be up for more bad news. Then he began: "Emergency. Hill Junction. This is bad. NEE freight derailed on main track diamond. Cars on the ground as far as I can see. Access blocked...."

Chapter 26: Red Board at Crawford

The engineer of Extra Fifty-Three South was getting uneasy. Only fifty miles into the run to Hill Junction, John Shanahan had been forced to reduce his train speed to 25 miles per hour and even that was risky because any semblance of visibility was gone. He checked his watch, which was now suspended by its fob on a hook above the throttle-housing console. It was seven thirty-one—no, seven thirty-two—and his projected arrival time at Hill Junction was being pushed back with each passing mile. The bus with the students would surely be there soon and he still had forty miles to go.

∞

The disheveled Henry Terrell stared blankly across the dispatching office. He had read the telegraph message from East Junction Tower as it clattered across the wire. Dispatcher Bill Westfield put his head down on the desk and there was silence, except for the wind, which howled around the eaves. Minutes passed before Hank spoke.

"Okay. Now what?" he pondered aloud. Westfield pushed his chair back, stood up and walked to a window. "Looks like snow, Boss," he observed without really looking.

"Uh huh," Hank replied. "I suppose so. Well, I guess we better notify Extra Fifty-Three about what happened at the junction. ... What's that young fellow's name; you know, the operator we called in at Crawford? How's he on the wire?"

Westfield returned to his desk. "Will Smith. Crackerjack operator. Great fist. He drove up from East Junction this afternoon because his work was done there. He was tickled to catch a trick at Crawford, even for one night. He comes from Eagle River. Can you imagine? Must have driven halfway across the state to pick up work at the tower."

"Yeah, at least. I remember him. He's a good man. Okay. Tell Will to get his order board out. Then give him a message for John. Tell him what you can, and make sure that engine doesn't go barreling into the yard at Hill. Stop him at the north semaphore above East Junction for sure. I've got to make some telephone calls to our people down there. Oh, and for God's sake, answer Harry at the tower, and thank him ... for the news."

"Got it," the dispatcher responded and cut his key into the telegraph circuit.

∞

John Shanahan had reduced his speed to 20 miles an hour and was straining to find a landmark somewhere in the whirling dervish of snow. He was able to pick up mileposts but that was all. He had passed the last County Road crossing and there were no more major hazards until East Junction Tower. For that, he was thankful.

180

∞

Relief operator Will Smith was stuffing paper into the cracks around the operator's bay at Crawford station to keep the snow out. He had reported for duty at 5:30 p.m. to be on hand for the arrival of Train Three, which disembarked several passengers for the tiny village about a half-mile away. The telegraph circuit had been unusually busy but there were no calls for his station so he tuned out the traffic and picked up on the paper-stuffing project. Before long it was apparent that the old station was no match for the driving snow that filtered through cracks and crevices. He gave up and was about to stoke the coal stove again when his station call, CR, rattled across the telegraph wire. He responded quickly: "CR here, Will Smith."

The dispatcher's message was terse: "Opr CR. Display order board ASAP. Be sure to stop light engine southbound. WLW."

Smith grabbed the order board handle and yanked it into the stop position. The board creaked loudly at first, caught up briefly and then slammed into position. The operator sensed the urgency of the moment and tapped out his response: "SD [signal displayed] at CR." After ascertaining that the board was indeed in the correct position and that the light atop the device was illuminated, he settled in to watch for the locomotive.

∞

Rob Rankin called the signal at Crawford, a tumbledown, long vacant wayside station 30 miles north of Hill Junction. "Red board at Crawford," he yelled.

"Red board? At Crawford? I thought that place was closed," John responded in disbelief, remembering the building. "Yep, so it is, a red board," he added after standing up to take a closer look. "What now, do you suppose?" He cut the throttle and made a sharp brake application. Snow that was piling up on the nose of the locomotive was beginning to limit his range of vision. There was probably a lot more on the front catwalk above the coupler. We'll have to knock off the snow when we stop, he thought, as he sounded the air horns in response to the station signal.

A minute or so later the engine pulled to a stop by a narrow walkway that had been shoveled from the track to the front door. There was no platform and the structure appeared about ready to fall down. The operator was barely visible hunched over the telegraph behind a windowpane that had been taped together. It was seven fifty-nine p.m.

"Place looks kind of dilapidated," Rob offered.

"Totally uninhabitable," the engineer said. "Well, you sit tight and I'll find out what's up." Then he grimaced and added, "I don't like the looks of this. Something has gone wrong, I think."

"I'd knock some of that snow off the engine, if you'd like," Rob offered. "It's kind of piling up on the nose."

"I'd appreciate that," John said as he opened the fireman's side door and let in a swirl of snow. "Oh, yeah," he yelled. "Toss my cane down, will you, after I fall off the ladder." He grinned and winked at the brakeman as he disappeared from Rob's view.

John made it down to the third step before reaching the bank of snow rolled up by his locomotive. He stepped back from the ladder tentatively, turned and sat down on the bank and slid to the walkway. Rob was at his side immediately, helped him up and passed John his cane. Retrieving his shovel, the brakeman said, "I'll get to work now," and began digging savagely at the snow on the front of the locomotive.

The telegrapher came to the door just as John reached for the knob. "Hi, Mr. Shanahan," Smith said. "It's good to see you again, but not under very good circumstances, I guess. Come in, please and take a seat. I have the dispatching office on the telephone and they need to talk to you."

"I think I'd rather just sit and talk to you, Will, but business before pleasure." John pulled up a chair and took the phone. "Hello, this is Shanahan the Younger calling in from the worst looking railroad station he has ever seen. When is this company going to loosen the purse strings and put some money into this thing, anyway?"

"This is Henry Terrell, purse-string holder and manager of sundry expenses extraordinaire," the voice at the other end of the line snapped. "I do my best, and all I get are complaints from ungrateful people." There was a short silence and then the trademark Terrell chuckle, followed by a burst of laughter. "Ah, but it's good to hear your voice, son; so good, especially on a night like this. I need to give you some updates on the situation and then if you want to find a pair of snowshoes and mush off into the night, never to return to this unbelievable place, I won't think the less of you."

John laughed heartily. "All right, Hank, I know it's bad but I'll listen, at least until I can find someone with a spare pair of snowshoes."

The engineer listened for the next ten minutes, uttering only an occasional "ah ha," "you don't say," "sure," "sounds good," "dumb enough to work," "really" and "hard to believe, isn't it?" In the background, Will hunched over the telegraph and copied a series of transmissions for Extra Fifty-Three.

The conversation ended with a salty remark about the storm. Then he added: "We'll see you when we get there, which probably will be next spring." He hung up the phone and peered at Will, who apparently had completed his duties for the moment. "Well, that's a fine kettle of fish. ... So, Will, you were planning to stay in this hovel overnight because you knew you could never get out of here in the storm and the dispatcher talked you into coming along with us so you wouldn't freeze to death in the night? That about it?"

"Yes, sir, Mr. Shanahan," Will said. "It's all there in the messages to you and Rob Rankin. They want me to report your estimated departure time south, and then get on with you and help out around the train down there. On the way back, they want you to stop here long enough for me to wire in your time and then go north with you to Summit. I'll come back after the storm to get my car. It wasn't my idea to inconvenience you."

John got up and clasped Will's shoulder. "We'll be delighted to have you. I understand they want you to ride in the coach on the way back and attend to the needs of the passengers. That's for pay, I might add; brakeman's pay, and, if we don't get going pretty quick that could net you a bundle. So gather up your stuff, give them our out time just before you close the door, and climb aboard."

John pulled on his jacket, gathered up his messages and stepped outside. Then he looked back in and added, "You'll probably want to clear the order board, or if you'd rather, we could just set fire to this place and let it burn down as we dash off."

"I think I should clear the board, Mr. Shanahan."

Extra Fifty-Three South was reported out of Crawford at eight-fifteen. Once under way, John briefed Rob Rankin on what he had learned. A New England Eastern freight train en route to Sunbury had been instructed to pull a string of boxcars destined for scrapping from an unplowed siding across the SB&Q main line at Hill Junction. There had been a derailment on the way out, the diamond crossing had been destroyed and some of the cars had been scattered onto the adjoining railroad's tracks.

To make matters worse, the NEE train crew, which was in danger of violating the 16-hour work rule, called in from a phone on their mainline and was told to proceed with haste to their home terminal with only their engines and the cars that were still on the track. They pulled out too fast and a second car derailed and fouled the east leg of the wye behind East Junction Tower. That made it impossible for the SB&Q relief train's crew to make even a circuitous detour around the wreck via New England Eastern track.

Henry Terrell had contacted conductor Joe Francis, who was vacationing at his family home near Sunbury. Joe made his way to Hill Junction by highway to help organize "Plan B," as the railroad manager called it. Francis knew there was a vintage combination coach-mail car in the back shop behind the engine house that was in excellent condition. A track, unused since the previous summer, led from East Junction Tower to the shop, a distance of more than half a mile.

"Now the deal is," John went on, "the railroad has rounded up a bulldozer from the Hill Junction Village Public Works Department and it is working right now on clearing snow off the track. A passel of townspeople—I mean a real army of them—showed up with their own hand shovels, along with all the railroad men they could find, even retirees, to get the flanges dug out after the dozer works it over. And SB&Q's shop crew and hostlers are there to see that the coach is shipshape.

"Our job will be to nose in on the back track after the switch is spiked over and fetch the coach from the shop," John continued. "They hope to have things ready about the time we get there … if we ever do. The students haven't shown up yet but the main road is still open south of Hill Junction, according to the bus driver who called in from a place about an hour-and-a-half away. That's under normal driving conditions, so it could be somewhat longer.

183

"Anyway, it looks like we'll load our passengers at East Junction Tower, after we get the coach out of the shop, and then we'll beat it back to Summit. How's that sound? Any thoughts on the plan, either of you?"

Rob looked uneasy.

"Something's on your mind, Robbie. Do you see a problem, aside from derailing on the back track, or not fitting through the old shop door or even getting the door open? How about if we get started on the way back and the station at Crawford decides to fall over just before we get there? Those things struck me as distinct possibilities."

"Ah, well, I was thinking about how we can turn the engine around to go back. If we can't use the wye and we can't reach the turntable and the train that's ready now can't get out, well ... I was just wondering about that, that's all."

"That's a good question," John said. "And the answer is that we can't turn the engine, not at Hill Junction. We'll have to run in reverse to the wye at Gatlin and turn there. All the way to Gatlin. ... All ninety miles in reverse ... with an old coach car on the rear and forty-five passengers inside. ... With the wind blowing in our faces. That's about it."

The engineer shrugged his shoulders and directed his full attention to the track ahead. "We'll give it our best shot, that's all we can do," he said as he notched the throttle ahead. He knew he was running completely blind but at least he had a handle on the track structure and the potential hazards that were ahead.

∞

At Summit, Henry Terrell had still another duty to carry out, the one that he had dreaded all day. He went into his private office, settled at his desk and poured a drink. He thought for several minutes about the words he would use, and then picked up the phone and asked that a call be placed to a party in the village at Quarry.

Chapter 27: The Mystery Coach

Extra Fifty-Three South limped by the south mainline switch of the sidings at Halfway at twenty miles an hour. It was nine-fifteen by John Shanahan's pocket watch, so they were at least half-an-hour overdue at Hill Junction. But he knew the next section of track particularly well and felt confident.

"All right, guys," he yelled to his companions. "Enough of this pokey-poke stuff. We're halfway to the equator here and I'm ready for a stroll on the beach. I want you two to pretend that you have X-ray vision when it comes to snow and let out a yell if you see anything in the way. I'm going to see what this engine can do."

With that, he drove the throttle forward. The branch-liner responded amazingly well, considering the weight of the snow it was pushing, and accelerated rapidly. Visibility was zero and the occupants of the cab could not see beyond the windshield. John tried to keep track of his location by looking down at mileposts as they whizzed by. At Milepost 9, the speed recorder inched past fifty-five and was locked on fifty-eight before the engineer eased off.

∞

Harry Hopkins' eyes were fixed on the clock in the tower at East Junction. It was only nine twenty-five and everything was set for the relief engine to attempt a run down the back track to the car shop behind Hill Junction yard where the combination mail and coach awaited pickup. An all-out effort by railroaders and community volunteers had resulted in the opening of the track and the readying of the passenger car for service. Twin coal stoves in the car had been checked, fueled and fired; all sixty seats in fifteen identical rows dusted; water chests iced and various machinery lubricants topped off. The gaslights were turned on and vintage kerosene train markers affixed to the rear of the car, which would be the mail section because the car could not be turned that night.

To top off their work, the villagers had rounded up an array of personal Christmas decorations—strings of garland, a number of ornaments, artificial icicles and lights that, even without electrical power, twinkled from the illumination of the car's gaslight fixtures. Balsam wreathes were hung on the insides of the coach doors.

The section crew was completing the last order of business, that of disassembling rods to the disabled switch stand that connected the main line with the back track. Once disconnected, the switch points were pried over with lining bars, held in place by the foreman, and spiked there by a pair of trackmen. When the job was done, the foreman stepped to the base of the tower and waved a clearance to the telegrapher.

Sandwiches and drinks provided by the Hill Junction Ladies Aid Society—enough for more than 50 people—were laid out on makeshift tables in the waiting room attached to the tower, and just across the track at East Tower Lunch—a railroaders' hangout—giant kettles of soup simmered in the kitchen. Many of the volunteer track cleaners gathered there, in the waiting room and in autos along the highway. Most roads in the area were snowbound by that time but the plowman for Hill Junction Public Works was still on the job, sweeping through the village every half hour or so.

"Plan B" was in place. Extra Fifty-Three would move directly up to the station, log in, pick up Conductor Joe Francis, Track Foreman Thomas Stacey and two trackmen and move onto the back track at restricted speed and only at the direction of the foreman. The engine would move up to the door of the back shop and stop. Shop workers would attach a cable between the couplings of the coach and the engine. The engineer would reverse the throttle and inch the coach out through the sagging car barn door, after which the cable would be disconnected and the engine and coach coupled. An inspection would be made and then the train would be returned to the tower. By then, the Hill Junction Public Works snowplow would have been dispatched on the main state highway leading south to meet and escort the bus carrying the students to their train. That bus should be in the station parking lot at train departure time.

It was all so simple but so fraught with uncertainty, Harry thought. The snow was still falling and the wind was blowing a gale and the efforts expended so far would be for naught before long. "C'mon, John Shanahan, notch that engine up a bit. Time's running out," Hopkins said aloud as he peered out into the savage storm.

∞

Still streaking along the mainline south of Halfway, Engine Fifty-Thee roared by mileposts five, four and three. "Okay, party's over!" engineer announced, and snapped the throttle into the slower speed zone. "Try to get a fix on the north semaphore at East Junction. We're supposed to stop there and call in."

"I see a light, I think," Rob called out in short order. "Yes. It's red. The semaphore is in the stop position."

"Very good. Hang on tight because I'm going to take a big bite on the brakes." With that, John made a heavy reduction and the locomotive shuddered violently when the brake shoes slammed against the wheels. The engine skidded on the rails and slid to a stop two rail-lengths beyond the semaphore.

∞

Joe Francis, who was seated in a swivel chair in the background of the tower, pulled his pocket watch from his vest, studied it intently and then placed it back in the vest pocket. "Extra Fifty-Three will be calling from the semaphore at nine thirty-one, Harry," he offered and said nothing more.

Harry nodded, never a man to doubt the word of Joe Francis. He focused on the tower clock and watched the second hand click past the numerals five, six and seven. When it reached eight, he reached across his desk expectantly. The second hand reached nine, and then ten. He clasped the handset. At thirty minutes and fifty-four seconds past nine o'clock in the evening the radio buzzer sounded twice in East Junction Tower.

"Hello," Harry yelled. "That you, Fifty-Three?"

"Fifty-Three's at the semaphore." It was John Shanahan. "How's about letting us come in?"

"You bet, John!" Harry exclaimed. "Come in slow and easy and pull right up to the station platform. There are a lot of people gathered here, so be careful. Joe Francis and some section men are going to get on and then we want you to fetch the coach. We'll talk about other details later."

"Got that. Coming in."

Harry went to the stairwell leading to the station waiting room and yelled, "Be alert, folks! Extra Fifty-Three is coming in. Stand back 'cause they have to go directly to the shop." Then he eyed Joe Francis. "All right, Joe. How the hell did you know they'd call in at nine thirty-one?"

Sitting straight in his chair and maintaining a stony countenance, Joe responded, "Indian know many mysteries. White man not understand Indian. Too bad for white man."

Harry burst into a gale of laughter. After regaining his composure and remembering an important duty, the night operator scurried to his telegraph instruments. "Good God, I've got to get on the wire to Summit!" he yelped. "Henry Terrell needs a little good news for a change. ... Oh, by the way, Chief, Indian is man of great wisdom. Gotta admit that."

Joe chuckled as he arose from the chair. He wasn't about to explain that he knew how the locomotive engineers running the mainline between Crawford and East Junction Tower managed their forward speed. Joe knew where they ran slowly, and where, like on the eight miles between Halfway and the Hill Junction semaphore, they tested their engine's mettle. Then he factored in the extreme weather and the fact that John's engine had no train. That, added to the formula, along with that engineer's remarkable ability to handle a locomotive, made it a simple mental calculation. It was really no great mystery, he thought, and chuckled again.

∞

The branch-line diesel locomotive was down to fifteen miles an hour and wallowing through snow on the approach to the tower at East Junction. Engineer John Shanahan was still trying to envision the scene ahead, particularly the scattered wreckage of Eastern's train that had snarled SB&Q's efforts to pull off an eleventh-hour passenger rescue mission. He thought of how Henry Terrell had worked so hard to get every employee home on Christmas Eve and how disappointed he must have been when the news came in about the bus delay, and worse, when he learned of the other railroad's derailment.

Hank had deserved better than that, he thought, and vowed that when he got back to Summit he would have a few kind words for his friend. And he would call his father in Chicago to explain how much work Hank had put into the Christmas shutdown.

∞

Although his night's work was to be that of a passenger train conductor, Francis had decided to forego the standard uniform and wear basic work clothes instead. A run on a stormy night with an unusual passenger train likely would involve some outside work, the down and dirty kind normally encountered on a freight train.

Joe pulled on an old sheepskin jacket and his railroader's winter cap. A scarf followed, and that was wrapped around his shoulders and tucked into the collar of the coat. A sheaf of railroad messages, pre-folded precisely to fit the dimensions of his personal time book, was inserted inside the back cover. The book went into the bib pocket of his neatly pressed Whitefield railroad overalls, which were worn over woolen long johns, a flannel shirt and heavy trousers, and a vest not unlike the one that went with his passenger train uniform. His SB&Q train timetable fit nicely behind the time book. The bottoms of his overall legs were fitted snugly over the tops of his insulated heavy-duty footwear and secured there with wide elasticized straps made and distributed by the railroad.

The conductor patted various pockets to ascertain that his railroad keys were readily available and that his pocket watch was deep in his vest pocket and its fob attached to a chain that, in turn, was attached to a vest button. His wallet was zipped in an inside pocket. He had already checked the traveling case that contained his conductor's ticket punch, various railroad forms pertaining to passenger services, his railroad rulebook and half a dozen more implements of his trade. He noted that his railroad lantern was at hand, along with his pack basket and the snowshoes that he had made long ago and carried religiously from the first day of November until the fifteenth day of April.

He had cut the ash tree and pounded out the strips of wood fiber that he had woven into the pack and the lunch basket carried through a lifetime of railroad employment. Inside the latter and designed to fit, were foods in jars and packages, dining utensils and Thermos bottles of varying size.

Joe Francis was ready to go to work. No railroader in the North Country was ever better prepared than Joe. He stepped up to the bank of windows on the north side of the tower when Engine Fifty-Three crept into view.

"Mother of God," he muttered, shaking his head in disbelief. The nose of the diesel unit was mounded in snow nearly to the top of the windshield and a swirling drift still in the making extended the length of the engine's roof. Icicles hung in wild profusion from the side of the locomotive that he could see. Almost a quarter of the locomotive seemed to be below the snow line and he knew that spelled trouble. It was more the scene of a moving mound of snow—the makings of an avalanche, perhaps—than a railroad diesel.

He picked up his gear, nodded to Harry Hopkins and descended the stairwell to the waiting room. He knew the improbabilities of this Christmas Eve venture better than anyone. His official workday was about to begin, and his destination, the station at Summit, was one hundred and eighty miles away.

∞

John stopped the locomotive and set the engine brakes. The crowd that had gathered cheered briefly and stepped back quickly to let Joe through. Rob climbed down to help with the conductor's gear and Will reached out to take the luggage aboard. Several track workers tackled the snow clinging to the nose of the engine.

Joe renewed acquaintances with the crew before reviewing the proposed move to the car shop. "I'm going up front on the platform with Tom Stacey, the foreman, and a couple of his men. I'll be in front of you, John, so you can see my signals directly. The track is old and in serious need of repair. We'll stop when we get a rail-length or so from the car shop. That's where we hook up a cable through the couplers. Everybody okay on that?"

"We're okay on that," John said. His companions nodded their agreement. "Very good," the conductor said as the snow-removal crew up front pried loose a huge chunk of packed snow. It slid noisily to the side and crashed on the station platform. "Rough trip?" he queried quietly of John.

"Hard haul. One heck of a storm, isn't it?"

"Worst I've seen in quite a while. Damned wind …" Joe broke off the conversation when the track foreman tapped on the windshield to indicate that the shoveling was done. "Well, let's do it, boys," Joe said, turning abruptly to the fireman's door. He opened it and descended the ladder two steps at a time.

"Joe's the best in the business, guys," John said. "Watch him, listen to what he says and do it, and you can't go wrong. … And look, for me, always be safe out there. I won't move this engine, ever, unless I can see each one of you, or your lantern, on the ground or on the cars. I have to know where everyone is all the time or I just sit there."

∞

J.P. Shanahan paced the great room in the estate at Seven Pines. The wind was howling through the hills around the town of Quarry. Apparently it was going to be an ugly storm—an epic nor'easter that would isolate town from town, house from house and family members from one another. It seemed that the only wheels still turning in the North Country belonged to J.P.'s Summit, Bolton and Quarry Railroad.

The wheels were those of Train Three, running north of Gatlin, and Extra Fifty-Three, just now fetching a coach car of improbable age from a track of improbable condition to bring forty-five stranded passengers more than one hundred and eighty miles through the brunt of the storm. To accomplish that with a locomotive he could not turn, the engineer would have to run in reverse for ninety miles.

And that task fell to a Shanahan, his flesh and blood, upon whose engine-driving skills those passengers, all high school students and their chaperones, depended. It would be a daunting task for the young man who had already

189

worked almost thirty-eight hours of the past fifty-four. Rest was many hours away.

It was nine forty-five in the evening and J.P's son, Engineer John Shanahan III, should be coupled onto the coach, about to pull it gingerly back to the main line at East Tower. If everything went as planned, they would be en route by ten-thirty, maybe later, the senior Shanahan figured. Or they could derail on the way out of the car barn and all would be for naught. There was no backup plan; all options had been exhausted.

He was angry with management at New England Eastern for having chosen such a night to move scrap freight cars across his railroad's tracks and derailing them in the process. "I can't imagine such stupidity," he had remarked to Ramon Martinez earlier.

The coach came to mind as J.P. envisioned the makeup of the train that had become the focus of the entire railroad. From the description Hank Terrell had given him, he was certain it was not his, and local officials of the New England Eastern assured him that it was not the property of that railroad. It was believed to have come in on a NEE freight train with no instructions as to where it should go, so it was placed in the car barn at the rear of the shop and forgotten. It had been there at least two years, probably more, but no queries were ever received from anyone claiming ownership.

Furthermore, it had no exterior markings designating ownership or car number. The employees hired by SB&Q to staff the shop after the sale inspected the car, even putting it on an air compressor to check the braking system. It passed with flying colors.

J.P. was annoyed that he could not come up with an answer to the mystery. He spied Ramon lying on the sofa. "Ramon, you're supposed to know a lot about passenger equipment," he said. "How do you move a coach car from here to there on a freight train and not know anything about the car?"

Ramon sat up and rubbed his eyes. "Dunno," he grunted. Then he yawned. "I suppose you just back into a siding somewhere and pull a block of cars out. Along comes a coach car mixed in with the boxcars and flat cars and pulp cars. You're the conductor, and you're tired and you're running out of time and you need to get where you're going so you just sort of neglect to note that you have an odd car in the mix."

"But what if the car is kind of fancy and doesn't have a number painted on the side?"

"All the more reason to pretend you didn't see it," Ramon reasoned. "But wouldn't you be curious, Ramon?" J.P. persisted. "Come on, I would be curious."

"Maybe not, Boss. If you'd been wallowing around in the snow all day and you were wet and cold and pretty well had it with the railroad business, you'd probably just want to go home and let somebody else figure it out. That figuring would have to come from someone making the really big bucks in management, maybe even the owner of the railroad."

J.P. burst into laughter and nodded in agreement. "Yep. I see your point. J.P. has to do the research. You're right about the train crews handling the car. That must be what happened, and as we say at the board meetings when all the brilliant minds plot strategy to outfox the federal inspectors, the paper trail ends in the boardroom. In the meantime, it looks like we have an addition to our collection of antique cars."

"Like that's something we really need," Ramon muttered under his breath. He had met the Shanahans—J.P. and Alicia—at Summit Regional Airport at midday on Thursday and driven them directly to Quarry. It was to be a quiet weeklong getaway, an unannounced reunion with their son who had spent the last Christmas in an Army hospital, too severely wounded to have visitors. They had vowed to make this Christmas a truly memorable one. Ramon had cut a giant balsam fir for a tree and assembled a dazzling array of ornaments and lights, both indoor and out. Hours had gone into the decorating and the place was ready just before the call from Henry Terrell.

Hank explained the situation in detail and J.P. reassured his railroad manager that he had handled the matter skillfully. The manager promised that the dispatching office would stay in touch with J.P. until the train arrived at Summit. Reports on the progress of both passenger trains would be given to radio station WSUM at Summit and to other media outlets as requested. "We need to be straight with everybody," Hank said. "The public, which is counting on us tonight, needs to know the situation all the time."

As the evening progressed it became evident that the whole North Country transportation system—railroads and highways—would be impacted by the storm so they agreed that the relief train should continue through to Quarry. There were eleven students on board whose homes were along the line, and J.P. knew there would be no way for the snowed-in residents to travel to Summit station to pick up their kin.

Hank said that if he had any qualified employees to man plow trains, he would dispatch them out of Summit to aid both trains. J.P. endorsed the idea but the manager was able to round up only three at Summit who would be rested— Engineer Bill Travers and Trainmen Carl Reardon and Stan Larrabee, who had tied up Number One, The Northern Express, at 4:30 p.m. at Quarry and driven out to Summit to spend Christmas there. Bill would be at Emma Cummings' house and Stan and Carl both lived just outside the town. Standby plowman Elmer Russell, who lived near the station and worked part time in the car shop also volunteered to work if needed.

The railroad officials decided that the plow train would report at Summit at twelve-thirty a.m. and run north ahead of Number Three as far as possible. That would provide greater assurance that the connection with the Canadian Eastern would be protected.

There could be no assistance for Extra Fifty-Three, so its crew would have to break track on its own. "When they get to Summit, Hank, look them all right in the eyes," J.P. had said. "If they look too beaten out tie up the damned train and book those passengers that can't get home in the best hotel in town. The rooms and eats will be on the railroad. They deserve nothing less."

Chapter 28: Godspeed, Fifty-Three

The air brake test was completed and railroad workers assisting in the movement of the passenger car from storage had stepped aside, their Christmas Eve duties completed. For want of an immediate storage place, they had coiled the cable specially cut for the tow from the car shop, and placed it in the mail section of the coach.

Brakeman Rob Rankin waved a go-ahead signal from the rear of the coach, and Will Smith waved another from the front. Engineer John Shanahan acknowledged the brakemen with two spaced blasts of the air horns.

John had settled into an awkward position in the engineer's seat, facing the fireman's side of the diesel, and, as he had expected would happen, fumbled for the controls. He was left-handed and could grasp all of the operating controls under normal operating conditions without looking. Now his reach was different. Everything was wrong about groping with his right hand to do what he could do so easily with his left. The seat was no longer comfortable because he had no place to prop his leg when it began to ache. He should find something to rectify that problem before leaving the junction.

In addition, he had to give up his wide-view windshield for a deep but narrow window that provided a limited view of the track ahead. Still, the rear-facing window was one of the unique trademarks of the branch line diesel and other road engines used in local service as it allowed an engineer at least a bit of visibility without having to stick his head out the side window.

In a way, he supposed, this was like running steam locomotives, in which the engineer's forward view was alongside the engine's boiler and not in front of the power source as was the case with many diesel engines. This one had been fashioned by its builders in a way that enhanced visibility for backup moves by the beveling of the top of the unit instead of adopting what rail aficionados had started calling the "covered-wagon" style of the Model F3s. Only it wasn't like a steam engine at all, he mused. He was not on the engineer's traditional right-hand side of the locomotive, and that was disconcerting.

But what difference would it matter? It was the darkest of nights and a blizzard was raging. He couldn't see anything outside and, at best, he was many hours from his destination. He was nagged by the notion that it would be better to call off the mission and try to find shelter for the passengers and crew. They could get on with the trip later, after the storm had run its course.

But this was the North Country and no tradition was deeper rooted than that of families getting together on Christmas.

John rubbed his eyes and shook his head as if to clear the cobwebs of doubt that were cluttering his thinking. He knew he was too tired to be responsible for passengers. The excitement of being engaged on this night in his chosen profession, the only work he ever enjoyed, was fading fast. He knew fatigue was taking its toll and this night's work was only beginning. This wasn't going to be an easy run, no piece of cake, he realized, as he released the brakes and inched the throttle forward. It would have been better if he had not answered the telephone hours earlier in Pleasant Valley.

Remembering a duty he needed to fulfill, he reached awkwardly for the radio but knocked the receiver off the hook. After nearly falling face down on the cabin floor in his effort to retrieve it, he called East Junction: "Fifty-Three coming out."

"That's good news," Harry Hopkins responded. "And you'll be glad to know the students are here and chowing down in the station."

"Good," the engineer answered, but his mind was elsewhere. "Harry, do you happen to have a foot stool around there?"

"Foot stool? Ah, gee, I don't think so." The operator was clearly puzzled. "Should I ask you what for?"

"I was just thinking of some kind of a prop upon which to rest my gimpy leg. It gets cramped up easy on nights like this and the ache raises hell with my sleeping once I kick the engine into overdrive. ... Aw, forget it, we've got too much to do; too little time."

"I'm working on the foot stool. Everything else is falling into place." Harry sounded confident. "I'll have something when you get here. Nobody on the railroad wants to deprive an engineer of his sleep, especially on a night like this. ... You fellows pull up to the station platform while I get to work on this."

∞

Henry Terrell sat at a desk in the dispatching office listening to the wind as it whipped savagely at the station. Bill Westfield was still at his telegraph console, hours beyond his shift, waiting for word of the progress of the two trains still running on the railroad system. Later there would be a third, an extra with a snowplow and a pickup crew that would depart ahead of Number Three at Summit to break trail north toward Boundary. They had hoped to put together a fourth, one that would leave Boundary with a plow to meet the northbound plow train somewhere along the way, but there were no qualified workers available.

Number Three was slogging north, its two passenger train diesels producing 4,000 horsepower, enough to drag their heavy load through the drifts encountered up to that point. They were expected to pass Blackwater station soon, and Westfield anticipated confirmation momentarily. Their progress was the priority of the hour, but with word from the Canadian Eastern that their connections were running some three hours late, the window for delays had widened considerably.

It was ten o'clock and the real concern was for Passenger Extra Fifty-Three, expected out of Hill Junction by at least ten-thirty. They had no deadline now. All Hank hoped for was safe passage and an arrival in the North County by Christmas Day.

But the manager of operations and the dispatcher knew that was a tall order. The engineer, the man least rested of all the company's operating employees, would have to run in the teeth of the storm not to Summit, as originally planned, but another 22 miles to Quarry. The Quarry line was not plowed nor had a train passed over it since the storm started. It would be heavily drifted by the time the extra arrived.

The condition of that line was something to be dealt with later.

Heavy snow had swept in from the sea in the late afternoon, engulfing most of the state as it moved from south to north. From what the dispatching office could learn from station agents and other sources, the heaviest snow bands were moving into the North Country slowly but with increased intensity. The storm still had not abated in the south.

The telegraph began to clatter. It was Agent Molly McCaslin, on duty at Blackwater as always. The message was simple: "Blackwater. Number Three, Engine Five-One-One by Blackwater at ten twenty-two p.m. McCaslin, Operator."

The dispatcher responded: "Got that, Molly, ten twenty-two. Sit tight and don't worry. Fifty-Three's almost ready to go at Hill." Westfield knew that Annie McCaslin, Molly's daughter, was on that train.

∞

Harry bounded out of the station at East Junction as Engine Fifty-Three crept to a stop. Joe Francis stepped off the engine and met him on the platform. "What do you have, Harry? Looks like a miniature stepladder. Indian not understand this mystery."

"Too bad for Indian!" Harry whooped. "Come with me. We need to make your engineer comfortable." The telegraph operator climbed to the cabin with the object under his arm and beckoned for the conductor to follow. Harry approached John, who was entering information in his time book. The telegrapher unfolded the wooden contraption, which appeared to be some kind of a two-step ladder or stepstool. The cushion of a small office chair fell out. "All right, Mr. Engineer, heist your leg and we'll slide your ottoman into place."

John grasped his leg and pulled. "I think somebody's pulling my leg," was his attempt at humor but there was no response. He needed to try something else. "So what the hell is an ottoman? I thought that was one of those barbarians back in the Middle Ages." Harry ignored him, placed the cushion atop the stool and pushed it into place. "There, try it out," he said.

The engineer shimmied around in the seat. "Son of a gun. By Jove, I think we've got it! Thanks. A real ottoman. This is what I've needed all along. Thanks!"

Harry grinned. "Anytime. Now we need to board some passengers pronto. After you, Joe. Look like white man solve big mystery. No?"

Joe chuckled. "Look like white man from big tower in sky also wise. Must be Indian in disguise."

John stepped across the cab and watched the students and their chaperones file out of the station and into the illumination of the platform lights. It was

195

obvious they had been on a tiring bus trip and there was more to go. Some seemed too young to be high school juniors. The seniors, on the other hand, stood out as mature young men and women. He stepped back into the shadows of the cab, not wishing to attract attention and was about to return to his seat when a man called from the platform.

He looked out. It was the bus driver. "Are you Mr. Shanahan?" he asked.

"I am, but just call me John," he answered. "Hold on a sec. I'm coming down." He stepped awkwardly through the cab door and hobbled down the steps. The driver came forward to offer a hand.

"I'm Tom Watson of Watson Bus Tours," he said. "I just wanted to say how sorry I am for getting here at this hour. It was late when we got the call, and the driving, man, I've been at it a long time and it's never been like this. Never."

"Well, I certainly want to thank you for the effort—for myself, and for my father. He owns the railroad, you probably know, and this means a lot to him, you pitching in and all, I can assure you."

"Thanks, John. And you're the soldier the kids talked so much about all the way up. They kept saying that John Shanahan was coming to get them and that seemed to indicate that the railroad was making a special effort with the best people they had. I guess most of the kids have railroad connections up there in the north. We've all read about you in the papers, even down our way."

Watson leaned closer to John as the wind whistled around the train. "My son's one of the soldiers that got out of North Korea ... down that road to the seaport. He remembered the firefights along the road and figured it was guys like you that got them out. He was wounded, too, and is still recovering at home. ... I'm honored to meet you, Lieutenant Shanahan."

John pulled out his time book, tore out a page and asked: "What's your son's name, Tom?"

"Thomas Watson, Junior. Just Tommy. That's what everybody calls him."

John wrote a message on the time sheet, re-read it and passed it to the bus driver. "Would you give this to Tommy? Read it, please, and forgive the wobbly writing."

Watson read the note: "From One Soldier to Another. Tommy, I just met your dad, who has provided his outstanding driving skills to help some passengers get to their destinations in the North Country. He tells me you went through Koto-ri just before Christmas last year. I was there, too, with the guys trying to guard the road to Hungnam and we got pounded on pretty good. I was wounded and it took a while to get back on my feet. I will be the engineer on the train that takes your father's passengers the rest of the way home. I wish you the best Christmas ever. I will think of you and all our comrades in my prayers. John P. Shanahan III."

The bus driver folded the paper carefully and tucked it into an inside pocket in his uniform jacket. He blinked back tears and cleared his throat. "Thank you," he said hoarsely. "My son will cherish this always. ... Always, he will. ... He's that kind of kid. ... You're kind, just like the kids on the bus said."

Watson retreated to the station door, opened it, paused and said, "I wish you the best on the trip north. The very best." He went inside quickly and closed the door. John was about to climb back into the locomotive when Joe Francis motioned for him to come to the front stairwell of the passenger coach.

"John, we're loaded and ready to go," he said. "We're going through to Quarry because Hank doesn't figure we should make this effort and then leave a few kids from down on the Eden line stranded that close to home. Are you up for another twenty-two miles?"

"Yes. We need to finish the job right."

"Good. I'm going to talk to the passengers now. I need to tell them what to expect as we go along. I'd appreciate you being there."

"Sure. I wanted to get a look at this coach from the inside. It's got a really nice exterior. Well maintained, I would say. It must belong to the Eastern, which seems a little out of character for them."

Joe shook his head. "Eastern had it in the shop but nobody seems to know why, or who owns it."

"What about the markings? Must have a company name somewhere."

"No name, no number. Nothing."

"So we're borrowing it without permission of the owner?"

"Indian know nothing, hear nothing, say nothing."

John grinned. "Okay. Well, let's climb aboard and let white guy hear Indian explain logic of plunging little train with stolen equipment into heap big snow-storm. This I gotta hear."

Joe climbed the stairwell and stood by the coach door. "It's one of those wonderful mysteries of Christmas, John. A gift, one might say. Nothing that needs any explanation." He smiled and stepped inside the coach.

John was taken by the rich interior of the antique coach, which was classified as a smoker-mail car combination. Gas lamps attached to the old-fashioned clerestory roof provided excellent illumination, not glaring but more than adequate for a trip into the night. Other lights along the windows could be extinguished easily, if passengers chose. Two gleaming chests filled with ice chips that would melt to drinking water were affixed to the wall along with containers holding disposable drinking cups.

The car was finished with a heavily lacquered veneer and the rollover seats appeared to be comfortable, and more than enough in number to seat the passengers. A door that separated the small mail section from the coach was open and John noted that the larger pieces of luggage were stowed there. There was a coal stove near the entrance to the coach section and another beyond the mail section partition. Coal boxes were rounded with fuel, and hods and various stove-stoking instruments were available. Rest rooms marked "Men" and "Women" were situated at the ends of the coach section. The car was an early 20th century creation fashioned for both utility and comfort.

What really caught John's attention were the Christmas decorations. "How splendid!" he whispered to Joe. He would certainly express his personal thanks, perhaps in a letter to the people of Hill Junction, after the mission was completed.

Joe delivered a straightforward assessment of what to expect. The trip would be long and the passengers should remain seated as much as possible, he said. Robert Rankin and Will Smith were the brakemen for the run and they would be responsible for stoking the stoves and attending to passengers' needs. The chaperones would be available to help, he added.

The conductor explained that the locomotive would be operated in reverse as far as Gatlin, where it would be turned on a wye. That was necessary, he said, because of the derailment that had occurred earlier at Hill Junction. Because the storm was particularly intense, he would ride in the engine to provide assistance to the engineer. Then he produced a portable radio acquired from East Junction Tower that would be in the care of the brakemen so they could communicate with the locomotive's occupants.

"That's about it," he concluded. "I'll ask John Shanahan to say a few words. He's quite a talker, so I may have to cut him off at some point so we can get under way."

Joe looked at John and winked. "Like the introduction?" he whispered to John, as the passengers burst into a loud applause.

"Ah. Well, I'm kind of at a loss for words, as usual. ... Naw, some of you know me better than that. That's not true. I'm a gabber but this is a serious time. I want to reassure you that we intend to get you home as soon as we can without endangering your safety. ... If you think we're going a bit slow from time to time, bear with us and understand that the visibility isn't very good. ... I think you have noticed that this is not a streamlined car but I can assure you that it is in excellent condition. I like the decorations and we can thank the people of this town for that. Think of this as a trip back in time, an enriching part of your education. ...That's about all. We have to hightail it now. Rest comfortably."

John returned to the engine, trailed by Joe. Harry followed them into the engine cab, presented their train order and more messages. "You'll need to watch at every station for possible updates," he said as he shook hands with both men, who read the order immediately. It was short and to the point. They would run as a passenger extra from East Junction to Gatlin with no need to protect against other trains. Train Three had left Gatlin at eight fifty-two and was well out of their territory.

"Got it, Harry," Joe said. John nodded in agreement. Harry returned to the tower.

The conductor picked up the radio: "Engine Fifty-Three calling the coach. You ready back there?" Will Smith answered. "We're ready, Mr. Francis. Rob's in the mail section about to give you a highball."

The highball was received at ten forty-four. John sounded the air horns in response, released the brakes and notched the throttle ahead. He touched the sander gently and the engine moved forward with ease. Townspeople that had assembled in rows several deep along the platform cheered and waved and the engineer sounded a series of blasts of the air horns. Joe radioed the tower: "Passenger Extra Fifty-Three North out East Junction at ten forty-five."

"Ten forty-five on the Fifty-Three," the tower man repeated. "Godspeed."

Chapter 29: Rule G on Christmas Eve

John Shanahan had adjusted to running the locomotive in reverse by the time they passed Halfway and was beginning to get comfortable again. His high-rise ottoman was quite the gadget and he knew it would become a permanent part of his gear. The storm was venting its fury and visibility remained a major problem. He was running blind at thirty miles an hour and was never sure exactly where he was. The engineer was continually reassured, however, that everything would be okay because his conductor seated across the cab knew the road like no other trainman.

He stole a glance at Joe Francis, sitting erect as always, his jaw set and eyes fixed straight ahead. He rarely spoke and when he did it was only to call out a landmark. John knew he was not a man to waste time in idle chatter when his mind was on his work. His forty years of railroad experience suggested that he was older than fifty-six, yet he looked younger than that. He had a playful streak and good humor, as John had noted back at the junction, but it was all business when he was engaged in train movements.

Joe broke the silence. "I'd take it down a little, John. We're coming up on Crawford."

Crawford? John had forgotten that they were to stop there to let Will Smith wire in their time. He shuffled about in the seat, pulled his leg off the ottoman and eased the throttle back, while fiddling lightly with the brake. The locomotive, which had been plowing an inordinate amount of snow, shuddered slightly and decelerated quickly.

"Good," Joe called across the cab. "Give it another couple car lengths and then let her coast to a stop. Shouldn't take much distance in that snow." He grasped the radio receiver and alerted his brakemen in the coach. The engine stopped almost in front of the old Crawford depot. "Well, at least the station is still standing," John observed as Joe opened the fireman's door and appeared to simply step off the engine into the snowbank.

Startled, John got up quickly and limped across the cab for a look. Will and Joe were already entering the building and he could hear Rob Rankin digging snow frantically from the engineer's side of the locomotive. John thought of the coach and attempted to take a look through the engine's big front window but there was no view to be had. Apparently the snow had drifted in over the nose to a level well above the windows. A claustrophobic sensation swept over him and he returned quickly to his seat.

∞

It was pushing eleven forty-five at the dispatching office and four train workers had joined Henry Terrell and Dispatcher Bill Westfield. The notion that

Hank could scramble another crew for a plow train at Boundary to assist in breaking trail ahead of Number Three had been dashed, so this crew, with two older diesel road units, would have to go all the way through. Because of that, the remote chance that the Summit-based plow train could make a quick turna-round at Aroostook, race back to Summit and run to Quarry ahead of Extra Fifty-Three was just so much fanciful thinking. John Shanahan and Joe Francis would be on their own.

Bill Travers had waded through the snow on the street from the Cummings home to the station, and Elmer Russell, the backup flangerman, had crossed the railroad yard from Shop Road on snowshoes. Carl Reardon's conveyance was his snow tractor, a homemade lagged contraption that was driven along the side of the state highway from his farmhouse. On the way in, Carl picked up Stan Larrabee, the other member of the crew.

Train Three had passed Spanish Junction at eleven-thirty and had reported heavy drifts and whiteout conditions from High Meadow on. Hank figured if the train could make the hill north of the junction tower, and that was a mighty big "if," he conceded, they should pull into Summit by twelve-thirty or so.

Travers paced the floor. His period of rest would not expire until twelve-thirty and Hank had decreed that the plow train would not leave Summit before then. "Dammit, Hank, you're a hard nose!" Travers exclaimed in exasperation. "Anyone would think you worked for the feds. I say we go now and get a head start on the passenger train. Otherwise, they'll be nipping at our heals all the way … and I get real agitated when some train comes nipping at my heals."

Carl Reardon stirred in his chair, got up and seemed prepared to speak. Then he shrugged his shoulders and slumped back in his seat. "Spit it out, Kook," demanded Travers. "You want to say it, don't you? You want to say, 'Let us go now, Hank, and you can book us out at twelve-thirty or any damned time you want.'… Go ahead, Carl. Say it!" The engineer kicked savagely at a chair and sent it careening against the wall.

Carl got up again, pulled on his sheepskin coat and walked crisply to the register book. The conductor turned to Saturday, December 25, and placed an entry on the northbound page: Work Extra 1080 and 1123, Engineer Travers, Conductor Reardon. Left Summit, 12:30 a.m. Plow X212, Russell, Flangerman. No caboose."

"There, boys," Reardon said. "Now somebody here needs to scribble out an order right quick, so we can get some work done." He looked at Westfield and then at Hank. "We're waiting," he demanded. "You got two minutes. Then we're gone, order or no order."

The dispatcher looked at Hank who was staring absently out the window. "Hank, what do you think? I say let's do it. I can touch up some numbers later."

The operations manager attempted to direct his sternest glare on the crew, each member in turn. But the twinkle in his eyes gave him away. Then he turned to Westfield, shrugged his shoulders and said, "Okay, Bill. Rip them out an order to wherever the hell they want to go. Alaska? Hawaii? Anywhere. The farther the better. We'll be rid of 'em. These particular guys can give you ulcers in short order."

"You're a good man, Hank," Bill piped in. "A little too careful sometimes, but a damned good man. And you, too, Carl. I'm an annoying twerp and I go a little ballistic from time to time. Sorry about that." The dispatcher passed the orders to Bill and Carl, who stuffed the onionskins into their pockets. "Aren't you going to bother to read your orders, guys?" Westfield asked.

"We're going to work extra between here and Boundary after twelve-thirty and we're going to protect against Number Three after twelve thirty-five and we're not going to protect against anybody else because nobody else in their right mind would be out there, anyway," Travers said. "You're going to see that Number Three signs this order, so somebody will know what the hell we're doing, even if we don't. Right?"

Westfield shook his head. "I thought I'd seen it all back where I come from, but those hoodlums have nothing on you guys," he said. "You're right, Bill. Take care of yourselves out there and do your best to make this Christmas merry. You've certainly given mine a shot of adrenalin."

Terrell waved as the crew scrambled down the stairs to the concourse. "Goodbye, you buffoons," he yelled down the stairway. "Sure, Hank can explain it to top management when some busybody notices that the plow extra averaged better than 60 miles an hour getting from here to there. But Hank's a good guy and what the heck more could you ask?"

∞

The stop at Crawford was brief and Passenger Extra Fifty-Three was moving again at eleven-fifty. A few minutes after John had eased the locomotive up to a steady forward speed of thirty-two miles an hour and was settled into his routine again when he noticed Joe get up and check his gear that was stacked against the forward bulkhead of the cab. He pulled out a paper bag and two coffee mugs and strode across the cab.

"Every year at midnight on Christmas Eve and again on New Year's Eve, this railroad suspends Rule G for five minutes for any employee stuck on duty," Joe announced. Then he opened a small bottle from the bag, poured two drinks, added dashes of mixer from a pop bottle, and passed a cup to John. "Since we're stuck on duty, we're bound by rule to observe this tradition. Merry Christmas, my good friend."

"And to you, my good friend, Merry Christmas, and thank you!" John touched his cup to Joe's. "Oh, my! This is what was missing on this trip."

John savored the drink, nursing it along as the miles passed. He couldn't remember that Rule G—the standard prohibition of the possession or consumption of alcohol on railroad property—had any exceptions, but who was to question the wise man that was his engine cab companion on this night. He had forgotten about Christmas, and the family tradition that it was for most people.

But when was the last time his family—father, mother and son—celebrated Christmas together? Certainly not the last—that painful one in 1950—when he was hospitalized far from home; nor the one before that when he was running a locomotive in Montana in a bit of a storm. He was hauling a wreck train into the mountains then and didn't recall anyone suspending Rule G at the stroke of midnight on that Christmas Eve.

Neither was it the Christmas before that, because he was on college break that year and idling away the holiday at a dismal train crew terminal on the wrong end of his usual run west of Helena. He thought hard and guessed his last Christmas with family was several years earlier. This year would be no different than many before. He would arrive at the little railroad town of Quarry on Christmas morning, trudge up the hill to Seven Pines and fall asleep on the sofa in the great room. He would sleep throughout the day. Later, he and Ramon would have a lunch and drink a few martinis—too many, no doubt—and retire for another night. But he would call his parents for sure, he vowed, and wish them a splendid Christmas.

Then he thought about the young woman in Summit and her little girl. Surely they would be at home with Emma Cummings at this late hour. Bill Travers would be there, too. Bill had spent a lot of Christmases in many God-forsaken places and John hoped this one would be special for him. Little Katie would be pretending to be asleep but really would be awake and wondering what Christmas Day would bring. He had assurances from Henry Terrell that the presents he purchased at Boundary and left in the railroad manager's care would be delivered to Emma and the girls well in advance of Christmas Eve.

Perhaps if this train had made it to the North Country before this storm approached he would have been able to visit the Cummings home at Three Railroad Street on Christmas Day. But that was no longer possible. He would place a telephone call from somewhere at some time, just to say hello. He could do no more. Damned storms take all the joy out of life, he thought, and attempted again to focus on the track ahead.

∞

Hank Terrell had another problem, as if the unfolding drama needed more. The crew of Extra Fifty-Three would have to drop the coach at Battle Brook Tower and run the engine around the wye, thus returning it to its correct nose-forward position. After re-coupling to the coach, they would run north to Gatlin and let their passengers off for a lunch break. Or they could take the coach to the station first, which seemed like a better idea, and then go about the same procedure to turn the locomotive.

But the wye had not been used since before the storm started. Hank had no railroad resources left at Gatlin for track-clearing purposes so he had called his nephew, Maurice Terrell, who was the paper mill manager, and requested assistance. There was a possibility, Maurice said, that he could find a machine operator who knew how to run a new pulpwood unloader, a lagged machine with a flat bulldozer-like blade designed to push wood from railroad cars. It had been used to push snow and the thought fired Hank's imagination. Maurice said he would call back if he could find the operator.

He had not called, and time was running out. Several trackmen were standing by at the tower, ready to do the best they could to free the wye switches of snow. Hank considered pulling on his topcoat and walking off into the storm when the phone rang.

"We got our man, Uncle Hank!" It was Maurice Terrell. "He's firing up the unloader as we speak. Where do you want him to start? Oh, and how much is it worth to you if he hustles right along?"

"My favorite nephew, the shrewdest cat in the Terrell litter!" Henry exclaimed. "I do owe you big time on this one, my boy. Thanks. You'll be rewarded, rest assured. ... Send your man down to the crossing at the mill entrance pronto and I'll see that our track foreman is there. Gotta go. Thanks, Mo." Hank slammed down the phone and yelled at Bill Westfield. "Tell the tower at Battle Brook to send the foreman over to the mill crossing on the dead run. We have the rigging to tackle the snow on the wye."

∞

"Crossing coming up," Joe called out. "Got it, Joe," John responded. It was the County Road just south of Carroll. He activated the engine bell and sounded the air horns while easing the throttle back. There was no sign of traffic and, upon crossing the highway, it was clear that the road was closed and had been for a considerable period of time. It was snowing hard but a faint glow of streetlights indicated they were nearing the station near the town center. He cut the speed to fifteen miles an hour.

A green light penetrated the gloom. "High green at Carroll," John announced. "High green," Joe repeated. "Watch for messages. The agent should be on the platform."

Agent Darrell Woodward was on the platform with a lantern and order hoop. John pushed the side window open, stuck his head and left arm outside and let the stationmaster line up the hoop. John's arm went through the loop in the device as the train slid by and he held it. Then he reached out with his other hand and pulled a red packet from the delivery pouch. He tossed the hoop back to the snow-covered platform and waved to the agent.

"Some news, huh?" Francis queried after John closed the window.

"Yeah, why don't you read the stuff, Joe, while I bring this beast back up to cruising speed?"

Joe unfolded several messages. "Okay, we have information here that says Number Three is between Spanish Junction and Summit and hitting heavy drifts. Then there's one about a plow extra leaving Summit ahead of Number Three to plow to Boundary. Engineer Travers, Conductor Reardon and Plowman Russell. That's Elmer Russell. He usually works in the shop."

"Those guys just couldn't stay away," John remarked.

Joe continued. "One message here for us says to turn the engine on the wye at Battle Brook Junction, if possible. The section men are at each switch, trying to keep the snow down. The tracks haven't been used since yesterday afternoon.

We need to use the wye tracks with extreme caution. Hank is working on some snow-removal plan but he's not sure he can pull it off.

"Our order runs out at Gatlin," Joe added. "They'd like us to go to the station first, let the passengers off for some eats that one of the churches has provided, and then attend to the turning."

"Okay. Yeah, those passengers need a lunch break. ... Speaking of eats, I've got some sandwiches somewhere in my gear. Probably a little stale by now. Whatever. I'm hungrier than a bear."

"Bear not eat now. Bear hibernate. Sleep out winter. Forage later."

"Smart critter, that bear," John suggested. "Bear in dreamland. Dumb engineer and conductor making strange tracks in snow. The logic escapes me."

"Big mystery."

∞

Will Smith, the telegrapher-turned-brakeman for a night, poked at the glowing coals in one of the stoves of Extra Fifty-Three's coach car. After adjusting the stovepipe damper he added half a hod of coal, shook the grates and closed the stove door. The car was warm but not uncomfortable. He noticed that many of the occupants appeared to be dozing as he walked back along the aisle to his seat. Others were gathered in clusters, engaging in quiet conversations. Two of the older girls were talking and laughing with Brakeman Rob Rankin, one of their classmates.

Will checked his watch. It was twelve twenty-five a.m. and the train had passed Carroll, the first large town north of Hill Junction. He was about to sit down in the double seat at the end of the car designated for his use by the conductor when one of the schoolgirls approached him.

"Would you mind company?" she asked. "You're so quiet. Perhaps I shouldn't intrude."

..."Gee, no. ... I mean yes," Will stammered. "Please, I would like company, and no, you're not intruding. I should sit on the outside, in case I have to get up quickly for some reason. I'm Will Smith and I really work as a telegrapher. ... I think the railroad made up this job tonight, just so I'd have a place to stay."

"I know you, Will, from last summer, when you worked with my mother at Blackwater station for a few days," she said, as she took the window seat at the end of the coach. She extended her hand. "I'm Annie McCaslin. Molly is my mother."

"Of course, Annie McCaslin, I do remember!" he exclaimed, recalling the girl who was in and out of the station often while he trained with the agent. She seemed older this night, he thought, but she was older, by a few months, of course. She was a senior in high school, after all, Will remembered, and he realized, for the first time, that she was really quite beautiful.

He sat in silence, trying to frame a coherent sentence. "Kind of a nasty storm," was the best he could do.

But it was quite enough. Annie seemed to sense his discomfort and led the conversation to his work on the railroad. They talked about telegraphy and she

205

told him that her mother was quite impressed with his ability on the wire. She asked where he had worked on the system and he told her about experiences at the stations where he had been leading up to Christmas Eve when he reported at Crawford.

"But enough about me," he said. "Tell me about you, Annie, what are you studying?"

She smiled and gave her seatmate a thumbnail sketch of her schooling. She would graduate in June, she said, and go home to Blackwater for the summer. In the fall, she would enroll in the community college at Summit and take courses that would lead to admission at an institution offering full degrees in transportation management. One day, she hoped, she would hire on a railroad as a transportation specialist.

Will was impressed. "You are so organized, Annie, and determined. I can see a secure future and happy life for you." She placed her hand gently on his shoulder and then withdrew it. "Thank you, Will. And maybe if you happen to be around Summit from time to time, I'll see you ... now and then?"

"I'd like that ... a lot," he said. "Yes, I'd like that. I expect I'll be in and around Summit from time to time ... as often as I can."

Chapter 30: Joy and Pain

Passenger Extra Fifty-Three was lumbering through the storm north of Carroll when Engineer John Shanahan realized the locomotive was beginning to struggle in the snow. When he begged more power on the throttle, the engine was slower to react. It was "bulldozing" snow now, a description he remembered from an old engineer in Montana.

"Lugging a little hard," he said to Conductor Joe Francis.

"Noticed that. Open country. Get into the woods north of here and it should be better."

"Make's sense," John said, never doubting the conductor's word. It was twelve-forty and their train should be at Collier by one a.m. It would be two in the morning before they reached Gatlin and at least two-thirty before they left. It would be daylight, at best, before they would reach Summit. He would have been on duty twelve hours or more by then and there still would be twenty-two miles of unplowed track ahead. He could envision bank-to-bank drifts in the rock cut north of Paradise and nothing but a mound of white well into the telegraph wires near the grade at Eden.

There would be time to speculate later. He had to focus on the immediate situation first. He asked the locomotive for more power and it responded, albeit reluctantly.

∞

The dim headlight of Train Three, the northbound North Country Express, broke through the snow on the hill south of Summit station at twelve forty-five. Henry Terrell turned off the lights in the dispatching office for a better look. Downstairs, Station Agent Larry Smith, who had come to work after midnight, stood at the platform door to keep a throng of townspeople inside, away from the oncoming train. Dispatcher Bill Westfield was with him to help passengers off and collect their baggage.

The headlight suggested that the train was barely moving. The light dimmed behind a swirl of snow and almost disappeared before re-gathering strength as the particular snow devil swept by. Finally the engine came into view under the station platform lights.

"God Almighty!" Hank exclaimed. In a lifetime of railroading in the North Country he had never seen locomotives so heavily laden with snow. Only the windshield wipers suggested life inside the white cocoon that crept along the track. Then, a side window opened in a shower of snow and ice pellets and Sam Wibberly's head appeared. "God bless you, Sam," the railroad manager muttered. "You made it this far."

There was no sound of brakes being applied as the train drifted to a stop alongside the platform. Smith and Westfield opened the station doors and allowed the people inside to step through and line up along the wall of the station until the unloading was completed. Trackmen who had gathered to assist wielded shovels at each stairwell to break away the snow and ice that had packed into each. Others tackled the front of the locomotive and helped clear a view for car inspectors who checked operating features beneath the train.

Flashbulbs popped up and down the platform as members of the local media, train aficionados and friends and relatives of those aboard Train Three recorded the arrival, one quite unlike any in the memory of those gathered at the station.

Engineer Wibberly descended the cabin ladder and walked to the front of the locomotive for a look. He ran a gloved hand across the icicles that shielded the engine's body and shook his head in disbelief. Sam shrugged his shoulders, pulled the collar of his jacket closer and made his way into the station. Hank met him at the door. "Sam, you made it! I call that one grand piece of work, my friend."

"I thank you, Henry. I've been around here a long time, you know, and never in my time have I ever seen the likes of this. We were hitting drifts back on the hill like little mountains. We went through a couple just the other side of Hillman, I swear to you, Hank; I think we made a tunnel. I know there's still snow hanging over the top back there. My God, those big engines have some power. Some unbelievable power."

Conductor James Grant and Brakeman Jack Demers came along with an express cart stacked high with suitcases and traveling bags. They pushed the conveyance into the waiting room and passed each piece of luggage to its owner as the passengers filed in. When their work was completed Grant talked to Hank and Sam.

"How's that young Shanahan doing with the extra, Hank?" he asked. "I understand he's running in reverse. That's got to be one bitch of a job. ... You know, he ought to be working in the main office, fellow with that kind of book learning. Not to say he's not one crackerjack engineer, because he is. But that's far, far beyond the call of duty."

"They're coming by Collier, I'd say. Yeah, one special lad, that gimpy leg and all."

Westfield approached the group and passed orders to Wibberly and Grant. "You've got Bill Travers ahead with a plow and two locomotives. He left here at twelve-thirty, more or less, but you know Bill. He's apt to be ten miles beyond the North Pole by now."

"So Wild Bill is out there," Demers joked. "Hold up your feet. You'll be getting calls about broken windows a hundred yards from the track halfway into Canada."

∞

The extra passed Collier at twelve fifty-five at a speed of twenty miles per hour. Agent Denny Chambers waved and retired quickly to the station. With one hundred and fifty-five miles logged already, Extra Fifty-Three had one hundred and thirty-seven to go.

John's fatigue increased with each passing mile. He wanted desperately to crack the side window for fresh air but that would only let in the storm. He shifted uncomfortably, then slipped his leg off the footstool and stood up. He stretched and yawned.

"Bear still hungry?" grunted the conductor who peered across the cab.

"Hungry bear sleepy," John answered. "Need burrow to hibernate for six weeks."

"That would be into February. Won't work," Joe said. "By then, you'll be on a little train like this somewhere in the middle of night, complaining about being hungry." He got up and pulled out his lunch basket. "Sit down and I'll rustle up some grub."

"Aha! Indian hungry, too," John teased. "If you'd just kick that ratty bag of mine across the cab, I'd get into those sandwiches I picked up earlier."

"What kind of sandwiches?" Joe queried as he re-stacked the gear stowed in the cab.

"I don't know. It was the special at the grill in Pleasant Valley this afternoon—yesterday afternoon, I guess it was."

"The greasy spoon by the liquor store?"

"Yeah. That's the one."

Joe pulled John's traveling bag from the stack of gear and opened it. "All I see is a pile of dirty clothes. You work on a train wreck lately? What a mess."

The conductor found the bagged lunch and opened it. He took out the soda bottle first. "Sarsaparilla," he noted. "Says here that it contains sassafras and oil of some kind of European birch tree. And sugar, a considerable amount." He held the bottle at arm's length. Then he checked the sandwiches, the grease of which had soaked through the bag. "Ah, yes. The special. Hot pastrami on rye once; crow food now. I remember. Had gas for a week. Not fit for human consumption." Joe returned the items to the bag, stepped to the fireman's side window, opened it and threw John's lunch bag into the maelstrom.

"Now, young man. Let's have a real dinner, American Indian style." Joe opened his picnic basket, pulled out two small trays and several glass containers that held a variety of multi-colored concoctions. Squat Thermos bottles, dishes, bowls, cups and eating utensils were produced, along with napkins. Using the bench normally reserved for extra riders in the cab, he laid out a tablecloth and began assembling food on the serving trays. He poured hot tea from a Thermos into the cups.

Dumbfounded by the proceedings, John had turned his attention again to the running of the locomotive. When Joe was ready, the conductor brought a tray across the cab, sized up John's ottoman and removed the cushion. He pushed the stool with his foot to a convenient spot by the engineer's side and placed the tray on top. "Okay, dig in," he said.

The fare, John would remember years later, was delicious. "Joe, you are a true chef. That was great!" he announced when the tray was empty. "So what do you call it? That creamy stuff was superb! And the soup—magnificent."

Joe responded with a word that John could not understand. "Say again, please." Joe repeated the name. "I guess I can't understand. Can you spell it?"

Joe shook his head. "Can't spell in English. Indian word."

John persisted. "Well, what about the ingredients? You could tell me the ingredients."

"Indian sworn to secrecy. Tribal law. White man cannot know."

"I see," John answered. "Well, anyway, Joe, it was mighty good and I thank you. Tell your family and friends that they have a good thing going there. I appreciate it. ...I'll never order hot pastrami from a fast-food place again."

"You'll live longer."

John sounded the air horns as the train rattled by the tower at Battle Brook Junction and the tower man responded with a highball. It was one forty-five. Passenger Extra Fifty-Three North had traveled almost twenty-four miles in fifty minutes for an average speed of less than thirty miles an hour, more or less, if his mental calculation was correct. But the engineer doubted his ability to cipher numbers without a pencil and paper.

"Hey! Look at that!" Joe stood up suddenly and pointed across a field behind the tower. The wind had eased momentarily and he had detected a large piece of equipment moving along the north leg of the wye. Startled, John pushed himself to his feet and looked. "I'll be darned! It's that big rig the mill bought to push pulpwood off the rack cars. That machine has some power. ...So what the heck are they doing around the track?"

"Plowing. That's what we needed. Things are looking up."

Joe called the brakemen in the coach to alert them as to their imminent arrival at Gatlin station. "How's everyone back there?" he asked.

"Fine," Rob Rankin answered. "Several passengers have slept most of the way."

"Good, that makes the time go by. Rob, you fellows need to go around and speak to everyone. Tell them we have a station stop here and there will be lunches available in the waiting room. We'll pull up shortly and you and Will escort them inside. John and I will take the engine back to the wye and turn it. You should have everyone inside for about fifteen minutes ... if we make it around the wye. So tell the passengers to step lively. And I want you two fellows to dig into the food with them. Okay?"

"Yes, sir! The food part sounds good."

∞

Operator Ken Wiley heard the train first and nudged the Gatlin station agent, Asa Chambers, who had dozed off. Asa, the older brother of Dennis Chambers at Collier, had come in to help his colleague when the passenger train

210

arrived. "They're coming, Acey, and you won't believe what you see!" Ken yelled as he grabbed his camera and bolted through the waiting room to the platform. Several women who had volunteered to serve food put knitting aside and went to the windows to watch the arrival.

Wiley was shooting film as the locomotive approached. The headlight was dimmed when the engineer saw him, and John sounded two short blasts of the air horns as a greeting. Ken clicked away, knowing that the pictures would be prize possessions in his home for years to come. His place was decorated with railroad photographs but none offered such graphic evidence of how truly hard railroading could be on a stormy night.

The branch liner, running in reverse, made him think of a giant gray Navy torpedo from his days in military service. It was impossible to say with certainty that the engine pulling the coach was a railroad locomotive. Snow had filled every odd nook and cranny of the car body, except for the little windows through which the engine crew had searched for landmarks en route to his station.

∞

The engineer's cabin door opened and Joe Francis tossed out a shovel before sliding down the side ladder's grab irons. He landed waist deep in snow the locomotive had rolled onto the platform, struggled free and began digging from the front stairwell of the coach. Will Smith worked his way down from the vestibule and when their shovels clanged, Joe stepped back. "Okay, Will, you finish up and let the folks off. I'll get the coupler pin free so John and I can get to turning the engine around."

Rob Rankin joined Joe from the other side of the train. The snow had packed between the engine and the coach until there was no visible separation between the two. It took several minutes to break a hole through. Both trainmen tossed their shovels aside and closed the angle cock on the air brake line from the engine. Joe pulled the coupler pin and signaled for John to ease away from the coach. The knuckle of the coupler opened and the airline separated with a whoosh. The coach's brakes were set and the engine was free. Snow cascaded from the nose of the diesel into a heap on the track.

∞

More than one hundred miles away Plow Extra Ten-Eighty North was streaking through the farmlands and wooded hills of the North Country, its two 1,600-horsepower diesel units running flat out and roaring in the night. Ahead, a new 50-ton steel plow, the best the Summit, Bolton and Quarry had at its disposal, ripped viciously through the banks of snow that had accumulated in the preceding hours. The plow shook continuously and the reverberations ran through the locomotives.

Engineer Bill Travers had a death grip on the throttle, then notched to the extreme, and watched the speed recorder waiver between forty-five and fifty miles per hour. He was running the engines blind, of course, relying on Conductor Carl Reardon and Plowman Elmer Russell to call instructions from the snowplow. It was a wild ride; one fraught with danger, he knew, but quite necessary for the passage of the passenger train that was still some distance behind. His train would reach Aroostook a few minutes after one in the morning, a time that would surely catch the attention of eagle-eyed bookkeepers perusing railroad records in the weeks to come.

"Oh, well, we'll cross that bridge when we come to it," he muttered, slumping deeper in the engineer's seat. Bill wanted to turn the plow at Aroostook, race back to Summit and plunge down the Quarry line to break track for John Shanahan's train. But he couldn't do that because without a plow running ahead of them, a much greater number of passengers on Number Three could wind up stranded in the snow in the North Country. This effort was really for the greater good, he knew, so his friend John would have to slog along on his own.

∞

Thanks to the assistance of the wood-pusher operator at Gatlin mill, the reversing of Engine Fifty-Three at Battle Brook Junction went as easily as it might have on a normal winter day. The move was made quickly and the locomotive was facing north again. The trackmen at the wye climbed aboard and knocked the heaviest of the accumulation of ice and snow from the diesel unit. When they were done, the engineer climbed down the cabin ladder to shake hands with each of the men and thank them. "If we didn't have you guys out here in weather like this we'd have to shut the railroad down," he said. "Thanks. Go home now and get some sleep and have the best Christmas ever."

John started back up the ladder when his left leg buckled. He slipped and struggled to regain his footing, but not before banging his right elbow hard against the diesel's car body. The joy of the moment had vanished. He held on to a grab iron tightly with his left hand, gripped first by pain and then nausea. Joe reached down with both hands, grabbed the engineer's jacket and pulled him the rest of the way into the cab.

Steadying his colleague, Joe guided John to his seat. "Cracked your elbow?" he inquired.

"Yeah, funny bone. Not funny." John was in excruciating pain. He sat immobile for several minutes, waiting for the discomfort to pass. It would not pass. He groped for the throttle and brake and sander levers with his left hand, found each and reached above his head to touch other cab controls. His left arm and hand worked fine, he concluded.

"It'll pass, Joe. Just a bit of a bruise, I guess. Never done that before." John shook his head to make the pain go away, but it would not. Then he looked sadly at Joe who was hovering nearby. "I suppose there will come a time when this cripple will have to call it quits. ... This is no good. I'm just a burden to my friends ... my fellow workers; someone always has to take up my slack. ... Maybe I can get a soldier's pension. Go away ... live out my time somewhere else. ..." Tears welled in his eyes.

John stared out the window for several minutes. Then he released the engine brakes and pushed the throttle forward. Relieved of some of its heavy load of snow, the BL-2 surged forward. He adjusted his elbow in his lap, planted his feet on the floor and focused on the track ahead. "We've got a job to do, so let's get it done," he said solemnly.

∞

Joe sat quietly and stared ahead. He could find no words to comfort his friend. There were no words. He could do nothing to help and he, too, was overcome with sadness.

Chapter 31: Irish Tea and Mulligan

The Christmas Train left Gatlin at two-ten a.m. The snow subsided as the front moved northward, and the storm became a series of sharp flurries with the wind quartered in the west-northwest. If the weather pattern followed winter tradition in the North Country, the temperature would drop and the wind would intensify, and drifting snow would become the main problem for the train. Indeed it had, for the occupants of the locomotive could detect no evidence of a passenger train having passed over the track but five hours earlier.

John Shanahan remained in the locomotive when it was reconnected to the coach in front of Gatlin station where the passengers re-boarded the train. Joe picked up John's copy of the train order—a straight run to Summit—and did not let on that his engineer had sustained a painful injury. The conductor begged a handful of aspirin tablets from the telegraph operator, complaining that he had a headache that needed attention.

John took two tablets but doubted that the nagging pain in his elbow would ever go away. Joe had rolled a pair of his overalls into a ball to serve as an armrest for the engineer, and as long as he refrained from sudden movement, John was able to achieve enough comfort to focus on his duties.

The visibility was decidedly improved as the train traversed the wilderness north of the Indian reservation at Mission. Despite the snow cover, John held the speed near forty mph. Joe called the approach light at Blackwater at three twenty-two a.m.

"Got it, Joe," John acknowledged, easing the throttle back.

∞

It was a day, and now a night, of ups and downs for Henry Terrell at the headquarters in Summit. When it seemed that things were going well, there would be a sudden and unexpected reversal in fortunes. When the situation began to look bleak again, something would happen to revive his spirit. Yet his concern for the crew of the passenger extra was growing. Hank had tried to facilitate their progress but there was always one more impediment. He had no alternative but to send them into Quarry knowing that the snow on the unplowed branch had been piling up for hours.

He was still grasping for a solution when he heard heavy footsteps on the staircase. It was after three a.m. and he had sent Bill Westfield off to his motel room for rest. Agent Larry Smith, in as dispatcher, was catching up records in the ticket office.

Hank waited for a head to appear at the top of the staircase but the sound of footsteps ceased. Another minute passed. He could stand it no longer, and yelled, "All right, whoever is out there! If you're a qualified plow operator or trainman, come right up and have a drink with Hank. If you're not, get the hell out of the building."

There was a roar of laughter and then a raspy voice. "Bah humbug! Okay, Scrooge. I call your bluff. Get out your best bourbon because Plow Operator First Class Charles T. Wilson is reporting for duty ... sir!" He appeared in the corridor and stepped to the door into the dispatchers' office. Charles stopped at the entrance and pulled out his tobacco pouch and papers. Time appeared to be of no essence and Hank watched as he crafted his trademark cigarette—the infamous "Two-Hump Camel"—with one hand. Charles pulled a wooden match from a trouser pocket, struck it across the doorframe and lit the cigarette. He crushed out the match between his calloused fingers and plunked down in Henry's favorite swivel chair.

"So aside from withdrawing your offer of a swig of Henry's best rotgut, what the hell do you have to say, Mr. Know It All?" Charles queried. "A plow man shows up all in a lather to go to work and you just sit there crabbing about a working-class stiff wandering around your fancy station."

"You know, Charlie Snowflake, if I didn't know an angel sent you on Christmas to help this old sinner, I'd probably call the police." Hank sprang up and embraced his friend. "Damn it, Charles! You're a sight for sore eyes! Yes, I've got a job for you, even though I promised to give you a long holiday. God knows, you deserved it."

"So the offer of a tad of holiday cheer still stands?" Wilson's eyes twinkled.

Henry pulled out the bottle. "By the authority granted me by whoever's the hell in charge right now, I hereby suspend Rule G for five minutes on account of this occasion, and I toast my good friend, Charles Wilson." He fetched two coffee mugs, poured generous portions of his best stock in each, and passed one to Charles. "Merry Christmas, you old reprobate," he said.

The toast was finished and the cups wiped and stowed in Hank's desk when he realized that there had been another miscalculation. He seated himself in disbelief and stared blankly at the nearest window.

"So what's nagging you now?" asked Charles, bewildered by Hank's abrupt change of demeanor.

"I can't let you go, Charles. ... The plan was to have everybody on the railroad home for Christmas this year. That's everybody. ... I've already failed one of my men—that young Smith lad, you know, the operator. I can't get him back to Eagle River. No, I can't let you go 'cause I can't get you back to celebrate with the grandkids."

"We already celebrated. The Wilsons do the Christmas present thing on Christmas Eve. Then Grandpa really celebrates by nipping a bit and sleeping most of the next day. The only cost to you, Henry Tightwad, is a place to stay at Quarry and I figure one of those snazzy rentals on Ten Commandments Street will fill the bill."

"Really? You're not putting me on again?"

"Have I ever put you on, Hank Terrell? ... Well, maybe once or twice ..."

215

"More like a hundred gazillion times, Charles Wilson, but I like you for it. Okay, go down to Quarry and hang out until you want to come back. ... Oh, and here, you might as well take this along to pass the time." Hank retrieved the bottle of bourbon, stuffed it in a brown paper bag and handed it to his colleague. "Stick that deep into the traveling bag of yours and leave it there until you go off duty. Rule G will now be strictly enforced."

"You're a good man, Hank, and you have excellent taste in liquor."

∞

Agent Molly McCaslin of Blackwater pulled a shawl closely and stepped from the warmth of her station as the passenger extra approached. Two track-men followed her out, shovels in hand, to clear the forward stairwell on the coach. She had messages and waved to display them to the engine crew as the train rolled to a stop.

Will Smith stepped off first with the one passenger's bags and set them on the platform. Then he reached for the passenger's hand and helped Annie McCaslin down from the train. She smiled at Will and embraced her mother warmly and said, "You remember Will, Mother. He's been a brakeman on this trip and has been wonderful company."

"Of course I remember Will!" Molly exclaimed. "He's the best young telegrapher I've ever met. ... You two talk for a minute. I need to dash to the engine with some papers."

Joe climbed down to meet Molly. "Some messages," she said. "Is John getting off?"

"He's hurting," the conductor said in a hushed tone and led her away from the engine. "Banged his elbow back along and I'm worried. I'm trying to keep him from any more climbing. Go up and speak to him, if you'd like. I need to check on the passengers."

Molly climbed into the dark cab. "John, it's Molly," she called. "I just wanted to thank you so very much for bringing Annie home safely."

"Hi, Molly." John reached above his head and fumbled for a light switch. "You're welcome. About Annie, that is. ... I was just kind of resting, you know, and letting Joe do the walking ... and talking. ..." His voice trailed off.

Molly stepped closer and peered into his face. He had gone unshaven for days and his eyes were bloodshot. She touched his forehead and he was noticeably warm. "Ah, just a little tired," he said, sensing her concern. "Not to worry. A good night's sleep again. ... I just need a good night's sleep ... all night for a change ...and I'll be fit as a fiddle."

"You sure?" she pressed, noting that he was holding his right elbow tightly against his side atop the rolled overalls that served as an armrest.

"Doing fine, Molly," he said, managing a weak smile. "Look, you and Annie have a wonderful Christmas. ... Now get back to work and finish up for the night ... so the two of you can talk over old times ... together."

216

"Bless you, John Shanahan," she said, and leaned down and kissed him on the cheek. She turned away quickly, crossed the cab and climbed back to the platform. "Bless you, too," he mumbled. "Good woman, that Molly. ... Salt of the earth. ..." He reached up, grimaced in pain and snapped off the light.

Joe made a final check of the passengers on Extra Fifty-Three North, assured them that everything was going well and returned to the waiting room door. Molly met him there with a Thermos and a carefully wrapped box. "Irish tea and a bit of mulligan stew for you and John," she said. "Always warms the heart. God be with you both."

Engineer John Shanahan had dozed off and was slumped down in his seat when Joe climbed aboard. He went to John's side, placed his hand on his shoulder and shook him gently. "Time to go, my friend."

John looked up. "Time to go? Oh, it's Joe. It's time to go. Go... Joe. ...What time is it?"

"Time for Molly's Irish tea and mulligan, if you will please get us rolling first."

"Sure. Mulligan and Irish tea. ... Ah yes. A definite pick-me-up." John smiled and assured his cabin companion that he was ready. "We'll just knock off those drifts ahead of us and roll on home." He released the brakes, touched the sanders and notched the throttle forward. "This Christmas train is rolling home," he said resolutely.

∞

Molly McCaslin cut in her telegraph key and clicked off word of the train's departure: "Blackwater. Passenger Extra Fifty-Three North departed three thirty-five a.m. One passenger off here. Thanks for bringing Annie home. Merry Christmas."

Henry Terrell responded. "Three thirty-five it is. Thank you for being part of the effort. A big part. The best to you and Annie this Christmas Day. HGT."

∞

"My gosh, Joe. I feel like a new man, wide awake and all revived," John offered after devouring the stew and wiping the bowl clean with a piece of Molly's homemade bread. "Looks like the storm is letting off," he added. "Bit of a wind though, and I suppose that'll pile it up a little higher. I don't know about the Quarry line. Well, we'll tackle each in its time. ..."

Joe cut him off sharply. "Read your messages, now that you've got your belly full again." The conductor chuckled as he picked up John's dishes, wrapped them and placed each carefully into the box from which they came.

"Oh, yes. The messages. So what's Hank up to now? Let's see. The plow train should be closing in on Boundary, it says here, and Number Three is nipping at Bill Travers' heels." He laughed gleefully. "Bill will like that. Anyway, everyone will make connections with Canadian Eastern. That's superb! My father will be pleased. ... Hey, Joe, remind me to give him a call when we get this mission done and behind us. Gotta wish the old rascal and my mom a Merry Christmas."

217

Joe chuckled again. "Sure, my friend. I'll remind you. ... Keep reading. There's more."

John fumbled through the papers. "Uh huh. Track Four at Eagle River is closed account of deep snow and ice, switches spiked. Hmmm. Must be snowing up in Eagle River. How odd. That place must be at least ten miles south of the North Pole. You planning to go up that way any time soon, Joe?"

"No. But I'll keep that track closure in mind."

"Good. ... Okay, so the safety rule of the day is to run no risks, always take the safe course. ... That's sensible, wouldn't you say?"

"Only way to go."

"Oh, here's one specifically for us. Says here, C&E Passenger Extra Fifty-Three North. That's us, isn't it? Enter Track One at Summit Station ... and so on ... and be prepared to nose onto Plow X401 ... and ... ." John stopped short and looked at Joe. "Am I reading this right?"

"You got it, Ace." Joe smiled broadly. "Charles Wilson is back. We're going to have a snowplow, at last. Going into Quarry. Imagine that!"

"All right!" John exclaimed. "Hey, this is going to work out okay. You know, Joe, I didn't want to think about that for a long time because, well, to be honest, I doubted that we could make it on our own. You?"

"I didn't think we could, John. Now we can. No doubt."

The engineer attached the messages to a clipboard, hung the board near the radio console and returned his attention to the track ahead. He began to whistle a tune, something he remembered that he heard Bill Travers sing not long ago. It was a railroad classic about a passenger train on a western railroad on a stormy night and it made him feel like his contribution this night was all worthwhile.

John notched the throttle ahead and achieved a forward speed of almost thirty-five before the locomotive began to get sluggish. He backed it off to thirty-two and the engine resumed its contented hum. They passed High Meadow and the woods operations at Camp Twelve, the Hayshed and Camp Sixteen. Now sheltered somewhat from the wind by the deep forest, the locomotive responded well and an additional notch on the throttle finally was achieved without difficulty.

The train was passing the flag stop at South Spanish when John thought again of the Charles Wilson and the snowplow. "Say, Joe," he called across the cab. "How'd they plan to get the plow out and take it over to the station? There can't be anyone left on duty now, except us and the Bill Travers gang, of course."

"Hank called someone and Charles was going to do the coupling up and switch turning. They'll drag the plow back out to the mainline and then plow out where they had dragged and then come down to the station and do the same. That's sort of okay in the working agreements that we have with management."

"Oh. I see. Makes sense. Good."

"And I suppose you want to know who the engineer was?"

"No. ... Well, yes, that occurred to me, I guess."

"It was foremost in your mind from the beginning of this conversation," Joe suggested. "Yes, it was who you hoped it was, and she stayed after her shift to arrange the service. She'll be there to help us get hooked up to the plow, and to offer any words of encouragement you might need. You satisfied now? If so, let's get back to business."

"Okay." John said. "A young fellow always had to explore the possibilities, but you know that, being the wise man that you are. Thanks for the information. Goodness, I'll have to tidy up a bit before we pull triumphantly into the station."

"Absolutely. But at this late hour I'd say that just wiping that silly grin off your face would do. Doll up in your tie and tails later and serenade the lady with more class."

The extra was making an approach to the tower at Spanish Junction when a violent gust of wind tore through the trees and slammed snow hard against the locomotive. There was no visibility again, and John cut the throttle and made a sharp brake application. He was startled when he heard a series of loud thumps and crashing sounds up front and looked quickly at Joe, who was already on his feet. "Something on the track!" the conductor yelled, reaching for the radio. "Hang on!" he called to the coach. "We're going into hard braking!"

John dumped the air reservoir and the engine and coach crashed and shuddered and finally stopped. One more problem, he thought, and closed his eyes as if to escape the likelihood that something had happened to bring the mission to a sudden end.

Chapter 32: Wire's Out South of Spanish

Operator Boomer Johnson was dusting his telegraph instruments in the wilderness tower at Spanish Junction when he was startled by a particularly strong gust of wind. The old wooden structure shook and planking in the floor creaked loudly in response. He knew the tower's days were numbered because years of neglect had made repairs far too costly to consider now. The station probably would be closed and he would have to move on or back to a railroad where he had been employed in the past.

He picked up his woolen coat and cap and was about to go downstairs to watch for the passenger extra when a crash of static around the telegraph instruments indicated a system interruption. He went back and clicked out the call letters "SU" for Summit.

Larry Smith answered: "Howdy, Boomer. Extra show up?"

"Not yet. Picked up crackle on the wires. Anything wrong?"

"We read you but you're weak. Let me try south of you. Molly's got a key upstairs at Blackwater."

Boomer heard the call but there was no answer. He tried from Spanish Junction but to no avail.

"Something wrong," Smith wired. "Cut the wire line south of you."

Boomer pulled a lever, which disconnected the system south of his tower. "Much better," the dispatcher responded. "It's south of you. Leave it cut a while, and watch for your train."

"Copy. Standing by."

Smith turned in his swivel chair at the dispatching office to face Hank, who was engaged in conversation with Jenny Boston and Charles Wilson. "Hank," he interrupted. "Wire's out south of Spanish."

"Wire's out south of Spanish?" he asked incredulously. "Why would the wire be out south of Spanish? I don't understand."

Larry shrugged his shoulders. "Don't know. It's been windy down that way."

The operator at Spanish Junction was still trying to put a finger on the telegraph disruption when the wind abated and he detected a ghostly figure pass under the most distant platform light. He groped for a pair of binoculars in a desk drawer, found them and focused on the figure. "Joe Francis, on snowshoes," he muttered. "What's wrong now?"

He hit the telegraph key. "SU SU SU. This SJ. Joe Francis coming on snowshoes. I'm going down. Stand by."

Boomer bounded down the stairs, coat and cap in hand. He wiggled into his coat at the front door of the tower and pulled his cap tightly on his head. Then he wallowed through the snow, stumbling often, until he reached the platform, which offered better footing. He was out of breath when he approached the conductor. "What's up, Joe?" he yelled.

"Wires are down. Wind pulled down a whole string of poles ... just below here. We ran into a couple of the poles and chopped everything up in good shape." Joe paused and caught his breath. "Boomer, let the dispatching office know and I'll get back to the train. I've got an idea how we can pull the poles out of the way and get through." The conductor turned abruptly and began snowshoeing back to the train. He was visible for only a moment and then disappeared in a gust of snow.

∞

John had slumped down in his seat when Joe told him of the predicament. At least the engine had not run over any large pieces of the poles but some of the telegraph wire was caught underneath the locomotive. The crew would have to attempt to remove other poles from the path of the train and then fish the wires from beneath his engine. And he would be of no help because he knew he would have trouble even getting out of the cab.

Joe had left with strict instructions for John to stay put. All he could do was watch as brakemen Rob Rankin and Will Smith and several high school boys struggled in the snow to push some of the poles aside. Rob had found a pair of heavy-duty wire cutters in a supply box in the nose of the diesel and was cutting wires in a frantic effort to free them from broken poles and cross arms.

John looked at his watch. It appeared to be two-twenty in the morning. Two-twenty? Why two-twenty? he wondered. It was two-twenty just after the train left Gatlin. He held the watch to his ear and realized that it had stopped. Then he remembered he had neglected to wind it when he checked the timepiece against the clock at that station where he and Rob set out on the mission so long ago. "Oh, boy, you're a dummy," he muttered. John needed another "pick-me-up" and remembered the last cigars he had taken from his father's humidor at Quarry weeks earlier.

But the cigars were gone so he sat silently and pondered the latest dilemma.

Lost in thought, he did not realize that several minutes had passed—probably fifteen or more—and Joe had returned and was tugging at a particularly stubborn pole directly ahead of the locomotive's headlight. He yanked it out with brute force, cleared it and then rallied his crew around the engineer's side of the locomotive. He signaled for John to open his window.

I'm going to be under the edge of the engine after we dig it out," he yelled. "You locked up good and solid?"

John checked the brakes and nodded. "Solid," he yelled into the wind.

"Good, this shouldn't take too long. ... Hold on, I'll be up. ... Can't talk in this wind."

Inside the cab, Joe explained his plan. The crew had rolled away what they could of the broken poles and wire. At least two of the supports were wedged in a way that they could not be freed by hand. The trainmen and volunteers would take the cable that had been used to tow the coach from the back shop at Hill

221

Junction earlier, wrap one end around the poles and attach the other through the front coupler of the locomotive. After freeing the tangled wires from beneath the locomotive the train would be backed up, pulling the embedded poles out of the way.

"I think we can drag them back and out of the way. Okay?"

"Yes," John answered. "I'm with you."

∞

Only the ticking of the station clock broke the silence at the dispatching office. Four people—the railroad's managing officer, a dispatcher, a snowplow operator and a yard engineer—waited for a telegraphic transmission from Spanish Junction. It was pushing on five o'clock in the morning and there had been no word from Operator Boomer Johnson for twenty-five minutes or more.

Twenty-two miles away, three others were tracking the train's progress with growing concern. John P. Shanahan, Jr. sat at the kitchen table in the estate at Quarry, his vision fixed on the snow that still swirled outside. Alicia was at his side and Ramon was preparing an early morning lunch. "You know, Alicia, there are times when I think this particular railroad venture was a really bad idea," J.P. said.

"Hush!" Alicia exclaimed. "This was a wonderful idea. A little problem has occurred and it is being resolved."

"I guess so. I never figured, not in my wildest dreams, that I'd be sitting here on Christmas morning worried sick about a train out there somewhere on the system. Most businessmen are just returning home from a Christmas Eve party about now, liquored to the gills, caring not a whit if some insignificant piece of machinery is working, or if it ever works again. ... What are we doing here, Alicia?"

She slipped her hand into his. "We're here because we're waiting for our son to come home from work." She smiled. "He's doing something he always wanted to do, and he's doing it with class, and that, John P. Shanahan, is what life is all about. Isn't that so?"

"You're right, as usual, Alicia. You raised one special young man. Yeah, that's what it's all about. Hang the inconvenience. What do you think, Ramon?"

"Hang the inconvenience, Boss," Ramon grunted in agreement. "And don't worry about John. He's pretty resourceful, and damn it, he is doing what he wants to do. And he's very good at it. I'll tell you both, he's the best public relations person Shanahan Enterprises has going right now. Folks love him up here."

∞

With the most dangerous and dirtiest work done, and the cable attached, Conductor Joe Francis motioned his crew to place themselves out of the path of the cable should it snap and whip back in their direction. He climbed into the cab and stepped to the front windshield. His overalls were smeared with grease and his face was smudged. There was little resemblance to the immaculately tailored conductor of the *Northern Express* John had met only weeks earlier.

222

"All right, John, take up the slack … real easy," he instructed.

After observing that the other workers on the ground were a safe distance from the train and clear of the cable's range, John released the brakes and eased the locomotive into reverse. He tapped the throttle gently and felt the engine strain against the cable.

"Okay, John. It's tight. Now some more on the throttle." The locomotive began pulling—slowly at first and then a bit faster. The poles were free. "Good, very good," Joe said. "Now cut some slack on the cable."

John reversed the locomotive again and inched forward. "That's good, John. We've got it. Lock the brakes now and we'll finish the job." Joe vaulted out the engineer's door and rounded up his helpers.

A few minutes later the train moved forward and the platform at Spanish Junction came into sight. Boomer was there with some papers that he passed up to Joe. "Good job, guys," the operator yelled. "Take care of yourselves and Merry Christmas."

John shoved open his side window. "Merry Christmas to you, Boomer," he yelled back and then turned to the task at hand. He had a long grade to climb, and the likelihood of deep drifts at the top near Hillman siding. But there were only sixteen miles between Spanish Junction and Summit, and he could surely make it through. Then, for the first time in many days, he could at least say hello to Jenny Boston.

∞

The long-awaited message from Spanish Junction rattled over the telegraph sounders in the dispatching office: "SJ. Psgr Extra Fifty-Three North in at four twenty-five; out at five-naught-five. Engr Shanahan, Condr Francis, forty-four psgrs. Coach number ..." Boomer paused and then tapped again. "Unable to see number. U have this?"

Larry turned to Hank. "Okay, chief. Are we going to give this car a railroad name and number or do we just keep putting off the inevitable?"

"Why am I always stuck with the dirty work?" Hank lamented. "I'm tired of hypothetical stuff. I don't have any clue what the number is." He turned to his colleagues. "I've told you about this problem. What do you say? You, Charles?"

Charles shook his head. "Beats me," he said, and went about making a cigarette.

Hank turned to the hostler. "All right, Jenny. You're a smart young lady, not a smart aleck like most of the people around here. What's your guess?"

"We should call it the Christmas Train—CT—and use the number one-nine-five-one. Years from now when we see the car we'll remember Christmas Eve in 1951 as a time that we all received a very special gift."

"Excellent!" Hank exclaimed. "That's it. ... Larry, tell Boomer ..."

Larry was already on the wire: "SJ, SJ, SJ. It's CT one-nine-five-one, for Christmas Train Nineteen Fifty-One. It is a name and number to remind us always about this night on the railroad."

"I like it. Good choice. I'll remember." Then Boomer added: "Joe will let you know later as to location of downed wires."

"Okay on that. Call it a day, Boomer. Thanks for being there when the railroad needed you. Been a great help. Chat next time. Merry Christmas."

"And to you, my friends, a Merry Christmas, too."

∞

After considerable tinkering, Engineer John Shanahan found a notch in the throttle that seemed to provide maximum sustainable output by the Fifty-Three, one that would produce a forward speed of thirty-five miles an hour under existing snow conditions without causing the locomotive to lug down. They plowed along at a steady pace, smacking drifts at angles that produced cascades of snow but seemed not to overly tax the diesel engine. It was going well, he thought, when Joe Francis stood up and peered ahead.

"Okay, John. A couple of trouble spots are coming up. Hank told me by wire back at Blackwater that Sam Wibberly was sure he carved a tunnel when he went by."

"I'd never doubt Sam," John answered. "I guess if we're going to get through it I need to coax a little more out of this old girl. Now, if there's stuff hanging over the top, it might come crashing down on the roof and ..."

"Right, I'll alert the coach." Joe grabbed the radio and transmitted the information to Rob Rankin. "Tell your passengers to sit tight and hang on ... and sit back to the windows. Snow could come crashing through. Got that?"

"Yes, sir. Will and I will see to it."

John shoved the throttle forward and the locomotive responded without hesitation.

"Here it comes! Hold on, John. There's a pile of it and it's hanging over bad!"

"I see it! Here we go!" The locomotive slammed into the drift at thirty-eight miles an hour and the impact sent shock waves crashing through the locomotive. Red wheel-slip lights flashed on and off and John worked the sanders unmercifully. The engine was bogging down but he begged still more power from the power plant. Visibility was nonexistent, of course, and they were feeling their way along in the dark. Chunks of snow crashed against the hood and windows and all along the roof.

They were still losing speed; the speed register dipped to eighteen, then fifteen and flickered down to thirteen. It stayed there for what seemed an eternity and then began to pick up. All of a sudden the drift was gone and the diesel's engine roared as the speed recorder rose to forty-two when John reined it in.

"All right, that was one of them, Joe. When's the next one?"

Joe exhaled loudly. "Hate to tell you, friend, but while you were pulling off that classy piece of driving, you rammed right through the both of 'em. Hear that clink? That was the south switch of Hillman. ... We're home free, my good man. Home free!" He grabbed the radio again. "Okay, gang. We're through. How's everybody?"

"Couldn't be better. Thank you, gentlemen. That was excellent." The voice was that of Roger Morris, a teacher at Summit High and one of the chaperones. "Listen, please. I want you to hear a reaction from the students. Go, gang!" On cue the passengers burst into a favorite cheer for the Summit Railroaders basketball team.

A few minutes later, as the train eased downgrade into Summit, the city lights came into view. Apparently, the storm was passing. John turned to Joe. "So what time is it?"

"White man have no watch?"

"Forgot to wind it yesterday. It stopped hours ago. I suppose there's a penalty for that."

"Definitely." Joe said, a smile playing at the corners of his mouth. "Well, let me see, I show five thirty-two in the morning," he said after a careful check of his timepiece. "That is the correct time. Exactly. Hasn't lost a minute in forty years. Good watch. I wind it every day at noon. Good practice. Always wind your watch."

"Thanks. Advice accepted. ... You know I can't figure much in my head at this time of day but it occurs to me that we knocked off that last piece of running at a good clip."

"That was one hell of a piece of running. I wouldn't be surprised if the feds come knocking on your door someday soon to review what you've pulled off here." Joe chuckled and turned his attention to the track ahead. "One hell of a piece of running," he repeated. "I think you found your place in the world, John. If this is really what you want, don't let anyone ever talk you out of it."

Chapter 33: The Doctor Makes Locomotive Calls

Henry Terrell alerted media outlets in Summit that Extra Fifty-Three had departed from Spanish Junction. He also provided the scheduled running time for a regular passenger train between the two stations but emphasized that conditions were much different. While the Christmas Train could make good time that was not a probability. Still, he said, people wanting to be on hand for the arrival should come right along. The railroad restaurant was open for light refreshments, he added, and observed that the Summit Public Works Department had cleared a narrow lane down the middle of Railroad Street to provide at least a pedestrian way to the terminal.

Hank watched as townspeople streamed into the station. There was a din downstairs after hours of silence, and that was comforting. Larry Smith and several volunteers had gathered in the stationmaster's office to attend to the public's needs. Bill Westfield was back in the telegraph office.

Track workers were clearing snow from switches and the station platform and car inspectors stood by to go over the locomotive and coach and to assist in the coupling of the train to the snowplow. Jenny Boston stood by a window in the dispatcher's office, her face pressed against a windowpane and her attention fixed on the tree line along the hillside to the south—the place from which the headlight of Extra Fifty-Three would first appear. Her thoughts were principally of the engineer.

Minutes passed and a hush fell over the building. Then, dimly at first, a light flickered on the hillside but only briefly. It reappeared, stronger the second time, and Jenny jumped and clapped. "They're coming! They're coming!" she cried. Hank smiled wearily and gazed at the clock. It was five-thirty in the morning on Christmas Day.

Westfield relayed news of the train sighting to Larry Smith. He reached for a switch on a long-silent public address system that he had spent many hours attempting to restore. Hoping against hope that it would work, he tapped the microphone and was rewarded with scratches of static. It had been years since the system had been used and this would be the ideal time for its reintroduction, he thought as he depressed the talk button.

"Ladies and gentlemen, your attention please. ... Your attention, please. ... Passenger Extra Fifty-Three... The Christmas Train ... from Hill Junction and points south ...now arriving on Track One. ... The Christmas Train now arriving on Track One. ...Thank you for being here on this special day ... and Merry Christmas to each and all."

Smith closed his mike and turned on a radio he had brought from home. It was tuned to WSUM where Christmas carols, interspersed with train updates, were the featured fare. He piped the sound to the PA system and a rendition of "Silent Night" drifted through the concourse, waiting room and restaurant and up and down the platform outside.

∞

Extra Fifty-Three rounded the curve at the approach to Summit station and crept slowly up to the platform. Engineer John Shanahan squinted when the platform lights came into his range of vision. His eyes had been blurry from time to time from lack of sleep and from the sparkling snow that had flashed wildly in his headlight for so long.

"Stand up and take a look, John," Joe Francis said from across the cab. "I haven't seen a crowd like this around here in years."

John got up and steadied himself with his good arm. The group was singing along with Christmas music that was coming from the background. "That's quite a sight, Joe!" he exclaimed. "Where's the music coming from?"

"The public address system. That thing hasn't worked since the Second World War."

John eased the throttle into idle and coasted to a stop in front of the station door. His conductor was already on the ground to see the passengers off when the engineer set the brakes. John struggled to his feet again and took an inconspicuous position near the fireman's side of the cab where he could view the activity on the platform. Mostly it was of railroad workmen shoveling snow from around the engine and the north stairwell of the coach. A few feet away the largest gathering of people he had ever seen at Summit station sang and clapped and strained to see more of the train.

All this fanfare for a little train made up of a new locomotive and an old coach car, both of which occupied no more than one hundred and fifty feet of track, John thought as he returned to his seat. There were forty-four passengers aboard, and a crew of four, making the aggregate weight of this train less than three hundred tons. A few nights earlier, he was at the controls of a freight train that passed this place at about the same time with six locomotives, two hundred carloads of potatoes and a caboose. It measured more than nine thousand feet in length and weighed more than thirteen thousand tons.

And there had been only a dispatcher, a pair of car inspectors and a railroad enthusiast with a camera to record its passage. This time was quite different, and he rejoiced silently as families embraced loved ones spilling from the train. The reunions were poignant and he was deeply moved. Thank you, God, for blessing this little train, he offered in a silent prayer.

∞

Joe was carrying luggage into the station when Jenny Boston bounded down the stairway from the dispatching office. He set the bags aside and grabbed her arm as she maneuvered through the crowd. "Stay right here, Miss," he said sternly. "I want to talk to you. Let me get this luggage to its rightful owner. Be right back."

227

Bewildered, she moved from the congested part of the concourse and waited near the station door. Joe returned and beckoned for her to sit on a nearby bench.

"What is it, Joe?" she asked. "What's wrong? It's John! ... Is John okay? Tell me."

Joe chose his words carefully as he described the incident on the wye at Battle Brook. Then he told her about his initial concern and his later realization that the injury might not be as bad as he first feared. He said he decided not to alert the dispatching office because Hank had enough on his mind. There was a need to keep the particulars quiet until they got to a point where medical help could be summoned, if needed.

"When he was really hurting at first, he talked to me about how he guessed he was not capable of being an engineer because of his wound from the war," Joe continued. "That made me very sad, because he is capable. ... In fact, he is a superior engineer—one of the best, the very best I have ever known. Later, he seemed to buck up quite well, but I noticed that he's not using that arm at all."

Jenny's eyes welled with tears. "Thank you, Joe, for telling me."

"Now that you understand, kind of observe how he's acting. I'm not sure he can get out of that engine now. Sooner or later I have to bring this to Hank's attention."

"I understand," Jenny said. "I'll find out and get right back to you."

Jenny pushed the door open, paused and then stepped outside. Engrossed in her concern for John, she almost bumped into a man who was snapping photos of the train.

"Jennie Boston! So what do you think about this train? Look at the snow on the locomotive. I've never seen the likes of that. What an adventure for that engineer!"

It was Jim Collins, the railroad's physician and a well-known rail fan, a man who took particular pains to be on hand for the arrival in Summit of unusual trains. "Doctor Collins! My prayer has been answered. Thank you for being here, at the right place at the right time. Can I please talk to you really quick and really confidential?"

"Sure, Jenny. Let's just slip back into the station really quietly. If there's something I can do, I'll do it." The conversation inside the station was straightforward and brief. Jenny would check on John while she inspected the locomotive's workings. She would report to Joe and they would report to Hank Terrell. The doctor would be hanging around in the waiting room and if the consensus were that he should examine John, he would just happen to be there. If not, he would see the engineer at another time.

∞

John wished he had set his watch by coordinating it with Joe's timepiece. It seemed that a lot of time had passed since the passenger unloading had commenced but there still was a buzz of activity outside so he was probably wrong.

He wanted to check the station clock but the passenger canopy would obscure the view and the effort would be vain.

He thought about trying to descend the cabin ladder when he heard a series of light thumps on the fireman's side of the engine. He craned his neck to see what was happening but could not. John was groping for his cane when a head appeared outside the cabin door. It was Jenny Boston. She came quickly to his side and grasped his left hand.

"Hi," she said. "So, you're back in town?"

"Yep. Back in town."

"And you're feeling well? You look kind of ... ah ... disheveled, I'd say."

"Say what you really mean, Miss Boston. I look like something the cat dragged in. ..."

She grinned. "That's true, but you're still the handsome rascal I remember the last time you came calling. ... Anyway, I must get about my duties. I'm being paid big bucks to check on your fuel and your sand and listen to all the motors and gadgets and see that everything is in proper operating order."

"Okay. I can tell you that we have logged two hundred and seventy miles since the fuel was topped off at Gatlin on the way out. I've been nipping at the sand pretty good, so that could be down a bit but we can't dally around here forever for a refill. Everything has been running well, considering the beating this locomotive has taken. ... This engine is an absolute peach, Jenny ... kind of like you, really." John winked and Jenny blushed.

John paused and then went on. "You said something about proper operating order." His face clouded. "I don't know if you know or anybody else knows— Joe does, of course—but I cracked my elbow back along and it really hurt— more than your run-of-the-mill funny-bone reaction, you know. It doesn't hurt now, much, but I haven't moved it since then, because, well, because ... because, Jen, I'm a spleeny cuss, really. ..."

"How would it be if Doctor Collins, who just happens to be here taking train pictures, hops on and takes a look? He might have a quick diagnosis and you could promise to pay his fee later and just roll on down the line like nothing happened."

John nodded. "Sure, if that's okay with Hank and Joe. I don't want to be the cause of any more delays on this trip. Maybe the doctor's got a bit of painkiller on hand. Actually, I'd settle for a snort of that prime bourbon Hank's got stashed ..."

"Enough, you fool! I'm off to consult with top management. But I'll miss you, John."

"I've been missing you for a long time, Jenny."

∞

Jenny went to Joe and they went to Hank. Hank called J.P. Shanahan in private to convey the news and ask his advice. "By all means, Hank," the senior Shanahan said. "Let the doctor decide. If John's done for this trip, take him off

229

no matter how much he hollers. But I hope he can go on because I know this means a lot to him."

"That's the way we all feel here," Hank responded. "We'll let you know."

The three hurried down the stairs and met Doctor Collins in the concourse. He had his medical bag in hand, something he carried even on rail fan outings. "Doc, could you go up in the cab and check on John?" Hank asked.

Collins nodded. "Sure, Hank. Am I looking for anything special?"

The railroad manager described the circumstance of the injury. "Uh huh. Yes, I should take a look," the doctor responded.

"How about that, gang? Here's a doctor who makes locomotive calls."

Collins grinned. "Here's a doctor who loves locomotives. Just the little boy in him."

∞

"Well, I'll be jiggered!" John chirped as the doctor opened the fireman's side door and stepped into the engine's cabin. "Here's a doctor who makes locomotive calls."

Collins shook his head. "That's the second time in the last twenty seconds that I've heard that line. Are all you railroading guys wired on the same wave length?"

"Yeah. I think it's a psychological problem, some kind of a genetic defect. None of us ever have an original thought. We just kind of bumble along, repeating things over and over, you know, just repeating things over and over, you know, over and ..."

Collins burst into a fit of laughter. "All right, cut it out. This is serious business. I understand you got careless around on the side of the locomotive and smashed your elbow. That so?"

"Yep. Just a dumb Irishman trying to make out that he was real slick around an engine. Anyway, I cracked my elbow, and it hurt, and I couldn't seem to shake it. Now I don't want to move because I don't want any more pain. ... I guess I've lost my confidence. I don't know how to get out of the engine right now. Joe pulled me back in at Battle Brook and I'm afraid of cracking the elbow again when I try to get out."

"Hmmm. That's a dilemma, isn't it? Well, one step at a time, so to speak. Let's look at the elbow. You have that coat and heavy shirt on and I don't want you to twist the arm around, so how about if I cut off the arm ... Sorry, careless use of words. I'll cut off the arm of your coat and your shirtsleeve. Would that be all right?"

"Sure. They're so dirty they'll probably fall apart in the next wash anyway."

The doctor cut away the sleeves and slipped both around John's elbow and down over his wrist. The elbow was black and blue and swollen. Collins ran his fingers around the bruise and directed John to call out if he experienced pain. "Okay so far," John said.

"Now I want you to slowly extend your arm. Stop when you experience pain."

John gritted his teeth and began to extend the arm. "Ah, right there, Doc. Pain!" he exclaimed. His lower arm was at about a forty-five-degree angle to the upper part when he stopped. Collins held his arm and moved it slowly back and forth, always stopping near the pain point. "Uh huh. And you've had your arm in a rigid position across your lap for a considerable period of time now?"

"Yes. My watch stopped back a ways so I'd suppose about four hours ago."

"Your watch stopped?" he asked incredulously. "Don't spoof me, John. An engineer's watch never stops. Let me see that watch."

John pointed at the timepiece, still suspended from the hook above the radio console.

Collins examined the watch. "Wow! Fine timepiece. A gift from an older railroader, I would say." John nodded. "Yes, a dear friend from my earlier rail-roading days. We worked out in Montana together. That was before Korea."

"I suppose if you wound it, your watch would work. Would it not?"

"Probably would. But while I'm left-handed, I always wind my watch with my right hand. Little superstition thing, I guess."

"I used to do that, too, when I worked … someplace else. … Now, to get back to business. You've definitely bruised your elbow, rather seriously. I doubt that it's broken, but I'd like to take an X-ray anyway. This is not the day for that, being Christmas and with the storm and all, so we should set that up at a time when life gets back to normal. I have some pain medicine here that would seem to fit your need, enough for a few days. I want to fix you with a sling, but I don't seem to have one in my bag, so we'll improvise. Let me call one of your colleagues over."

Collins strolled across the cab and signaled to Jenny. She bounded up the side ladder and entered the cab. "Is he going to be all right, Doctor? Please, is he?" she pleaded.

"Well, Jenny, aside from a genetic defect that all railroaders seem to have, I'd say yes. I need to fix a sling, so could you rummage up a piece of cloth, say a clean bed sheet?"

"Certainly, I'll be back in a jif! And Doctor Collins, tell that good-looking guy with the really funny shirt that I'll be around anytime he needs assistance." Jenny hopped down to the platform and sprinted inside the station.

"Sounds like Miss Boston has taken a shine to you, John," Collins remarked. "Some women have strange tastes when it comes to men. That observation, I might add, comes from some really high-level research in the medical field."

∞

The dispatcher's office clock read six-fifteen when Joe Francis walked out, orders in hand. Larry Smith flicked on the public address system: "Your attention please. … Ladies and gentlemen, may I have your attention please? This is the final call for passengers boarding Extra Fifty-Three North, The Christmas Train, for Swenson's, Johnson Farm, Bolton, and Quarry. … This is the last call for Extra Fifty-Three North on the Eden Valley line. … Merry Christmas and thank you all for this marvelous homecoming."

231

Several operating plans for the completion of the run of the Christmas Train had been considered and scrapped before Hank came up with his final solution. Engineer John Shanahan would complete his run to Quarry with his right arm in a sling and Jennifer Boston would go along as fireman, specifically to be there to assist John because she was qualified to run locomotives if the need arose.

She had added her traveling bag to the personal effects stacked against the bulkhead in the cab. Unlike the others, her bag, inherited from her father, contained mostly school clothes from which she changed to overalls, schoolbooks and other workers' gear when she went to work at four o'clock each afternoon.

Joe Francis would ride in the snowplow with Flangerman Charles Wilson. Brakeman Rob Rankin would be dismissed and would be home for Christmas. Will Smith would continue as brakeman, attending to the eleven students remaining on the train.

∞

Rob climbed into the cab and approached John awkwardly. "I'm going home now. ... I just wanted to thank you for doing this ... this difficult thing for my classmates, and I wanted to say thanks for helping me ... on all the trips we have made together. ..."

John pushed himself to his feet and embraced the young brakeman. "I wouldn't have wanted anyone else, Rob. We've had some great times together. You take care of yourself, buddy, and you and your mom and family have a wonderful Christmas."

∞

Hank had resolved the problem of how to get Jenny and Will back to Summit. Plow Extra Ten-Eighty was en route in from Boundary after opening the main line for Train Three and that crew would be dispatched to the Eden line for another sweep through the snow. It would also be within range of the Christmas Train in the event of an emergency. The plow extra would turn at Quarry, pick up Jenny and Will and return to Summit.

Hank talked to Ramon by telephone about another detail. "I don't believe John can climb down out of that engine when the run is done. He might be able to work his way out through the nose, or the door beyond the power plant, but the ladders ... you follow me?"

"No, but not to worry. I'm on that situation as we speak. It's a work in progress," Ramon concluded.

"I see. Well, good day, man of mystery," Hank grunted as he flipped the telephone receiver into the air and watched it make a loop before crashing into its cradle. Then he smiled. Hank knew that Ramon would resolve any problems that came up.

Chapter 34: A Helping Hand at Eden

The Christmas Train cleared the switch at Quarry Junction as traces of a reluctant dawn teased the eastern sky. It was not night anymore, but not quite day; the air was still and cold, and the snow that had swirled across the land without mercy was at last at rest, heaped in drifts that went on, it seemed, without end.

"I make it six twenty-five at the junction," came the call from Conductor Joe Francis in the cupola of the steel snowplow, the latest addition to the train. "How's that match your watch, John?" Engineer John Shanahan detected a chuckle.

He checked his watch. Then he depressed the engine radio's talk button. "Why, yes. It is six twenty-five. Exactly. Must be a good watch. Never needs to be wound. You just shake it because it has a perpetual-motion winder." He looked across the cab at his fireman, Jennifer Boston, who returned a disapproving stare. "Joe didn't see me wind your watch and set it with the station clock, John. You should tell him, you know."

"You're too honest to work for the railroad. You've got to string people along a bit."

"You're a buffoon, John Shanahan."

As the train rolled into the curve beyond the highway crossing at Summit Heights it was apparent that there would be a sunrise, quite a glorious one across the Eden River valley, at least from early indications. Jenny clapped her hands. "It's going to be a beautiful day, John. A beautiful Christmas day!"

"Sure," John responded. "If we can just burrow through another twenty miles of snow." His earlier visions of the rock cut at Paradise and the grade at Eden came back ever more vividly. The impending sunrise was an illusion, he supposed, a distraction from the task ahead. They would plow into the drifts, lose their momentum and stall, and the snow would come crashing down on the train and they would be smothered in a sea of white.

He shook his head and slumped into his seat while straining to see ahead as the train nosed into the river valley. The only view he could get was an occasional glimpse of the rear of the snowplow; mostly it was one of chunks of snow being propelled through the air all around him. He was tired and dirty, and uncomfortable. At least his injured arm, strapped tightly against his body in a makeshift sling, was reasonably protected against additional bruising. A woolen shirt borrowed from Hank that had been fitted over his left arm, slung around his right shoulder and buttoned by his fireman provided warmth, something that was missing after the arm of his jacket and work shirt had been cut away.

Having the company of Jenny in the cab was pleasant and for that he could be thankful. But she was missing Christmas morning at home with Katie and Aunt Emma, and that was sad. Still, they assured her that they could wait until this important duty was done.

"Rein it in a little, John. We're coming up on Swenson's." It was Joe again, ever-alert Joe, John's eyes for most of the harrowing trip through the dark of the night and the blizzard that had been so taxing. John cut the throttle and the train slowed considerably. From his blind spot behind the plow, the engineer couldn't even guess how they could stop anyway near the little flag stop in the wide-open plain near the Swenson farmstead.

But Joe directed him in and the train was stopped precisely in front of the shelter. He pulled open his window and looked back to see Mr. Swenson shoveling furiously through the wall of snow rolled aside by the plow. A path to the coach stairwell was carved through the bank within minutes, and father and daughter embraced. The girl saw John and waved. "Thank you, Mr. Shanahan!" she called. "Merry Christmas!"

"You're welcome, Angela!" John yelled. "Sorry it took so long. Merry Christmas."

Brakeman Will Smith waved a highball after the Swensons retreated to the shelter of the flag stop. John answered with a quick blast of the air horns and Joe acknowledged the move with a similar signal from the snowplow. The scene was repeated at Johnson Farm.

"We're getting there," John observed as the student departed and the train resumed its course. "Paradise will be next and that could be trouble. Yep, trouble in Paradise." Jenny knew about the rock cut and how the wind could render it impassable in a severe storm. "I know you can do it, John. Think positive."

"Yep. But I'm thinking we might consider …" The crackle of the radio interrupted him. It was Joe. "John, Charles and I are thinking we ought to consider dropping the coach near the siding and make a run on that cut to break through first. How about you?"

John looked at Jenny. "As I was saying, Jen …" He reached for the radio and completed the thought as a shared conversation: " … We ought to consider dropping the coach near the siding and make a run on the cut. … Oh, you said that, Joe, and you wanted my opinion. Capital idea! Let's do it. Need to notify the coach. … Calling Will Smith, you still back there following us or did you get off and walk back to Summit?"

"No, sir. … I mean yes. … Ah … I'm here and I copied Mr. Francis. We're prepared to stop. You want me to stay back here with the passengers?"

"That's right, Will," Joe responded. "Have everyone sit tight."

The coach was dropped and John adjusted his position in his seat. The ottoman was pushed aside, and various instruments checked. Then he gripped the throttle tightly, released the brakes and sounded the air horns. He saw Charles turn in his seat and give him a "thumbs-up" sign. "Go!" the flangerman yelled into the radio.

"Charlie Wilson loves this stuff," John said to Jenny. "I do, too, in a negative sort of way, I guess."

"Think positive, my friend!" she yelled back but the rumble of the diesel engine precluded additional communication between the two.

Engine Fifty-Three struck the drift at forty-one miles an hour. Charles held the steel wings of the plow out as long as possible. When the locomotive speed fell off sharply, he withdrew the wings, leaving the flangers down at first and then lifting them. Joe yelled, "Cut the speed now. Sharp! And then reverse the engine quick and pull back."

John grinned. "Yes, sir! That's the way to do it. Slam ahead, stop quick, back up, and do it again. Don't get stuck that way. Gotcha!"

The move was repeated several times and each effort gained a little ground. On the eleventh pass, running at eleven miles an hour, the Christmas Train broke free of the snow in Paradise. They backed through, stopped, retrieved the coach, revved the engine one more time, dropped the flangers and extended the wings, and roared through the cut.

"All right, gang!" John yelled into the radio. "We knocked the bastard off!"

"John Shanahan!" Jenny exclaimed. "There's a lady present. Mind your tongue."

"Oops, sorry, Jen. A real fine lady, too, I might add." He winked. She blushed.

Extra Fifty-Three North pulled into Bolton at seven-twenty and departed at seven twenty-two. John was nearing his fourteenth hour of continuous duty and had eight miles to go. He remembered the adage about there being a light at the end of the tunnel. That would be the tunnel in the snow his train would have to create or become snowbound just short of its destination. He pushed the thought from his mind and nursed the BL-2 to a forward speed of twenty-eight before it began to lug down again as snow continued to pile up on the plow, engine and coach. He backed off with the throttle.

"Hard going," he muttered. Jenny had returned from an inspection of the engine room. "How's everything back there?" John asked.

"Okay. This is a fine locomotive. None the worse for wear. So, my gentleman friend with the sparkling personality, how's the engineer doing?"

"Well, I'd say not bad for a fellow who's been on an all-night toot across the great northern New England outback. Not bad, really. Craving a bit of Christmas cheer, I suppose. I imagine Ramon is up and about now, so I should be prepared to have a little toddy with him and dig into a fine meal. ... Say, you ever been to the grand mansion?"

"No, I've seen it, though, from a distance. It looks like a lovely home."

"Someday, if you'd like and could work out the time, maybe you and Katie would like to come and visit. My father and mother might come up in the spring, and well, I'm sure they'd like to ... meet you, you know, if you wanted to do that. ... I would like that. ..."

"Maybe they'll come sooner than you think. Anyway, a meeting would be nice and proper. And I'd certainly like to meet them, being an employee of the company and all. If they do come sooner ... and we're both able to work out the time, I should like an invitation to see that home." Jenny sat down, blushed a bit and set her attention to the track ahead.

∞

J.P. Shanahan donned his winter coat and cap at the front door of Seven Pines. Alicia followed him to the door and he helped her with her coat and hat. They stepped outside, viewed the sunrise over the Eden Valley and remarked at the extraordinary beauty of the snowy scene. But their minds were on their injured son, the engineer of the Christmas Train, now on its last lap of the long journey home.

They trudged hand in hand down a narrow path to the garage where Ramon was idling a station wagon, one of the several vehicles available at Seven Pines. He had rigged chains on the wheels and assured the Shanahans that the vehicle would take them to Quarry's railroad station and back. A Quarry Village Corporation snowplow had broken through the heavy snow on the road and left a one-lane passage into the village center.

A heavier piece of highway equipment was at work on Main Street and in the parking lot at the station. The road was open in a southerly direction but only to the entrance at the Army test site whence the machine had come. Two soldiers were operating the plowing machine while an officer familiar to the Shanahans stood on the station platform and appeared to be supervising the work. He came over to their car and opened the door.

J.P. jumped out and shook his hand. "Major Adams! It's so good to see you again."

"Welcome home," the officer said. "We didn't know you were here."

"It's a secret from our son," Alicia said, as the major helped her from the station wagon. "We wanted to surprise John and have Christmas together for the first time in several years. I'm thrilled."

"So, young John is bringing the Christmas Train in? From what I've seen of the snow around here, it must have been some adventure."

"You don't know the half of it, Bob," J.P. said. "I can't even begin to relate what has occurred along the way. But if you'd like to come by later, after the dust, or snow, has settled, I'd fill you in. And thanks for your help with this road-plowing project."

The officer nodded. "We have some passengers on the special train and just wanted to do something in appreciation. ...I'll tell you, J.P, news of this train is spreading across the country like wildfire. It's really unbelievable. Some brass in Pentagon circles picked up reports in the national news during the night and they called our little outpost when they found out this special train thing was happening right here in Quarry."

"When I first heard about it I didn't think the boys could pull it off, Bob. I have some fine workers all across the country, but I'll tell you, the fellas up here seem to come up with the darndest ways to make the impossible work."

"So what is all the talk about a mystery coach? Some kind of an antique car you picked up for the museum down here?"

"Truth is, I swear to you, Bob, nobody knows where it came from. It has no railroad designation or car number, and apparently no identifying marks. It's like... well, like a gift that just sort of appeared when we had no way left to make this mission work. It's almost spiritual, you know. I can't explain it."

Adams smiled. "It's Christmas. God works in mysterious ways. We don't need to know the hows and whys. Just be thankful that it all worked out. Listen, we have three rail-fan types from the site that plan to film the train when it comes in. They know trains pretty well."

"Excellent! How have you got them set up?

Adams explained that one had snow-shoed out to the rock cut north of Eden, another was hanging around the Army station at the entrance to the test site and the third planned to patrol the station grounds at Quarry. "We have a classy photo lab at headquarters—that's classified, of course— and I've granted permission for them to develop the film there. That's mainly because I want to see it, too. If the film comes out okay and you're interested, I could bring it over later for a premiere viewing."

"Fantastic! I love it. And look, we'll pay for as many copies as your guys would be willing to produce. We'll pay top dollar because this is something special for all of us at the railroad."

∞

Engine Fifty-Three was struggling by the time the train passed Eden siding. The load of snow was the worst yet and the engineer knew he was losing momentum. Joe noticed the drop in speed and grabbed the radio. "What's up, John?" he asked.

"Sluggish. Dragging too damn much snow. I can't find my running notch on the throttle. Damned if I can find it. You noticed it, too, and if I read you like I'm beginning to be able to do, you're thinking about some solution."

"Yes, I think we've got a choice now because we're so close to Quarry. It is either uncouple the coach again and do the back-and-forth routine or we stop, back up for a ways, knock some snow off the train, and you wind her up for all she's worth. ... Make it a go-for-broke move, a one-time shot. Charles is geared up for the second option. I think he's right but you're the guy that has to make it work."

"Let's go for broke, Joe," John said. "We need to get this thing done. I'll take her back to the north switch at Eden. That's right at the pitch of the hill. When we're ready, I'm going to set the brakes there, rev her up for all she's worth, hit the throttle hard and then release the brakes. I saw that work once or twice and always wanted to try it. But it'll jolt the coach a goodly wallop, so what do you think?"

237

"I think that's the way to go." Joe called the coach. "Right here, Mr. Francis," Will responded. "We heard your conversation. Perhaps we should get down on the floor and hold on to the legs of the seats?"

"Exactly, and tell everyone to stay there until I call again. But first, you go to the rear through the mail compartment and watch the track as we back up. Let us know when we're at the north switch of Eden."

The move was made and John set up the engine for the charge while the entire crew, including Jenny, shoveled furiously at the train. When everyone was back on board at seven forty-five and he had confirmation that the passengers were in secure positions, he hit the voice button on the radio. "Now!" he yelled, slamming the throttle forward and releasing the brakes. The jolt was sudden and loud and the whole train shook wildly. The locomotive burst forward and the speed recorder shot into the twenties and thirties and had passed forty when the plow impacted the first deep drifts.

John figured he had found his notch as the train burst through the first of the piles of snow and emerged with the speed recorder still flickering between thirty and thirty-five. Then the train hit another wall of snow and faltered badly. "I'm losing it, Jen!" he yelled. "Can't get enough power. We're going to stall and that damned snowbank's gonna fall in on top of us. ..."

Instinctively, he mouthed a silent prayer: "Please God, reach down and give this little Christmas train a helping hand. ... Just a nudge would do."

He was unable to understand what happened next. With his momentum gone and his engine stalling, John knew there were no options left. He gripped the throttle tightly and tried to pull it back. But it wouldn't move. Something was holding it or he just didn't have enough strength left to move the lever. He peered at the speed recorder again. It was flickering when he felt a slight bump from behind the engine. The speedometer inched upward, slowly at first, and then as the snowplow burrowed into the deepest drift on the longest cut on the Quarry Branch, the train burst forward like a tiger unleashed. When the speed reached forty, he tugged at the throttle again. It slipped two notches at the touch of his hand and the locomotive's power plant resumed its contented hum.

John put his hands to his face. Thank you, God, he murmured. Thank you for the helping hand. Only then did he look up in an attempt to find a landmark.

But there were no landmarks because the locomotive apparently was encased in snow. Even the windshield wipers had stopped, stuck midway across the panels, so he quickly cut their power source. The cab was cloaked in darkness and he began to panic. "Jenny, you there?" he yelled.

"Right here, John," she called from the dark. "I think we're dragging a whole mountain of snow along with us. I can't see anything but snow."

John grabbed the radio. "Hey, guys, just checking in. I can't see anything. You, Joe, what's going on? How about you, Will, how's everybody back there? ... You, Will, answer me first."

"We're all fine. Just waiting for word to get back into our seats. ..."

238

Joe cut in. "Everything's fine, John. We broke through and we're cruising right along. Will, the crisis has passed. Thank our passengers and tell them it's time to get ready to get off. How's your visibility back in the coach?"

"We have none, sir; none that I can see. Just snow."

"And you, Mr. Engineer, you found your notch, didn't you?" Joe chuckled.

"I thought so, Joe, at first. But no, that wasn't it. ...Did you feel that little bump just before we regained our momentum?"

"Yeah. ... Like a little push?"

"Exactly. A helping hand, I think, Joe. One of those wonderful Christmas mysteries."

"A mystery that begs no explanation, my friend. We know what happened. Just a gentle push on Christmas Day, that's all."

"An answer to a prayer," Jenny offered quietly from her dark corner of the cab.

Joe was figuring the next move, his final in regard to the train that was but minutes away from its destination. "Now, since you can't see from the cab any more, John, I'll tell you what we ought to do. It's clear sailing right on into the yard at Quarry. Unless you want to stop for half an hour or so to shovel off the snow again, I'd just as soon slow down a little and creep on in. Charles and I can guide you by radio. For some reason most of the snow fell away from the windows up here and we have very good visibility."

"There's a reason for that too, Joe. Something connected to that push we got a few minutes ago. I'm mighty thankful. ... Now I'll haul it back to fifteen or twenty and you holler if you see anything unusual up ahead."

Chapter 35: Home at Last

J.P. and Alicia Shanahan sat in the station wagon, which Ramon had parked in a way so they could see an opening in the forest near Quarry through which The Christmas Train would emerge. Stationmaster Harland MacMillan alerted them to a call by a track watcher that the train had passed Eden siding at a slow rate of speed, stopped and backed up. After some snow had been removed, the train barreled forward and disappeared in an explosion of snow. The caller could offer no more.

The railroad owner looked nervously at his watch. It was eight o'clock in the morning and if the train was able to break through the drifts north of Eden it should appear soon. He looked at Alicia and she smiled and patted his hand. "Patience, my love. It will be soon, I'm ..." She stopped short and screamed, "There, John, what's that, over there?" She pointed at what appeared at first to be only a mound of snow. But it was moving slowly across an open field. It was as strange a wintertime apparition as either had ever seen.

"That's it, Alicia! I see the cupola of a snowplow at the front of a huge snowbank. Holy cow! The whole bank is trailing along. My God, the whole train is inside and dragging that drift along!" He jumped out of the car and hopped onto the platform for a better look. Alicia followed. "I see it, John, but I still can't see the engine. Where is our son?"

"He's there somewhere, honey. That snowbank needs an engineer, and a good one, to drag along that much tonnage. And, man, that snowbank has a great engineer!" He waved his arms and motioned the crowd gathered in the station and near the front entrance to come down the platform. "They're coming, folks! The Christmas Train is coming!"

∞

Conductor Joe Francis was standing up in the cupola of the snowplow, his head out the window, as the train approached Quarry Road crossing. "Quarry Road coming up," he radioed to the engineer. "You want to sound it out?"

"Sure!" John Shanahan responded. "With great joy!" He pulled the cord sharply and precisely: two long blasts, a short and another poignant long finale that echoed against the rolling hills as the engine rumbled across the road. He couldn't see anything but he knew exactly where he was. He sensed the location of the end of the platform, gauged distances in his mind, cut the throttle and let the snow-laden train roll ever so slowly on.

∞

The crowd on the platform had burst into applause as the Christmas Train neared the station but fell silent when the plow, engine and coach crept up to the platform. It was like a ghost train, almost indistinguishable from the

240

landscape in its heavy cloak of white. Only the cupola of the plow was clearly visible along with a rear side door that Joe Francis had jimmied open from the inside. The rest of the train was mostly sheathed in ice and snow and no movement was visible inside.

Joe leaned out and waved a shovel. J.P. stepped forward and grabbed it as the train inched on. "Get that snow away from the front stairwell!" the conductor yelled and then jumped off, another shovel in hand, and headed for the locomotive cab.

∞

When the train stopped John set the brakes, slumped into his seat and pulled his cap visor down over his eyes. "Thank you, God. Thank you so very much," he muttered and closed his eyes. He was at peace at last. Fireman Jenny Boston took off her cap and bowed her head. "I thank you, too, for helping us and for watching over this good man through this storm ... and the others, too," she offered in a quiet prayer.

∞

Joe dug furiously at the snow rolled onto the platform and knocked more off the ladder leading to the cab. When he reached the top, he scraped at the engineer's side windows with his mitten and the sunlight began to filter into the cab. He pried at the ice formed around the entry and was about to put his weight against the door, but Jenny wrestled it open first. "Thanks, Joe," she said. "I couldn't get it from the inside at first. I guess the snow was packed in too hard. ... John fell asleep the minute we stopped. ... I've checked the brakes and they are set solid."

"Good," he responded. "Stay with John. I'm headed for the coach." He descended the ladder rapidly, and sprinted down the platform when he spied J.P. Shanahan digging hard at the front stairwell on the coach. "I'll take it from there," he ordered. "Go to the back and see to the rear stairwell."

The owner of a network of railroads and one of the country's most influential financiers responded instantly and had the stairwell open in a matter of minutes. Then he knocked an accumulation of ice off the outside of the rear vestibule door and slammed it open. "Everyone all right in here?" he yelled as he barged through the mail compartment and into the coach section.

A schoolgirl met him in the aisle. "We're all fine. Our brakeman is working on getting the front door open now. It has been a wonderful trip ... and very exciting!"

"Young lady, I thank you. And your classmates, here, I thank them, too. My name is John P. Shanahan and I have what you might call a vested interest in your comfort when you ride on this railroad's trains. I'm your engineer's father and that is, well, that's what I'm most proud of. ... I'm very happy that you are all home at last."

One of the boys stepped forward and extended his hand, which J.P. clasped in a firm handshake. "We know you, sir. You made this educational experience possible for us and made everything work out in spite of the storm. The

241

accommodations have been excellent. Because I was going to be one of the last passengers to get off, I was asked by my fellow students and our chaperones to give the railroad these expressions of our appreciation."

The student passed J.P. a paper bag containing forty-five handwritten notes of gratitude. "These are for you and all the management people involved, and especially for all the train workers—John, the engineer, and Joe Francis, the conductor, and our two brakemen Robbie Rankin and Will Smith. We thank you all sincerely."

∞

The banging and scraping sounds outside the locomotive, accompanied by a cacophony of shouted commands caused John Shanahan to stir. He sat up and tried to remember where he was. His fireman came to his side. "Too noisy out there for a tired man to get his forty winks?" she asked, as she put her hand on his shoulder.

"I must have dozed off," he said, rubbing his eyes with his left hand. "I fell asleep in the aftermath of a violent storm and I woke up in the company of a gorgeous woman. I must be dreaming. And what is your name, by the way?"

"John Shanahan!" Jenny exclaimed and tweaked his cheek.

"No, you're not John Shanahan, because I'm John Shanahan, or I was when I fell asleep. Besides, John Shanahan doesn't go around tweaking people. You must be mistaken." John pulled his visor down and slumped back into the engineer's seat.

"You exasperating scalawag! Wake up! There are some people outside who want you to come down from your locomotive. Now!"

"They're agents from the federal department that enforces railroad hours of service laws. Open fire on them. I have absolutely no intention of being dragged away in chains."

Jenny was about to shake John when Ramon Martinez appeared in the doorway. "Ramon, he's being silly again!" Jenny exclaimed. "Do something!"

"There is nothing that can be done for this man, Jennifer, I'm sorry to say. Let's you and I sneak off to a bar somewhere and see if the sleeper picks up the trail."

"A bar, you say?" John asked, peering from beneath his visor. "Gee, I don't seem to be sleepy anymore." He pushed himself up, spied his cane hanging over the radio console and grasped it. "I guess we're at the end of the run and I'll have to climb down a ladder to get on with my life. I'd like to do that, but I think I'm somewhat incapacitated. ... Maybe if Ramon and Jenny would mound up a bit of snow down there I could jump off ..."

"Step to the door." Ramon commanded. "The Quarry Travelers' Aid Society has just what you need. Come."

John looked out. What appeared to be a stairway, complete with banisters, was set against Engine Fifty-Three's cabin door. "Well, I'll be darned, a disembarking device, just like at the airports. And you are responsible. Thank you." John shook hands with Ramon and then stepped out onto the stairway and into

242

the bright sunlight. The onlookers, many who had greeted the handful of passengers with warm embraces, pressed forward and burst into a rousing round of
applause. A soldier standing atop an Army truck recorded the moment with a
tripod-mounted movie camera. Stills were taken by other villagers who had assembled for one of the most captivating events in Quarry's history.

∞

J.P. and Alicia slipped into the shadows of the platform canopy and watched
teary eyed. In one arm he cradled the paper bag presented by the student spokesman minutes earlier. He held Alicia tightly with the other. "I'm so proud of our
boy," he whispered. "His grandfather ... would have been proud, too." His voice
broke and Alicia sobbed and gripped J.P.'s hand.

∞

Ramon reached for John's cane and he passed it to his friend. The engineer
pulled his borrowed woolen shirt tighter, squinted in the sunlight and adjusted
his cap. Then he reached tentatively for the banister with his left hand. Once
assured of a solid grip, he eased himself down to the first step, paused and looked
back. Jenny was near his side and Ramon was in the cabin door. John's fireman
smiled and clapped her hands and he smiled back. Then he turned to the crowd
and waved weakly.

The onlookers waved back and cheered and then fell silent. He gripped the
railing more firmly. "I guess ... I should say something ... on behalf of my fellow
workers ... and the railroad," John stammered. "It's difficult now ... a long trip,
you know, but, well, we all really thank you for coming here ... and supporting
us. Thank you for that ... and for your prayers and wishes ... all, everybody
along the line. Good people, you are, good people, and I must say, the students
and chaperones, our passengers—well, they were special. ... Understanding of
the situations as they came up ... and they did come up, one after another, like
you wouldn't believe ... but everything worked out.

"When we were there just a little ways back ... in that rock cut up near Eden,
well, I thought we were losing it, the ability to keep going on this long, long
journey through the storm ...and so close to the end of the trip. Some kind of a
little miracle occurred, I think, ... I know ... and our little train seemed to get a
push, somehow, and well, here we are."

John paused, rubbed his eyes, and grasped for words. "Personally, I will remember this day ... this welcome ... always, and I accept your thanks on behalf
of this crew and others ... with deep humility. ... You'll remember us, I suppose,
but I hope you'll really remember those out there who go to work every day
without fanfare. ... So many that put in a hundred percent all the time, a lot
more when needed, and don't complain. You know, we all know those kinds of
people. ... They are the ones who really make good things happen."

John smiled. "Anyway, God bless you. ... Thanks. ... Now go home and
enjoy the best Christmas ever."

He shuffled down the stairs, leaning heavily on the railing as the boisterous crowd continued cheering. His friends followed and Ramon handed him the cane when John reached the bottom.

The onlookers stepped back to clear a path across the platform to the station door. John acknowledged their presence with nods and repeated expressions of thanks. He scanned the gathering but could not see Joe or Charles Wilson or Will Smith, and Ramon and Jenny had slipped back into the crowd. They all should be here, he thought, because they were the heavy lifters in the effort. But he knew they still had work to do, after all they had done. He vowed he would thank them later, personally and on behalf of the Shanahan family.

John reached the station door, stopped and leaned on his cane. He took a long look back at the train he had just brought in. Even in the wildest of the winter stints he had served in Montana railroad yards there had been no scene quite like that before his eyes. Snow was caked in eerie swirls and layered from the nose of the plow to the rear vestibule of the old coach—that Christmas mystery car that so caught the people's fancy. When the image was sufficiently committed to memory he turned back to the station.

He was about to plod on when a hand gripped his shoulder from behind. He stopped, studied the hand and placed his hand upon it. It couldn't be, he thought. Not here, not now. That person was a thousand miles away or more. … Another place. Another time. Far away … John blinked and peered at the man whose hand was upon his shoulder.

"Dad!" he cried. "It's you. … You're here!"

J.P. gathered John in a firm embrace. "It's me, son. Let me look at you again." J.P. held John by the shoulders at arm's length. "Yes, it's really my son, John. Wow!" Then he remembered Alicia. "And there's someone else here who wants to say hello. I think you remember this lovely lady." J.P. stepped aside and summoned Alicia from the shadows.

"It's my mother! You came too, Mom! Oh, what a lovely Christmas gift!" John dropped his cane and groped for his mother's outstretched hands. She burrowed into his woolen shirt and held him closely. "John, it's been so long … too long … I was so worried and then we saw the Christmas Train, coming through the snow, all that snow, and it was you coming … coming back to us." Alicia smiled through her tears of joy. "We're all together now and I thank our Lord for that. … This is the best Christmas of my life."

∞

Dispatcher Larry Smith logged Passenger Extra Five-Three North off his books following the train's safe arrival at Quarry. Plow Extra Ten-Eighty was being turned on the wye at Summit and would be at the station in a few minutes for an order to run down to Quarry and back. He placed his feet on the desk and lit a cigar. Hank was sound asleep in his alcove at long last and things were falling into place as planned. Then, in the middle of a yawn, Smith detected the faint sound of a buzzer in a distant corner of the room.

244

He got up and traced the source of the sound. It was an old railroad telephone; one he assumed had been retired long ago. "What the heck," he said aloud as he knocked a thick accumulation of dust from the wooden box housing the device. He picked up the receiver. "Hello!" he yelled. "Who's there?"

The line was scratchy. Then he made out the voice of Carl Reardon, conductor of Plow Extra Ten-Eighty. "Dispatcher, you there? I can't hear you."

The dispatcher ran his fingers along wires leading into and out of the telephone box and discovered a loose connection, which he tightened. "Right here, Carl. I think I fixed it. Talk again, please."

"Yeah, got you, faintly. Problem out here at the wye. The plow jumped the track in the east wye switch. We definitely have a broken axle on the rear trucks of the plow and it's sitting on the ground crosswise. We ripped up the switch and the frog and derailed the front trucks on the lead engine."

"Rats. Everybody okay, Carl?"

"Yep. We're good. But I don't think we're going anywhere real soon."

"Carl. Stick by the phone and let me ring you back. ... Hell, there's no buzzer knob on this gadget! Just stick by the phone, will you, and I'll get Hank."

"Break it to him easy. Poor guy's had enough for a lifetime this last day or so."

∞

Families and friends of the passengers at Quarry had trickled away. John sat between his father and mother on a settee in the waiting room, fielding one question after another. They seemed enthralled by the adventure so he tried to give them enough details to satisfy their curiosity without elaborating on the difficult parts. After a while, the rest of the crew followed Joe Francis into the room. Ramon brought up the rear.

Joe shook hands with J.P. and tipped his cap to Alicia. They were all longtime friends, John remembered. Then Joe introduced the Shanahans to the crew. J.P. knew Charles Wilson well and watched while the plowman fashioned a homemade cigarette for him. The senior Shanahan lit up; inhaled sharply and blew the perfect smoke ring. "I like your taste in cigarettes, Charles. This is a dandy smoke."

The young people were next in line. Will Smith, who appeared to be somewhat in awe of the railroad tycoon, stepped forward and nodded when he was introduced. "I'm pleased to meet you, Will," J.P. said. "Henry Terrell speaks most highly of you." The young man swallowed hard. "Thank you, sir. Mr. Terrell is kind. I enjoy my work for the railroad." He stepped back quickly.

Jenny was next. John watched and squirmed. He stole a glance at his mother who appeared to be quite taken by the young woman garbed in working man's attire.

"We have heard a lot about you, Miss Boston." J.P. began. "I must say that you have stepped into a most unusual profession for a young lady. Hank says your father taught you well as a youngster and you know more about

245

locomotives than just about anyone on the system." He turned to John. "Would you say that is true, son?"

A flash of color came to the engineer's face. "Ah ... oh, yeah. Jenny knows engines better than anyone I ever met. She's got the mechanics down to an art; knows her stuff. In the engine, she makes the right moves ... all the time. ... I mean that part about the moves to mean, you know, what to do at the right time ... when it comes to engines. ..."

Alicia came to his rescue. "I'm pleased to meet a young woman who embarks upon a career doing what she really wants to do. It seems that this young lady has found a special niche and that is wonderful. I would like to sit with you some time, Jenny, and talk woman-to-woman about your work. These men get my mind all muddled with railroad nonsense that nobody can understand."

"I would love to visit with you, Mrs. Shanahan, at the earliest opportunity," Jenny offered. "Thank you for the kind words. Like Will, I like my work, especially when I have a chance to operate locomotives. And I'm aware of how muddling railroad men can be. I just rode down from Summit with one." She looked at John and grinned.

John was trying to keep an eye on the station clock as different conversations around the room continued. He had expected to hear that Bill Travers's train was en route from Summit to tidy up the plowing his train had done and then get back home to enjoy Christmas. Time was passing and there had been no word on any progress on that front. Jenny and his mother retired to a corner of the station and appeared to enjoy each other's company.

His eyelids grew heavy and he was starting to doze off when the station telephone rang. The stationmaster was on an errand and J.P. picked up the telephone. "This is the station at Quarry," he said. "May I help you? ... Oh, it's Hank! I hope you're finally on the way home to get some long-overdue rest. ..."

J. P.'s features paled suddenly. "No, not that, Hank! Not another setback. Damn it, not another. ... But the boys are okay? ... Good, thank goodness for that. Yeah, well, that changes things. ... I'd say let's shut it down for now. Those guys can get home for Christmas anyway. Just leave everything where it is. You and Larry go home, spend some quality time there, and let's say we'll all talk by phone tomorrow. You call when you're ready, but don't hurry. ... You need your rest now. ... All of this other stuff will have to wait. God bless you, Hank. I'll make the calls from here that need to be made."

Chapter 36: Christmas Day in Quarry

J.P. Shanahan stood by the front window of Quarry station and tapped his fingers on the windowpanes. He was lost in thought after his disconcerting telephone conversation with Henry Terrell and felt bad that Hank's plan to phase down operations for the Christmas weekend had fallen short of expectations. Every element of the plan was crafted well and carried out with the best of intentions and yet, in the end, an equipment failure derailed the effort, both literally and figuratively.

Could he have directed the railroad manager to have Bill Travers and crew to take the locomotive that escaped the derailment at Quarry Junction from the accident scene, move it around Summit yard, forcing it through drifts by way of the back track from the shop to the connection with the Quarry Branch at Summit Heights, and run to Quarry to pick up the stranded employees? That thought passed through his mind but it was far too risky.

"No, we've pushed the envelope far enough," he said aloud and slammed his fist on the window ledge. He had to tell one of his youngest employees that the railroad's effort to get her home would not come to pass.

∞

John Shanahan knew his father was wrestling with a problem that he could not solve. He was sad and sat with his head bowed. Sensing his concern, Jenny and Alicia seated themselves next to him. The rest gathered nearby to hear J.P. speak.

He cleared his throat but did not turn from the window. "First, you must know that nobody was injured, and I thank God for that," he said, choosing his words deliberately. "The plow extra derailed while turning at Quarry Junction. … An axle broke on the plow and it ran across the main track. One end of the first engine is on the ground. We have decided to send the crew home. They all live nearby."

He turned and stared at his family and friends. "The problem is, some of you are stuck here at Quarry on Christmas Day and we intended to have everyone home. I understand Charles was okay to stay anyway and Will wasn't going to be able to get home so we planned to offer him the best accommodations we could find in Summit."

J.P. turned to Jenny. "That leaves you, young lady, and I'm so sorry. You have an aunt and a young daughter at home and I have no way to get you there. We can't get a train down that branch line because of the derailment. If we could, I would get a business train to take you home. The highway is blocked by snow, probably for quite a while, but when it is open I can promise that I will personally drive you home. Do you understand?"

Jenny nodded. "I understand and Aunt Emma and Katie will understand." She stood up, walked to J.P. and hugged him. "I'm quite all right with this. If I could have one of the railroad units over on Ten Commandments Street, I'll be more than comfortable. Bill Travers will be with Emma and Katie, and I'll get back when I can."

Ramon cleared his throat and stepped forward. "It's not for me to say, but I was thinking that since we have that big house on the hill, maybe we should invite …" He paused and looked directly at Alicia. She jumped up and clapped her hands. "Yes! They all shall be our guests. John, what do you think?"

"I couldn't think of anything better," J.P. said. "A nice gathering of family and friends on Christmas. How about you, young John? Are you up for visitors?"

John was seized by the idea. "I think that would top off this Christmas in a special way. And I'd want Joe to come along, at least for the evening, even though he has a nice peaceful place back in the woods. I'd consider it a personal honor if you'd come, Joe."

"Joe will honor his friend. Yes, I would be delighted."

"Are the rest of you okay with this?" J.P. inquired. "No other plans?"

Charles, Will and Jenny shook their heads. "Very good. Then, Ramon, if you'd be kind enough to bring the station wagon around, we'll all pile in. … Well, maybe not all at the same time. How about if you and I take Alicia and Charles and the baggage up the first time? Then we can come back for the young people. Okay?"

"Good plan," Ramon said. "And Joe will come along when he's ready, but well before supper because Ramon plans to present an exquisite banquet the likes of which the North Country has never seen."

∞

Henry Terrell turned out the lights and closed the office door at the Summit, Bolton and Quarry's dispatching office. Always the first to come and the last to leave, he was leaving this time with many things undone, he realized as he descended the stairway to the station's concourse. There was the problem of the New England Eastern's wreck in the middle of Hill Junction yard, a matter that management at Eastern had no intention of dealing with until Monday morning. That would create havoc for SB&Q, which expected to be running full-scale service—both passenger and freight—by then.

Snow removal was another concern. The entire system would need to be plowed—some locations several times, and freight yards cleaned up and that snow hauled away. There was the matter of the condition of Crawford station, which the company needed to staff in order to facilitate train movements into and out of Hill Junction.

There was to be a police investigation of an alleged attempt by the crew of an emergency train to ram a highway snowplow on a railroad crossing, and as preposterous as the claim was, the railroad would have to prove its innocence.

There was the downed telegraph line at Spanish Junction, which was needed for efficient train service. Just north of Summit, a plow train was disabled, its plow resting askew of the mainline to Quarry and one locomotive was grounded in the wye switch. There were no plows available at Summit to resume snow-removal operations.

There was a mysterious antique coach car on the system and nobody knew why, but it surely had come in handy. Two employees were stranded at Quarry, and that troubled Hank greatly.

But J.P Shanahan was right. Christmas Day was no time to worry about to-morrows. Hank crossed the concourse leading to Railroad Street and picked up a sign he had left in a chair near the exit. The railroad manager affixed it to the inside of the station door before stepping out and letting the door lock behind him. The wording on the sign was his and left no doubt as to his deep Christian faith: "This Railroad Station is closed Saturday, December 25, in observance of the Birth of our Lord and Savior Jesus Christ. 'Glory to God in the highest and on earth peace, good will toward men.—Luke 2:14.'"

∞

The traveling bags of the crew of the Christmas Train were loaded into the station wagon at Quarry station. J.P., Alicia and Charles climbed in, and Ramon whisked them off to Seven Pines. Joe had gathered his gear for the trek by snow-shoes into the forest northeast of the train yard. Satisfied that he had balanced each piece in the most comfortable position, he waved to John and Jenny and struck out along the track beyond the station. Will was still sweeping the coach and bagging trash that had accumulated during the nine-and-a-half hour over-night run from Hill Junction.

"Want to call home now, Jen?" John asked. "My father left the key to his office and said you'd be welcome to use the phone."

"Yes, please," she said. "Will you come in with me? I know a little girl that would like to say hello. She thinks the world of you, but I think you know that."

"I do. Let's go in." John unlocked the door to the office in the north end of the station and pushed it open. "Welcome to the executive office of the Quarry Division of Shanahan Enterprises. Take a gander, Jen. It's quite the place."

Jenny stepped inside as John groped for the light switch. A chandelier that hung down from the station rafters flashed on at the snap of the switch and illuminated a grand—albeit compact—replica of as plush an executive suite as could be found anywhere in the industry. Mahogany paneling glistened from each wall and the officer's desk of solid oak was a stunning centerpiece. A dozen chairs upholstered in red leather rimmed the room. There were gold ashtrays near each chair, and several deep bronze cuspidors were available for tobacco users of a different bent.

Thick drapes were drawn over the four oversized windows, one of which faced the main line track. Wooden filing cabinets that reached to the eaves lined the back wall and a ladder on a trolley was stationed nearby to provide access to the topmost files, some twelve feet above the floor. Several framed pictures hung from the other walls, each featuring equipment assigned to the original Summit, Bolton and Quarry line. An operating telegraph was in place and a telegrapher's green eyeshade hung over the back of the stubby chair that was pushed into the recess under the instruments.

"My Dad takes pride in being a first-class telegrapher," John offered as an explanation.

A large station clock was built into the wall that separated the office from the waiting room. The gong sounded ten times in succession as the couple watched. "Must be ten o'clock," John said, and checked his pocket watch to be sure. "Yep. It's ten o'clock. J.P.'s clock is ticking right along on time."

"Doesn't the employee check his—or her—watch against the station clock?" Jenny queried. "The employee doesn't presuppose that his—or her—watch is accurate and the station clock is not. Is that not correct?"

"Never heard such nonsense. Where did you ever get a notion like that? I always check the station clocks against mine, which happens to have an automatic winder—one of those perpetual-motion gadgets, and I tell the stationmaster if his clock is wrong."

"I'm not going to argue with you," Jenny said sharply. "It's right in the rule book. ... You have read the rule book, haven't you?"

"Well, no. Not really," John grinned sheepishly. "Maybe that's why I didn't know about that exception to Rule G on Christmas Eve."

"I cannot take any more of this! You are impossible, John Shanahan! There is no exception to Rule G! Absolutely none. Now, I want to use that telephone immediately."

"Okay, if you insist." He stepped to the overstuffed executive chair and rolled it back. "Sit down, Jen, and I'll wheel you up to the chief's desk. Then settle in, reach to your left and open the top drawer. I believe you will find a telephone inside. Fetch it out and follow the dialing instructions on the card that is attached. ... Oh, and while you're at it, grab that humidor right next to it. If I figure right, there ought to be a stash of Cuban Delights inside."

Jenny laughed. "And what, might I ask, is a 'Cuban Delight'?" she asked, after placing the telephone atop the desk.

"Oh, that's just some slangy name I made up for the best cigars I've ever smoked. You go about your telephoning and I'll just rummage through the Shanahan cigar stash." He pulled out the humidor and selected a fat cigar, unwrapped it and sniffed the tobacco. "Oh, yes! Cuban, for sure. J.P. Shanahan, you sure know your cigars." He bit off the end and spit the piece across the room into the nearest cuspidor.

"Oh, how awful!" Jenny exclaimed. "John, how could a girl ever take a shine to you?"

"Beats me. What do you think, Jennifer?" He slouched down in one of the red upholstered chairs, puffed on the cigar and winked an eye. "Watch this, my friend. A Shanahan specialty. Something that an expensive education produced for this ne'er-do-well." He raised his head and blew several smoke rings that floated into the rafters.

"You're a buffoon! Now I've called the wrong number. I'll have to start over. Please hush with the babble and let me make this call."

Jenny followed the instructions again, dialing each number deliberately. Finally she heard the sound of a telephone ringing. "Hi, Auntie Emma. This is Jenny. I'm calling from the railroad station at Quarry. ..."

"Yes, I'm fine. It was a difficult trip. We hit a lot of snow, Emma; you would never believe it! It was up into the telegraph wires at Eden. ... John did a tremendous job. He's a fabulous engineer. ... We're in his father's office in the station. It's a fantastic place. ... Oh, he's here blowing smoke rings from a Cuban cigar that he filched from his father's stock. ... When he's serious, he makes a lot of sense. When he isn't, well, I don't know what to make of him. You never know what he's going to say next."

The jovial exchange continued and John realized how strong the bond was between aunt and niece. The whole thing about family ties was real, especially in the North Country. John began thinking about what it might have been like if his father and mother had moved to Quarry when they first found the place and had brought him along. He might have met this young woman before the war and dated her in the normal fashion of the time. But that time was gone, he knew, and suddenly he felt old and tired.

His attention had been distracted. Jenny was talking to Katie. "Yes, honey, I'm disappointed but I will be home as soon as possible. ... I know you understand, sweetheart ... Do you really want to wait until I get home? Is that okay with Aunt Emma? ... It is? Well, that would be grand, and we could open presents together. I'd love to do that. ... Mister John? Sure, he's right here. ... Okay, I'll put him on the phone. Well, thank you. I do, too, but let's make that our little secret. I love you, darling, and I'll talk to you later."

"Would you talk to Katie, John? She misses you."

John took the telephone. "Hi, Katie, it's Mister John."

"Hello, Mister John. Mama said you are tired. Are you tired? Was it a long trip? How long was it?"

"Well, yes, Katie, it was a long trip, and yes, I must say that I am tired. We left Gatlin at six o'clock last night and we arrived here at about eight o'clock this morning."

"Wow! That's a long time. Did it snow hard along the way? It snowed hard here. And the wind was blowing very hard. Was the wind blowing very hard where you were?"

"Wow! I'd say it was. Blowing and snowing all night long! And it was hard to see in the snow. ... I would like to come over to your house someday soon and tell you all about it. Would that be okay?"

"I will ask Auntie Emma first. You wait, please. ... Auntie Emma, would it be okay if Mister John comes over to tell us about the snowstorm? ... It would? Okay. ... Hello, Mister John, are you there?"

"Right here, Katie."

"Auntie Emma said to tell you to come over as soon as you can."

251

John pulled out his time book and scribbled: See Katie real soon. "There, Katie, I wrote that down in my time book. It says, 'See Katie real soon.'"

The little girl giggled. "Thank you very much, Mister John. I must go now. I love you very much. Thank you for calling. Goodbye." The little girl hung up the telephone.

John placed the receiver back in its cradle and returned the telephone to the top drawer. "She's a precious little girl, Jenny," he said. "You're truly blessed."

Jenny held his hand tightly. "Thank you for caring for my daughter the way you do. Yes, I am truly blessed."

Christmas Day turned out to be more than John expected. After finally shedding his work clothes, soaking in the tub and exercising his injured arm ever so gently, he dressed in fresh clothes in his sloppy sort of way, shaved and combed his hair. "Wow! Some suave cat," he remarked at the image in the mirror. Refreshed, he hung his cane over his left shoulder and sauntered—somewhat unsteadily at first—to the great room. He detected a low wolf-whistle from somewhere in the gathering and looked directly at Jenny. She pretended to ignore him but he detected the makings of a smile.

Having the family together again, along with many newfound friends was the highlight of his Christmas and the presence of Jenny made it all the more special. A lunch prepared by Ramon was exquisite, and the drinks for those of age, quite exotic. Presents were exchanged among family members and Ramon, and each was a simple token of esteem, in keeping with long family tradition.

Unexpected guests each received a complimentary packet of literature produced by Shanahan Enterprises. Included in the packets were photographs and data on all railroad operations, including spectacular scenery, stations, operating equipment and people at work. Several photographs focused on the *Northern Express* and its first crew—Engineer Bill Travers, Fireman Jim McDermott, Conductor Joe Francis and brakemen Carleton Reardon and John Kelly, and Postal Clerk Dan Stubbs.

John's gift from Jenny and her daughter was a framed portrait of the two with a notation that brought tears to his eyes: "You have touched our lives in many special ways. With deepest affection, Jenny and Katie." Another package contained a pair of long gantlet engineer's gloves, a bright red bandanna and a black silk railroader's cap like those worn on the Canadian Eastern, a style that had struck John's fancy.

There was also a new time book stamped with the gold letters "SB&Q RR" and his name and position: "J.P. Shanahan III, Engineer." Jenny had tucked a note inside: "Please try to keep your time reports in order. You cause nightmares for the people who have to figure out what your hen scratching means. You can confuse your dearest friends, including me, and get away with it, but have pity on the bookkeepers, please. Adore you, Jen."

John's presents to Jenny and Katie were under their tree at Summit.

Alicia took Jenny on a tour of the house and J.P. entertained the men in the great room. He began by attempting to limit the topics of discussion to anything except the railroad but his curiosity about goings-on from the perspective of the people who knew best led to his scraping of that notion quickly. It soon became a free-for-all at which proposals and counterproposals about better ways to do things dominated the proceeding.

"You know, fellows, this has been a frank and productive airing of views," J.P. concluded after more than two hours. "You have provided the kind of analysis that I would pay plenty to get, only to find out that analysts didn't have a clue as to what they were talking about. I learned a lot here today, and many of these suggestions will be pursued, I can assure you. ... Oh, and I will talk to Miss Boston later and get her thoughts because she belonged in this conversation. It's just an old habit railroad men get into—forgetting about employees because they are women. We'll learn in time, I guess."

"If you don't, Dad, women like Jenny will remind you," John offered.

Fatigue caught up with John by two o'clock and he dozed off while sitting on the sofa in the great room. His mother and Jenny helped him to his feet and led him to his bedroom at the end of the first-floor hallway. Within minutes, he was abed and asleep. Jenny lingered a moment after Alicia left, and came back to his bedside. She smoothed the blankets, leaned down and touched his face. "Bless you, my love," she whispered.

Chapter 37: Movie Night at Seven Pines

The evening banquet in the formal dining room was a special part of Christmas Day at Seven Pines even though John was sound asleep in his room. Jenny Boston, whose time on duty in the freight yard at Summit and in train service later had spanned sixteen hours, was still wide awake and enjoying the opportunity to build a bond with John's parents. Joe Francis arrived promptly after sleeping for several hours at his home. As for the banquet, Ramon's legendary cuisine appeared to be a big hit and his alcoholic concoctions served to all but Jenny and Will were savored. For them, milk shakes made with more cream than milk had to do.

The telephone rang not long after the meal was over and the kitchen cleanup completed. J.P. picked up the receiver. "Merry Christmas!" he exclaimed. "This is the Shanahan residence. ... Ah, Major Adams. I trust that you and the missus have had a pleasant day. ... I do remember. Really! That is great. Oh, yes. Please come now. And bring your photographers along. We'll be waiting. Thank you, sir. ..."

J.P. hung up, his face aglow. "They have the film of the Christmas Train and Bob says it is superb! They filmed the arrival, all of it—out at the cut near Eden, going by the station at the site, coming into Quarry! It's all spliced together and ready to show."

Major Adams and his entourage arrived in an Army Jeep twenty minutes later. The officer hopped out first and shouldered some of the heavy moving picture equipment. Three enlisted men followed with film reels, a projector and screen and various stereo sound devices. Before they could reach the door, J.P. was on the veranda to welcome the men and usher them inside. "How would our great room do for a movie theater?" he asked as they entered the house.

"Fits the bill, J.P.," the major said. "First, let me introduce you to the three best filmmakers in the United States Army. We have here, from the right, Staff Sergeant J. W. Cooper, Corporal Billy Walters and Private First Class Hiram Miller III." J.P. shook hands with the three and welcomed them to the home. Then he introduced the others, beginning with Alicia.

"Did I miss John?" Major Adams looked around the room after the introductions.

"He's beat out, Bob," J.P. replied. "Totally exhausted. The railroad had to wake him yesterday afternoon in Gatlin after a little more than five hours of sleep following a sixteen-hour run. He had eight hours of rest before that ... and another sixteen in a locomotive before that. ... I've gone back over the records of the last few weeks, and I'm telling you, he has been there and back many times. ... Then, on the way up with the Christmas Train, he slipped on the ladder to the cabin and smashed his elbow. You probably noticed that when he got off at Quarry."

"I did, indeed, J.P. He's one tough hombre in my opinion, and I know the others here agree." Turning to the soldiers, Major Adams continued: "My men know about Lieutenant Shanahan and his service in Korea and he's been an inspiration to all of us ... Well, we'll show this film now and leave this copy with you. It's yours and John's and at the right time, you can all sit together and enjoy it."

The military contingent went about setting up the equipment. "You won't believe what my men have produced," the major said. "This is one great piece of cinematography. We haven't written a script yet but you will hear the actual sounds of the train. Each photographer will offer comments as his portion of the film is presented."

The lights were dimmed and the film began rolling. It was titled "The Christmas Train: December 25, 1951." The filmmakers were identified by name and rank and a brief printed description preceded the opening shots. Appropriate music played in the background and sounds of trains that emanated from the strategically-placed speakers reverberated throughout the lower level of the residence.

∞

The train sounds reached John's room and he sat up suddenly. "Time to go," he mumbled. "Yes, Joe. I'm ready. ... Miles to go before we sleep. ... Let's get this job done right." He reached for a pair of crumpled dungarees and pulled them on. Then he grasped a shirt folded on a chair. He worked his left arm into one sleeve and flung the other over his right shoulder and the sling that was wrapped about his injured right arm. He noticed a pair of slippers beneath the cot and slipped his left foot into the right one and the other foot into the other. "Close enough," he said, and grasped his cane.

The film was just beginning with a long-distance sequence of a train laboring near the top of a grade when John reached the room. He slipped quietly into a chair by the fireplace and stared at the screen. A soldier he did not know was talking about the train when he realized the setting was familiar. He stood up suddenly and, in doing so, knocked his cane across the room. Startled, the soldier stopped the film and all eyes turned toward the fireplace.

"That's the Christmas Train!" John exclaimed. "That's our train! But how did anyone get pictures of our train?"

Jenny came quickly to his side. "It is your train, John, and these soldiers are from the test site. We wanted to wake you, but you were sleeping so soundly that no one had the heart to do so. The Army is giving us this copy of the film so we can watch it as often as we want."

Major Adams approached John and shook his hand. "If you're up to it, considering your lack of sleep, we'd be honored if you would join us for the premiere showing."

"Yes, sir. I would be honored. Thank you for doing this. I was a little dopey when I got home and sort of dozed off this afternoon. I'm fine now and I look forward to the film. … Maybe I'll be able to figure out what we were doing out there thrashing around in the snow. It's all a little hazy now."

Adams reintroduced the soldier-photographers for John's benefit and asked that the film be rewound to the beginning. John settled in between Jenny and his mother on the sofa. Jenny pushed a footstool in front of him, grasped his left ankle and lifted his leg onto the stool. "I think someone's pulling my leg," he joked.

"You tried that one last night and it fell kind of flat." The voice came from behind John. He looked back at Joe Francis who winked his eye. John grinned and Joe patted him on the shoulder. "Seriously, I'm glad you're going to see this film."

The long-distance shot of the train struggling over the grade at Eden was taken from the engineer's side of the track. Then the camera, operated there by Sergeant Cooper, zoomed in on the nose of the plow. Joe Francis was clearly visible standing up at his post. Charles Wilson had his window open and was peering out, apparently trying to estimate the size of the drifts ahead. Joe picked up the radio receiver and seemed to be talking to someone in the engine. The antique coach was quite distinctive despite layers of snow that clung to the car.

The film showed the train being stopped and the direction reversed. It was backed to the north switch of Eden where several people climbed onto the snowbanks and began shoveling the heaviest cover of snow from the train. Cooper related how he stopped filming and, using his snowshoes, found a more advantageous point when he realized the train was going to attempt to charge through the drifts in the cut. He found that place, he said, and focused on the front of the train.

The film resumed when the engineer sounded the air horns. That action was audible and visible. The engine roared and snow was blasted high about the locomotive's roof. Black smoke representing diesel exhaust also shot into the sky as the train surged forward.

Skillfully maneuvering his close-up lenses, Cooper caught the charge in graphic images. The collision with the first drift produced what a witness had described earlier, an enormous explosion of snow that landed up to two hundred feet away. Cooper kept filming by cupping his hand above the lens despite being blasted by the snow.

The locomotive seemed to barrel on even as snow rose to the apron of the plow and beyond. The train, which was identifiable as such at the beginning of the sequence, all but disappeared in the onslaught. Still it rolled on, with only the top of the plow and the side windows of the engine visible in the sea of white.

"Right here, folks, watch real close," Cooper instructed the audience. He had flipped to a particularly strong close-up lens, he said. The viewers noticed the change and watched as the cameraman focused on the side of the train, as near as he could calculate to the level of the engineer's window. The view was mostly of snow until the camera reached the side window. There the camera lens was locked on John Shanahan, whose head and shoulders were clearly visible. His hand was frozen on the throttle, jammed into its final notch, and his eyes were fixed on what was ahead. His heavily-whiskered jaw was clenched and he seemed to be begging more from the locomotive than it was built to stand. The intensity of the moment was so vivid, so poignantso, that Alicia and Jenny broke into tears and sobbed.

Joe Francis was glued to the scenes in the film, particularly those of his engineer. "God almighty!" he exclaimed. "That is some piece of filming."

At that point, Cooper said, the train began to slow down. He had looked up and the end of the cut came into his view, but he still had doubts that the engine had enough left to get through. The engineer had bowed his head as if in prayer with his left hand still glued to the throttle. Then the engine seemed to make a last-gasp effort—something unusual seemed to have happened, certainly—and the train surged forward, smashing through the last drift and speeding up rapidly before the engineer reined it in. The train virtually disappeared from sight as the snow kicked up by the plow wings came crashing back on the locomotive and coach car.

"The major asked me to explain that sudden pick up, seeing as he and I share great interest in trains and know a bit about them," Cooper said as he froze the film again.

"I am a man of faith," he continued. "I told Major Adams that. I know in my heart that the hand of Heaven reached down for just a second and boosted that little train along. I believe that. As hard as that engineer worked to coax a little more out of the locomotive, there just wasn't enough left. It is Christmas after all, folks. What better time for a little miracle?"

Cooper looked at John. "Perhaps I've surmised something that didn't really happen, Lieutenant Shanahan. I've filmed a lot of trains over the years and I saw something like that only once before. It was in a pass in northern California and this train with a lot of cars and a full load of passengers was having a real struggle in the snow. A year or so later, I found that engineer and asked him about it. He said, 'Son, you saw a miracle out there. I was stalling and all of a sudden there was this thump behind my engine and everything picked up. It was like I was being pushed along. We got out of that scrape but it was certainly not my doing. I had some help from on high.'"

"We had some help too, sergeant," John said solemnly. "It was the same thing—a little bump from behind. Honestly, I had given up. I was trying to shut it down only I couldn't pull the throttle back, as hard as I tried. Then the little bump—I know it was nothing mechanical—and, doggone it, the locomotive just took off."

"Let me show you something in the movie, sir." Cooper flicked a switch and rolled back a number of frames. Then he set the control to a slow motion forward mode. "Watch close now, folks. The engineer knows he's losing it. See how the speed is falling off. Still falling. Get ready!"

The images were clear. There could be no mistake. There was a sudden forward movement of the locomotive, as if another engine had slipped up behind the Christmas Train and pushed it forward ever so gently. It was almost imperceptible at first and then John's train picked up its momentum and charged forward.

Cooper's segment ran through and Private Miller stepped forward to explain where he was when the train came into view. "I was told to find a good vantage point," he said. "The roof of our station at the junction to the site was the highest place, so I found a ladder and climbed up there. That gave me a good view of the curve in the track south of here and also of the train as it passed in front of the station."

The footage began when the train emerged from a grove of trees south of the test site. At that point the train was almost indistinguishable from the landscape. Again, close-up lenses were used, bringing the train much closer. It took several minutes to run the segment because the train was operating at a low rate of speed.

"I thought something was wrong with the engine," Miller said. "I couldn't understand what was wrong until Major Adams pointed out that the engineer could not see anything because his windows were covered all the way around. The men in the plow were talking to the engineer and guiding him in. That really impressed me."

Miller's lenses were fixed on the fireman's side of the train. As it passed the station there was no way to see anyone on board except the plowman. The coach, also sheathed in snow, caught the soldier's fancy, he said, and he got as much detail as possible as it passed. Only the rooftop jacks that expelled smoke from the coal stoves were visible. The rear of the car was supposed to have stairwells and a vestibule but there was no evidence of either. The film showed nothing but an extension of the snow on the roof that ran well beyond the end of the car. Chunks of snow and ice were falling off and exploding in clouds of snowy particles behind the train as it crept by.

Having had more latitude of movement than the others because the Army had plowed a short section of the main highway into Quarry and roads in and around the freight yard, Corporal Walters filmed the longest portion of the movie. It started with long-lens footage of the train creeping out of the forest south of Quarry, where the engineer was running blind. From various vantage points in and about the station, he recorded the actual arrival when Conductor Joe Francis passed a shovel to J.P. Shanahan and then jumped from the rear door of the plow with another snow scoop and tackled the door and windows of the locomotive. Walters raced back and forth between the two shoveling operations, catching highlights of both.

Then he climbed atop the cab of an Army truck and filmed each passenger as he or she got off the train. He focused on tearful family reunions and on the well-wishers who stood by and cheered. His footage showed Ramon Martinez and two track workers setting up a stairway leading to the engine and he chose to stay at that spot to film the engineer and fireman as they came out from their cocoon.

"I'll always remember that," Walters said, his voice suddenly choked by emotion. He stopped the film. "You folks were there and so you're familiar with the next part. There was this young railroad man, dirty and unshaven ... and just about as bone-tired as any human being I've ever seen. He stood there, God bless him, that soldier back from the war ... leaning on that banister and squinting into the light like he wasn't sure quite where he was. ... Then he started talking to us—in that tired voice—and thanking everyone, and ..." Walters' voice broke and he rubbed tears away. "I'm sorry, Major, sir. I get kind of emotional when I see something like that. I'll just let this play through."

The film continued and the audio picked up John's words clearly. "...You'll remember us, I suppose, but I hope you'll really remember those who go out to work every day without fanfare. ... So many that put in a hundred percent all the time, a lot more when needed, and don't complain. ..."

The cameraman stayed with John as he made his way to the bottom of the stairway and through the crowd. A particularly moving scene was captured on the film when his father placed his hand on John's shoulder and the two embraced. The scene of his reunion with his mother evoked more emotion still and even the stoics, Charles Wilson and Joe Francis, dabbed at their eyes with their handkerchiefs. Sergeant Cooper's eyes were red, the major was misty-eyed and J.P. went quickly into the kitchen to conceal his emotion. Jenny went to Alicia's side and they sat together on the sofa, hands entwined, and sobbed.

After the onlookers had drifted away Corporal Walters filmed the train extensively, even entering the coach to capture the ambience—from the clerestory roof to the gaslights to the two pot-bellied coal stoves that served so well. The Christmas decorations provided closing scenes for the film.

The film ended and Ramon turned on the lights in the great room. The guests stood up and clapped loudly. J. P. made the rounds, shaking hands with each of the soldiers and their commanding officer. "I can't possibly tell each of you how meaningful this film is to my family and my co-workers, especially those here who were on that train," he said. "That film is a true work of art and I want you to know how much it is appreciated."

John, who was visibly moved, talked to each of the soldiers at length, congratulating them for the extraordinary filming and thanking them for their many kind words. Finally, overcome by emotion and weariness, he excused himself, went down the corridor and tumbled back into bed.

Sergeant Cooper went through the equipment the soldiers had brought for the screening of the movie and selected several labeled packets, which he passed to the colonel. "Folks, when we were editing the film this afternoon we decided to freeze some frames and develop them into pictures suitable for framing," Cooper said. "We have prepared these packets, which contain one of each selected. It is the desire of the photographers that each of you receive a set. The major will do the honors."

"I think I will skip our traditional way of doing things and just let our friends from the railroad step up to the coffee table here and select the packet upon which their names appear," Major Adams responded.

Alicia and Jenny picked up their photograph packets and placed the contents on the table after the men had moved to the kitchen for refreshments. "These are so beautiful!" Jenny exclaimed as she examined a photograph taken of the snowplow crew in the cut at Eden. "Oh, and look, you and Mr. Shanahan with John! Those are priceless. … And, Alicia, look! It's John in the engine up in the cut at Eden." Tears welled in her eyes. "He looks so determined," she mused, "and so handsome."

But the last—the one showing John emerging from the cab, tired and grimy and groping for the handrail, touched her like no other. She held the photograph to her heart and cried. Alicia held her closely and stroked her cheek. She knew that this was a match meant to be, and that made Christmas Day in 1951 one of the best days of her life.

Part VI: North Country Roots

Chapter 38: Into the Snow Again

When John awoke early the day after Christmas he was unsure as to his whereabouts. It had become a routine of life to be in an exhausted state after long hours of work and to simply tumble into a strange bed in a strange place and not remember at the end of a rest period the place at which he had arrived eight hours earlier.

The room in which he had slept this time had high tin ceilings, large richly-draped windows and well-appointed furnishings. It definitely was not just another train crew dormitory, crossroads motel or aging downtown inn to which transients came, slept for a while and moved on. This was different. It was a lovely home and there seemed to be people talking in a distant room. He detected the smell of bacon, scrambled eggs and percolating coffee, and heard the familiar voices of family. He knew then that he was home again, even if the place was far from the Shanahan residence in Chicago.

John closed his eyes contently and slipped back into a deep sleep. It was midmorning before he awoke again. Refreshed at last, he rolled the covers aside and eased his legs over the edge of the bed. His right arm seemed to be caught in the bedding and he struggled to pull it free before remembering that he had suffered a painful elbow injury in the not-too-distant past. He wiggled his fingers, flexed his wrist and lifted his right arm within a confining makeshift sling. The elbow was stiff but there was no pain.

He offered a silent prayer of thanks and was about to push himself to his feet when his eyes focused on a picture that he must have placed on a bedside table the night before. It was of a woman, young and stunning, and a little girl, also beautiful. Both had sparkling eyes and were look-alikes in many ways. "Jenny and Katie!" he blurted out loud, and memories of the events of the last twenty-four hours came back vividly. Jenny was there with him, at the end of the *Christmas Train* odyssey, and now she was somewhere in this house, he remembered as he groped for his clothing.

John arose and dressed but couldn't find his cane. He sat down again and tried to remember where last he saw his trusty walking stick. He kept it at his side for months after recovering sufficiently from his war wounds to use it instead of crutches. He clung to the cane at first because he had great difficulty maintaining his balance. After adapting to his disability, the cane gave him a sense of security. Of late, however, he had been less careful and misplaced it from time to time, and, so far, had been able get to where he needed to be, if it were a short distance, without aid.

It might be in the last locomotive in his charge, he thought. That was the one he pushed hard on Christmas Eve and on into Christmas Day. But no, he had the cane after that because he had hung it over his shoulder and tried to show off by sauntering down the hallway of the Shanahan estate without using it on Christmas afternoon. That was a crystal-clear memory because Jenny had whistled when he limped into the great room. He had the cane later in the evening because he accidentally kicked it across the room where family and friends had gathered to watch a movie of the *Christmas Train*.

John had not been out of the house after that, as best he could remember, so the cane had to be nearby even though it was not within his immediate range of vision. He resolved to stand up and walk out through the bedroom door and down the hall like anyone else under the roof on that day. He would spot the cane along the way and the mystery would be solved. Otherwise, he eventually would have to call for help.

John got up tentatively and leaned against the wall to chart his course. Then he shuffled from the side of the bed to the door, which he pulled open while balancing unsteadily on his feet. He focused on the wall across the corridor, stepped forward through the bedroom entryway and reached back to close the door behind him. Then he stood straight, took a deep breath and walked methodically down the center of the hallway, and did not waiver.

He spied the cane leaning against a coffee table where the film had been shown on Christmas. John walked over cautiously, retrieved the walking stick, rested it on his shoulder and continued across the great room. He leaned the cane against a wall and stepped quietly into the kitchen. Those were the most steps he had taken unaided since that day in December 1950, more than a year before, when he fell in battle in Korea.

His mother was seated in a kitchen chair, deeply engrossed in a part of a newspaper that had been separated from the rest, the sections of which were laid out on the table.

"Good morning," John said simply, and awaited a response.

Startled, Alicia looked up over her reading glasses and saw her son standing in the entryway. "Oh, John!" she exclaimed as she sprang up and embraced him. "My dear son! Standing here so straight and tall without your cane!"

John grinned. "Yes, I walked from the bedroom to here ... with God's help, of course. The walking stick is nearby, but for the first time since ... well, back then, I kind of ... well, just sort of put one foot ahead of the other ... and, you know, I moved my arm around and ... it's kind of stiff, of course ... but I moved it without great discomfort."

"Thank God," his mother whispered. "This has been a Christmas when many, many prayers have been answered. ... Now sit, please, and I will make a lunch and fill you in on what has been going on. ... Oh, and you must read the morning paper. They have the most wonderful accounts about all of you and the *Christmas Train!*"

John sat down at the table and turned his attention to the front section of the Summit Sentinel that his mother had been reading. The bold headline on Page One was riveting: "SB&Q Defies North Country Blizzard." Subheads added more: "Christmas Train Delivers Stranded Students" and "Weary Railroaders Challenge Fierce Nor'easter." A panel of gripping pictures provided graphic evidence as to the storm's severity. One at the left of the page was taken from the second floor of Summit station and showed Passenger Extra Fifty-Three coasting up to the platform. The locomotive and coach were barely visible beneath layers of ice and snow. The photo at the right focused on Conductor Joe Francis digging at a stairwell to clear a path for the passengers. In the background, family and friends stood by anxiously to greet loved ones about to step from the train.

Then he focused on the centerpiece, a close-up of the engineer who had pushed his window open and was staring absently into the distance. John remembered the moment and appreciated the words of the editor who had written the caption: "Engineer John P. Shanahan III, near the end of a 292-mile Christmas Eve mission to pick up 42 high school students and their three chaperones stranded by the blizzard, contemplates another 22 miles of hard running between Summit and Quarry. The nearly exhausted engineer was in his thirteenth hour of continuous service."

John pushed the newspaper aside as his mother brought his lunch to the table.

"What do you think about the coverage?" Alicia asked.

"It's flattering and appears to represent a lot of hard work by talented writers and photographers. ... I haven't seen it all yet, but I hope there are references to the others ... many people ... who had a lot more to do with making it work than me. I just happened to be along. Luck of the draw, you might say. There was Joe and our two brakemen and Hank and the dispatchers and station people along the line ... and those village folks down at Hill Junction who came and pitched in, and that bus driver who went out in the storm and got the kids who were stranded in the backcountry ... and the railroad workers everywhere along the line ... so many of them."

John put his hand to his face and rubbed his eyes. "There were so many of them, Mom ... so many good people. ..."

"You will be pleasantly surprised when you read it all, my son," she said, patting his arm. "Henry Terrell's brother, Nolan, wrote a lot of the material and he is very good at what he does. He has called once today and he would like to meet you. There have been other calls, too, by the national media, because this event, they all said, is one of the best-ever Christmas stories. Your father was on the telephone into the night with the press."

"Speaking of my father, and all of the people who were here ..." John paused and stared at his mother. "Where is everybody, anyway? Jenny was here.

Where's Jenny? And what time is it? There's a lot to do ... with all that snow and the wreck at Hill and the downed telegraph lines ..."

Alicia pulled a chair up close to John and put her arm around his shoulder. "Everything is under control. You eat now, slowly, and I'll fill you in. Jenny was up into the night, writing notes to the students who were so kind in their remarks about the *Christmas Train*. She is home now and has had Christmas with her family. The Army opened the highway to Summit earlier to one-way traffic, and your father and Ramon took her home. They are at the station in Summit now to help Hank get things moving again."

"Okay, Mom, I'll eat because I'm hungrier than a bear, and you please fill me in on the latest goings-on. ... But first, I really need to know how you feel about Jenny. It seemed that you two hit it off. I hope that's true."

"Jenny is a kind, sincere and delightful young lady. She's very special and I'm so happy that you met her. Your father is also very impressed. I know that she really cares deeply for you and I think the feeling is mutual, isn't it?"

"I'm fond of her, Mom. I've thought a lot about it and there's no doubt now. You know, of course, about Katie, but probably not about the circumstances involved ..."

"I do know, John. She told me everything and I understand. Those things happen and she did the right thing to keep her child and give her a loving home. Mrs. Cummings seems to be an extraordinary woman to be there the way she has been. And you seem to care for little Katie like your own daughter."

"There is no question about that, Mom."

Alicia nodded. "You're a fine young man. Now eat and I'll tell you about the railroad."

John's mother explained how Army personnel at the test site in Quarry had received permission to move heavy snow-removal equipment onto community and state roads between there and Summit. That was because the state had marshaled its northern district equipment on the Hackmatack Highway. As a consequence, most roads in the North Country except for downtown streets in the larger communities were still closed.

But so was the entire railroad and that was why J.P. and Ramon stayed over at Summit to help Hank plan the quickest possible resumption of service. The train crew involved in the derailment of the plow train in the wye at Quarry Junction—Bill Travers, Carl Reardon and Stan Larrabee had reported earlier with SB&Q Engine One, the yard switcher, and had broken through drifts on the track along Shop Road to reach the site of the plow derailment. Shop crews were summoned to fire up the wrecker, pick up the plow and place new wheels under it. The derailed locomotive was declared to be a low priority issue and would be taken care of later despite the fact that it was blocking the south leg of the wye at the junction. The second locomotive was stuck in the snow.

One plow train had reported at Boundary and was already plowing yard tracks and the interchange with Canadian Eastern at St. Anne's. A second was working in Aroostook yard and would run south to Summit to finish clearing the mainline. A third had reported at Eagle River and would attempt to clear that branch line through to Summit although snow depths were such that the work would be difficult.

At Hill Junction, a switcher crew had been called early to use a snowplow and open tracks between the roundhouse and the scene of the New England Eastern wreck that had destroyed the diamond crossing and fouled SB&Q's tracks in the yard. Eastern officials said that railroad would not dispatch wreck equipment before Monday morning so J.P. Shanahan authorized his railroad's personnel to remove enough damaged equipment from SB&Q tracks to provide access into Hill Junction yard. The diamond crossing was to be replaced with straight rails, leaving the leased Eastern spur tracks without access.

Two crews reported at Gatlin. One would have a snowplow and clear the mainline as far north as Blackwater, where crewmen would await further instructions. The second would go south with a plow to clean up the mainline between Gatlin and Hill Junction.

The principal mission of the day was to clear the entire mainline in time for a six p.m. departure of the southbound *North Country Night Express*, the connecting link for southern New England-to-Halifax passengers and the only scheduled train for the day. There would be no switching of potato cars for at least another day.

"I see," John said after his mother had concluded her summary. "Sounds like an impossible mission. There's still the downed telegraph line at Spanish Junction."

"Yes," his mother said. "Your father is not optimistic. … "

"One reason is that Charles Wilson is marooned here at Quarry," John interjected. "Say, where is Charles and the young operator who stayed here last night?"

"Charles and Will Smith are in the freight yard shoveling snow. They both wanted to do something to help and that was the best Hank and your father could offer. He wanted to start them out of here but they don't have enough men to make up a train crew."

John stared at his mother. "What they really need is an engineer, isn't it? Joe Francis is here, I think, and then there's John Kelly out at Bolton who might be able to come in, and Will, who had a bit of brakeman's experience the other night. But there are no engineers in town at the moment. Jim McDermott must be working elsewhere or he's out of town."

"That's true. Jim's away on vacation," she said as she gathered up John's dishes. "I know what you're thinking, my son, and … well, it's not for me to say."

"I should call Summit station and suggest something," John said. His mother turned on the faucet and prepared to wash the dishes. "If you really want to do that, John, perhaps you should," she said over her shoulder. "But you've done more than enough already."

John made the call and Bill Westfield answered.

265

"Hello, Bill," John said. "This is John. John Shanahan."

"I beg to differ with you, caller. Someone using that name is here in this building right now. Who are you trying to kid?"

John chuckled. "Okay, let me approach this from another angle. I am sort of a no-name loafer lazing in a little abandoned mining town in the North Country. I noticed that you have a snowplow and engine sitting around down here and maybe those pieces of equipment would be useful if you had someone with a tad of experience to drive the locomotive."

"Uh huh. And for the right amount of money, you might be willing to join the team and dig this railroad out of the storm of the century?"

"You might say that. I'm expensive but it appears you folks are in a bit of a bind."

"Yep. That's the one part of this conversation that is based on fact. Tell you what, the fellow that I was led to believe is the real J.P. Shanahan is entering my place of business at the moment. Let's suppose that he is the real McCoy for the sake of argument, so why don't you run this notion by him? I'm mighty glad you're up and around after that last workout. That was some piece of railroading. … Hang on and I'll get J.P."

John's father picked up the phone. "John, my boy, is that really you? Bless you, son, it seems you feel up to a little workout in a locomotive. God knows we need you but I need to know that you're okay. How about that elbow?"

"Hi, Dad. Yep. I'd like to offer a little assistance, seeing how everybody else is doing more than their share. The elbow is stiff, but the pain is gone. Besides I've figured a way to crawl up the cab ladder one-handed if I have to."

"You sure?"

"Yes, sir. No doubts."

"All right, young man. Gather up your gear. … Oh, Bill wants to talk to you again. … Thanks, son. I'll see you later. I need to go harass the Eastern again about their failure to grasp the significance of their wreck in the middle of Hill Junction yard."

Westfield returned to the telephone. "My thanks, too, John. You get yourself ready ASAP and I'll call Harland, the agent, and get him over to the station so he can talk to Charles Wilson and Will Smith. Then, I need to get Clem Morse at the engine house to run up to fetch you. We'll see about rounding up Joe Francis and John Kelly. … Must run. … Thanks again. … See you later." The phone clicked.

At one-ten p.m. John was sitting in Engine Fifty-Three, adjusting his new black Canadian railroad cap that was a gift from Jenny. The locomotive and snowplow had been turned and the Christmas coach had been placed in the engine house. The engineer had walked to the side of the locomotive, loosened the sling on his right arm, reached up to the grab irons leading to the cab, gripped one on his left and pulled himself aboard. There was no pain.

There was no caboose, so the crew's gear was stacked in the snowplow. Included were four pairs of snowshoes that Joe Francis had brought along. The conductor was in the plow with Charles Wilson, and John Kelly occupied the fireman's seat, across from John. Will Smith had the rider's bench. All had read their train order, which directed that they work extra between Quarry and the east wye switch near Summit Heights.

Joe turned in the plow's cupola and waved a highball to John, who responded with two quick blasts of the air horns. "One-fifteen out," the conductor said over the radio. John responded: "One-fifteen. How do we want to approach the hard going up ahead?"

John watched through the window as Joe handed the radio to Charles. "Let's just wind her up and attack as savagely as possible," the plowman responded. "If it bogs down too badly, ease it off and we'll do the back-and-forth thing. How's that sound, young man?"

"I like it," John responded gleefully. "I feel savage today," he added as he jammed the throttle forward. The train bolted out of Quarry yard and was crossing the main road leading to Bolton before the engineer completed the standard crossing approach signal.

The locomotive was up to forty miles an hour when the plow smacked into the first heavy drift east of Eden. The diesel unit shook convulsively and the snow flew wildly in all directions but the plow train lost little of its momentum. The second drift came up immediately and the train burst through that one as well, slowing only to twenty miles an hour. The crew decided to come to a stop at Eden and back up along the line far enough to observe track conditions after the initial sweep.

Joe and Charles stepped down from the plow and waded in the snow to the back of the locomotive in the company of the two brakemen. The plowman judged the plowing to be adequate and Joe agreed. "It worked," he called to John as the crew re-boarded the train.

Work Extra Fifty-Three barreled on through the heavy snow and pulled to a stop at the east wye switch near Summit Heights. Carl Reardon, conductor of the train re-railing the derailed snowplow, met Joe Francis at the switch and advised him that the Shop Road running track was clear so that Joe's train could move into the yard and get additional updates from the dispatcher at Summit station.

Upon Joe's go-ahead signal, John inched the train forward and the conductor climbed into the cab. "Carl says they want to send us south on the mainline to break drifts at Hillman," he said. "They plan to send a crew of linemen and equipment along with us to try to get started on repairing the telegraph line. There will be another plow train coming north from Blackwater so we'll need to figure out some game plan with the dispatcher."

John checked his watch. It was two-thirty in the afternoon. "Looks like it will be a long night, Joe," he suggested. Joe Francis nodded.

"Long night," he responded grimly. "You sure you're up to it?"

The engineer grinned. "I wouldn't want to be anywhere else," he said.

Chapter 39: 'Time Flies When You're Having Fun'

Work Extra Fifty-Three out of Quarry crawled over the running track adjacent to Shop Road in Summit freight yard. The snow that had been mauled earlier by the yard switcher was hard and difficult to move, even for the big plow manned by veteran plowman Charles Wilson. Joe Francis waved a stop signal when the train reached the office center at Summit Shop and Engineer John Shanahan slipped the throttle to the idle position, set the brakes and went to the fireman's door to look out.

Joe strapped on his snowshoes in the plow's doorway, judged the distance to the top of the bank of snow rolled back by the plow and jumped across, after which he conferred with the engineer at almost eye level. "I'll call the station from the shop office," he said to John. "If we're going to pick up equipment cars for the linemen, we'll do it on the way out. The snow's hard and deep and a derailment would really gum up the works."

Joe mushed across the tracks leading to the shop and disappeared behind the buildings. "Amazing man, that Joey," Brakeman John Kelly offered. "Fifty-six years old, forty years on the railroad and as spry as they come. There isn't a finer railroad conductor in the world. ... And Charles, too, he's sixty-four now and tougher than a boiled owl. Started on the railroad in 1904 and he's been here forty-seven years, with time out for the First World War. He was thirty-one when he fought in the Ardennes Forest. ... You probably knew that he's Fred Wilson's father."

"I didn't know. I'll be darned! ... And Joe and Charles together have worked for railroads a total of eighty-seven years. That's remarkable."

Joe returned to the train a few minutes later, dropped his snowshoes on the bank and climbed into the cab two steps at a time. He advised the crew that they would pick up a rider-sleeper coach for the linemen and shop workers that would accompany them to Spanish Junction to repair the telegraph line. They would also have a standard forty-foot boxcar with tools and equipment and a flat car with a mechanical posthole digger, spare poles and cross arms, a portable generator and floodlights. The supply cars would be in the train between the locomotive and coach.

The conductor reported that four trackmen from South Spanish had snow-shoed four miles to the work site that morning and were engaged in shoveling off the main line track and removing broken poles and wires that had been struck by the *Christmas Train*. Their trek had taken them over the high bridge spanning the Spanish River. John shook his head in disbelief.

When the switching was done, John backed the locomotive and plow along Track One to the station where he had to climb down from the cab to sign the train order. "You okay on climbing?" Joe asked.

"Absolutely. It's a matter of a formidable approach to a positive problem ... or is it a positive approach to ... whatever," John winked and backed into a position at the top of the ladder. He gripped a grab iron with his left hand and held on tightly. It was painstakingly slow but he focused on a step at a time. "Hot dog!" he exclaimed at the bottom and walked across the platform with his cane atop his shoulder. Joe was at his side and held open the door leading to the waiting room.

Bill Westfield and J.P. Shanahan were inside. His father burst forward and embraced John. "I watched you from inside, son," he whispered. "Good job. Always keep focused. Good job!" Westfield patted the engineer on the back. "Well, my friend, you're out and about. Now we need to do the bookwork. Read these train orders, understand them and sign your name."

"Did I understand that there is a handsome bonus for volunteering to work on a cold winter day?" John queried.

"Read the papers when your turn comes and sign them, Shanahan," Bill barked. "Shenanigans come later."

The first order canceled the one issued at Quarry for work on the branch. The second instructed the crew of the plow train to work between Summit and Spanish Junction until nine p.m. A third was a copy of an order delivered at Blackwater to the plow train from Gatlin, instructing that crew to work between there and a point south of Spanish Junction where a red flag would be placed because of the debris from the downed telegraph line. Orders at all stations south of the junction were being transmitted by telephone because the telegraph system was inoperable.

Joe read the orders and passed them to John. He read each aloud, nodded and signed the three. When he looked up, Jenny and Katie Boston were standing nearby. They stepped forward and curtsied and giggled and then Jenny came to John and clasped his hands.

"Hi," she said, and smiled her Irish smile. She was wearing the fancy Canadian Arctic winter coat, and the wool-lined, leather-covered gloves that he had found in an exclusive store in Ste. Anne when he had gone Christmas shopping on a run to Boundary. He also had purchased identical child-sized pieces for Katie so the pair looked much like sisters—one grown up and one very young—in their finery.

John hugged Jenny and held out his hand to her daughter. "I missed you, Katie," he said to the little girl.

"I missed you, Mister John!" she exclaimed. He stooped, picked her up and cradled the youngster in his left arm. He raised his other arm carefully, clasped his new cap and placed it upon her head.

"Now you're the engineer, but it's not the *Northern Express*," he said, pointing at the engine and snowplow outside. "It's the best we could do on such a wintry day."

"I know about that engine, Mister John. That's the engine for the *Christmas Train*. I like your new cap. Mama said you would be handsome with your new cap." Katie giggled. "He is handsome like you said, Mama."

Jenny blushed. "Yes," she whispered to her daughter. "He is quite handsome."

A wolf-whistle came from the cluster of trainmen and station personnel gathered in the waiting room. John suspected Bill Westfield or Larry Smith but wasn't sure. Sporting new Canadian winter footwear, Larry stepped forward to inspect Jenny and Katie's winter wear and John's new railroad cap. "I wonder if some railroaders around here have been shopping at that fancy trading post in St. Anne," he mused. "Do we know which ones smuggled the goods into this country, perhaps on a train?"

Joe Francis entered the conversation after eyeing Larry's flashy boots. "Man with fancy mukluks make big footprints. Easy to track to Canada." Then he grinned at the station agent and said that his train would be out of Summit at four forty-five p.m. "Last call for Work Extra Fifty-Three South, now departing on Track One," he declared, mimicking the public-address announcer as he stepped through the station door.

John clasped Jenny's hands again. "Hope you had a great Christmas," he said. "Best ever," she said, and kissed him on the cheek. "Take care of yourself for Katie and me," she called as he walked across the platform and mounted the ladder to the engine cab.

The plow train rumbled immediately into the hill south of Summit. Joe was still in the plow with Charles but John Kelly had moved to the rider coach on the rear with the men being dispatched to Spanish Junction. Will Smith took the fireman's seat. Before long it was apparent to John that the snow dragged around by the two northbound passenger trains early Christmas Day was getting more unmanageable by the mile.

He lifted the radio mike from the console. "Lugging hard, Joe."

"We noticed that," the conductor responded. "We have those bad drifts coming up so I think we'll stop at Hillman and leave the cars until we can punch a hole through."

After the train was set off John backed the engine and plow about half a mile, stopped, revved up the diesel power plant and charged forward. They rolled by the cars on Hillman siding with the plow wings pulled in until they passed the south switch, after which Charles set the wings at their most extreme position. They went into the first drift at forty-one miles an hour but lost their momentum quickly and almost stalled. The engineer reversed the movement and retreated to the south switch of Hillman. They tried again but gained little.

The third and fourth tries were failures. Joe was on the radio. "John, let's take it back to the siding, pick up the cars and push them back to the semaphore.

We'll leave them there so we don't pelt the cars with snow anymore and then run full bore into the drifts."

"Good. We needed more speed before. That's what we need, a lot more speed."

The engine and plow hit the drift at forty-six miles an hour on the fifth attempt and went almost through before the diesel began to stall. John stopped and went back for a sixth attempt. They gained only one rail length that time. After another five tries, the plow broke through the first drift before stopping, after which they returned to the point where the equipment cars and coach were located.

John knew they had lost an inordinate amount of valuable time. On the next attempt the speed recorder reached fifty miles per hour at Hillman and the train surged into the heavy snow at almost fifty-five. The diesel engine whined and shook and slabs of snow crashed against the train. John could see nothing from the engine as it went into the deepest snow. When it seemed that the diesel would surely die, they broke through the last drift and the engineer pulled to a stop.

John opened his window, leaned out and gulped the cold air. His vision was blurry and he leaned forward to regain his sense of equilibrium. Will Smith came across the cab and placed his hand on John's shoulder. "You okay, Mr. Shanahan?" he asked.

The engineer looked up weakly. "Yeah. Okay, Will. Got a little woozy … back there. I didn't think we were ever going to hammer a hole. … That was a workout."

The cabin door on the fireman's side opened suddenly and Joe Francis burst in. "You fellows okay?" he asked of Will, who pointed to John. "John, speak to me. You okay?"

John rubbed his eyes. "Yeah. Just got a little overanxious, I guess. Damn, that was hard going. How are you and Charles? That must have been one hair-raising ride in the plow."

"Yeah. Pretty rough. We made it okay but the left wing on the plow collapsed. Bent a pneumatic ram on the left wing. Made a helleva crack. Charles is looking it over now so we'll have to sit tight a few minutes while he investigates. … You sure you're okay? I'll call this mission off in a second if you're feeling poorly."

"No, I'm good now. Pumped too much adrenalin back there, I guess."

"Happens to good railroad men all the time. I've got an Indian dish that will cure what ails you. I'll be right back." Joe went down the ladder, wallowed through the snow and climbed into the snowplow. He was back soon with a covered bowl, spoon and Thermos.

"This is like a bit of mulligan, not good like Molly makes, but not bad. Tribal secret, so don't ask. You eat this and have coffee from my Thermos. That should light up your life until we reach civilization again. I'll be back when we figure out what to do next."

John nodded and checked his watch. Then he held it up, looked at it and put it to his ear. He shook the watch and peered closely at the dial.

Joe, who observed the performance as he was about to step out of the locomotive, came back to take a look. "Forget to wind your watch again?" he queried.

"No. Don't think so."

"So, what's the problem?"

"It's running way too fast. Must be that perpetual-motion winder. All this crashing around with the engine kicked it into high gear and now time is flying by as we speak."

"Really? How odd." Joe pulled out his watch and held it up next to John's. Both read six-thirty p.m. "I don't follow you, John. It is six-thirty. What's wrong with that?"

"It can't be six-thirty," the engineer stated flatly. "We're sitting here in the snow and cold about seven miles from Summit. We left there at three-thirty. Now you're convinced it's six-thirty. If so, we have taken three hours to get here. Seven miles in three hours?"

Joe's eyes twinkled. "Well, let's go with six-thirty anyway," he offered as he prepared to climb down the ladder again. "Time flies when you're having fun. ... Eat your mulligan so your adrenalin will stop pumping. Maybe that will slow down your watch."

After retrieving the rear of their train, Work Extra Fifty-Three moved again to Hillman where Will Smith dug out a trackside telephone for Joe to report their delay and problem with the plow. Henry Terrell, who was sitting in as dispatcher, advised them to continue to Spanish Junction while top management figured out the next step.

The train limped into Spanish Junction at seven-fifteen with the disabled left wing of the plow pinned in the closed position. The northbound plow train, headed by Engine Fifty-Four, another branch-line locomotive, was already on the mainline under the tower lights. A brakeman on that train opened the switch to the east side siding and waved the Fifty-Three into the track. Then Joe signaled for a stop so that the snowplows would be alongside each other, after which he boarded the other plow to talk with the conductor. Boomer Johnson, the telegraph operator, followed Joe to join the conversation.

Five minutes later, Joe, Boomer and Brakeman John Kelly trekked to the tower to provide an update for the dispatching office and then came back to John's locomotive and climbed inside the cab. The Gatlin-based plow train pulled out en route to Summit.

"Aha, my friend Boomer from out Montana way!" John exclaimed as he shook the operator's hand. "Looks like a lively night in your neighborhood."

"It's good to be busy," Boomer said. "Make's the time fly. Speaking of time flying, I have instructions to check my watch against that one you carry. Rumor is that you have one of those automatic winder gadgets that makes it gain the faster you go."

Boomer held out his watch and compared it to John's. "Hmmm, seven-thirty. Both the same. Wonder why. I wind mine by hand."

John grinned. "I think now that it has to do with atmospheric conditions, not speed." He opened his window and stared at the pitch-black sky. "Yep. There's definitely a low-pressure system moving in. Lows slow everything down, even railroad watches."

Boomer stared at John. "Doggone, I think you're right. The weatherman on the radio said there's a low-pressure system headed this way. That means more snow."

Joe Francis placed his hands over his ears. "I didn't hear that."

"Me, neither," John chimed in and covered his ears. "Sorry I brought it up. ... Now for the task at hand, where do we go from here?" he asked Boomer.

"The Gatlin plow makes a run through to Summit immediately to clear the *Night Express*, which is running on time. Here, the section men from South Spanish cleared both the mainline and siding of telegraph wires and poles so the dispatcher wants you to plow down through this siding, drop the cars with the repair crew near the work site and continue to Blackwater where you'll probably need to go into a siding for the passenger train. Beyond that, everything is hypothetical."

Boomer handed orders and several messages to John and Joe. All were read aloud. Their plow would continue in service without the wings but the flangers would be used to remove snow that had tumbled back over and between the rails. Boomer stepped off and Joe called to him. "Let's call our departure from Spanish Junction seven-forty. Add ten minutes for dropping the cars and coach," he yelled. Boomer responded with a highball.

The plow train re-entered the main running track at seven fifty-two. Joe returned to the snowplow and after Will re-aligned the switch and climbed aboard John cracked the throttle open. They clicked off the miles rapidly and were approaching Blackwater just before nine p.m. when Joe spied agent Molly McCaslin on the platform with two order hoops. She waved a highball, which the conductor relayed from the plow.

John reduced the speed to fifteen miles an hour, watched as Joe snagged his hoop from the snowplow's side door, and reached out for his. The catch was clean and he waved to Molly as he pulled the hoop inside, detached the information from the pouch and tossed the hoop back to the platform. Joe waved another highball with his lantern and closed the plow door. John pushed the throttle forward, snapped on an overhead light and read the order aloud: "Engine Fifty-Three run extra ahead of Train Three, Engine Five-One-One Blackwater to Gatlin. Train Three will not leave Summit before nine-naught-one p.m. Extra Fifty-Three South need not protect against extra trains Blackwater to Gatlin."

There was also a message advising the train crew to drop the snowplow at Gatlin and to be prepared for the possibility of making an emergency light-engine run through to Hill Junction. A SB&Q wrecker crew had cleared and repaired the main running track through that yard and New England Eastern was finally working to re-open the east leg of the wye. If Conductor Francis and crew could reach East Tower by two a.m. they should expect to be called at ten that morning to handle a special train out of Sunbury that would carry groceries and other commodities for the communities of the North Country. The move was necessitated because the state had failed to reopen the Hackmatack Highway and might not have it reopened until the next weekend. The message was signed "JPS."

"Who is JPS?" John asked Joe on the radio. "That's a new one."

"J. P. Shanahan. Know him?" There was a long silence. "Hello, anybody home back there?" Joe asked.

"Just a dumb engineer making small talk. That's because I'm coming back to normal, Joe. Thanks, by the way, for the mulligan. That was very good. What was in it?"

There was another long silence. "Sorry, nobody home up here" was the eventual response.

∞

Extra Fifty-Three had nosed its snowplow into a siding and then pulled to a stop at Gatlin station at ten-thirty, just as Train Three was arriving at Blackwater. Hank Terrell made a split-second decision that the light engine would make good enough time to stay ahead of the passenger train through to Hill Junction and instructed Larry Smith, who was sitting at the nearest telephone, to advise both trains of the change of plans.

J.P. Shanahan, who was still at the station, slapped Hank on the shoulder. "It was yours to make and that was a damned good call, Hank! The priority definitely needs to be that commodity train for the North Country. If we can make that work, any doubts about this railroad's ability to handle a crisis will be long forgotten." Then, as an afterthought, he added, "This innocent bystander observes that the general manager of this fine railroad needs to suspend Rule G for a few minutes and let us break into that cache of fine liquor I just happened to notice in your office desk."

"Now that is a damned good call," Hank said and stood up behind his desk. "By the power vested in me by the powers that be, I declare that within the walls of this room Rule G is suspended until this executive order is annulled."

Chapter 40: The Commodities Train

Extra Fifty-Three South, operating as a light engine with four trainmen and a stack of personal gear in the cab ran the ninety miles from Gatlin to Hill Junction in two hours and thirty minutes and arrived at one-fifteen in the morning. The crew went off duty there and was asked to report at nine-fifteen a.m. to handle an urgently needed special commodities train back to the snowbound North Country. The night hostler drove the men to the Railroad Motel, after which he returned to attend to the locomotive.

John fell asleep thinking about Jenny Boston, dreamed about her while he slept, and when he awoke at seven-thirty a.m., his first thoughts were of the young lady who had made such an impact on his life in a short time. He had forgotten to ask if she was lined up for work the next day and then remembered that she held the engineer's job on the Summit switcher at four in the afternoon. There was no school this week, he remembered, so perhaps she would be out walking with Katie. The walk likely would be down to the station to see the *Northern Express* depart for Sunbury.

If they walked to the station, they would go by Emma's house, and then the vacant Ryan place, each of which was just north of the imposing station and its grounds at the end of Railroad Avenue. The arrangement was so American: Three town houses in a row and just steps from a train depot. If he were to stay in the North Country, he thought he would enjoy living in the Ryan place. If he didn't stay, the house would be a wise investment because another railroader would likely make an offer for the property.

Maybe he should contact the owners or a real estate agent and inquire about the house. But he wasn't much of a barterer, he realized, and would probably settle for a price that would saddle him with debt. He would get taken and be the laughing stock of his friends. But then, in a flash, the dilemma was resolved.

John P. Shanahan the elder! The shrewdest barterer he knew and that gentleman was only a phone call away. John smiled. "Why not? I'll call my father and run it by him," he said aloud. It was almost eight o'clock when he reached for the motel room phone and placed a collect call to the Summit, Bolton and Quarry Railroad in Summit.

The call was transferred to the dispatching office and Larry Smith answered.

"Hello," John said. "Is John P. Shanahan up and around today and in a chatting mood?"

"I don't fall for that old line anymore, John P. Shanahan!" Larry exclaimed and then burst out laughing. "You're a jewel, buddy. Obviously you're up and around and enjoying life this morning. By the way, you guys turned in a great day's service again yesterday and early this morning. Now, if you'll hold on, I'll summon your father."

J.P. answered immediately. "Hello, J. P. Shanahan here. How may I help you?"

"Let's buy the house at One Railroad Avenue, Dad."

"It's John! I'm glad you called! Are you rested now? That was some piece of work you fellows pulled off yesterday. Tell the boys I really appreciated the effort."

"Thanks, Dad. I will. Now about that house I mentioned. I'm just ... well, thinking ... you know, like a shrewd businessman might ... well, like you ... and I figured that a fellow ... young guy like me ... might invest in something ... in the line of real estate."

"I see. You say that's One Railroad Avenue? Sure. I know the place. The Ryans used to live there but they moved to a new home at Summit Heights. One Railroad Avenue is next to the station. Also, it's just two doors away from the Boston residence. But that probably would be only a coincidence."

"Well ... yes, of course. However, you see ... well, in my work with the railroad, I kind of figured I'd be running here and there on the line. Out of there sometimes and other times, well, you know, somewhere else ... and I thought I might like to have my own place to stay ... instead of a hotel or motel room, you know. ... Not that I don't like Seven Pines ... because I really do, Dad, but it's a little out of the way for a guy that doesn't drive a car or walk long distances to work."

"I think I see where you're going. Really, I must say you've put some thought into this and I applaud you for that. Hey, if I were a young lad and, you know, looking around, so to speak, I'd move into a house as close to the Boston residence as I could get."

"Uh huh. Well, we seem to see eye-to-eye on that point."

"Not to change the subject, but you probably know Jenny is the engineer on the *Northern Express* today. In fact, they just pulled out with a full load of passengers. I'm telling you, business is looking up despite the trouble we ran into with this storm."

"Ah ... well, no, I didn't know that Jenny was on the *Northern Express* but I guess the regular crew is scattered hither and yon. Joe Francis and John Kelly are with me, come to think about it. And yes, I'm quite excited about the business, both passenger and freight."

"So far, so good. Well, I have to run. Need to earn my keep around here."

"The house, Dad, do you think that, well, maybe ...?"

"That's my first business. I know Harry Ryan very well. I'll make him a generous offer, more than the house is worth, because he was a first-class railroader. Consider it done. When you get back here we'll do an inspection and see what we'll want to invest in improvements. We might be able to move your gear in later today if things go okay. I'll spring Ramon to handle the moving. But always feel welcome at Seven Pines, because that's your home, too. ... Now I really have to go. We'll talk later. See you."

The line went dead and John put down the phone. He got up, walked across the room, whistled and peered out the window. "Piece of cake," he said and smiled contentedly.

A runner from the shop drove the train crew down Depot Road to the New England Eastern's station after they had breakfast in the motel lunchroom. While there, they also purchased sandwiches and drinks for the trip north.

The Eastern agent presented two tallies listing eighty cars coming in from Sunbury for interchange with the Summit, Bolton and Quarry. Surprisingly, the cars were lined up by destination: Blackwater; Summit, including cars for Bolton and Eagle River; Aroostook; Lyndon and Boundary. The train was made up of thirty-two flat cars carrying truck trailers with a variety of consumer goods, fourteen refrigerator cars with other foods, sixteen tank cars containing fuel and gasoline, four cars of building materials and fourteen new SB&Q cabooses from Pennsylvania that had been handled through to Sunbury in error. Conductor Joe Francis took a copy of the tally and gave the other to John Kelly, who was head brakeman. Will Smith would be the flagman and ride in the rear caboose with Joe.

John shook his head in disbelief at the size of the train. "That's a lot of supplies. I guess the stores were running low on goods. ... So what do we have for power?"

"Looks like six units," John Kelly responded, pointing across the freight yard. There, new general-purpose diesel units bearing numbers five-eighty through five eighty-five were idling in a ready-to-go mode. The diesels were pure white with a sky blue trim and red letters denoting them as property of Shanahan Lines Northwest. The locomotives were on a track adjacent to local cars from the *North Country Night Express*.

"There's a bundle of money tied up there," John observed. "And I was hesitant this morning about asking my father to help me with a little house I'd like to buy in Summit."

Joe smiled. "That would be the Harry Ryan house at One Railroad Avenue," he offered. "Nice place. Good shape. Wise investment. Two houses down from the Boston place."

John shook his head. "No secret is safe from the native American. By the way, I'm the scalawag who smuggled the Christmas gifts across the border. But you knew that, Joe."

"No. Thought it was Larry Smith."

Joe and John received clearances from the Hill Junction agent at nine-fifteen to move the six engines slowly through the wreck-littered yard to East Tower. After the northbound *Northern Express* pulled away John backed the engines down the wye to the NEE mainline, arriving there minutes before the freight train from Sunbury pulled in.

The Eastern locomotives were stopped, uncoupled from the cars destined for the North Country and pulled ahead to let John back his engines onto the mainline and couple to Eastern's train. The train for the North Country pulled forward to a point where the last interchange car was near the switch. The Eastern brakeman uncoupled the rest of the train and advised Joe Francis that he could go ahead.

Joe and Will Smith tossed their gear into the last caboose in the string and climbed aboard. The conductor carried an SB&Q portable radio issued by the agent at Hill Junction and after a satisfactory test of their train's air brakes was made, Joe radioed his engineer. "Okay on the rear, John. I make it out from the Eastern junction switch at nine-thirty. You're pulling sixty-six loads and fourteen caboose cars, four thousand five hundred tons. We'll take our running orders on the fly at East Tower."

"Okay on the time and the orders, Joe," the engineer responded as he notched the throttle ahead and tapped the sander lever. John Kelly caught the order from the operator when the engines passed East Tower and moved into the mainline grade. John Shanahan observed that the new engines ran well and handled the eighty cars with ease.

John Kelly passed John Shanahan the train order, which he read aloud: "Engine Five Eight-Five run extra East Tower to Carroll not protecting against other extra trains. Train One Engine Five Naught Two left East Tower at nine-fifteen a.m."

The radio crackled. "I make it by East Tower at nine thirty-eight," Joe reported. "How's she hauling?"

"Smooth as silk. Good rail. Mainline looks great but I guess the sidetracks are a mess."

"That's true. We'll probably have to contend with a spreader train or two before this day's done. ... You happen to notice that cloudbank off to the southwest?"

"No, but John Kelly's making a meteorological observation. ... Uh oh. He's not smiling that handsome Irish smile of his. ... Ah, now he is, and he says, 'Let's hurry home before the storm hits.'"

"Good idea. Let's make tracks while the tracking is good."

The goods train passed Halfway and Crawford running at forty-five miles an hour and was nearly into Carroll when Joe called again. "Need an order at Carroll," he reminded the engine crew. "I have a feeling that we'll have to stop because there's got to be a spreader train working somewhere around here."

"We'll ease into the yard and keep our eyes peeled."

John Kelly spotted the order board first. "Red board at Carroll," he called. Then he bolted upright. "Hey, the *Northern Express* is in on the north end of Track Two! The agent is giving us a signal to pull up to the station and stop."

John sounded the air horns and made a brake application. "Hey, Joe," he called on the radio. "Train Two's on the siding. Looks like they're putting us out ahead of them."

"That's different. I like it. I'll be standing by for more good news."

John stopped the train directly in front of the station door and stepped out to the catwalk on the fireman's side, after which he descended the stairwell to the platform. Agent Darrell Woodward came forward to shake his hand. "Good to finally meet you, Darrell," John said. "Seems like I go by here quite a lot but never get a chance to stop."

"It's good to meet you, John," Woodward said. "Unfortunately, we have no time to talk. I need you to sign a Form 31 train order pronto and get you moving ahead of Train One." The agent passed a clipboard to John, who read the order: "Engine Five Eighty-Five run extra ahead of Train One Engine Five-Naught-Two from Carroll to Blackwater, not protecting against extra trains. Extra Five Eighty-Five use main running track and meet Train Two Engine Five-Naught-One at Gatlin. Train Two take siding from north end Track Two at Gatlin." The engineer signed the order and the dispatcher at Summit was advised of the signing. Additional paperwork was completed and the order became official. John's copy was bundled with messages and he hurried back to the locomotive.

John sounded the air horns indicating that the train would move forward. He notched the throttle up and the train responded well. Then he passed the order and messages to John Kelly and called Joe to advise him that he would be getting orders on the fly as the caboose passed the station. "We're running ahead of Train Two. Busy now. Talk later."

"Roger on that. I made us into Carroll at ten-forty and we'll say ten forty-five out."

John had the commodities train up to twenty-five miles an hour when it passed the northbound *Northern Express*. He shoved his side window open, waved to the engine crew on the passenger train and notched the throttle ahead again. Then he turned to John Kelly. "Hope you're okay on the order," he said. Kelly nodded.

"And the messages? Maybe you'd run through them while I nurse our horses along?"

The head brakeman read each aloud. The first, directed to all employees on the Hill Division, specified that Extra Five Eighty-Five was now a priority train carrying rush commodities to community centers in the North Country and would take precedence over all other trains. The engineer was directed to exceed freight train speeds at his discretion by up to ten percent on tangent, or straight track. Another advised the train's crew to disregard the setoff of one commodity car at Blackwater and handle it through to Summit, where it would be switched to the next train going south.

"I see," John said. "Does being a priority train qualify us for an upgrade in pay?"

John Kelly grinned. "I hope so," he said. "This is a tremendous responsibility. Responsible people should expect to be paid handsomely for their work, and if you're going to buy yourself a house, young man, I'd think any extra income would help, even if you have certain connections with important people in the company."

"Well said, John. I'll advance that notion next time I sit down to supper with the man who pays the bills."

The commodities train rolled by the clear order board at Gatlin station at eleven fifty-five a.m. A minute later, the locomotive of the southbound *Northern Express* appeared on Track Two in the distance. As the trains drew closer John suddenly remembered that Jenny had been assigned as the passenger train's engineer. He opened his side window and peered ahead. A head also appeared in the engineer's side window of Engine Five-Naught-One. John tugged the throttle back and the speed dropped to fifteen miles an hour. Another figure appeared in the doorway of the passenger train and held a tightly rolled newspaper at arm's length. John stepped to the door of his engine, opened it and held his left arm out with his hand open. Then he recognized Rob Rankin, who apparently was the head brakeman on the train.

John grabbed the newspaper and turned his eyes quickly to Jenny as his engine rolled by. "Hi, handsome!" she yelled. "Hi, beautiful!" he yelled back. She blew him a kiss and he returned one.

John squirmed back into his seat and jammed the throttle ahead, just as Joe called. "The rear passed Gatlin at eleven-fifty," he said. "Did I detect a slight slowdown when we passed the other train?"

"Yes. I was admiring the attractive engineer."

"Good move. No engine malfunction then. … By the way, I also noticed a couple of plow and spreader trains over on the back tracks in the yard. One was faced north and the other south. They must have been on hold until the traffic passed."

"Yep. Avoiding gridlock."

John checked the track ahead and then unwrapped the newspaper to find some significance for the unusual delivery. After scanning the front page he realized the paper was published on June 23. He held it at arm's length, pulled the sections apart and was refolding it when a pink envelope fell out and fluttered across the cab. The head brakeman reached down and picked it up. Then he looked at John and flashed the Kelly smile. He got up, walked across the cab and passed the envelope to John.

"Lovely handwriting and a most enticing scent," he observed, his eyes twinkling. "I'll watch the track ahead for a bit so you can focus on your mail."

"You caught us romancing on the job, John Kelly," John said sheepishly. "I'll take up your offer of track-watching while I read and daydream for a few minutes."

Kelly chuckled and resumed his post. John removed his gloves to open the envelope. "Hey, it starts 'Dear John,'" he observed. "That's the first 'Dear John' letter I've ever had from a gal." He looked at his colleague and noted the beginning of another smile. "Not to worry, lad," John Kelly responded. "That young lady is genuine."

John read the letter. Jenny wrote that she was thrilled to be engineer on the *Northern Express* for the first time. Bill Travers had worked a sixteen-hour shift the day before and was not rested in time to resume his regular run out of Quarry in the morning. When the re-railing of the plow was completed the previous afternoon, the crew went on plow and spreader service in Summit Yard and had reopened more than half of the sidings.

Jenny explained that the passenger crew, which also included Elmer Knowlton as conductor and Rob Rankin and Roland Evers as brakemen, was transported by Ramon to Quarry that morning. Upon arrival in Gatlin, she wrote, they would transfer to the northbound passenger train for the first time under the two-train arrangement and return to Quarry in the afternoon. She understood that the regular crew—Bill, Jim McDermott, Joe Francis, Carl Reardon and John Kelly—would take over again the next day and her crew would run a special round-trip freight train between Quarry and Summit at the request of Major Robert Adams at the transportation test site. For that reason, John's father and mother had invited Jenny to stay over at Seven Pines and asked her Aunt Emma and Katie to join them by traveling to Quarry on Jenny's train from Summit.

"It's all so exciting, John!" she wrote. "I'm very fond of your father and mother. I also should say that I'm especially fond of you and miss you every hour you are out of town. I should close now, but I hope we have an opportunity to get together again soon. Most affectionately, Jenny."

John folded the letter and re-inserted it in the envelope, which he placed in an inside pocket of his frock jacket. "Well, I guess it's time for this daydreamer to get back to work. Give me an idea where we are, John Kelly, and I'll attempt to keep my attention on the track ahead."

Chapter 41: One Railroad Avenue

The commodities train took its last order and a message on the hoop at Blackwater at five minutes after one. The order granted running rights through to Summit ahead of the passenger train with no trains to meet en route. The message added particulars: The train would not have to stop at the semaphore and would be aligned into Track Five in Summit Yard. The northbound *Northern Express*, about fifteen minutes behind the special freight, would come in on Track Three and the connecting passenger train to Boundary would be on Track One.

John Shanahan was directed to stop the locomotives alongside the platform where a relief engine crew would take over immediately. The new crew would move the train ahead so a similar exchange could occur at the caboose. John and his colleagues would be dismissed upon arrival and Joe Francis and John Kelly could expect to resume their jobs on the *Northern Express* at Quarry the next day. Will Smith would report for duty as an operator in the dispatching office again and John would be held "for later assignment."

The engineer accelerated quickly after leaving Blackwater and reached a running speed of forty miles an hour. He slowed to thirty at the approach to the crossover near High Meadow and re-opened the throttle again on the upgraded northbound track where the refrigerator cars had been stored when he arrived in the North Country. Here and there, cars destined for scrapping were set on the ground away from the track and would be removed at a later date. The commodities train came back to the original one-line mainline at Spanish Junction and ran the grade to Hillman with relative ease.

Extra Five Eighty-Five rolled to a stop in the Summit passenger terminal yard at two forty-eight p.m., at which time the engineer and head brakeman exited the cab. They had been on duty slightly more than five-and-a-half hours, and the trip marked the shortest shift of any since John began running locomotives for the Summit, Bolton and Quarry.

He worked his way through several clusters of passengers on the platform to find a place near the station wall from where he could observe the arrival of the *Northern Express*. He found the place, leaned against the wall and had his attention fixed on the hill to the south when he felt a tug at his coat sleeve.

He turned and looked down. "My little princess!" he exclaimed and took Katie's hand. She was wearing her new hooded winter jacket and gloves. "How is my favorite young lady?" he asked. She giggled. "I'm very well, Mister John. I am going for a ride on my mama's train today. Did you know that?"

"Yes, and I see them coming in now," he pointed and then realized that the view from the little girl's perspective was obstructed by the adults who had crowded into the outdoor waiting area. "You need a better view," John said as he planted his feet firmly on the platform, braced himself against the station and lifted her into his arms. There was still tenderness in his right arm, so he relied mostly on his left. "Is that better?" he asked.

"Oh, yes. I can see the train! Here it comes, Mister John!" She began waving in the direction of the cab just as her mother opened the fireman's door, spotted John and Katie and waved back. Then Jenny retreated quickly to attend to bringing the train to a gentle stop alongside the platform.

John and Katie watched as the passengers began stepping off. John put her down and Emma Cummings, who had been standing quietly nearby came forward to grasp her hand. John doffed his cap and then clutched her other hand. "So Mrs. Cummings and Miss Boston are off into the country for a train ride," he offered.

Emma smiled. "Yes, John. This is our first ride with Jenny. We're both excited," she said as she reached for her traveling bag. John snatched it up and directed Katie and Emma toward the rear stairwell of the coach *Sunbury*. Joe Francis, who was deadheading to Quarry, stepped to John's side and took the grip. "I'll take that," he said. "Conductor Knowlton has reserved seats for the ladies in the dome car and I'll see that they get settled in. … I don't know when I'll see you again, John, but I want you to know that it was a pleasure working with you these last few days."

"The pleasure has been mine," John said. "White man learn much from Indian." Then he grinned slyly. "But not tribal recipes. Education incomplete."

Joe chuckled. "Maybe in time." He climbed aboard and took the traveling case into the dome car *Aurora Borealis* for safekeeping. Emma, Katie and Joe waved from the dome as the train pulled away. The freight already had proceeded to the north end of Summit yard to set off the cars for Summit, Bolton, Eagle River and Blackwater. The *Northern Express* connector to Boundary left next and the premises were strangely quiet again.

John went inside, lost as to what to do next. Then he remembered that he should book off, so he limped up the stairway to the dispatching office. A somber Bill Westfield hailed him and motioned for John to follow him to an office in the west wing.

Puzzled, John followed. They stopped at Room Twenty-Eight and Bill rapped on the door. J.P. Shanahan pulled it open from inside. His face was flushed and it was clear that he was not happy. "Come in, John and Bill. This is not a pleasant situation."

Hank Terrell, Larry Smith, Fred Wilson and several others, mostly representing the transition team for dispatching, were gathered inside. Two men that John did not know were seated at desks in the front of the room. One wore the uniform of a state police officer, while the other, a surly looking man, was attired in a pinstriped business suit.

John and Bill sat down in chairs placed in front of the SB&Q personnel. The man in the suit glared at John. "John P. Shanahan the Third," he snarled.

John pulled down the visor of his railroad cap and peered back. "If what you said, and I believe I am quoting correctly, 'John P. Shanahan the Third,' was a statement as to your identity, that is a suspect statement. If you were asking me if I am said Shanahan, I will wish to see some identification as to who the hell you are as I do not talk to total strangers. Your companion appeared to be a uniformed officer of some law enforcement agency but I don't see any specific identification there either."

The man in pinstripes slammed his fists on the table. "I am asking if you are John P. Shanahan the Third. You will answer."

John stared at the man and responded in a measured tone. "And I beg to differ. I am telling you that until you produce some identification and state the purpose of lolling around here and taking up office space I shall not talk to you. Period."

The uniformed officer got up, stepped forward and held up a badge. "I am Officer Matthew Martin of the State Highway Patrol," he said in an affirmative but polite manner. "I am accompanying Special Investigator Maurice O'Hara who is assigned to the attorney general's office." The officer stepped back.

"I see. Your badge and your courteous manner suggest that you are whom you say you are. As for the bozo in the zoot suit, he has yet to identify himself." John drummed his fingers on the arm of the chair and tapped his cane on the floor. "I've been working out on the line for quite a while the last couple of days and I'm tired and hungry, and I've had enough nonsense. Present your credentials now, pal, or I'll walk out of this room."

John watched his father from the corner of his eye. He was somber at first but a smile began to play at the corners of his lips and his eyes started to twinkle. Bill Westfield was fighting hard not to burst into gales of laughter.

Officer Martin leaned over the desk and whispered to the investigator. O'Hara groped in a suit coat pocket and shoved several folded papers at the policeman who carried the material to John and presented it to him. John perused the documents and passed them to his father. J.P. reviewed the information and passed the material to a young man in a business suit who was standing next to him. Then he stepped forward and faced O'Hara.

"I'll tell you what, Mr. Bureaucrat. My name is J.P. Shanahan Junior and I own this railroad. The young man sitting there is my son and one of our locomotive engineers, a damned fine one. This man at my side is our counsel here in Summit, Mr. Robert Murray, Esquire, and he will represent us in any legal matters that you hope to generate from this affair. Now that you have finally identified yourself, much against your grain apparently, we are prepared to accept you as who you claim to be. I believe Engineer Shanahan is satisfied and will answer your questions. Is that right, John?"

John nodded. "Perhaps our attorney would stand nearby to make certain that Mr. Bureaucrat plays the game right. Wouldn't you say so, Owner Shanahan?"

"That's right, Engineer Shanahan. We'll play the game on our terms. Now, my good man for the state bureaucracy, tell us just what the hell you are doing here on our property."

Despite his anger, O'Hara attempted to compose himself and stated the purpose of the visit. It had to do with the matter of a railroad engineer attempting to ram a state highway snowplow with a locomotive. The incident occurred on Christmas Eve on the Country Road crossing south of the town of Pleasant Valley, he said.

O'Hara identified the engineer as John P. Shanahan the Third. The snowplow operator was the first to report the incident to the Highway Patrol office in a telephone call from somewhere in the town of Collier. Later, he said, a Mr. Henry Terrell of Summit, claiming to represent the railroad, had attempted to distort the earlier account by blaming the road plowman.

"What a bald-faced lie!" Hank screamed and charged forward. The officer held up his hands quickly and asked the railroad manager to return to the back of the room.

"If we can have order here," O'Hara snarled, "I intend to ask questions of Engineer Shanahan. Can you give me a specific account of what happened, from your point of view, on Christmas Eve at that crossing?"

"I will tell you exactly what happened from no specific point of view. Your plowman was operating recklessly and at high speed despite limited visibility, and almost caused an accident." John pulled out his time book and turned back to the Christmas Eve event.

"After my colleague and I ascertained that a collision had not occurred I wrote a message regarding the event and dropped it off to our agent at the nearest station, who telegraphed it to this office. The following is an exact copy of that message: "Agent, Collier. Denny, please advise dispatcher of 'near miss,' County Road crossing, Mile 84.9, at 6:17 p.m. this date. Southbound highway snowplow truck failed to yield to flashers. Engine bell and horn in operation. Set brakes at 26 mph. Truck cleared engine by approximately two feet, no more, and continued without stopping. Engine 53 stopped south of crossing, engine checked over and run resumed at 6:21 p.m. Signed/ J.P. Shanahan III, Engineer.' The next train over the crossing reported that the crossing signals were in operation when that crew passed the location."

"I will have that book for the investigation," O'Hara said. "Officer Martin, the book."

John put his time book back into the inside pocket of his overall jacket and shook his head. "Not on your life, O'Hara. If you had conducted any kind of an investigation so far, such as interrogating the plow driver, and paying attention to Mr. Terrell who relayed this information word by word to your man at headquarters, you would have this already. Either you have it or you don't, and if you don't, then the state needs to launch an investigation of your investigation."

O'Hara slammed his fist on the table again. "We can't investigate the plow driver because we can't find him. The person who took the call at our office quit the next day and left town. So we're investigating the sources we can find. We have a case here, and the governor knows that, and he is determined to move this matter to court."

J. P. arose again, his face florid. "The governor!" he screamed. "This governor is furious because I purchased this railroad to help the people here get around and get their freight moving to markets. This governor wanted the railroad for the purpose of building a highway on the right of way to make up for the broken promises to the people in these parts when he was elected. This governor has seized on this incident that nearly crippled our effort to rescue forty-five stranded passengers—stranded I might add because the state was not able to remove snow from the Hackmatack Highway and make it suitable for road travel. That poor excuse of a road is still closed and we're out here working day and night to get goods in, potatoes out and people back and forth, and you people have the audacity to blame us to cover for your continued failure to provide adequate highway service."

"Is that the end of your political speech, Mr. Shanahan?" O'Hara retorted. "If so, let's get on with the questioning."

"No, let's not! I have a staff here tied up with your nonsense when they'd prefer to be getting their work done so they can get home for supper. ... By the way, how the hell did you get up here, O'Hara? I know Officer Martin works in these parts but I think you came from downstate, which likely accounts for your crude manners."

"What's it to you? I took your train today. I wasn't impressed."

J.P. turned to Larry Smith. "Larry, I'm closing this inquisition and ordering these intruders off the property. Would you refund the price of this gentleman's train ticket? Oh, and you might advise the gentleman that since he wasn't enamored with our train service we will not sell him any tickets in the future. Maybe he can get home with the state plows if they ever clear that highway. Meeting dismissed, folks! And O'Hara, if you have any more questions, direct them to our attorney, Mr. Murray. But stay the hell off my property."

"Yeah!" Hank Terrell yelled. Bill Westfield got up and yelled, "Absolutely!" The railroad personnel cheered loudly and then filed back to their respective workstations.

John and J.P. followed Hank into his office and closed the door. "By the power vested in me by the powers ... etcetera," Hank announced, "I declare that Rule G is suspended indefinitely while the three of us down the kind of booze needed to bring this marvelous day in railroad history to a close." With that, he rummaged in a liquor cabinet hidden in a coat closet and pulled out a very expensive bottle of liquor.

J.P. held it up and chuckled. "Henry Terrell, you are a true connoisseur of exquisite liquors. I'm thinking that I'd like to have you on my immediate staff back in Chicago once we get this operation fine-tuned. In the meanwhile, we need to celebrate this day."

An hour later, J.P. called a taxi to take Hank home and helped guide the railroad manager to the car when it arrived. Cabbie Richard Smith pretended nothing was amiss and promised to see to it that his fare was safely into his home before he departed. J.P pressed several extra bills into Richard's pocket, patted him on the back and thanked him for many years of faithful service to the railroad. John watched from the station door.

"Hank's a good man, John," the elder Shanahan said when he returned.

"He is, Dad. A wonderful man. ... You know, I've been thinking, in my inebriated way, that you and I are here and home is down the road a fair piece, and you are in no condition to drive. ... I don't have a hotel fee, and ... well, I'm pretty well beat out ... and ... Duh, I don't know where I'm going with this conversation. Do you?"

J.P. peered at John. "No," he responded seriously. Then John noticed the twinkle in his father's eyes. He liked that. "Okay, you're hatching a plot. Gonna let me in on it?"

"Think you could lean on me and stagger along the sidewalk leading toward town?"

John sized up the street, which seemed a bit blurry. "Dunno. Probably. Maybe we could stivver along and find a diner. I know there's a diner down there somewhere. Food. Yeah. That's what I need to neutralize the booze. Sure, let's stivver down the street ... and eat."

The night air was cold and snowflakes had started to fall. The two walked slowly along the west wing of the station, staying in the shadows to escape the notice of an occasional walker. John's head was beginning to clear when his father stopped suddenly and turned into a walkway. "Whoops, Mr. Shanahan of railroad acclaim, I believe you zigged there when you should have zagged. Hold on, now, and I'll follow my footprints in the snow back to where you are and get you steered in the right direction again."

J. P. was already at the door of a house that appeared to be occupied. He was knocking loudly when John reached his side. "I say, Dad, I think we best make tracks before someone finds out that we're intoxicated and calls the police. ..."

The door opened and Ramon Martinez peeked out. "I heard a rapping, tapping at the chamber door but I figured it was that doggone raven looking for another handout. Instead I find two wayfaring strangers who appear the worst for wear. Enter please, before the evening patrolman arrives and whisks you off to the hoosegow."

J.P. stepped inside and held the door for John. "Come on in, my boy, and feast your eyes on the new home of one John P. Shanahan the Younger. There's more paperwork but it's yours. We even had a telephone installed this afternoon. What do you think?"

"I think I've awakened from a long sleep and found that one of my dreams has indeed come true. You got the place, Dad, and Ramon has been hard at work moving things in. I don't know what to say. ... Thanks, I guess, is the best I can

287

do right now. He embraced his father and then Ramon. "Super father and super friend. I am truly blessed."

After removing his work clothes and splashing water on his face, John found a pair of jeans and a loose-fitting flannel shirt in his gear that was stacked in boxes in the hallway. Then he wandered around to see what was now his. The little house looked much like Jenny and Emma's places with a living room, kitchen-dinette and small bedroom and bath downstairs and two bedrooms and a bath on the second floor. The residence was tastefully appointed and well furnished.

He stepped back outside and noted the address affixed above the front door: 1 Railroad Avenue. The perfect address for a railroad man, he murmured and closed the door quickly when a gust of wind pelted him with snow. He was still brushing off the snow when he heard a telephone ringing. "Answer the telephone, John," Ramon yelled from the kitchen. "Ramon is not contracted to provide answering services at this residence."

John picked up the phone tentatively. "Ah, I'm not sure I should be answering ..."

"Hi, sweetie!" the caller exclaimed. It was Jenny. "I called several times already and Ramon said you and your father were in an inquisition, but I think he was funning me. I'm so excited for you. ... I had no idea you were interested in the Ryan house or that you really intended to stay here. Your mother told me about it and I can't even begin to tell you ... well, I'm so excited. And we're going to be neighbors! That's really special. ..."

"You really like the idea, Jenny? Really? I didn't know how you'd feel about it. I had second thoughts on the way up from Hill Junction today. It was like this little voice was telling me that I was intruding in a neighborhood that was really yours and your Aunt Emma's and Katie's, and Bill's, of course. I got to thinking that Bill might have an interest in the place and well, I certainly would see that he would have it, if that were so."

"Not Billy. No, he's quite content staying with Emma when he's in Summit and in one of the Ten Commandments when he has to be in Quarry. What he really wants to do is build his own place out in the Heights or maybe down in the Eden Valley."

"Well, that's good to know. ... How are Emma and Katie taking to the castle?"

"We love it here, all of us, and we're having the very best time. Your mother has invited us to stay the rest of the week. Apparently I'll have work on the freight several more days because the Army has a number of shipments in and out of the test site and then there's the potato loading going on at Bolton, and more switching than ever at the box and barrel company. Things are really looking up, John, and I'm so very happy."

"Me, too, Jen. ... And now Ramon is waving his arms in the kitchen and threatening to cut the phone line if I don't get to the table. Uh oh, here he comes with a meat cleaver. Back off, Ramon! Dad, disarm that man! I've got to run for my life. Sweet dreams, honey."

Chapter 42: Reliable Sources

John slept soundly in an upstairs bedroom the first night of residence in his new home and did not wake until the Summit station clock sounded the hour of ten in the morning. He pulled back the window drapes and looked out across Railroad Avenue. The street and sidewalks had been plowed and the sun was shining brightly. Apparently, the storm had passed sooner than expected, leaving but a few inches of fresh snow to sparkle in the sunshine. That was a welcome development because only yesterday railroad crews and contractors worked the length of the line to clean up after the Christmas Eve blizzard.

He took his time descending the stairs knowing that every staircase was a new adventure. He gripped the banister tightly against a misstep. When he reached the first floor he stepped into the compact living room and made his way to an easy chair where he sat down to savor his new domain.

The thought that he actually owned a piece of real estate he could call home was dizzying at first. Although his family was wealthy, he had never owned anything of substance. Suddenly he was the owner of a little house in a nice neighborhood in a community that truly caught his fancy. There were still papers to sign and file with government offices but payment had been made and the bill of sale was in his hands. John was sinking roots in the North Country and he was pleased with his progress.

The Ryan place was plain and utilitarian, yet warm and friendly. He marveled at how quickly the acquisition had been made after he had suggested it to his father. The house came with enough furnishings to make it comfortable so his only task would be to add personal decorative touches to make the statement that John P. Shanahan the Third resided there, his father had observed during supper the night before.

"Just pile the dirty dishes on the table and strew your clothes around the living room," Ramon suggested. "That's how I know you've been on the premises."

John smiled, knowing Ramon was right. "But it will be different this time," he vowed and tried to imagine how he might decorate the house. A hook near the door that the Ryans had placed there for some purpose caught his eye. He got up, walked over and hung his cane on the hook. "That should do it," he said. "John Shanahan's trademark."

Then he limped to the kitchen to see what was in the refrigerator. That was when he saw a note taped to the door. It was in Ramon's handwriting:

"Sleep in, friend. You need the rest. We're over at the station, taking care of the business of the day. J.P. said you should drop in on Dr. Collins to check the bruised arm. Traffic is moving well at the railroad but the highway is still closed, so it looks like another busy day for us.

"We stayed over last night but plan to go back to Quarry this afternoon. You'll notice that Ramon stocked your refrigerator and cleaned up the kitchen. Don't get used to this catering service. You'll find some lunch stuff around so don't try to do any fancy cooking. You're a good engineer, but I have serious doubts about your hot stove abilities. I wouldn't trust you to boil water. We'll talk later. Ramon."

John rummaged around the kitchen, figured out how to operate the toaster, found bread and butter and settled for a glass of milk rather than attempting to boil water for tea. After eating, he washed and shaved and wiggled into long johns, a fresh sweatshirt and trousers, and a comfortable pair of winter boots. Then he pulled on the fancy parka and cap that his father had insisted that he bring from Chicago and struck out for the doctor's office, which was more than a half-mile away.

Doctor James Collins was talking with a patient in the waiting room when John arrived. After the man left, the doctor came across the room and shook his hand. "Well, John Shanahan, we meet again and you appear to be looking chipper. Word has it that you bought the Ryan place yesterday. That's certainly the ideal location for someone who plans to make railroad work a career."

John grinned. "Yes, it's a lovely house that was well cared for by its owners. It's small, but just right for me now. I must say that word really travels fast around these parts. I'll have to call on you regularly to keep up on local doings.

The doctor chuckled. "A little tactic I learned in medical school: Listen when people talk and tune in to what they're saying. Medical folks are nosy critters and like to keep a handle on what's going on in their territory, so to speak. ... Now, I suspect you came by for me to look at that arm you bruised on the Christmas Eve adventure. I know a little bit about railroads, being the railroad's doctor in these parts plus the recognized No. 1 railroad enthusiast in the North Country. From what I've heard, that was an incredible piece of work under the worst of conditions."

"Ah, Doc, you do what you can do and hope it works out. In the railroad business, success is the result of the work of many people. On that outing, believe me, there were many, both railroad workers and community volunteers. I just happened to be the engineer, and, well, there was a lot of help, especially from the big railroader in the sky."

The doctor peered into John's eyes and nodded. "The hand of heaven touched your little train and give it a shove in the hard going."

"Sure did. I have no doubt, absolutely none."

"Neither do I," Jim Collins said. "I remember an incident once ... some years ago ... quite well. ... Anyway, step inside my office and we'll take a look at your elbow."

The examination went well and the doctor pronounced John to be in good health. "The soreness may linger for a few days because that was a nasty, painful

291

bruise, but I'd venture you're already climbing up and down the sides of loco-motives. I know quite a lot about railroad engineers and I've known none who ever wanted to give up that business."

"Yeah, I've been climbing up and down, awkwardly, of course. And no, I never had a colleague who gave it up voluntarily."

The doctor nodded. "Now, since you're going to be around here, at least for a while, you probably should have copies of your medical records forwarded to a local practitioner, one of your choice. I'm on call for the railroad, but that doesn't mean I have to be your choice. Understand that, please."

"Actually, I chose you for my doctor Christmas Day when you made that locomotive call. I will have my medical records forwarded to you. I have a war wound, a bum leg, as you probably know, so I'd say there's a lot of paperwork that you should have."

"I'd be interested in taking a look at your leg, if you're really settled on put-ting me on your payroll," Doctor Collins offered.

John nodded and exposed his scarred leg and reconstructed knee. "I had to go on crutches for quite a while after a long time in the hospital," he said. "Then I graduated to the cane, and, once in a while, like when I'm alone at home and can be as clumsy as I want, I take some steps unaided. I'm always a little unsteady at first, but once in a while, I even think about running a marathon," John joked. "I was a cross-country runner back in college, not great, but usually nearer the middle of the pack than the rear."

"Don't sell yourself short, young man," Collins said. "Always keep working on goals such as that. You had a life-threatening injury in the war. I imagine the Army medical corps had doubts that they could save your leg. Some surgeons did an incredible job of rebuilding that knee because it appears to function quite well. That is one critical factor in future rehabilitation."

The doctor paused and looked closely at John's knee again. "Flex your leg for me and bend the knee as much as you can. ... Ah, that's good. ... Yes, that was a marvelous piece of surgery. I'd say you'd regain more mobility as time goes on. Regular exercise is important, starting with plenty of walking. As I remember, an engineer on a long run can get pretty cramped up. Get up once in a while and walk around the cab."

"If I could just race up and down the side ladder on a locomotive the way I used to do, wow! That would really be something."

"I suppose you're thinking about getting in and out of the cab of a basic 1948 version of a Class F3 or an E8 in the 2,000-horsepower class with a vertical side ladder and a fairly narrow door?" Jim Collins asked in a somber tone but John detected a twinkle in his eyes. "Or perhaps a road switcher with short lad-ders and narrow runways?"

John looked at the doctor in amazement. "I know you're the railroad's doc-tor and quite the train-watcher but I didn't know the qualifications for either involved an intricate knowledge of diesel-electric locomotives."

"Let me show you something, John," the doctor said. He rummaged through a filing cabinet and produced several documents and a photograph and handed the material to his patient. The documents included a seniority roster from a Gulf Coast railroad, listing a James A. Collins as a qualified engineman. There also was a citation for meritorious service at the scene of a wreck in Louisiana in the early 1940s and another letter of commendation for averting a collision in Alabama. The photo was of an engineer about to climb into the cab of a well-known Gulf Coast-to-Chicago passenger train at the New Orleans terminal. It was a younger Jim Collins, John's new physician.

John stared at the doctor. "Well, I never imagined ..."

"Hey, don't look so surprised," Dr. Collins said. "We all have a past life, John. Medical school is expensive, and I wasn't born rich. I knew that railroad wages were usually quite good. Yes, I did a stint with the railroads and was in a quandary when I had to make a choice. I was engineer on the *Bayou Flyer* at the time—the train in the photo and a prize assignment—when I knew it was time to move on. It was a difficult decision."

He picked up the commendation for averting a collision. "This one, John, was really the doing of a higher power. I believe that with all my heart. There was a scheduled meet at a siding inland from Mobile. I was running a short passenger train at the time and had the right to the mainline because my train was running in the superior direction. The opposing train missed the meeting point and for some reason, I think we both know why, I looked out across a bayou at the right time and saw it coming in the distance."

The doctor continued in a serious tone. "We were approaching a spur track that led to a mill and I yelled at my fireman to get down on the front steps and run for the switch when we got close, and throw it. I had the train slowed down pretty well and he jumped and ran ahead and heaved the switch over. Then I juiced the engine for all I could and we cleared the other train by less than a rail length. I had a dickens of a time to get my engine stopped as we raced down the spur, but all of a sudden, through no doing of mine, something snubbed us and we stopped before hitting the freight cars in the mill. You couldn't step between the couplers of the engine and the first car when we stopped."

"The hand of heaven," John offered. Jim Collins nodded his head. "The hand of heaven touched my train that day," he said.

Doctor Collins reassumed his professional demeanor. "You appear to be getting around quite well considering the extent of your combat wound. A lot of effort and courage, which you obviously have exhibited so far with the injury, will go a long way toward achieving your goals. You know, you might even be dancing with that beautiful girlfriend of yours before long."

"I guess my girlfriend is about the worst kept secret in Summit," John said. "If I could dance with Jenny that would be a great step forward. I'll work on this exercise stuff."

John left the doctor's office and limped in the direction of the station. He stopped frequently to flex his leg and thought about the possibility of dancing with Jenny one day. Things seemed to be looking up, he mused, and he began to whistle a railroad tune.

When he stopped for the pedestrian light at the corner of Railroad Avenue and Sentinel Street he spied a building that he had not observed before. It was a two-story brick structure, much like an office building, with a parking lot at the side. Set among several retail businesses, it seemed somewhat out of place. When he looked closer he saw a sign overhanging the sidewalk that identified it as the home office of the North Country's daily newspaper, the Summit Sentinel.

Then he remembered that Nolan Terrell was the owner and editor of the paper and that he wanted to meet John. Not one to seek publicity, he had not given any more thought to the matter. But he should meet Hank's brother, make his acquaintance and refer him to his father, who reveled in "good press," as J.P. Shanahan put it.

"What the heck," he muttered and turned down the street to the newspaper office. John entered the building and walked up to the receptionist-telephone operator at the front desk. The woman looked up and smiled. "May I help you?" she asked.

"Ah, well ... yes, I guess," he stammered. "Mr. Terrell called the railroad some time ago to inquire if I could talk with him about ... well, some of the railroad work that we're doing. I just work there ... and wouldn't be a very good source ... but, well, I was out and about today and noticed your building ... from over at the street corner and ..."

"You're John P. Shanahan, the engineer that we've all heard so much about," the woman said as she stood up quickly and offered him her hand.

John nodded uncomfortably. "Ah, yes, I'm John ... ah, Shanahan, from the railroad and I operate locomotives ... at times."

"I'm Wilma Rogers, the mother of one of the girls you brought in on the *Christmas Train*. She said you were a handsome young man and very nice and she was quite taken by you. I want to thank you sincerely for that special effort you made that night." She shook his hand again and then embraced him.

"Believe me, ma'am, I just happened to be available to help out. Really, a lot of people did a lot more than me. I can assure you of that."

Just then a tall man with graying hair came down the hallway. Although his white shirt was rumpled and his tie was undone, he seemed to be an authority figure at the business place. "Wilma," he said to the receptionist, "I believe you're talking to that young John Shanahan who came to town recently."

"I am, Mr. Terrell," Wilma said. "Mr. Shanahan, this is Mr. Nolan Terrell, editor of our newspaper, and Mr. Terrell, this is indeed Mr. John P. Shanahan."

The two men shook hands. "It's a pleasure to meet you, Mr. Shanahan. My brother, Henry, has nothing but good words to say about you. And I talk frequently with your father about the railroad. Welcome to Summit. Oh, and I understand from some highly reliable sources that you have acquired the Ryan place next to the station. That's a mighty fine home for a young man starting out in our community."

John grinned. "I'd say you have highly reliable sources, at least regarding real estate transactions in town. I'd guess that reliable sources are a key resource for a journalist."

"Most are, John," Nolan said. "Sometimes we get burned, however, so we have to be dead sure of our facts. We have good relations with the Summit, Bolton and Quarry through both your father and my brother. Both are square shooters and even when the news isn't exactly the kind of publicity they'd like, they are up front with the staff here."

"They both speak very highly of the Sentinel, Mr. Terrell," John said. "And from what I've read since coming here, your paper seems to state the issues clearly and fairly. Anyway, I don't wish to take up your time. I came by in response to a request you made a few days ago but I've been out on the line a lot and this is the first time I've had off."

"Hank tells me about a lot of your comings and goings. If you have just a few minutes today, would you share a little time with me?"

John nodded and they went to Terrell's office on the second floor just outside the newsroom. "This place is quiet right now," the editor said. "In a while the reporters will start coming in from their assignments, along with the editors. By suppertime it really gets humming and by ten o'clock we crank up the presses to roll our first edition. We go on into the night and usually have the city edition on the street by three in the morning."

John chuckled. "About the closest I ever came to being a newspaperman was when I was twelve and delivered papers in my neighborhood in Chicago. I was pretty good about getting the papers out early but my collecting habits weren't so hot. My mother usually wound up paying out of her own pocket to balance my books."

"Didn't we all!" Nolan exclaimed. "My son, Maurice, was the same way. Who would believe that he's now the mill manager down at Gatlin Pulp and Paper?"

The two had just begun talking about John's work with the railroad when a telephone rang. "Excuse me, John. I probably need to take this call," Nolan said. "It's a private line that I have for calls that are urgent. Sit right there, please. This should take but a minute."

"Okay with me. Take as long as you need."

The editor answered the telephone. "Oh, it's you, Hank. I can't imagine why you'd annoy your hardworking brother in the middle of the day like this. Usually your frantic calls come just as we're going to press or early in the morning when you know we're behind on deadlines. So what the heck do you want this time?"

Nolan tapped his pencil on the desktop. "I see. … Uh huh. … Well, look, bro, I'll put him on. … Sure. Yes, I've heard. He's the new heartthrob in town, according to Wilma at the switchboard. Hold on, Hank. … It's for you, John. Hank has a favor to ask."

"Hope he's prepared to dish out big bucks, calling this time of day," John grinned as he reached for the phone. "John Shanahan, ace reporter for the

Sentinel here. So what's the hot tip? I just got a lecture from my editor about being sure my sources are reliable."

"Reliable?" Hank chuckled. "Heavens, no. You know better than that. I work for the railroad. Nobody that works for the railroad is reliable. You should know that."

"I think you're right, Hank. So why are you ... Say, how did you know I was here?"

Hank was seized in a fit of laughter. "Reliable sources, my boy. Reliable sources. Listen, are you rested enough to go to work again? Would you consider doing Hank a big favor? How about hauling a rush order of reefers to Aroostook? The job reports here at three-fifteen, just behind the passenger train. It should be a piece of cake, and I expect you'll be home later this evening. I'll have someone come over in ten minutes, pick you up and drop you at home for a change of clothes. You will? Thanks, John. I'll ...

"Hold on, Field Marshal Ludwig von Terrell! Let me catch my breath. ... Say, I have an idea but I need to run it by my editor." John put the telephone down on Nolan's desk. "I need to run a job to Aroostook in a little while," he said. "If you could go along we could talk about railroads and you'd be able to see what we're talking about. Afterwards, maybe you could explain it to me because most of the time by the time I figure out what we're doing, we've already done it."

Nolan looked puzzled. "I didn't quite follow that last line, John, and if I were editing you, I'd demand you put that thought in better order." Then he smiled. "Sure, I'd be tickled to go, if it's okay with Hank. If you've decided to go, let me talk to my brother and I'll run that by him."

"Good idea. I'd get the message tangled up and we'd both miss the train. And sure, tell Hank that I'll go along, too, but just for the ride."

John was at the station at two-fifty and was reading bulletins in the dispatching office with Conductor Stan Larrabee and Brakeman Rob Rankin when Nolan Terrell arrived, camera and reporter's notebook in hand. The assignment had the earmarks of a routine, short turn-around run, the engineer thought, and that would be a change of pace for him.

Chapter 43: Switching in the Heartland

The assignment for the crew of the extra train was to move seventy-five heated potato cars to Aroostook to supplement a dwindling supply at that critical railhead. During a briefing in the dispatching office, John learned that the train, already made up by a yard switcher, would have two road units for power and handle a caboose. The regular train on the Heartland Branch had been out since three that morning and would have to terminate their workday by seven in the evening. A second train from Boundary had arrived at eight a.m. and was also working on the line to help switch out some of the one hundred cars that would be loaded by evening. John's train would pick up any loads available at Aroostook and move them back to Summit for pickup by the next southbound train.

His train left Summit at three-twenty in the afternoon, twenty minutes behind the passenger train to Boundary. Nolan Terrell rode in the caboose with Conductor Stan Larrabee for the first leg of the trip and Rob Rankin occupied the lead locomotive with John Shanahan. The cab was silent for the first dozen miles and it was getting dark when Rob spotted the order board at Siberia. "Red board," he called to the engineer.

John responded with appropriate blasts of the air horns and slowed his train. When the agent appeared in the station door and waved a stop signal with a red lantern John notched the throttle back and made the first of several air-brake applications. The radio crackled and Conductor Stan Larrabee inquired as to the reason for the surprise stop.

"Don't know, Stan," John said. "The board's out at Siberia and the agent wants us to stop. Must be some hitch in the plan. ... I'll let you know shortly."

John stepped out on the catwalk on the engineer's side and walked to the rear of the locomotive where he climbed down the short stairwell on the fireman's side to the platform. Agent Robert Murchison was at the telegraph when he entered the station so John stood outside the ticket window. Murchison beckoned for the engineer to come inside after the wire business was completed.

"There's been a three-car derailment north of Travis Farm on the branch and both trains are trapped behind it," he began in a matter-of-fact manner. "At first, the dispatching office wanted you to drop your train here on Track Two and go back to Summit for the Big Hook. Now they think you should take the cars through, go down the branch with your engines and try to re-rail the cars without the hook." The operator passed John a message and folded a copy to deliver to the conductor when the caboose came by.

"Thanks, Robert. We'll get right to it," John said and returned quickly to the engine. He passed the message to Rob to read and called Stan to alert him to the change of plan.

"Okay," Stan responded. "That sounds like something we can handle."

"Roger. How's your passenger standing the suspense?"

"He's writing down everything I say. I talk too much. … I think we're in trouble."

"I think we've been in trouble before, Stan," John chuckled.

The train pulled into Track Eight at Aroostook where the cars were set off, after which John backed the engines along the mainline to retrieve the caboose. Then they stopped at the station at five-thirty p.m. and the crew went inside to get an update on the derailment. Several car inspectors and track workers who were being dispatched to the derailment scene were on hand to board the train. A flat car loaded with jacks, blocking, cables and other re-railing equipment would be picked up to take in on the branch.

Stan and John signed a work order giving their extra train exclusive rights on the Heartland Branch between Aroostook and the derailment at Travis Farm until twelve-thirty a.m. The regular branch line freight crew would be dismissed by the time the Summit train arrived and would leave their train on the mainline beyond the derailment. The train from Boundary would continue to pull loaded cars from sidings near the end of the line at Heartland and marshal them there, after which that crew would go off duty.

The train crew from Summit would have until seven in the morning to clean up the derailment and bring all loaded cars to Aroostook. Carroll Bartlett, a veteran trainman with extensive service on the Heartland Branch, joined the crew and advised them that the branch had been poorly plowed after the Christmas Eve blizzard. In addition, the last storm had apparently hit hardest in the Aroostook-Heartland area, where upwards of a foot of snow had fallen and drifted.

"Hit us hard," Carroll said. "The plow we usually use on the branch clunked out the day after Christmas so the track crews hired farmers around the area to scoop off the worst of the drifts with farm tractors. The boys tell me it didn't work very well. The derailment was caused by packed-down snow that they couldn't get cleaned up today."

John and Rob got back aboard their lead locomotive and were joined by Nolan Terrell. Carroll Bartlett and the track- and car-repairmen rode in the caboose. After picking up the tool car behind the caboose, the train departed Aroostook at six-ten p.m.

Ten minutes into the run John knew that operating conditions were less than satisfactory and he cut his speed to fifteen miles an hour. The farm equipment had been adequate enough to clear drifts down to the tops of the rails, but the flanges remained full of packed snow. In places, drifting snow had re-covered the track and the movement of trains earlier left only the slightest of wheel impressions. Ragged snowbanks pushed around by the tractors encroached on the track and crunched against the engine.

While traversing a cut through the drifts, the train lurched and went into automatic braking. John closed the throttle as a whoosh of air indicated that the brakes had set. The train stopped and the air pressure indicator stood at zero. "Big hole," John muttered.

Nolan Terrell looked at John quizzically. "Big hole," the engineer repeated. "The air got dumped from the braking system and the brakes set. That will happen sometimes if the snow lifts a handle to uncouple a car. The air-brake line will separate when the train pulls apart and that sets the brakes."

The radio crackled. "We lost the tool car, John. That hard snow must have lifted the coupler handle on the rear of the caboose. It looks like the car is five rail lengths or so behind us. I hope it's still on the track. We got a thump back there so maybe the snow lifted the front end of the car, which was the light end. … Carroll is going back."

The occupants of the cab opened their windows and watched the relief brakeman's lantern bob as he walked toward the errant tool car. Then Bartlett swung the lantern in a rapid back and forth motion parallel to the ground indicating the car was off the track.

"Yep," John said. "The tool car derailed."

Stan was on the radio again, confirming John's observation. "I've closed the angle cock on the caboose so you can pump up the air again. When we get our sixty pounds, we'll take the train back to let the car knockers off so they can figure what we do next."

John recharged the brake line. Then he reversed the diesel units and inched back along the track until Stan signaled for him to stop. Rob and Nolan walked back to observe the proceedings. John pulled out his time book and scribbled a notation that a tool car in his train had derailed three miles in on the Heartland Branch at six-thirty.

The re-railing work took the better part of an hour, most of which was spent by the crew digging out snow around the front trucks of the tool car and setting a heavy steel re-railer device firmly in place. Then the brakemen signaled for John to back up to a point about six feet from the tool car. A heavy cable was looped through the rear couplers of the caboose and the derailed car. When the cable was in place John inched the train forward to make the cable taut. After receiving verbal assurance that all employees were well away from the area where whiplash could be a factor if the cable broke, the engineer opened the throttle and hit the sander lever. The car crept up over the re-railer and then slammed down abruptly with all four wheels on the front end back on the rails.

The air brakes on the tool car were bled off and the air hoses reconnected. A fresh charge of air was pumped through the train line from the diesel locomotive and a brake test was made. Assured that no damage had been done to the car or the track, the workmen restacked their tools on the flat car. Then they climbed aboard the caboose, Stan waived a highball and advised John by radio of a departure time of seven thirty-five.

"I guess the slower we go, the better," Stan said. "I don't trust that tool car worth a damn. When we get done with it, I'd like to drop it at Travis Farm and not try to drag it back to the junction with a string of loaded cars."

"Agreed," John said. "Hope someone routes a snowplow down here eventually."

"Spring will come … eventually."

John chuckled. "Really? Does spring really come this far north of the Arctic Circle?"

There was a pause. "I'm thinking about that, John. You know, I can't remember. But I think it does. I'm thinking tonight I'll plan my next vacation in the dead of winter—say along about this time of year. Then I'll book off for another two months so I wouldn't have to come back much before the first of April. … Just a second, Carroll is chirping something about the best time for vacation. Hold on. …"

John glanced over his shoulder and noted that Nolan Terrell was jotting down notes furiously. The engineer grinned and pressed the radio mike. "The reporter and the engineer are eagerly awaiting Carroll's contribution. I bet he says if you start vacation on the fifteenth of February you can drag it on until the snow is but a distant memory."

"That's amazing!" Stan exclaimed. "That's just exactly what he said. I swear to you, John, word for word. You guys must be on the same wavelength."

"I take that as a complement, Stan. … Well, we have the horses up to a nice comfortable gait of fifteen. How's that work back there?"

"Suits me. … Yep, I'm going to apply for vacation beginning on February fifteenth and fly down to a resort in the Caribbean. Can't you imagine just lying on a beach and taking in the bikini stock and soaking up the rays? No trains around for a thousand miles. …"

"You sold me, Stan. I think I'll do the same thing. In fact, maybe I'll run the notion by management that we shut down this railroad adventure in mid-February and all of us, the whole doggone SB&Q team, charter a bunch of airplanes and head for the tropics."

The work extra pulled up to the station at Travis Farm at eight twenty-five p.m. The task at hand was only about two hundred feet ahead and from the cab John could see that one of the derailed cars was blocking a siding leading to a string of potato houses from the main line. It appeared to him that the only way to approach the problem was to clear the siding of cars from the south end and then attempt to re-rail the car from the sidetrack. If initial reports were correct, he told Nolan, there were two derailed cars beyond the first.

The train crew and the newspaperman entered the station while the car repairmen and trackmen headed to the site of the derailment to inspect the damage. The agent, Wilbur Jones, who was busy at the telegraph key, waved a greeting. They were about to go to the ticket window when the door slammed open and a man clad in a heavy hooded parka burst in. "All right, where the hell you guys been all night?" he bellowed.

John turned and grinned. "You look like a polar bear and sound just about as mean but I'd recognize that raspy voice anywhere. You want to know where we've been? We've been hanging around that bar next to the station at Aroostook getting liquored up good before we had to face the wrath of Harry Travis."

Harry shoved back his fur-fringed hood, beamed broadly and pulled off a mitten to shake hands with the railroaders. "Ah, boys," he said, "I was just funning you. Might as well laugh instead of getting boil-over angry like I usually do and break some windows around here. Let me assure you that the shippers on the branch are mighty glad you're here and appreciate the efforts being made on behalf of the lot of us."

The station agent emerged from his office and sat down in the waiting room. The regular Heartland Branch crew had been dismissed at seven and their train was on the mainline beyond the derailment, he said. The train from Boundary was expected to have its switching done by eight-thirty and would go off duty at Heartland. It would fall to the train from Summit to re-rail the three cars and finish the switching at Travis Farm. John and Stan's train would marshal the loaded cars they switched out on Track Three, along with the train already made up by the crew that had been dismissed earlier.

The next step, Wilbur Jones said, would be to run to the end of the line, couple their engines into the train from Boundary and work out to Aroostook, picking up loads already switched from sidings at Travis Farm, Singer, English and Jackson.

"Summit wonders how long the whole job will take, Stan?" the agent asked sheepishly.

Stan sat back, clasped his hands behind his head and stared at the ceiling. Then he shrugged his shoulders. "Well, we have a deadline as you know, Wilbur. It's February fifteenth because my good friend, Engineer Shanahan, plans to shut down the railroad then for a month-long vacation in the Caribbean. That right, John?"

"Absolutely," John said as he got up and introduced himself to the station agent. "And it will be your responsibility, Wilbur, to notify Harry Travis and his cohorts to that fact. February fifteenth, at eleven fifty-nine p.m.—that's the hard and fast deadline."

Wilbur chuckled and turned to Harry. "Well, you heard the word, Mr. Travis. Your game is up in mid-February. If you haven't got your spuds all shipped by then, it's back to your trucking buddies, just like the good old days."

Harry grinned. "You know, John Shanahan, if I hadn't taken a liking to you early on, I'd get the shotgun out of my pickup truck and blast that locomotive of yours to kingdom come. Instead, the shippers around here are going to give you fellows a hand here tonight and see if we can get this show on the road. I've got a couple bulldozers down by the derailment and I figure we can push or pull

301

as you see fit and move things along a little. ... And if we aren't satisfied, well, I've still got that shotgun in the truck."

Stan got up. "Okay, boys. Time to get to work. We'll appreciate any help you can give us, Harry. And, Wilbur, tell the dispatcher that I figure we can be out of here on the way back to Aroostook by, oh, let's say midnight, if everything goes okay. And tell the dispatcher that we're going to leave that damned tool car we've been trying to keep on the track right here. John and I refuse to haul that wreck another mile."

"Very good," Wilbur said. "And you probably know the railroad doesn't expect you to classify the train tonight. Just scrape it together the best you can and take it all out—engines, caboose cars, the whole works. The classifying will have to come later."

On the way back to the train, Stan asked relief brakeman Carroll Bartlett to go to the site of the derailment to advise the men there of the work schedule. "We'll go in on that siding from the south end and pull all the cars out and drop them on the mainline. Then, we'll nose in with the locomotives and re-rail that first car from the siding. After that, we'll work on the other two. When you're done, Carroll, it would be a big help if you'd work your way back along the siding to make sure none of the shippers still have the conveyors set up between the potato houses and the cars. Rob will work down from the other end." Turning to John, he asked, "You good with that?"

"Master plan, Stan," John responded and winked at Nolan Terrell who was standing at his side. To the brakemen, he added his standard safety message: "I'll be watching you guys all the time and I never move the engine until I can see all of you, or at least your lanterns. If I can't account for somebody, I won't move and I'll start sounding the air horns until I'm sure you're all clear of the cars. It's just one of my quirks, I guess."

The re-railing went a lot faster than anticipated. After the grabs, as the re-railing device was called on that railroad, was positioned, the locomotive was coupled to the refrigerator car and moved in a reverse direction. The car re-tracked easily and it was moved via the siding to the mainline. At that point, Stan decided that while the car repairers went about placing the rerailers under all of the wheels of the second car, the train crew would re-set cars at potato house doors along the siding.

That done, the locomotives were moved down the mainline to re-rail the next two cars. The procedure went smoothly and the bulldozers were not needed. After the loaded cars were assembled on Track Three, the Heartland Branch caboose was placed on the rear of the string and the two locomotives were moved to the other end. Then the train from Summit moved on down the line to Heartland, arriving there at ten-thirty.

The train was reassembled with the Summit-based locomotives ahead of the two from Boundary. The car inspectors coupled the control hoses so that the train could be operated from the leading unit on the southbound run and Stan's caboose was placed on the rear behind the caboose from Boundary.

The procedure was repeated at Travis Farm, where the agent presented the engineer and conductor with a final Heartland Branch running order to Aroostook. There was also a message for the crew to pull up to the depot at Aroostook, where a switcher crew would take out the two extra caboose cars that were assigned to Boundary and Heartland. After a lunch, the crew would take the train through to Summit, using all six locomotives. Substitute power for the Heartland service would arrive a few hours later.

Stan booked the departure from Travis Farm at eleven forty-five p.m. with six diesel units, eighty-two loaded refrigerator cars and three caboose cars. Pickups were made at Singer, English and Jackson sidings, rounding out the total count at ninety-eight cars.

The train pulled into the yard at Aroostook and John set the caboose in front of the station, after which Stan booked the train in at one in the morning. Brakeman Carroll Bartlett was offered work through to Summit, where he would be dismissed and deadhead on the morning passenger train back to Aroostook. Their work done for the night, the trackmen and car inspectors were dismissed upon arrival. Stan and Carroll had lunch in the depot and John, Rob and Nolan Terrell opted to have their lunches in their locomotive as the switcher crew shuffled the engines and made up the train for the run to Summit. Ten more potato cars loaded at Aroostook were added to the Summit-bound train.

After the northbound *North Country Night Express* cleared Aroostook station at one thirty-five a.m., Stan called John from the caboose. "Looks like we're ready to go south," he said. "I'll make us out at one-forty. Six locomotives, one hundred and eight loads, all potatoes, and the caboose. I figure eight thousand, nine hundred tons."

"Heavy load," John responded as he released the brakes and pushed the throttle forward. The train moved slowly at first but gradually gained momentum. Eventually he got the train up to thirty miles an hour and held it there for the duration of the run. They arrived at Summit at three twenty-five in the morning, where the crew was dismissed and told they would be called later, if needed.

John sat in the waiting room with Nolan Terrell after the others had gone home. They talked about the trip and the engineer answered questions about particulars of the work. "I don't attempt to tell anyone their job," John said. "I hope you'll emphasize that this run was the work of a lot of people who care about what they're doing."

"That was my impression, John," Nolan said. "I'll put my notes away for tonight, or what's left of it, and work up my story over the next few days. I'll need to talk to Hank again and check some sources that I contacted a while ago." He closed his notebook and stuffed it in a jacket pocket. "Thanks for a splendid trip," he added as he shook John's hand and then walked to the station's Railroad Street exit.

John sat for a while longer to catch up his time book. The station clock was sounding four in the morning when he finally got up, stepped into the cold night air, and walked down the street to his new home at One Railroad Avenue. As he

303

was about to step inside he noticed a newspaper in a plastic wrapper lying on the doorstep. A note affixed to the wrapper stated that the publisher and managing editor had entered a complimentary subscription to the Summit Sentinel in his name. "Thanks, Nolan," he murmured as he stepped inside.

Part VII: Considering the Future

Chapter 44: An Interlude in Summit

John Shanahan was cold and too tired to climb the stairs to his bedroom after the eventful run on the Heartland Branch. He pulled off his work boots, sheepskin jacket and overalls and scattered the gear across the living room floor. Then he dragged a blanket out from the downstairs bedroom and curled up on the sofa.

He heard the tower clock at Summit station sounding the hour but dozed off and lost count of the peals. John likely would have slept all day had the sun's rays not broken over the buildings across Railroad Avenue sometime after eight in the morning and flooded his living room.

Still weary and achy, he sat up and rubbed his eyes and thought he heard a train moving somewhere although the sounds were faint. He pulled out his pocket watch, tried to focus on it but the second hand didn't seem to be moving. He held it to his ear to determine if it was ticking. It was not and John shook his head. Obviously he had forgotten to wind it again and since he had no clock to set the timepiece by, he returned it to his watch pocket. "Got to get a definite routine going here, Shanahan," he muttered. "Wind your doggone watch once a day at the same time every day. This is ridiculous."

John limped to the kitchen and began rummaging through the pantry shelves. It was then that the sounds of the train became more distinct. He peered out the back window and could see a locomotive approaching from behind the station so he opened the back door and stepped onto a small porch for a better look. The train was a northbound two-unit freight carrying the white flags of an extra. John waved and the engineer responded with short blasts of the air horns. Asa Adams stuck his head out of a side window.

"I like your place, John!" he yelled. "Me, too, Asa!" John yelled back as the engines slid by. A string of empty pulpwood cars followed and the caboose appeared. The side door swung open and Jack Demers bellowed: "Gotta team up again sometime, mon ami!"

"I look forward to it, Jack," John responded and returned a wave. He watched as the train faded in the distance and a feeling of sadness swept over him. After having been an intricate part of train movements in the North Country for weeks he was an outsider again. There was no train assignment this day and the young engineer wondered why. Suddenly he became aware of the biting cold and was seized by a fit of shivering. John stumbled inside but the shivering continued and he drew a blanket around his shoulders.

"Dummy," he muttered. "You stood out there in the cold to watch a stupid train go by and caught a chill." Even his hands were cold and he rolled them into recesses in the blanket. John tried to focus his thoughts on Jenny and knew she must be working somewhere on this frosty morning. But where was that? He still didn't know what time it was so he listened intently for the sounding of the station clock. But he dozed off and did not awaken again until a sharp knock came at the front door. He got up and stumbled across the living room. The knocking continued. "All right, I'm coming!" he grumbled loudly and was reaching for the knob when the door swung open and Jenny Boston looked in.

"Oh, I woke you," she said. "I'm sorry, John. ... I was just in town and ... well, I'm sorry." She stood in the open doorway and the cold air swirled in.

"Come in, Jen, and close the door," John responded, his teeth chattering. "I picked up a chill a while ago and can't seem to shake it." He returned to the sofa and pulled the blanket tighter.

Jenny closed the door, slipped off her sheepskin jacket and hung it with her railroad cap on the coat rack in the entryway. She approached John quietly and leaned over to touch his face. His skin was cold and his eyes were bloodshot. "I ... just got cold a while ago and I can't ... seem to get warm," he muttered.

"You'd be a lot more comfortable if you got that work gear off and stretched out on the sofa," Jenny offered. "I'll get more blankets and pillows." She sprinted up the stairway and returned immediately with the extra bedding. Then she helped John to his feet and fixed a place for him.

"Now lets get rid of that filthy flannel shirt and the woolen trousers," she said after lifting the blanket from his shoulders. Jenny unbuttoned the shirt and helped him pull it off, after which she re-wrapped the blanket around his shoulders. Then she reached to unbuckle his belt when she caught herself. She turned crimson and looked away. "I'm sorry, that was ... very forward ... of me," she said. "I was so concerned about you getting warm that ... " She put her hands to her face.

"Ah ... that's okay, really, Jen," he said awkwardly and patted her on the shoulder. "I definitely need to shed the trousers and get under the blankets before the damned shakes come back." Jenny kept her back to him as John struggled out of the woolen pants. Still clad in his long johns, he slipped quickly under the blankets. "There, I'm decent again."

Having regained her composure, Jenny came forward and tucked the blankets tightly around him. "Okay," she said. "Now I'm going to brew some coffee and scramble a couple of eggs. You're exhausted and hungry and run down from the day and night routine you've been on for so long. You don't take care of yourself, you know, and I really wish you would. When was the last time you ate anything?"

"Ah ... well ... I can't ... remember. I went on some run yesterday afternoon, I think, and got back ... ah ... about four this morning. I had a couple of sandwiches in the night. Aroostook, I think. That was the last time. ... Say, Jen, what time is it anyway?"

"Don't tell me you didn't wind your watch again. John Shanahan! I cannot believe you. The neatest engineer I ever met and you never know what time it is." Jenny pulled out her pocket watch. "It's twelve-twenty. Now hush while I rustle up some grub."

John attempted to focus on Jenny as she scurried about the kitchen but his vision was blurry and he finally closed his eyes. He was warm as long as he stayed burrowed deeply in the blankets, which he pulled over his head. He had nodded off when she returned and pulled an end table to his side. Then she brought a plate of scrambled eggs and toast, a mug of coffee and eating utensils.

When everything was in place, Jenny pulled up a kitchen chair, sat down and touched his cheek. "Wake up, sleepy guy, breakfast is served," she whispered in his ear. He stirred slightly, groaned and then peered from beneath the blankets. "Oh, it's the beautiful lady," he murmured. "I've been missing you a lot lately."

"Me, too, John," Jenny said wistfully. "We always seem to be going in different directions." Then she smiled. "So, would you please emerge from your burrow and eat?"

John slipped his feet to the floor and sat up. She reached around him, pulled the blankets up against his back and let her hands linger on his shoulders. He peered up at her and grinned sheepishly. "You know, Jennifer, you're really a very nice lady," he said. "Thank you for coming today and for preparing this scrumptious-looking …" He stopped short. "So, what the heck are you doing here, anyway? I thought you were working … somewhere. I can't remember where, come to think of it. Wasn't it … somewhere …"

"Quit your babbling and eat, John Shanahan! Your eggs are getting cold." Jenny stamped her feet. "You're the most confusing human being I've ever met. I made you a hot lunch, so eat it or I'll have to spoon feed you." She reached for his fork but he grasped her hand and pulled her toward him. Caught off balance, she stumbled and landed awkwardly on the sofa beside him. Jenny tried to get up but John wrapped his arms around her. Their eyes met: His were pensive and Jenny's teary.

"Jenny, I wanted to say … well, what I've been wanting to say for days and days. …" He paused and clasped her hands. "I love you," he finally blurted out. "I babble a lot and don't make much sense most of the time but I know I love you. Do you understand that?"

"Oh, John, I love you so very much; truly I do," Jenny said through a cascade of tears. She pulled him close. They embraced tenderly. He drew his blanket around her shoulders and held her close. "I love you, Jenny," he murmured again.

They were still wrapped in each other's arms when the station clock struck one in the afternoon. She bolted upright. "Oh, my gosh! It's one already. I need to be back at the station in ten minutes. There are some rush cars coming in that we need to take back to Quarry." She scurried across the room and pulled on her sheepskin jacket and cap.

She went to the door, then stopped tentatively and turned to John. "I love you, darling," she said. "May I call you this evening, after work? I understood that you were not to be called for work today unless an emergency came up."

John pushed himself to his feet, realized he was standing in sight of his girlfriend in his long johns and pulled the blanket closer. "Sorry ... for my appearance," he mumbled as he grasped Jenny's hand again and kissed her. "Please call. God be with you, my love," he said as she turned and stepped out into the cold.

"God be with you, too, sweetheart," she called from the walkway. He closed the door and watched as she turned at the end of the walkway and faced into the west wind. Just a wisp of a girl doing a man's job, he thought as she disappeared from sight. That should change, he reasoned, but he knew that Jenny was doing what she wanted to do and was accomplished at that calling. He vowed he would never intrude in that part of her life.

The eggs were cold but John savored Jenny's breakfast just the same. After he was done he contemplated cleaning up the kitchen and unpacking the boxes that had been brought up from Quarry. But the whole procedure was overwhelming and he decided to develop a strategy first to deal with the situation, as his Army colleagues used to say.

"Yes, sir, I need to plan this out in an orderly manner," he said aloud. "I should strategize by maximizing my resources, minimizing duplicative efforts, weighing options and improvising as I carry out the mission. Hmmm. ... Perhaps I should sleep on this and conduct a thorough review at a later time. ... Damned good thinking, Lieutenant Shanahan, you're definitely officer material."

John pushed the end table away from the sofa, rearranged the blankets and burrowed back into his cocoon. He thought about rewinding his watch and setting the time by the station clock but he fell asleep before it tolled the next hour.

It was dark outside when he opened his eyes again. John remembered that he had dreamed about Jenny and he wished he had not awoken when he did. He looked out from beneath the blankets and noticed that the clutter around the sofa had been removed, along with his boxes of personal belongings. Someone was whistling a tune in the background and the pleasant smell of a freshly-baked pastry permeated the room. He still didn't know the time and decided then that he should make the purchase of a clock his next priority. It would be an electric model because winding timepieces didn't seem to be his forte.

He was about to get up when the telephone started ringing. He had pushed his legs over the side of the sofa and was trying to remember the location of the phone when a familiar voice boomed from the kitchen: "Answer your damned telephone, Shanahan. There's nobody here but you."

John's eyes lit up. "Aha, it's Ramon, my good buddy. So that's the reason my home has taken on such a bright new look. And I detect the smell of exquisite food, prepared by the best chef in the land. What more could a man ask, I ask you, my friend?"

"Nothing, I hope," Ramon snorted as he sprinted across the room and picked up the telephone. "Good evening," he said. "You have reached the residence of Rip Van Winkle, who, unfortunately, will not be awake for twenty years. May I take a message?"

"C'mon, Ramon!" John yelled. "Hold the caller right there. Old Rip is coming back to life after his twenty winks. Just a little patience, please."

Ramon grinned. "Well, I guess you heard that, officer," he said to the caller. "I'd say he's been on a bender with those strange little fellows that make the moonshine and reside in yon hills. ... Oh, you don't think that's funny? Obviously you wouldn't because you can't catch them. Hold on, your suspect is here."

John paled. "So, who is it, really, Ramon?" John whispered.

"Police. You're in deep trouble." Ramon boomed and returned to the kitchen.

John picked up the phone tentatively. "Hello" was all he could think of saying.

"Hello," a deep voice responded. "Is this the legend of Sleepy Hollow?"

"Ah, no, officer. I'm sorry for the tomfoolery. I guess we were expecting a call from someone else. I apologize ..."

"You and Ramon are a couple of absolute hooligans, John Shanahan. But I truly love you, you buffoon."

"Jenny! How nice of you to call. I was just kind of stirring from a long sleep, sort of like Rip Van Winkle, I suppose. But I was dreaming about this enchanting young woman and it was just too spellbinding to leave off to answer the telephone."

"Really? Is this enchanting young woman someone I would know?"

"Well, possibly. But I get disoriented easily and have difficulty at times sorting fact from fantasy. ... I think that's what I wanted to say, but now I'm not so sure. ... By the way, what did you say your name is?"

"Ah, gee, I can't remember. And yours?"

"Don't know anymore. But I'm in love with an enchantress named Jenny Boston, so keep that in mind if we ever happen to run into each other."

"I'll do that. It could be tomorrow. We have another run for Major Adams from Quarry to Summit and back. So if it works out, we'll have a lunch break around noon and I'll treat you at the station restaurant. Your father says you'll be working in the office for a couple days. He's here and he said to tell you that Ramon has the details."

"Okay. Well, until tomorrow, keep me in mind. ... Oh, and tomorrow, too, please."

"You'll be in my mind forever, darling. Thanks for this very special day. I must go now. Love you."

"Good night, Jen. I love you. Tell Katie I love her, too."

John went into the kitchen, sat down at the table and stared at Ramon. "You know, that was a pretty good stunt we pulled, wasn't it, Ramon?"

Ramon grinned. "Yeah, we ought to think seriously about going into vaudeville with that Rip Van Winkle thing. Slick performance, I must say. How did Jenny cotton to it?"

"She's a good sport. She's also in love."

"And that's good with you, John?"

"It is."

"So who's the lucky guy?"

"I can't remember his name. Rip Van Winkle, or something like that."

"You don't say? Sleepy fellow, that Van Winkle guy. Jenny seems to be kind of a live wire. Oh, well, they say opposites attract. ... Since I was eavesdropping on your conversation with the lady, I remember that I'm supposed to tell you about tomorrow."

"That would be the day after today?"

"Ah, possibly. I'm not terribly up to date on the passage of time. You know, Rip missed twenty years while he was napping. That was a while ago and everything seems to be moving faster nowadays. Perhaps the day to which we're alluding could be the day after tomorrow, or to explain it better, two days after yesterday."

"Ah, yes. I think I'll take the second option. Now what did I do yesterday?"

"I would venture a guess and say very little. ... Let's eat in absolute silence and when we're done let's talk about tomorrow's game plan. So, shut your yap and eat."

John savored the supper—a superb beef roast, gravy, baked North Country potatoes and homemade bread. The dessert was apple pie. John leaned back in his chair when he was done. "Ramon, I can't thank you enough," he said sincerely. "Someday, after I grow up, I'd like to watch you cook things so I can learn to feed myself. It's embarrassing. I couldn't even make tea this morning."

Ramon grinned. "Sure," he said. "Trouble is, you're never going to grow up."

John nodded. "Now, about that game plan you mentioned before I took the vow of silence?"

"Barring the unforeseen, there will be no call as an engineer tomorrow so your father suggested that you work in his office up in the tower. About midday we need to go to the shop and get Fred Wilson to show us some equipment that's needed this weekend."

John sat silent. Ramon began whistling a tune and several minutes passed before John spoke. "About this equipment, can you be more specific?"

"No. It's a company secret."

"Okay. Would it have anything to do with what I might be doing the next day, which I guess we agreed would be two days after yesterday."

"I wouldn't agree with you about anything." Ramon's eyes twinkled and he waited for the next question but John appeared to have lost interest in the topic.

"So where do you want to go with this conversation now, John?" Ramon queried.

"I was thinking about that booze that Rip got into with the strange fellows in the mountains. They had a keg as I remember."

310

"True. They started with a keg and then poured the contents into two large flagons."

John shook his head. "I guess I don't know what a flagon is. You?"

"No, but I know what kind of liquor it was. Dutch gin." Ramon's eyes twinkled again.

"I don't suppose that you ..."

Ramon got up and opened a kitchen cabinet. He pulled out an ornamental liquor bottle and held it up gleefully. "Found this in one of J.P.'s secret stowaways," he said.

John peered at the label. "Gin distilled in Holland. Must be Dutch. I'll be jiggered."

About an hour later, John fell asleep on the sofa, goblet in hand. Ramon took the glass, capped the half-full bottle and returned it to the kitchen cabinet. Then he yawned and walked unsteadily toward the downstairs bedroom. He stopped at the doorway, looked back at John and said in a serious tone, "Sleep well, friend Rip. See you in twenty years."

Chapter 45: Lunch with Jenny

John settled behind the mahogany desk in the ornate third-floor office that rose above the sprawling railroad depot in Summit. Ramon had taken him there for a first-time visit and John found that the windows rimming the room provided a breathtaking panorama of the community. The office looked out to the south over the Summit, Bolton and Quarry Railroad's new mainline that ran to Hill Junction. There were a few residences near the right of way but the long grade and the dark evergreen forest were the dominant features of the landscape.

To the right was more of the city with rows of houses defining the main residential part of the town. In the foreground was the Eagle River branch of the railroad and just visible beyond the west wing of the station was the roof of his newly-acquired home. Two houses beyond his was the residence of Jenny, the young woman that he loved.

To the left were the many sidings of Summit freight yard and the rambling car and locomotive repair shop that his father's company had restored and expanded. Beyond the shop was the dilapidated neighborhood of Shop Road. As he took in the view he thought of his friend, Rob Rankin, the young brakeman whose widowed mother and children occupied one of the Shop Road houses and struggled hard to make ends meet. She had been ill of late, Rob had told him on their last outing.

In the distance, juxtaposed against the Shop Road district, John could see the edge of the new development known as Summit Heights, an increasingly valuable piece of real estate with commanding views of Eden Valley to the east and north. There certainly was a disparity between the haves and the have-nots in this North Country community, he thought, and he could see it plainly in that panorama on the other side of the tracks.

He turned in the swivel chair to savor the view toward the north. There, from the intersection of the two wings of the station below the tower, Railroad Avenue, the city's main thoroughfare, extended into the distance, and its shops and sidewalks were just coming to life on the cold winter morning. It was an enchanting view for a visitor accustomed to city life, and a pleasant surprise, he knew, for the occasional outsider after a long train trip through great tracts of wilderness.

Twenty feet or so above his head was the four-faced station tower clock that could be seen by nearly every resident in the city of Summit.

John leaned back in the chair and his thoughts returned to the dark-haired woman and her little daughter. He had told Jenny just yesterday that he loved her and Katie and now he was glad that he did.

John was seated at his father's desk. The sign on the door indicated that the senior Shanahan's position with the railroad company, one of his many holdings, was that of superintendent, which for bookkeeping purposes he was. But Henry Terrell, the line's general manager, ran all operations almost single-handedly although after the recent acquisition of the Hill Division, that might change. Ramon had said that morning that J.P. was about to make certain "major pronouncements" about railroad management.

"Ah, he's just going to invest in some more of that gin from Holland that we sort of got hammered on last night," John had offered. "By the way, how did you sleep, Ramon?"

Ramon's eyes had narrowed to slits but a smile played at his lips. "Quite soundly, I would say. I fell asleep near the end of December 1951. When I woke up this morning, I noticed that the calendar at your place was for 1971. But you probably didn't notice because you have no understanding of the passage of time."

"Well, I certainly do," John had insisted and instinctively pulled out his pocket watch. He studied the face intently and then quietly slipped the silent timepiece back into his pocket and looked away.

"Maybe if you'd wind it once in a while you'd understand time a little better," Ramon had snorted as he returned to the station elevator and went downstairs. His friend left without even a hint of the work John was expected to do that day.

He thought he should wind his watch for a start. But that would mean finding an authorized railroad clock to ascertain the correct time. The best one was above his head in the tower but he couldn't see it from where he sat. John would have to go downstairs to the dispatching office to inquire as to the time of day. People would look askance at first and chide him about it later. No, he would forego that embarrassment.

Satisfied with his reasoning, he rummaged through a desk drawer and found a humidor that he knew would contain the best Cuban cigars in the American marketplace. He pulled one out, peeled off the protective wrapper, bit a chunk from the end and spat it into a nearby wastebasket. Then he leaned back and placed his feet atop the desk.

"Thanks, Dad," he said aloud as he struck a match and lit up. He inhaled, savored the experience and then blew the perfect smoke ring. It hung above the desk like a halo before drifting across the room. He watched the ring float away and then made several more while he reflected on events of late and the people he had met, especially Jenny. Quite content with his progress in that matter, he stubbed out the cigar, slumped down in the chair and fell asleep.

It was then that he found himself carrying a heavy keg of liquor up a hilly trail. It was just off the railroad track on the grade south of Summit. He stumbled and dropped the keg and despaired of how he would raise it to his shoulder again when a small, strange man in a Dutch costume appeared on the trail. The gnome wore wooden shoes, which intrigued John because he had no shoes. The stranger held up the keg and stuck a tap into the side. Then he produced two giant mugs, drew liquor into each and passed one to John.

They drank a toast to "New Amsterdam" although John could not understand why. The liquor overpowered his senses quickly and he fell down on the trail. While he struggled unsuccessfully to get up, the stranger hoisted the barrel to his shoulder and disappeared in the forest. John fell asleep in his dream while yelling, "Stop, thief, stop! That's my gin!"

He was next aware of gentle hands clasping his. He opened his eyes and Jenny was there. "Wake up, John," she coaxed. "You're dreaming. Please tell me you are okay."

"Just an odd dream, I guess. I don't know why I fell asleep. I had every intention of working today and accomplishing something significant." He smiled and leaned forward. "Well, there is one thing I can do and maybe that will atone, in part at least, for this day's idleness," he said and kissed Jenny gently on the lips. "Now that the smooching matter has been attended to, perhaps you'd tell me where I am, why and what I should be doing next. And by the way, do you happen to know what time it is?"

Jenny folded her arms and glared at John. "Let's see. How do I answer your flurry of questions?" She pondered his queries and then responded: "No, no and no on the first part, and no on the second."

"I know you know about the second part—the time of day. Don't spoof me. You have a fine timepiece and all you have to do is pull it out and look. The little hand at the bottom clicks off the seconds, but I wouldn't care about that. The long hand ..."

Jenny stamped her feet. "Why did I fall in love with you, of all people?" she asked.

"I can't answer that because I'm still hung up about why you keep cutting me off when I ask relevant questions and make astute comments? Why?"

"Okay," Jenny mumbled. "Let's backtrack to why I'm here. I seem to have forgotten."

John smiled. "That's an easy one. You came to tell me where I am, why and ..."

Jenny interrupted again. "No, that's not true! I came to see if you remembered that we have a lunch date in the restaurant, which you promised to pay for, and ..."

"Hold it right there, you panhandler!" John exclaimed. "I distinctively remember that you, Jennifer, promised to treat me. You're cuter 'n a button, but you're also a slick cat."

"If you keep babbling along, Mr. Shanahan, we'll miss lunch because I'll have to go back to work. Now, because I'm ahead of you on certain intuitive matters, I have a nice lunch already prepared in the locomotive, while you, because of your inability to even boil water, have no such backup plan. So, unless you're confident that you can forage for grub on your own, I'd suggest that you follow me downstairs to the restaurant. If you're the cheapskate that you appear to be, I'll pay. But only this time."

Jenny stepped into the elevator and closed the door without looking back. John watched it descend to the lower level and stood by the door to wait for its return. By the time he arrived at the restaurant door the waitress was leaving for the kitchen with Jenny's order.

She looked up and flashed her best smile. "Why, what a pleasant surprise! John Shanahan has arrived to pay for Jenny's dinner. So what are you having today?"

"Crow," he said simply. "You're right, sweetheart. I'm a doofus. And, by the way, I was going to ask you what time it is now but I just happened to remember this station is the clock center of the universe. There are clocks everywhere in this place. Did you know, Jen, that the time gurus in Green Witch, Connecticut, check in here every day to ascertain that their clocks at the observatory are ticking along in unison?"

"I didn't. But that's certainly good to know. I also didn't know that the time center was in Connecticut. I thought it was in England. And I think the place is Greenwich, pronounced 'Gren-Itch.'"

"I think you're right." John smiled and winked. "Gosh. I love talking to you, Jen. Honestly, you're witty and bright and beautiful and a real ray of sunshine in my life." He grasped her arm and looked intently into her eyes. "I really mean that. Really."

The waitress returned with two identical luncheon specials and passed the bill to John. Jenny winked at him. "Thanks so much for inviting me out to dinner," she said. "Now tell me what your mystery assignment is for today. I didn't pick up on any particulars."

John shook his head. "Beats me. Ramon led me up to my dad's office and left. There were no phone calls, no visitors, nothing. I fell asleep and dreamed about this little man in a Dutch costume who stole a keg of gin that I was carrying barefoot through the woods. We had a drink before he took off on the run. That's when you came in."

"That's sort of like the story of Rip Van Winkle that was on your mind last night when we were on the telephone." They continued to talk as they ate until Jenny pulled out her pocket watch, shielded its face from John and checked the time. "I have to go back to work," she said. "This is going to be a short day because we have some things to do at Seven Pines."

"Really? What could possibly need to be done there?"

Jenny smiled mischievously. "Can't say, my love. It's a company secret."

John walked Jenny to the door leading from the station concourse to the train platform. He was about to kiss her goodbye when Ramon pushed the door open and stepped in. "C'mon, you two. Time's a wasting. We need to make that shop run now, Jen." She nodded and climbed into the yard engine, SB&Q 1, which had been assigned as the power on the Summit-Quarry military equipment shuffle. John followed her up into the cab. Ramon hopped on the caboose, which was coupled to the engine, and signaled a smart go-ahead. They ran down Track Three to the south ladder of the freight yard and then backed to the area of the parking lot at the shop's administrative building.

Jenny set the train brakes and observed that the locomotive was idling properly. "We need to follow Ramon and the rest of the crew over to Building Eight after we check in at the administrative office," she said.

"Ah, yes, about that Building Eight. Let's see now, that would be the place where … ah … you know, the place. …"

Jenny smiled. "Yes, that would be the place."

John persisted. "That would be the place where …" He paused and waited.

"That would be the place where we are going!" Jenny said sharply. "Only we're not going to get there if you don't be quiet and start walking. If you were a nice gentleman, you would step down from this engine ahead of me, extend your arm and assist a lady down the steps."

"I could do that." John descended the stairwell carefully, stepped to the ground, planted his feet solidly and held both arms out to Jenny. When she got close enough, he gathered her in his arms, and carried her over the rails of the next track to the path leading to the shop office. After placing her on the walkway, he kissed Jenny's hand and smiled.

"You are a gentleman, John," she said softly. "That must be why I love you." He smiled and they walked arm in arm to the administrative center. Fred Wilson was at the door and led Jenny, John, Ramon and the train crew inside. "It's good to see all of you again," he said. "I've had several people working on this project this week and we're ready to show it off."

Fred went to his desk and pulled out an artist's rendition of a bright new locomotive and an antique coach car. John looked closely and the others, who knew about the project, watched as he traced his fingers across the drawing. "That equipment, my friend, represents the first pieces for a new Shanahan Enterprises entity to be known simply as The Christmas Train," Fred said. "Look familiar?"

John studied the rendition again, nodded and looked up at Jenny. There were tears in his eyes and he reached for her hand. She came to his side and put her arm around his shoulders. "It's beautiful and very special to us," she said to Fred. John nodded and wiped his eyes. "Very special," he murmured.

Fred pulled on his jacket and led the group through the office to the back door and the walkway to Building Eight, which was a part of the paint shop. He unlocked the door, opened it and ushered the visitors inside. Then he turned on the lights and stood back.

Engine Fifty-Three, the BL-2 that John had driven hard through the blizzard on Christmas Eve, had been transformed from its dull gray factory finish to a glistening high-gloss white, trimmed by red and green. The red lettering under the engineer's and fireman's windows had been changed from SB&Q to CT while the number 53 was retained. A name, "The Christmas Train" was applied to each side of the locomotive in Old English script. That inscription was repeated in the same style, only smaller, across the nose of the locomotive and across the back. The wheel sets were painted jet black, unlike the usual silver trucks of most diesel-electric locomotives.

On each side of the locomotive's body, near the bottom, in two crisp lines, the shop's paint artists had scripted words from the Gospel of St. Luke: *"Glory to God in the highest and on earth peace, good will toward men."* Next to the quotation was a depiction of a stable against a landscape that could not be mistaken for any other than the Holy Land. Directly above that depiction was a bright silver star. Jenny broke down. "That is … so very precious," she sobbed and buried her head in John's jacket.

After leading the viewers around the locomotive Fred directed their attention to the coach. The exterior had received a fresh application of light green paint and then gold letters to spell out "The Christmas Train" along with the numeral "1951," as recommended that Christmas morning by Jenny Boston. Touches of filigree in bright reds, dark greens and gold had been added around the letters and numbers and at corners and ends of the car. The handrails and most of the metal works were done in black. All paints used were of the high-gloss variety and the car sparkled under the shop lights.

"I think you're going to like this," Fred said as he beckoned the group to the back of the coach car. Work had been done on the narrow rear vestibule and a train name board, or drumhead, had been fashioned specifically for the train. "Oh, my!" John said, his voice quavering. "Oh, my goodness. This is … just … so very nice. …"

The circular drumhead featured the Christmas star near the top. A superb manger depiction with a skyline image of the Bethlehem of the Bible for a backdrop was the principal focus. The drumhead also featured the name of the train. Many of the better-known passenger expresses in America had drumheads but John knew of none more striking than this.

The interior of the car was already well appointed in its lacquered style so the only addition was bright red carpeting in the passenger aisle. All Christmas decorations except the evergreen wreaths were still in place. The mail section had been refurbished and officials from the Department of the Post Office had approved the use of the car in regular mail service "for certain specified occasions," Fred Wilson said.

"Are any such occasions coming up any time soon?" John asked.

"Yes," Fred responded, but on a signal from Ramon, added quickly: "That is top-secret stuff limited to top management. I don't know anything about it."

"Uh huh. It seems that I'm hearing a lot about secrets among the higher-ups. Would you say these secrets may be revealed soon or will they be revealed at some future time?"

"I defer to Ramon on that question," Fred said.

John looked at Ramon quizzically. "Quit staring at me, Shanahan," his friend said sharply.

"Fred suggested that you might answer a question that I asked. Is that so?"

"Sure," Ramon answered. "The answer is no."

"It was a two-part question," John persisted.

"The answer is still no."

John shook his head. "Okay. I really don't need to know." Ramon nodded.

The train crew returned to its duties and Ramon and John went back to the shop's administrative office where a shop employee was waiting to take them to the station. They stepped quickly inside the concourse when they arrived and Ramon directed his companion to check in with the dispatcher, after which he would be free for the day.

"You're headed back to Quarry, I take it," John said.

"Yeah. Your father has a lot of things to iron out and tie down before we head back to Chicago next week."

John nodded sadly. "Next week, huh? I kind of figured the time was coming."

"Yeah." Ramon blinked and looked away. "Anyway, get upstairs and confuse the dispatching office. After that, call a cab to go home because it's cold and the cold eats right through those damned parkas your old man saddled us with. ..." Ramon grabbed John's shoulder. "I mean that about the cab, buddy, ... and stay inside tonight. It's going to be a cold one. Don't worry about food. You'll find the place outfitted for a king; well, at least for a pretender to the throne."

"Thanks," John said simply and was about to walk away. Then he stopped, turned and added: "I wish you could stay longer. We came here together to do a job, and I wish ... well, heck, Ramon, I just wish ... the very best for you, always." He blinked back tears, stepped quickly into the elevator and was whisked upstairs.

Chapter 46: Company Secrets

John stood in the passenger entryway and looked back along Railroad Avenue to the little house beyond the west wing of the depot at Summit. It was December 31, the last day of 1951, and it had dawned bright and cold but he was dressed in his winter railroader's gear and had not noticed the bite in the air as he walked from his new home to his place of employment. He had carried his cane but was learning each day to rely on it less and less. He was steadier on his feet than at any time since coming to the North Country and was eager to take on the unusual assignment to which he had been posted.

He would be the engineer of a special running of the *Christmas Train* and that was about all he really knew. He would pick up the locomotive and coach at the shop and bring it across the yard to the station, where it would be placed on display for most of the day. The purpose, he was advised by the dispatching office, was to respond to a deluge of calls from townspeople who wished to see the equipment again and learn what function it would have in the railroad's future. He didn't know what that would be but Henry Terrell would be there to explain what J.P. Shanahan Jr. had in mind. John's role was to be available to answer questions about the train that had so captured the fancy of all who were there and those who learned about it later through the media.

John had reported to work early but even then people were gathering in the concourse, thanks to a splendid write-up in the Summit Sentinel and bulletins about the event that had been aired over the local radio station. He slipped into the elevator unnoticed and went up to the dispatching office. When he arrived on the second floor, Hank met him at the door and led John to his office beyond the dispatchers' quarters.

"So, young man, you're looking quite spiffy today," Hank offered as an opener.

"Thank you," John responded with a grin. "I did my laundry last night for the first time in quite a while, and even took a crack at ironing. When an awkward guy like me focuses on something, well, I even surprise myself. Note the nifty creases in my overalls."

Hank looked at the overalls. "You sure surprised me," he chuckled. "I half expected to see you show up in gear that would stand by itself. Good job, my boy, good job."

The railroad manager reached into a box on his desk and passed John an elaborate printed program that featured a cover with the artist's rendition of the *Christmas Train*. Inside was a description of the Christmas Eve run and the new locomotive and old coach. "I understand you saw the equipment yesterday," Hank said. "Any comments?"

"It's fantastic, Hank!" John exclaimed. "I have an idea you had a lot to say about the design, and it certainly touched me. And that write-up in the Sentinel this morning was really great. I'd guess my dad liked it, too."

"He did. I've been down there about all week—we've been going over a lot of things about the future, you know—and he wanted this little presentation to be a kind of prelude to some announcements he plans later today."

"I see. You couldn't offer a few hints as to what those will be?"

Hank shook his head.

John chuckled. "I know. Company secrets. That's all I ever get when I ask. … Oh, not to change the topic, but I believe you're a connoisseur of fine liquors. Am I correct?"

Hank's eyes twinkled. "Hmmm. Well, yes, you might say that."

"I've been told by someone that a particular brand of gin distilled in Holland is … what's the way to say this … a spirit sought by those who know their booze?"

"I suspect the scalawag who told you that was Ramon who apparently uncovered a cache while re-stocking the larder at Seven Pines. Is my suspicion well founded?"

John tried to keep a straight face. "I wouldn't be at liberty to comment on that supposition. I could say, however, that particular brand has a certain effect …"

"Yeah. It makes you sleepy. There is a piece of classical literature about a Van Winkle character that tapped into the stuff and fell asleep for twenty years. Know that story?"

"Uh huh. I think I know why he fell so sound asleep but that's all I can say."

"You sufficiently recovered to work today?"

"Absolutely, Hank. But I wouldn't be averse to tapping into a keg of that stuff sometime when we all have plenty of time to sleep off the effects."

"I'll take you up on that, chum. … Now back to the business of the day. I don't think you're up on the details." With that, Hank outlined the schedule. The train crew that was on the original *Christmas Train* would gather at the shop after the departure of the morning trains and board many of the original passengers. The train would be moved to the station where Hank would address the gathering. After that, tours of the coach and the locomotive would be offered. Then a series of short runs from the station to Summit Heights and back through the shop yard to the station would be provided for onlookers.

After the departure of the *Northern Express*, the *Christmas Train* would run as the second section of the regular train to Quarry with stops along the way. After tying up, a rented school bus would be available to bring crewmembers and others back to Summit if they desired. Some would be afforded overnight quarters in the Ten Commandments or at Seven Pines. A New Year's Eve event for guests would be held at the end of the day.

"You might find this interesting, John," Hank continued. "The U.S. Post Office has authorized the use of the mail section of Coach 1951 during the day

320

here and on the trip to Quarry. We're giving out stamped postcards to all our guests so they can have commemorative postmarks of this event. You remember that Dan Stubbs became the regional inspector when we added the night trains? Anyway, he will be the clerk for this run and will show our visitors what a postman does in a mail car. We thought it would add a really nice touch."

"What a great idea!" John exclaimed. "And Dan's a fine choice." Hank nodded.

"Now about this crew. You did say the original crew would be aboard?"

"Uh huh. Joe Francis is coming up on Train Two this morning from Quarry and will be relieved from the rest of his regular run, so he'll be your conductor. Rob Rankin and Will Smith will be your brakemen. Oh, and Charles Wilson will be a guest even though we can forego the plow this time, thank God. I guess that's it. Am I missing anyone?"

"Yeah, I don't think I can do this without a fireman ... you know, a fireman is really essential on a passenger train. Wouldn't you say so?"

Hank smiled. "Well, I don't know. You ran all the way from Gatlin to Hill Junction and back to Summit without a fireman the first time. We're still not up to snuff when it comes to a fireman's roster, you know."

"I see. Well, it was just a thought."

"Good thought. Who'd you have in mind?"

"Well ... ah ...oh, nobody, I guess."

Hank laughed. "Come on, John. You want Jenny along. We all want Jenny along, and, yes, she should be along and has agreed to be with you, which is not surprising. She'll always be a key crewmember when this train goes out on the road. She's coming in on Train Two today. They should be arriving shortly. ... By the way, what time is it?"

John paled. "Ah, well, your office clock seems to indicate that it is seven-forty."

"And your personal timepiece, I would guess, agrees with my office clock."

"Well, not quite," John said sheepishly. "I might as well fess up. My watch stopped a couple days ago and I've been so busy, I haven't had time to wind it and re-set the time."

"Busy? Come on, John. I'd say now is as good a time as any. Otherwise, you'll forget again and someday a federal inspector will call your bluff and fine the railroad. I'll pretend I know nothing about your winding habits if you'll fix it now. Now, damn it!"

"Yes, sir!" John responded. "By the way, don't you think an engineer ought to be paid overtime for winding his watch? It's mostly done when he's off duty, and really ..."

"Really, you give me migraine headaches, John! I think I'll go somewhere where I can stare at a blank wall for fifteen minutes or so. You, on the other hand, better get down to the platform and see to your fireman who should be arriving momentarily."

John scrambled down the stairway and worked his way through the clusters of people in the concourse. He reached the platform door and slipped through just as Train One pulled up to the station. Engineer Bill Travers waved as he throttled down and let the train roll to a stop. Conductor Joe Francis stepped from the coach *Bolton* and began helping passengers disembark. The first person to appear on the vestibule was Jenny who spied John and rushed into his arms. He held her closely and stared deeply into her eyes.

"Hi," he said. "Hi," she responded and kissed him gently on the cheek. Relieved of his responsibilities by Brakeman John Kelly, Joe Francis joined Jenny and John. "So we're going on a new adventure," he said. "Our train is going to be quite an attraction today. I have to book in Train Two and then Hank has a car lined up to take us over to the shop."

Ten minutes later the three entered Fred Wilson's office and met brakemen Rob Rankin and Will Smith, who had been relieved of his duties in the dispatching office to make the run. Both wore new trainmen's uniforms. "You guys look exquisite!" Jenny exclaimed as she hugged both young men.

Fred advised the crew that a school bus was en route to the shop with all forty-five of the original *Christmas Train* passengers. Annie McCaslin had come up from Blackwater the night before and the students from Quarry and Bolton and the flag stops along the branch had arrived on Train Two that morning. The special train had been moved from Building Eight and was idling on the spur behind the office building where it had been inspected and pronounced ready for service.

John and Jenny climbed into the locomotive and Joe took Rob and Will to the coach to discuss boarding passengers from the parking lot. On Joe's hand signal, John moved the train ahead just as the bus appeared.

John watched from the engineer's seat and Jenny from the doorway as the students and chaperones lined up to enter the coach. Joe and Rob took positions at the stairwell and Will held the coach door open. Jenny waved to her classmates from the locomotive and called off their names to John as each passed. When everyone was boarded and seated, Rob waved a highball and climbed aboard. "I make it out of the shop at eight naught five," Joe called on the radio. "We'll pull out onto the south ladder and then proceed slowly in reverse to the mainline."

"Eight-naught-five. Got that, Joe," John responded and moved the train forward slowly. After clearing the spur, he stopped the locomotive and watched Rob throw the switch. Then the engineer reversed the locomotive and backed along the ladder track. The switching maneuver was repeated and the train backed onto the mainline.

We want to give the folks back at the station a little extra," Joe said over the radio. "Let's back to the south semaphore and then you can make a smart little charge down the hill to the station. When you pull in, watch for a couple of stairways that will be set up so the visitors can enter the locomotive from the station side and exit through the engineer's door to the second platform. Okay?"

"Roger on that, Joe."

The reverse move was made, after which John stopped and then notched the throttle forward sharply. He sounded the air horns as the train accelerated down the grade. The train's speed had reached twenty-five miles an hour when he cut the throttle and make the first of several brake applications. The train slid up to the platform and the locomotive stopped exactly between the stairways.

"You really are a marvelous engineer," Jenny said in admiration.

"Ah, just dumb luck," he said. "The next time I'll overshoot and have the embarrassing task of jigging back and forth to get it right. Usually when I think I'm on top of things, I forget how to do them and feel like an idiot. ... But anyway, thanks, sweetheart."

John set the engine in idle, checked the brakes and walked to the fireman's side to observe the goings on. Hank had taken a position at the station door and picked up a microphone that Stationmaster Larry Smith had wired to the station's public-address system. He welcomed the assembly to the railroad program and talked about the train.

"Most of you probably recall the difficulty we encountered a week ago when we were faced with a nearly impossible mission. These students and their chaperones were stranded after a transportation conference, which this company sponsored and helped organize. When it was apparent that we might not be able to get them home for Christmas because of an unforeseen blizzard, we gambled that we could dispatch a locomotive—this one—from Gatlin, pick them up at Hill Junction and bring them home."

Hank paused and put a hand to his head. "It wasn't easy ... and the storm came on faster and far worse than we expected. Then there was the Eastern freight train wreck in the terminal yard down there and we were cut off from the equipment we needed to bring our scholars home. Ah ... it was difficult and I was about ready to call off the mission ... really, I had just about given up hope ... when our people found this wonderful old coach car in a back shop at Hill Junction. It took a lot of work by some fine railroaders and some extraordinary people in the village there ... to pull this mission off."

The railroad manager stopped and looked up pleadingly at John. Hank's voice broke and he wiped his eyes. "I'd like my colleague, my dear friend John Shanahan, to come down and pick up this story because I get so emotional ... still ..."

Jenny turned to John. "Please, John," she whispered. "Please help Hank."

John hobbled down the visitors' stairway. Jenny held his cane until he reached the platform and then passed it down to him. He walked toward the station door and grasped Hank's shoulder. "I'd be proud to stand here with you," he said quietly. "Let's bring the rest of the crew down, too."

Hank motioned to Joe and the two brakemen to come forward and then beckoned for Jenny to join them. John took the microphone, cleared his throat and scanned the audience. "Ah, it's difficult ... to talk about this now," he began hesitatingly. "First, you must know that the ... trip ... at Christmas had a successful conclusion only because a lot of people pulled together ... and willed it

323

to happen … and prayed … and that's really the only way anything can work when the odds are … so much against what … you're trying to do. Those of us on the train had our doubts … when the storm worsened … that we could get through, me, the most of all. There were times when I really wanted to stop along the way and find shelter for our passengers … out of the storm, where they would be safe and sound … even if it meant missing Christmas at home."

John paused, coughed and tried to continue. His voice broke at first and he wiped his eyes. "But we knew how much Christmas … and family and friends means to each of us. I … must tell you that I … we … all of us … had some help, much help, because of our faith … and that we can never discount. There was a place … several places … along the way where the snow was so deep and our little train seemed so … so frail, so very frail … and … well, I know, God's hand was on us at those times. Our prayers were answered … time and again … and I'm sure that you—the parents and loved ones of these passengers—know that your prayers were answered, too."

John studied the faces of his audience. "I don't know what else to say. … This little train is dear to me and I'm sure to all of you who had family aboard when we came through the storm. I am so pleased … personally … that the railroad has chosen to preserve it in this way. I understand that it will be brought out from time to time … to remind us all about the miracle of Christmas. It brings joy to my heart … to see how some very talented working people in this company's employ have embellished the Christmas message this year through their work on our little train. I just … want …"

John choked up and Jenny stepped forward quickly and placed her arm around his waist. She took the mike and continued: "I'm Jenny … Jenny Boston … and I had the very wonderful opportunity to complete the last part of the trip with this crew. On behalf of Mr. Henry Terrell and John and this train crew, Joe Francis, Rob Rankin and Will Smith, who worked so hard that night, I thank you for coming and participating in this event that is so special to those of us who were there at the time. God bless all of you."

John had slipped away before the crowd broke into a loud and sustained applause. He retired to an alcove between the waiting room and the restaurant. Jenny found him several minutes later slumped in a corner at the end of a long passenger settee. She sat down close to him and held his hands tightly. "God bless you, my love," she murmured as she wiped the tears from his cheeks with a handkerchief.

"I hope I said the right words, Jenny. I'm not a very good speaker … because I get emotional, especially about Christmas. It's hard sometimes … for me to pick the right words to … well, to find the words, that is, to state what's in my heart. …"

"You said it so … very beautifully, my love. It was so precious. Nobody ever doubts your sincerity and your strong beliefs," she said. "Your words touched my heart. You are an extraordinary man and I'm so blessed that you came into my life when you did."

After John regained his composure, Jenny led him back outside where the train crew was escorting the visitors through the coach. The engineer and fireman returned to the locomotive and welcomed small groups to the cab. Children were invited to sit in the engineer's seat to ring the engine bell and pull the cord that activated the air horns. John sat down often and held the younger ones as they came through with their parents. Jenny watched and smiled, knowing that he cared deeply for the youngsters.

The short train rides followed and more than a dozen trips were made before the last of the visitors left the station grounds at one in the afternoon. The crew was dismissed for lunch and told to come back on duty at two-fifteen. John and Jenny took their postcards to the mail car and she mailed one to him and one to Emma. John mailed his to Jenny and Katie. After that, they sat alone in the engine cab and shared a lunch that she had brought from Seven Pines. They were still holding hands when Larry Smith activated the public address system to announce that invited passengers could start boarding the train.

The student passengers who had made the first trip on the *Christmas Train* climbed aboard first. Plowman Charles Wilson came along later and climbed into the cab with John and Jenny. John hadn't seen him since the night after Christmas when the extra train he was running had set off Charles's crippled snowplow in the freight yard at Gatlin. The men shook hands and John asked where his friend had been since that night.

"Flew out to Pennsylvania," Charles responded as he set about rolling a cigarette. John waited until he had completed the project. "Learn anything out there?" he asked.

"Yep. Remember those old rotary snowplows when you were working out West?" John nodded his head. "Kind of pokey but they sure could move the snow."

"J.P. had a new one built in Erie. Diesel-powered. I was out looking it over. It's coming in next month. That beauty really can move the snow!"

Chapter 47: Reunion at Quarry

The station at Summit was crowded with passengers and onlookers again at two forty-three in the afternoon when Larry Smith activated the public address system: "Ladies and gentlemen, your attention please. Train One, the northbound *Northern Express* is now arriving on Track Three from Gatlin, Hill Junction and Sunbury. Further announcements will follow regarding our expanded services today. Thank you."

John Shanahan watched from the engineer's seat of Engine Fifty-Three as Bill Travers pulled Train One to a stop beside the *Christmas Train*. Fireman Jim McDermott opened his window and peered out. "Hey, that train of yours is a real nice piece of work, John. That mystery coach is a beauty! Anyone ever figure out who really owns it?"

John shook his head. "No, Jim. But we know it was where it was at the right time and there's something spiritual about that."

"That's for sure," Jim said. "Well, I need to find our green flags. See you later on tonight." The fireman disappeared inside the cab to find the markers to signify that Train Two was the first section of two passenger trains running from Summit to Quarry. A couple of minutes later, Bill Travers appeared in the fireman's doorway. "Hey, John. You got any green flags in there? We don't seem to have any. I don't think we ever did."

"Hold on, buddy," John said. "Jenny's looking. ... Yep. We got 'em." Jenny brought the flags to the door and passed them to Bill. "Like our train, Billy?" she asked.

"That's really something, Jen. That engine is one stout locomotive. Nice paint job, beautiful message, and that coach, man, that's an American classic! Hey, thanks for the flags." Bill reached through the fireman's window and inserted one in the holder on the left side of the engine. Jim McDermott put up the other one on the engineer's side.

"So you're gonna be running ten, fifteen minutes behind our schedule, John," Bill said when he came back to the fireman's seat and settled in.

"Yeah. We have the students who came up with you this morning, and we're carrying some mail so we should stay comfortably behind you."

Bill nodded. "Okay. Probably see you around Seven Pines this evening." The engineman waved and closed the fireman's window.

"Why is it that everybody seems to be planning to visit the family homestead tonight?" John asked. Jenny smiled. "Gee, I hadn't noticed," she said.

"Okay. Anyway, it looks like Jim's going to be running for a while. How about you? I suddenly feel very tired and might doze off if I sit here much longer."

Jenny looked at John sternly. "Tired? But you haven't even started yet. Aren't you the guy that ran day and night so much that the girl back home hardly ever saw him?"

"Well, I suppose. But I don't see the correlation between my being sleepy today and my busy schedule before that. I guess I don't understand a woman's way of thinking. Let me try to puzzle this out."

John got up and limped across the engine cabin. He picked up Jenny, carried the fireman back across the cab and deposited her in the engineer's seat. "You drive and I'll sit over there and try to fathom out what we're talking about."

Jenny grinned. "You're impossible. Why do I love you so?"

John wiggled in the fireman's seat to get comfortable, leaned back and pulled his visor down. "Be quiet, please. I'm factoring the various elements of our recent conversation."

Jenny sat up straight and closed her eyes. "You be quiet, please," she said as she reached for and grasped the various controls on the engineer's console, naming each in order. "Okay," she said. "Everything's there. I learned that routine from a handsome young engineer I met once. ... Now, you were saying?"

John was silent.

"Hello, anyone over there in the fireman's seat?" she queried.

"No, not that I can see from here," he responded without looking up.

Jenny was about to continue the conversation when Larry Smith's voice boomed again over the public-address speakers: "Your attention, please. Trains now boarding at Summit station are Number Twelve, the *Potatoland Connector* for Aroostook, Lyndon and Boundary on Track Five; First Number Two, the *Northern Express* for Bolton and Quarry on Track Three; and Second Number Two, also known as *The Christmas Train* for Eden Valley destinations and Quarry on Track One. Train One Twenty-Two, the *Wilderness Flyer* for North Branch and Eagle River is on Track E, on the northwest side of the concourse. First call for Trains Twelve, Two, Second Two and One Twenty-Two. All aboard please."

"Okay, Larry, you got that out of your system," John mumbled. "Now that I am totally distracted and have lost my train of thought, Miss Boston, I should say that I love you. Other than that, anything I've said in this conversation is unintelligible babble."

"I'm glad that my love is an honest man!" Jenny giggled. "Now be a good engineman and watch out the window for any activity on our train's platform, please."

John peered back through the narrow rear window of the cab. "Well, how about that? I see Henry Terrell boarding, along with Fred Wilson, Bill Westfield, Charles Wilson, Doctor Jim Collins and ... let's see ... that looks like Nolan Terrell. Yes, Mr. Terrell from the newspaper. And now Larry Smith is getting on. Hey, and isn't that Boomer Johnson from Spanish Junction. So where the heck are they going?"

"Company secret," Jenny responded and her eyes twinkled.

After a last call announcement offered by a voice unfamiliar to John, coupled with a New Year's wish and the playing of "Auld Lang Syne" over the station's public address system, Train Twelve pulled away, followed by First Number Two. Then, behind the station, Train One Twenty-Two was set in motion. Several minutes later the radio crackled in Engine Fifty-Three. "Okay back here, Jenny," Joe Francis said. "Go when you're ready. I make it out at three-fifteen p.m. First passenger stop is Swenson's."

"Okay, Joe," Jenny responded. "First stop is Swenson's." She released the brakes and nudged the throttle forward. Turning to John, she asked, "How did Joe know I was over on this side?"

"Indian endowed with mystic power. Great chief sees what white woman does not."

"Men!" Jenny exclaimed. "Oh, by the way, I met three of your old friends at your parents' home after work last night."

"Men or women?"

"Men, of course." Jenny flashed a smile as she notched the throttle forward. "Company secret. End of conversation. I'm busy now." The train clicked up through the yard, rolled slowly through the junction switch and then stopped so brakeman Will Smith could realign the switch that had been left open intentionally by the *Northern Express*.

John watched the track but frequently stole glances at his fireman. It appeared that she was at ease in the engineer's seat and happy to be there. She began whistling a tune and he realized that she was also musically gifted. "Any words to that tune?" he asked.

She nodded and fell silent.

"You going to sing it for me some day?" John pressed.

"Perhaps. ... Ah, I see the little flag stop at Swenson's coming up," she added and sounded the air horns. Joe was on the radio immediately. "Rob is going to signal you in."

The fireman reduced the train speed appropriately and grasped the brake control handle. As she was working the brakes, she spotted a large gathering of people around the passenger shelter. "John, come over here quick!" she exclaimed. "It looks like the whole Eden Valley is on hand to see the *Christmas Train*. This is exciting!" Jenny radioed the conductor with the advisory.

"Good, Jenny. We'll stop here a few minutes and give everyone a tour."

Brakeman Rob Rankin signaled for Jenny to stop, after which Will Smith hopped off with a step stool and helped passenger Andrea Swenson to the platform. A male classmate followed. Then Joe and Hank Terrell climbed down and motioned for the onlookers to come forward. "We'd be pleased to stop here for a few minutes so you folks can come aboard to see our train from the inside," Hank said. "After you go through the passenger section, the postal inspector, Dan Stubbs, who I think you all remember, has agreed to show you the inside of the mail section. We're delighted to see all of you today and want you to know that you're all highly valued customers of this railroad."

Fifteen minutes later, after the last of the visitors climbed down from the coach, Rob waved a highball and stepped back aboard and Joe came on the radio. "Okay, Jenny, you can skip the stop at Johnson Farm. The Johnson boy got off here, so Bolton is next."

Okay, Joe," she responded. "Bolton next." Jenny flashed a broad smile and giggled.

"So, what's amusing?" John asked.

"Carl Johnson got an invitation from the Swensons to have supper with Andrea. She's been eyeing him for quite a while. He's the Eden Valley heart-throb, you know."

"Uh huh. So we add a little young love to the intrigue of this day, Miss Matchmaker." John slumped in the fireman's seat and pulled his visor down. "Wake me up at Bolton."

"Well, bah humbug to you, John. I'll be excited for Andrea and Carl all by myself."

One student got off at Bolton and the postal clerk delivered a mailbag and a piece of express to the station agent. At that point, Jenny suggested that John should complete the run to Quarry. "If you don't," she added, "you'll soon forget all those wonderful moves you make in the engine." She got up and was crossing the cab to return to the fireman's seat when he gathered her in his arms.

"Perhaps you haven't forgotten ... those moves," Jenny whispered and kissed him. The radio crackled and John reached for the mike. "Engine Fifty-Three here," he said. "I'm indisposed at the moment but I'll be with you shortly."

Joe chuckled. "The delay is quite understandable. There seems to be a certain amount of romance in the air today. We can wait."

Jenny turned crimson and returned to her seat. John grinned and slipped into his seat and depressed the radio mic. "There, that matter has been attended to. Now, you were about to say something, Joe, when I cut you off."

The radio was silent for a moment. Then Joe chuckled again. "I was going to say that if you're up to the challenge perhaps we should press on. Does four-ten p.m. sound about right for our departure from Bolton? And your watch, does it compare to mine? Mr. Terrell wants to know."

"Oh, my goodness, I forgot he was there. My watch stopped a long time ago but I'll set it to four-ten. ... Let's see. The short hand goes to four, or is it ten? No, that's not right. ... There, close enough. ... Fasten your seatbelts and we'll taxi down the runway."

The *Christmas Train* rolled through the hill country north of Bolton and by the deep cuts in the snow near Eden. The banks still towered above the engine where the train struggled earlier. The memory was still vivid and John knew it would be long lasting.

The train passed Test Site Junction and broke out of the evergreen forest just south of Quarry Village. John activated the engine bell and blasted the air horns for the highway crossing at the end of the freight yard while noting that the *Northern Express* had been turned and was on the siding across from the station. He cut the throttle and coasted to a stop at the lower end of the platform where a crowd of village residents had assembled.

Jenny went across the cab and opened the engineer's door while John entered notes in the time book Jenny had given him at Christmas. She placed her hand on his shoulder and he looked up and winked at her. "How do you spell 'smooched'?" he asked slyly.

"John! You are not writing that in your time book!" she exclaimed.

"Of course I am. You know that an engineer has to account for all of his delays. I'm entering five minutes for smooching at Bolton and attributing the cause to the amorous fireman on the *Christmas Train.*" He closed the book, tucked it into his jacket pocket and was getting up when Jenny directed attention to his father who was standing with three well-dressed men outside the waiting room door. "Your father has some special people he wants you to meet," she said and watched intently for his reaction.

John squinted out the window and then gasped. "Oh, my God!" he exclaimed when he recognized the men. "That's Glennie Lightfoot ... and Harvey Williamson, the guy on the left, from the South Montana ... and Rick Vandergrift, the president."

John buried his head in his hands as memories of an incident in the mountains came flooding back. "Harv, he was with me, Jen ... in the dark ... inside that ... caved-in snow shed in the Bitterroots. ... And Glennie, he met us ... God bless him ... he met us with the relief train. He came west from Missoula ... wide open ... and met us at Timberline when we were bringing them ... the passengers ... some hurt ... and terrified, most of them ... we were bringing them down off the mountain. It was the day after Christmas, Jenny, and I was eighteen, I guess, and running a steam job with a rotary snowplow. ..." John's voice broke, his shoulders shook and he could say no more.

Jenny helped him to the cabin door and held him by his jacket as he climbed slowly down the ladder. When he was standing on the platform, the fireman passed him his cane. "Go see your friends, my love," she said. "I'll come along with the rest of the guys."

John had only made a few tentative steps when Harvey, a slight, gray-haired man, ran up, grasped his hand and drew him into an embrace. "John, it's great to see you again! Seems like it's been a lifetime." He stood back, held John by the shoulders and peered into his eyes. "We read about you and the *Christmas Train* in the papers back home and your dad told us more and, man, it all came back—you and me, crawling around what was left of Snowshed Seven up there on the east slope, us trying to find a hole ... so we could fish those folks out. ... You found it and we crawled in like a couple of rats. ... Dark, it was pitch black in there ..." Williamson paused and shivered.

So intent was his reunion with the South Montana conductor that John didn't notice that Jenny and the rest of the SB&Q train crew had gathered nearby.

"When I saw you there on the platform, Harv, it all came back for me, too," John said. He wiped away more tears as he remembered his conductor on the plow train and how they engineered the rescue of more than 100 passengers and crewmen trapped in the collapse of the snow shed. "You and me, buddy. ... We were a good team back then. Remember when we crawled out of that little hole we found and sat there in the snow and tried to figure what to do next ... and I looked at you ... and you know ... you looked so doggone funny covered with that soot that fell out of the broken beams in the ceiling. ..."

"You think I looked funny? Don't think you weren't a sight! I've seen some dirty railroad men in my day, but you, John Shanahan, really took the prize. Soot and grease and ... my God ... we did figure out how to get 'em out, didn't we?" His voice broke and he blinked away tears.

John nodded and embraced his friend again. Then he turned and clasped the extended hand of Glendon Lightfoot, a legendary engineer in the high country west of Helena. He had ridden in Lightfoot's cab in the later days of steam locomotives as a young high school observer and later as a fireman. The Blackfoot Indian, in his early 60s, stood tall and straight on the platform at Quarry, his long silver hair bound in a ponytail. He peered into John's eyes and then gathered him in a bear hug.

"Damn, it's good to see you, Johnny," Glennie said. "Everybody on the South Montana talks about you. Like Harv said, we been reading the papers about your Christmas Eve run and I'll tell you right now that was some piece of railroading. I knew years ago, when you rode with me the first summer out there, that you had the right kind of stuff."

"I learned whatever I learned from the very best in the business when I worked with you," John said. "I've got some rough edges but I guess I finally got the basics down."

"I have a lot of good memories of you, John," Glennie said. "But I'll tell you straight up when I saw you that day at Timberline backing down off the east slope with those busted-up cars from the *Intermountain Flyer,* with no brakes, I turned to my young fireman and I said, 'Bub, commit this day to memory. You just seen the best engineman I ever knew and you seen him here today at his very best.'"

"You're kind, Glennie, you were always kind. I remember when the medics you brought up were transferring the injured passengers to your train across the platform at Timberline and I ... I just lost it ... and broke down on the platform. You climbed down and we sat there on the planks together ... and you put your arm around my shoulders. We talked quite a while and you encouraged me, because I really was going to put this locomotive engineer thing to rest."

"Mighty glad you didn't. Our business needs the best and you're cream of the crop, son. ... Now I think you have another person to meet. We'll get together this evening and talk some more." Lightfoot stepped back and motioned Rick Vandergrift forward.

"Hi, John," the railroad president said as they shook hands. "Golly, you're looking great and I know you've been through some really difficult times since we last met. The South Montana is very proud of what you did in the service of our country and we're envious of the Summit, Bolton and Quarry for having you on their roster now. I can only echo my colleagues' words about your service with us. You gave us the very best and, from all appearances, you continue to be a key part of this railroad's fine, fine work force."

"Ah, you're too kind, Mr. Vandergrift ... Rick. ... I have colleagues here who plan out the moves and carry the load and ... well, like it was there in Montana, I'm really just along for the ride. ... Gosh, it's good to see you guys again. You know, if I hadn't run into that difficulty in North Korea, well, my heart was in the Bitterroots and my intention was to go back there and pick up my railroad career." John paused and looked around.

He spied Jenny, whose eyes were red from crying, and waved to her. Then, he continued, "I came here, Rick, on a short-term, office-type project for my father because I believed then that I could never climb into a locomotive again. My dreams had been dashed, there was no doubt about that, and I figured ... well, that maybe I could get a little pension from the military and do some odd jobs to make ends meet. One thing led to another over the past two months, and, well, I'm back doing something that I love. And I met a girl, that pretty fireman over there, and ... well, I guess that's it in a nutshell."

"I shouldn't say this in front of my boss and friend, your father, but you ever want a change of locale to pursue your dreams, the South Montana will always have a place for you," the railroad president said and clasped John's hand again.

Chapter 48: Bitterroot Memories

John sat stiffly in a straight back chair in the library at Seven Pines awaiting his father's return from a private meeting in the dining room with several employees of the Summit, Bolton and Quarry Railroad. The evening had been a whirlwind of activities highlighted by a reunion with Katie Boston in the room where J.P. and Ramon had set up a model railroad for the little girl. She demonstrated her trains to John—there were several—and her talent for operating them. They talked and he fulfilled his promise to tell her about the Christmas Eve storm and the difficult trip of the *Christmas Train*. Afterward, she fell asleep in his arms and he carried her to the room that she shared with her mother.

There had been no time to be with Jenny because she had pitched in to help Ramon, John's mother and Jenny's Aunt Emma in the preparation of the supper meal, another Ramon special. There were twenty-eight people in attendance and the fare was exquisite. He looked forward to more conversation with his friends from the South Montana Railroad and several of his colleagues from the SB&Q. But there was business to do first and his father was running late.

He stood up, leaned on his cane and tried to massage his leg to soothe the ache that had come on in the evening. He also had a nagging headache that he attributed to the excitement of the event-filled day. He had enjoyed the trip down to Quarry in the cab of Engine Fifty-Three with Jenny and his reunion with Glendon Lightfoot and Harvey Williamson of the South Montana Railroad and wanted to spend more time with each.

John sat down again and fidgeted with his suit jacket and vest that Ramon had squirreled from his bedroom closet at One Railroad Avenue in Summit. Then he smiled, remembering how his friends, even Jenny, had kept the evening's affairs from him. It had been "a company secret" well kept. And now his father wanted to talk privately to him, but he did not know why.

He was about to get up again and go wandering around the estate when J.P. Shanahan burst into the room. "I'm sorry I'm late, son," he said as he tossed a sheaf of papers on the library desk. He found two cigars in the desk humidor and passed one to John. They both lit up and J.P. leaned back in the office chair and placed his feet on the desktop.

"Enjoy the day so far, John?" he asked.

John nodded. "Yeah, but I'm beginning to wind down. I don't have your stamina, Dad, I'm sad to say. That's probably why I'm not executive material."

"I can't think of anyone with this company who has shown more stamina than you these last two months," his father responded sharply. "I keep track of the records and you have logged more duty hours than anyone. Hard duty, too! Just when I think we've reached a place where I can order you to take some time off we need you again. ... At least the traffic finally slowed down yesterday and today for the holiday weekend, but we expect it to double in early January. Which leads me to what I want to talk to you about."

"Okay, Dad. So we get down to the hard negotiating." John grinned and blew a smoke ring that drifted off across the room.

J.P. laughed heartily. "I've always been envious of you because you create the best smoke rings in the family. Your grandfather had that ability; only he developed it on those cheap dime-store cigars he used to smoke and they failed the ring test. I spend a lot on the best smokes made and I still can't create anything near the perfect smoke ring."

"That's true, but you make the best business deals and even grandfather admitted that. Never sell yourself short in that department, Mr. Shanahan."

"Ah, you know how to get on the good side of the old man." J.P. smiled broadly and added, "We don't spend enough time together and I'm going to try to fix that. First, though, I need to talk seriously about a few things."

"I know. I suppose Jenny is the primary issue."

"Well, I hadn't thought of it that way, but I suppose you could enter that factor into the general equation ... in order ... to create a hypothesis that would lead to an overall. ...

"C'mon, Dad! You're beginning to talk the way I do. When I get through I can't remember what I said or why I said it."

"You're right. That's me, sometimes. Okay, let's talk about Jenny but first let me tell you that your mother and I love the young lady like a daughter, and little Katie, now that's a very special little girl. Smart and sweet, like her mom."

"I've fallen in love with Jenny and little Katie," John said. "I'd like to propose to Jen someday but I think that should come after she graduates from high school. I'd like to encourage her to go to college and get some kind of a degree. The problem is that she loves her work and is superb at it ... and needs the work. There are a lot of considerations here, but mostly I don't want to be an impediment to her."

J.P. nodded in agreement. "Your mother and I have talked to her often lately. Really heart to heart, and we know that she adores you. Skeptics would say, 'Ah, she's a poor girl just looking for a man with money, or access to it.' But that's not so, in our estimation. She is genuine and she really is in love with you, John. Emma agrees, and so does Bill Travers."

The conversation continued for more than fifteen minutes and then J.P. broached the topic of John's future with Shanahan Enterprises. The senior Shanahan pointed out that he planned to continue managing the corporation indefinitely but his eventual successor would be his only son. "I'm not that old, but I'm getting there, son. At some point—sooner, not later—we're going to consider the future—yours and this business venture."

"I know that, Dad," John said. "I guess I'm just hung up on what I do. I love what I do and it's something that I have learned to handle with a modest degree of skill, I guess. I know that it's just a common workingman's job but, doggone it, it's where I fit ..."

There was a light tapping at the door. J.P. got up and pulled the door open. "Jenny! Come in, please."

"I apologize for interrupting you," she said. "Alicia said you wanted me to join John and you as soon as I could."

"I did. We're talking over some business matters and I'd like you to sit in. Is that okay with you, son?"

"Sure. Jenny's my business agent. Don't try to pull any fast ones on us." He got up and offered Jenny his chair and fetched another for himself.

"I was just about to tell my son that there's no doubt about his engineering talent. I think that conversation on the station platform with the men from the South Montana confirms that. I've never been entirely clear on that incident at Snowshed Seven in the Bitterroots and I wanted to ask John more about it."

John shifted uncomfortably. "I don't know what else to say. ... It's not easy to talk about. ... We were in the siding at East Slope with the rotary plow to clear the *Flyer*, which was running behind us. They went by and disappeared around that curve east of the shed."

He rubbed his eyes. "Oh, boy. It's hard to think about it. Our head brakeman opened the switch and we pulled out on the main, basically to follow the passenger train along at a safe distance. ... I can remember the brakeman ... I can see him now walking back to climb into the cab when there was this ... sickening, sliding sound ... and the wind came up and then there was this earth-shaking crash ... and everything went deathly quiet."

John swallowed hard. "It was a hard time, Dad. ... Awful hard time. ... We knew something bad had happened at the snowshed. Then I heard this faint crackling on the radio. You remember, the radios were new back then, and, well, not very good. In fact, it was unusual that we had a radio hooked up in a steam engine. I could hear this voice, faint and scratchy. The person kept calling, 'Help us. Somebody please help us. Please, we're trapped inside Snowshed Seven. ...'"

John got up and walked across the room. "It was Engineer Albert Goodine on the *Flyer*. It was his last trip, Dad ... his last trip ..." John's voice quavered. "He was going back home to Idaho for the last time ... to retire ... and his engine was ... buried in an avalanche ... with that wooden snowshed all busted up on top of his train."

John wiped his eyes and came back to his chair next to Jenny. She grasped his hands. John took a deep breath and continued. "We made a run for the east end of the shed ... but when we saw it all smashed down under the snow, well ... that was hard to face. I left my fireman to hook up the field telephone we had and told him to call Timberline, the nearest station. The rest of us ran up to the place where the snowshed was and started digging but the damned timbers were tangled everywhere and we couldn't even ... see the train. ...

"I climbed up on top and tried to find a hole somewhere. Someone, I know it was a guardian angel ... led me to a little hole and I could make out what

335

looked like the top of that fancy observation car, you know, the one that used to be on the end of that train."

"*The Mountain Star*, first car of its kind," J.P. interjected.

"Yeah, that's right; I forgot the name," John continued. "So, to make a long story short, I crawled down through the timbers and finally got a good footing on the roof of the car, which was all banged up. It was awful … down there. I never want to go to a place like that again. I knew there would have been little chance of getting many of the people out through the little hole we found. … Probably none …"

John's voice caught and he fell silent. He coughed and wiped his eyes. "Harv found a couple of flashlights somewhere and some rope and worked his way down to where I was. We had a little crawl space on top of the car so we looked down over the sides until we found a broken window. Harv lowered himself on the rope and stuck his head inside and started hollering. … There were people in there … a lot of them … who had made it back through the train to the last two cars.

"After we found out that everyone including the head end crewmen had made it on their own … or had been carried to the back cars, we tried to give them some words of encouragement and then went down to track level. The track looked okay around the two rear cars and then I noticed a speck of daylight right next to the rail. After that, we climbed back through the hole in the shed above the train."

John dabbed at his eyes again with his handkerchief. "We didn't know what to do, Dad. … Then it struck us that we might be able to run some cables through the debris for about ten feet or so at the east portal and hook the cables to the rear coupler on the *Mountain Star*. … And then, well, maybe we could yank the cars out through the debris with our locomotive.

"We took the rotary back to East Slope and set it out of the way and then put our caboose in ahead of it and beat it back to the snowshed with the engine. … Then Harv crawled back inside. …"

John paused and peered at Jenny whose eyes were teary. "Harv," he continued, " bless him; he unhooked all the train lines and jimmied the second car coupler loose from the rest of the train. … Down in that black hole all alone … Harv did that … all alone." John broke down and sobbed and Jenny and J.P comforted him.

"We, ah, got the cables through the debris and wrapped them through our engine's front coupler. We knew we needed to agree on a time and make the pull then because I wouldn't be able to talk to him. … That was the hardest part and something I could never do again. … When the time came, I whistled several times and took up the slack the best I could … and then I rammed the throttle to the end and prayed like I never prayed before. The cars came a little bit and then they snagged. I was going to shut it down and then something let go and, man, those cars came out in a cloud of soot and snow and broken timbers. Once I got her stopped I bailed out of the cab and ran looking for Harv."

336

John's face was suddenly wreathed in a smile and he chuckled. "I went around to the back and looked up and there was that goofy Harv standing in the open doorway with his arm around Al Goodine's shoulder and grinning like a Chessie cat. Dirty, man, I'll tell you; I know I never saw a steam fireman as dirty as my conductor was that day.

"You know the rest of the story," John concluded. "We backed down the grade to Timberline relying on the engine brakes. It was a little ticklish and the rear coach was banged up so bad we kept losing pieces off the sides. Most of the windows were broken out and the roof was jammed way down in a couple of places. But we needed it to handle the passengers we had. ... What became of those cars, Dad? I never saw them again."

"We scrapped them right there the next spring. The coach had a broken frame. God knows how it ever held together to get you all down off the mountain."

Jenny had nestled her head against John's shoulder and her fingers were intertwined in his. J.P. smiled and knew then that he couldn't take his son back to Chicago as he had been contemplating.

"Well, young people, I have a few more details to go over with our other guests before we get to tonight's entertainment," he said. "I'd like you both to sit here as long as you like and consider the offer I'm going to make to John. ... I need you in management, son, desperately, and it can start right here. I want to announce to the media—that would be Nolan Terrell—that you will be interim superintendent of the Summit, Bolton and Quarry Railroad effective immediately. The union has already agreed that you can remain on the engineer's spare board at Summit as long as you pay your union dues. But we've got to get on with a new learning experience. Will you consider my request?"

"I suppose so," John said tentatively. "What does a railroad superintendent do? If it involves any particular management skills, I'm afraid that I'm ..."

J.P. glared at his son. "You're my man. Do it for yourself and do it for Jenny and Katie." Then he smiled and winked and left the room.

When J.P. was out of earshot, John responded, "Yes, sir, Mr. Shanahan, I'm your man. No doubt about that." He got up and gathered Jenny in his arms. They held each other tight and she kissed him. "I love you, John Shanahan," she whispered.

"Uh huh," he responded but his mind was elsewhere. "Seriously, what do railroad superintendents do, Jen? I know they have certain responsibilities but danged if I know what. Shanahan Enterprises doesn't have many management people at the local level and they sort of work together, I guess, to make things work. I hear that some of the big railroads have all kinds of management types with offices and assistants and fashion models for secretaries and they send interoffice memorandums back and forth and rarely leave their offices. I don't think that's the kind of superintendent I want to be."

"I'm sure you'll be the best one anywhere," she said. "Take you father's offer, please, and if it involves going back to Chicago eventually as I imagine it will, then do it for me. I'll always love you … and … we'll get together … when we can. …"

"Perhaps I should. I really owe my father some time … and it would create opportunities … well … for you and me and Katie … you know, that is if … and we should … ah … you know. …"

Jenny burrowed into his arms. "Yes, do it for us, because … well, just because. …" She looked up at John. "Because we should … we will … make a life together. I hope."

John and Jenny slipped quietly into the great room just as J.P. announced that Rick Vandergrift, president of the South Montana Railroad, now had an added duty as chairman of the Board of Directors of Shanahan Enterprises. Rick offered a short report on his railroad operation's financial health, which was sound, and then introduced Glendon Lightfoot and Harvey Williamson again.

"Glennie has worked for us in train service for many years and is now our senior engineer," he said. "We recently had a retirement in management and are pleased to announce that he will become our new superintendent. As for Harvey, his service as a brakeman and conductor has been exemplary, the highlight of which was and will always be the rescue that he and John Shanahan carried out at Snowshed Seven some years ago. Harv will join our management team as a trainmaster. I brought Glennie and Harv along to meet with J.P. Shanahan, and especially John, whom we all had longed to meet again."

After a round of applause, J.P. took up the issue of management of the newly-expanded SB&Q. "This railroad, from its modest beginnings as a 22-mile short line, has always been managed locally by Henry Terrell. Those of you who have been around here over the years know Hank to be a workaholic. We just barged into this expansion when we took over Eastern's Hill Division and I failed to realize that this dedicated man was running the whole shooting match by himself and working day and night.

"That's going to change effective right now," J.P. continued. "The directors of Shanahan Enterprises have confirmed the choice of Henry Terrell as the new president of the expanded Summit, Bolton and Quarry Railroad. I also have added a provision and that is that Hank will be required to work no more than forty hours a week because if the rascal doesn't slow down he'll wear out and we can't run the railroad without him."

The meeting attendees arose and cheered loudly. Afterward, J.P. continued by announcing the choices of Charles Wilson as roadmaster, responsible for track maintenance; and Joe Francis and Bill Travers as trainmasters, responsible for two divisions of the line that would be created. Bill Westfield, a member of the transition team, had agreed to stay in the North Country and would be chief dispatcher. J.P. also announced that Fred Wilson, superintendent of the shop, was chosen as a new director of Shanahan Enterprises, along with Hank Terrell.

"Let's see, now, who else do we have?" J.P. looked around the room. "We can't appoint Nolan Terrell to any position because he's editor and publisher of the Summit Sentinel and is here tonight to report on this business session. But

338

we can salute him as a diligent pursuer of news and a fair and balanced journalist. He asks tough questions and digs into our doings like a beaver but he's straight with us and we appreciate that." The senior Shanahan grinned and peered at Hank. "He's also Hank's brother."

"That leaves one more person. He's my son, the fourth in a line of railroading Shanahans. I guess we've come full circle because my grandfather was an Irish immigrant who went to work on the first transcontinental line as a very young laborer. Patrick died in a terrible accident when his son, my father, was just an infant. That boy, John Patrick, eventually created Shanahan Enterprises years later and was an extraordinary businessman. Then I came along and tried to follow in his footsteps.

"Next was John, sitting over there, and he decided early on that he wanted to be a locomotive engineer. I've always been baffled by that decision but I've come to understand his passion and realize that he has remarkable skills in his craft. As you know, he served his country in Korea and came home wounded, not expecting to ever resume ... the only work he ever wanted to do. ..."

J.P paused and cleared his throat before continuing. "His mother and I are proud of him, especially for his perseverance. I've hesitated to do this because I never wanted to interrupt his career choice but I need him in another capacity, at least for a while. ... Our directors have agreed that we should offer him the position of superintendent of the SB&Q on an interim basis."

J.P. looked directly at John and Jenny, who sat quietly in the background. "Jenny," he said, "I need to do this and I have selfish reasons for it. I need John to learn management skills and Hank can lead him there better than anyone. I need him to be prepared someday to carry on the work of Shanahan Enterprises. And most of all, I need to know that your futures—his and yours and Katie's—will be as secure as I can possibly make them."

Chapter 49: A Song for John

J.P. Shanahan concluded the New Year's Eve meeting by reviewing several bookkeeping matters. The first, he said, concerned the circumstances of the near ramming of an SB&Q light engine on Christmas Eve by a highway snowplow on a main road crossing between Gatlin and Collier.

"We had a representative of the governor arrive here the other day to conduct an investigation, so called, of the incident. He leveled ludicrous allegations against the engineer but failed to produce evidence of ever attempting to gather statements of other witnesses. I made the most of a marvelous opportunity to order him off the property ... and to make a few comments about the governor, who instigated this nonsense."

J.P. said the railroad's attorney was advised that the snowplow operator had surfaced—he had been missing for several days—and had admitted fault in the incident, thus ending the investigation. The information had come from the governor's office directly and J.P. asked the attorney to demand a public apology. "We won't get it, of course, but we'll be on record with our demand," he concluded.

J.P. thumbed through his notes. Then he chuckled. "Oh, here's an advisory from the state Department of Highways. At six this evening, the bureaucrats are pleased to announce, the Hackmatack Highway has been re-opened to traffic, which they say now makes it possible for North Country folks to get back and forth between here and Sunbury again. That's amazing news. If memory serves me correctly this debacle began a week ago and this railroad has been providing remarkable service for most of that time."

Then J.P. called on Carleton Reardon to discuss what the railroad owner described as a "very compelling issue" that Carl had brought to his attention. "I've already asked our newspaper friend, Nolan Terrell, to keep this information confidential and he agreed," J.P said. "He is also prepared to participate anonymously in what we plan to do."

"What's this?" John whispered to Jenny.

"Honestly, sweetheart, I forgot to tell you. But listen, please, because I know you'll be thrilled."

Carl explained that one of the railroad's youngest trainmen, still in high school, was helping his mother raise several siblings. "Several of us who have worked for the SB&Q for a while knew about the struggle Delores Rankin had to keep her family together. She's Rob's widowed mother and for you who don't know, Rob has been working as a spare brakeman for several months. He's a crackerjack trainman and he's a top student in this year's senior class. And he's the most sincere and mannerly young man that I have ever met, and one of the hardest workers. Our group has been making personal donations to a trust fund that will be available if and when Rob can go to college."

Carl looked around the room sadly. "But it's not enough, folks," he continued. "I learned a few days ago that they were way behind on their rent on Shop Road and have received an eviction notice. Mrs. Rankin broke down when she received the news … and the poor lady is now under a doctor's care. Hank, bless him, he went out and personally hired a good woman to be with the young children when Rob is working and to help around the house at other times. So I went to J.P. and asked what, if anything, can be done. I believe he has found some answers that will help a lot and he should be the one to tell you about it."

J.P. joined Carl at the center of the room. "I had our people in Chicago check some records and we ascertained that Mr. Rankin had worked for the Eastern some years ago, before he became ill and passed away. He didn't have quite enough time in railroad service to qualify for any benefits but because he should have been issued a leave of absence at the time of his illness, a matter that seemed to have been overlooked, we find that Mrs. Rankin is entitled to a modest benefit each month."

The railroad owner said the directors of Shanahan Enterprises decided to match the monthly amount because of Rob's affiliation with the railroad. In addition, they decided to help find a better place for the Rankins to live and agreed to cover the initial payment for them. "From this point on, I will personally match the donations that those of you who are contributing to Rob's college fund are making. Depending on how long you plan to continue this wonderful gesture, you might consider splitting the money on a percentage basis by placing a certain sum in the trust and making the rest available on a regular basis toward the family's basic living needs until they get on their feet again."

Dr. Jim Collins stood up. "If I may, Mr. Shanahan, I'd like to say that I am Mrs. Rankin's doctor. As a physician I do not discuss my patients' conditions outside of the family but I will tell you that what all of you are doing is just about the best kind of medicine this lovely lady can have. And I would like very much to join your cause by providing some personal financial assistance. I remember Mr. Rankin when I first came here and I was taken by his commitment to his work and to his family. God bless you all for caring for them now."

John raised his hand and J.P. pointed to him. "I think the other Shanahan would like to make a comment. Go ahead, son."

John stood up. "I'm ashamed to say that I learned about the effort to help Rob some time ago and, quite naturally, completely forgot about it. Please count me in from here on out. I've had the pleasure to work with Rob a number of times including the trip on the *Christmas Train* and I cannot begin to tell you what a fine young man he is."

Boomer Johnson, who was sitting with his old colleagues from the South Montana spoke after John. "I know this young lad, and he's what everyone has said, and more. Count me in. We always need to help our own."

After Boomer sat down Rick Vandergrift asked to speak. "We have a joint employee-company fund for such occasions on the South Montana Railroad. As the current treasurer for the organizers I can tell you that we have been well endowed and have a considerable amount of cash on hand. I'll talk to our principals—I have two of them here—and I believe you can count on us to cover some immediate, short-term expenses. I salute all of you for your efforts on behalf of one of your own and I suggest, as Boomer has, that railroad men and women are always protective of their own."

Glendon Lightfoot was next. "I rise to speak as a tribal leader of a Blackfoot Indian band in south Montana. I understand from my new friend here, Joe Francis, that Mr. Rankin was a Native American, like the both of us. We have a particular interest in the welfare of our people in general and this Rankin family in particular and have certain tribal resources that can and will be applied in this circumstance. We will coordinate our assistance with you and appreciate your deep concern for this young member of our culture, his mother and all of her family."

"Well said, friends, and thanks," J.P. said. "Then it's settled. We'll see that young Rob and his mother and brothers and sisters get the help they need to pick up their lives again. God bless them and all of you good people here. ..."

J. P. looked around the room. "If there is no more business, I believe a round of refreshments is in order. I have a particular alcoholic drink that I stashed away for such an occasion and it is one that I recommend most highly. There are a couple of guys in this room who have already sampled it without authorization but we caught on early and will deduct the cost of what they consumed from their next paychecks. I won't name the culprits."

John stood up. "While not admitting guilt, I must tell you that Mr. Shanahan's specialty is from Holland and it makes you very sleepy. I have a buddy, whose name I shall not mention, that downed a flagon or so and he claims he slept for twenty years. I tried a little myself ... not knowing, of course, where it came from specifically ... well, sort of, actually ... and ... ah, well, I woke up later thinking I was Rip Van Winkle."

Jenny grabbed John's arm and pulled him back into his chair. "You are a buffoon, John Shanahan!" she exclaimed loudly. The men in attendance burst into gales of laughter.

"Ah, the little lady is reeling in the ball and chain!" Bill Westfield exclaimed. "Better escape while you still can, Shanahan!"

"It's a little too late, Bill. Looks like our plans to stake out territory on some beach with lots of bathing beauties is, well, just a pipe dream now." He leaned over and kissed Jenny. "I found someone here in the North Country who is far too precious to give up," he added.

Jenny and several of the SB&Q railroaders slipped away while Ramon and J.P. circulated with the drinks. John was puzzled and when he noticed that Hank had taken a seat in front of him, he tapped the new railroad president on the shoulder. "Excuse me, sir, could you advise me as to what has become of my colleagues all of a sudden?"

Hank shook his head. "Company secret," he grunted.

"Uh huh. Will this be the last secret of this long period of secrecy?"

"Dunno."

John's father pulled up a chair beside his son. "How was the drink?" he asked. "Get sleepy yet?"

"No, but that's because you watered it down. Last time ..."

"Last time you were operating in the dark. You're a great engineer and I expect you'll be a great superintendent and you're a darned good son but you don't have a clue about mixing drinks. ... Oh, by the way, your mother is in the library and she's been inquiring about you. Would you give her a few minutes before we go on with our program?"

"Of course I would, Dad. And thanks ... for everything ... especially lately."

"You're welcome, John. Now go see your mother, please."

John made his way to the library, relying on his cane more than usual. It had been a wonderful day for many reasons—the renewal of old acquaintances, the blossoming of a relationship with the only woman he had ever loved and the possibilities that a management post would offer—but it also had its downside. He would leave his dream job, the only one he had ever wanted, the one that had been his because of skills he developed on the way to becoming a locomotive engineer.

He stopped in the hallway leading to the library and leaned against a wall. He had been truly happy in Montana and had gained the respect of his peers in the railroad business there. Then the Korean War drew him away and it was near an innocuous village called Koto-ri that his dreams had been shattered in a horrific battle. He came home crippled in body and spirit, and despaired of ever climbing into the cab of a railroad locomotive again. But he had overcome that handicap and had found that his skills had not failed him even though his war injury made the work more challenging.

He knocked at the library door. "Mom, you there?" he called. The door opened and Alicia Shanahan embraced him. "I just don't see enough of you, my dear son," she said. "It seems that this family is always on the go, from one business to another, and we never have enough time together."

Alicia drew him to a settee and sat down beside him. "You've met old friends today, John. What was it like to remember those times with them?"

"It was wonderful, Mom. We had some hard times out there and we had some mighty good times, and it was a great experience. And then I came here, and sort of regained what I thought I lost forever."

"And you met a lovely young woman here and fell in love. You seem so happy now after having been so unhappy all those months after you came back ... from the war."

John nodded. "I've been blessed in so many ways, Mom. I have the best parents in the world, some great colleagues from out west and now here in the

North Country. And now Jenny … and little Katie. I couldn't be happier. … I guess you know that I want to ask Jen … sometime soon … to marry me …"

Alicia's eyes twinkled. "Of course, my son. I believe with all my heart that she is right for you, and you for her."

"Your approval means a lot to me, Mom. Thank you."

They talked until Alicia glanced at the library clock. "I think we should return to the great room for the conclusion to our New Year's Eve celebration. Jenny had some business to do, but she'll be along soon."

John opened the library door and escorted Alicia into the hallway. Emma Cummings met them there and the three walked hand in hand to the place where the others were gathered. John peered around the corner and realized that the setting had been transformed. In the background a low stage had been set up and a variety of musical instruments were assembled behind a battery of microphones. The Christmas tree was still in place but streamers proclaiming New Year's greetings had been added to the festive setting. Ramon came forward and escorted Alicia, Emma and John to seats near the stage where Katie Boston was waiting. She hopped up and dashed to John's side.

John steadied himself, bent down and pulled her into his arms. "Happy New Year, little princess!" he exclaimed. "Happy New Year," she murmured and kissed him on the cheek. "I love you, Mister John, and my mama loves you, too," she added. "I love the two of you with all my heart, Katie," he said, blinking away tears of joy.

Ramon seated Alicia and Emma and held Katie while John settled in the seat between the two women. Then he placed the little girl in John's lap and took the chair next to Emma. J.P. came across the room and sat down next to Alicia. "We have a grand family here, my love," he whispered to his wife. "The grandest in the world," she said and squeezed his arm.

Fred Wilson stepped to a microphone, attired in the garb of a railroad shop worker. "It's my pleasure to introduce a group that some of you have heard before. For those that haven't, we make up a local country-and-western band that performs from time to time around the North Country when we're not tied up running a railroad." Fred knelt and retrieved a circular sign from beneath the corner of the stage. He placed it on an easel that was set to one side of the musicians' instruments. It was similar to a passenger car drumhead and was emblazoned with the group's name: Bill Travers and the Northern Express.

"Oh, my gosh!" John exclaimed. "This is fantastic!" He arose holding Katie and began clapping. The rest of the audience joined in.

Fred grinned. "Thanks, folks, let's meet the band: Bill Travers, our leader who plays guitar and sings; Carleton Reardon on the bass fiddle; Jim McDermott on the piano; Larry Smith, with the electric guitar, and myself, I'm Fred Wilson and my instrument is the banjo. You'll notice that our outfits are basically our work clothes, which is how we were dressed the first time we gathered in the station restaurant at Summit to see if we could play together. We're the Northern Express now, and, of course, you know the origin of the name, which we have the permission of Shanahan Enterprises to use. … That's enough from me. We hope you enjoy our music."

After another round of applause, the group went through a series of legendary railroad songs and performed each flawlessly. Bill sang several strictly country pieces and John marveled, as he had once before, at his friend's musical ability. Larry, billed as the "Voice of Summit Station," belted out a couple of humorous tunes; Jim offered solo instrumentals and Fred followed with a medley of banjo music. The segment concluded with instrumentals by other members of the band.

After a brief intermission, Fred returned to the role of emcee. "And now it's time for everybody's favorite when our band performs. It's that little songbird that we all love. Ladies and gentlemen, the North Country's own Miss Jenny Boston!"

John sat stunned as Jenny stepped to the stage. She wore blue jeans, a tailored railroad jacket, a bright red bandanna and her new black silk railroader's cap. Her repertoire ran from lively popular songs to classic country to spiritual music, all of which was interspersed with railroad ballads. She sang of legendary railroaders and legendary trains and the happiness and heartache experienced by those employed in the business. Occasionally she asked the audience to join her in song.

When it seemed that her spellbinding performance was over, Bill Travers walked across the stage, put his arm around her shoulders and took the microphone. "Jen has one more, folks, and it's a special piece she wrote for a special friend. I've been a country music fan all my life and have heard some big-time entertainers sing some mighty fine songs. But I'll tell you, this piece speaks from the heart and I guarantee you'll always remember 'A Song for John.'"

Katie tugged at John's arm. "My mama wrote this for you, Mister John, because she loves you," she said.

John held Katie close and fought back tears as Jenny sang about a handsome stranger who had stolen her heart when their eyes met at Summit station for the very first time. It was, he knew then, the tune that she had whistled when they rode together on the train en route to Quarry earlier that day.

His tears flowed freely as she told of her love in the simple words of her song: "He was a soldier from the war, / a humble man who said no more." … "He told me not of his acclaim / but he was my hero just the same." … "This man who came to Maine … one night upon a train; / he looked into my eyes … and made me realize …/ that God had sent this man … to make me understand …/ that on this special day, true love had come my way. …"

Jenny bowed and Bill Travers led the gathering in a rousing round of applause. He hugged her and escorted Jenny off the stage to John and Katie. "I think this lady loves you, Shanahan, if you hadn't figured that out yet," he said. "Be good to her, pal, or I'll make your life some kind of miserable." Then he gripped John by the shoulders, grinned and bounded back on stage to lead the Northern Express in a closing medley of railroad music.

John and Jenny continued to sit together, their fingers intertwined around Katie, who slept soundly in his arms. They mostly watched each other in adoring ways. As the hour neared midnight, Bill Travers came by and tapped John's shoulder. "We're about ready to do the New Year's bit, buddy," he said quietly. "Let me take the little princess off to her room while you unleash my cousin so we can have her for one more song. After that, the little twit is your responsibility."

The countdown to the midnight hour had begun when the band struck up the music to "Auld Lang Syne." Jenny sang the words with John at her side, leaning heavily on his cane. When it was done and several of the guests tossed confetti on the stage, she burrowed into his arms and professed her love for him again. "Are you happy tonight, my darling?" she asked as she peered up into his eyes.

"Never happier, and you, my darling?"

"Never happier. Never in all my life." They embraced and Bill, still at the microphone, raised a glass. "A cup of kindness for John and Jenny," he announced. "May this year bring them a stout locomotive, a clear rail down the track of life and a high green at every signal on their run."

Epilogue

John Shanahan and Henry Terrell stood by the east-facing windows of the third-story office in Summit station and watched water droplets form and fall from icicles still clinging to the eaves. It was late afternoon on a day in early April 1952, and winter was finally loosening its grip on the North Country. The sprawling railroad yard was full of freight cars, and the second switcher, one of three in around-the-clock service, was shuffling loaded cars into one section of the terminal and empties into another. Snowplows, including the new rotary that had proven its worth during its inaugural use, and spreaders and winter equipment cars had been trundled into the back shop yard for eventual summer servicing and storage.

"Spring is coming, John," Hank remarked.

"I believe it is," his colleague responded. "You know, I was getting tired of winter, Hank, especially when that blizzard roared through here a couple weeks ago. It was sort of like the Christmas Eve storm, although that one was definitely in a class of its own."

"No doubt about that. But, by golly, we slogged along, kept everything on the track most of the time and didn't inconvenience the public unduly. You know, I believe one of our best accomplishments is that we made a lot of friends across the region. My brother, Nolan, over at the Sentinel commissioned a poll a week or so ago regarding how the people judge our service since the takeover. How would you guess it came out?"

John shook his head. "Gee, I don't know. There are always detractors. They're everywhere across the country. I'd hope that half the respondents gave us good grades."

Hank chuckled. "The newspaper will release the figures in the weekend edition. What would you say if I told you that ninety-eight percent of the 1,500 people contacted gave us top marks across the board?"

John pondered the numbers and frowned. "I guess thirty people didn't think we were so hot."

Hank rolled his eyes. "That's true, John. But one thousand four hundred and seventy endorsed us. Wouldn't you say that was … you know … quite good?"

"Oh, absolutely, Hank. … Sometimes when I'm working here at night and look out across the city I wonder if anyone really cares about the railroad. Obviously they do."

"They certainly do," Hank said. "Now, changing the topic, did you know that as of last weekend we'd moved thirty thousand carloads of potatoes?"

"I didn't, but I'd believe you. Let's see … there are twelve hundred fifty-pound bags in a reefer so we've hauled thirty-six million bags … if I have all the zeroes in the right places. I can't do the math in my head, but that's a fair amount of potatoes."

"That's true. And despite the cost of operations, we're looking at a banner year."

John nodded. "Yep. And we provided jobs for folks, some who were down and out."

"That really was the best part," Hank agreed. "Well, I could stand here and gab with you all day but duty calls. I think I'll ring up Nolan Terrell and suggest that he call you. Got any yarns you can spin that would put us in a good light with the media?"

John shook his head. "Honestly, Hank, I'm about spun out. ... Well, we could tell him about the thirty-six million bags of spuds we've handled. If that's some kind of a record ... an enterprising journalist like Nolan might want to do a series of interviews with shippers to get their assessment, and, my goodness ..."

"Right! Call him tomorrow and plant the seed. I think I'll sneak downstairs and check out my liquor supply. I have a new cache that I know you'll never find. Cheerio, my friend!"

John returned to the swivel chair behind the mahogany desk of his office, lit up a cigar from the stock his father had left in January and thought about how things had changed since he arrived almost six months earlier. He had come to this distant place under the impression that he would be in the North Country no more than a month during which time he would close down a Shanahan railroad. Then he would go back to Chicago, where he would get on with his life, certainly in another calling.

But along the way, he remembered, he had met people who urged him to stay. There was Molly McCaslin—wonderful Molly, and Carl Reardon and Joe Francis and scores of station, shop and track workers. He had finally made the acquaintance of the soldier, Bill Travers, who saved his life in the hills of North Korea and a deep bond had developed between them. John had an opportunity to be a locomotive engineer again and that had provided considerable personal satisfaction because he had been convinced for almost a year that his war wound would preclude further engagement in that calling.

Afterward, he had accepted the post of superintendent of train operations for the railroad and figured out significant operational changes to enhance train movements. He proposed the re-introduction of the *Hayride* as a mixed freight and passenger train between Summit and Gatlin to speed up the schedules of the railroad's two name trains—the *Northern Express* and the *North Country Night Express*. He designed a small interim station in the shop at Summit and had it delivered by rail to Crawford to replace the tumbling ruin at that location.

John had remembered how the people of Hill Junction had turned out to help the railroad with the *Christmas Train* and made an appearance at a special town meeting to thank them personally. He also presented the selectmen with a check from Shanahan Enterprises to apply to any town project the townspeople desired.

He had operated locomotives when he was needed and that was often during the course of the winter months.

Best of all, he had met a beautiful young woman and they had fallen in love. John and Jenny Boston were engaged in March and had begun planning for their wedding later in the summer, at which time formal adoption proceedings would be completed and little Katie would become his daughter. They loved Summit and both John and Jenny owned homes there but it was likely they would have to move to Chicago—at least for a while—so that he could learn about managing the railroad empire that his grandfather had created before the turn of the century. He knew now that he was ready for that challenge and it was a decision that his beloved Jenny supported wholeheartedly.

John worked late into the night on an engineering study for rehabilitation of the closed section of former Eastern track between Eagle River and Boundary, which was one of several ongoing projects for the railroad superintendent. Finally satisfied that the blueprint and supporting documents were suitable for the level of service expected by shippers in the region, he placed the material in an envelope addressed to Henry Terrell.

He was pulling on his topcoat shortly after midnight when a knock came at the door. He opened it and Jenny, who had finished her tour of duty as engineer of the third Summit switcher, stepped into his arms. "Ah, the best time of day," he murmured in her ear. "Umm, the very best," she whispered.

The pair was about to exit the office when she drew his attention to a bright signal light alongside the track on Summit grade. He hadn't noticed it earlier and then remembered that railroad linemen had been upgrading semaphores in the area. He snapped out the office lights and they lingered by a window to get a better look.

"It's a high green, John," Jenny said softly.

"High green!" he responded. "It's surely for us, Jenny," he added, and kissed her again.

About the Author

Herb Cleaves is the son of railroad employees and worked his way through college and beyond as a trackman and station agent-operator. He published a railroad history titled *Bangor and Aroostook: The Maine Railroad* (Flying Yankee Publications, 1986). An updated sequel was produced a few years ago.

He became a reporter for a Maine daily newspaper where he also served as a bureau chief and copy and layout editor during a 25-year career. Herb has written numerous articles for various magazines and has been associated with a weekly newspaper on the coast of Maine for 16 years where he recently wrote a weekly column.

www.ingramcontent.com/pod-product-compliance
Lightning Source LLC
Chambersburg PA
CBHW030557020726
47494CB00005B/1653